By Dean Murray

Ambushed

Dean Murray

Ambushed is a work of fiction. Names, characters, places and incidents are the products of the author's imagination or are used fictitiously. Any resemblance to actual events, locales, or persons, living or dead, is entirely coincidental.

Published by Fir'shan Publishing

ISBN 978-1-9393632-8-2

www.FirshanPublishing.com

First Edition

For Tim

This isn't what you thought I'd end up doing, but I appreciate everything you taught me along the way.

Chapter 1

Alec Graves
Deutsche Bank, Cayman Office
George Town, The Cayman Islands

You don't get to be a Senior Vice President in a bank the size of Deutsche Bank without learning to do at least a reasonable job of concealing your emotions, but that doesn't mean that you don't feel them. It was obvious to me that the man sitting across the massive mahogany desk from me was very nervous.

The simple fact that Mr. John H. Ford had failed to introduce himself would have told me he was feeling off balance, but there was more than that to it. When it came to me—to my kind—there was almost always more to it than just simple observation.

I could hear Mr. Ford's heartbeat stuttering, could smell the stress-induced perspiration that was hidden so well by the jacket of his thousand-dollar suit. Someone watching us from outside of Mr. Ford's luxuriously appointed office would have probably thought there wasn't anything unusual going on, but this wasn't just another day at the office for him. Days like this were the sole reason that he'd been assigned to this branch.

The Cayman branch of Deutsche Bank was a big branch—it had to be given the sheer amount of money that flowed through it on a daily basis. As Switzerland's banking laws had become less and less protective of the identities of account holders, more and more of the black-market money that had once hidden in Switzerland had shifted to other offshore locations like the Cayman Islands.

Just having an office in the Cayman Islands no doubt caused problems for the banks that operated here, but the simple fact of the matter was that there was too much money to be made for most of them to pass up a slice of the action. Deutsche Bank probably made more money out of their Cayman branch than they did out of the next three biggest offices combined.

Each of the big multinational banks that operated here tried to insulate themselves from repercussions in slightly different ways, but it all boiled down to the same thing. They needed a fall guy, someone to throw to the regulators if something came back to bite them. Mr. Ford was the sacrificial lamb in Cayman and he knew it.

There were offsetting perks, of course. Mr. Ford probably made three or four times what other people at his level in the bank made, but I could tell that he was getting to the end of his endurance. It had to be hard to sleep knowing that he could go to jail at some point because of transactions like the one that we were about to make.

"Everything seems to be in order, Mr. Peterson."

I was nervous too, but the fact that I was using a fake identity that was strong enough to fool even the head of the U.S. National Security Agency meant that I didn't have as much on the line as Mr. Ford did. If everything went against me then I might lose the money in the account he was looking at, but it would take more than a dozen human police to have any hope of capturing me, and even then, I'd probably hear them coming from a long way off.

I leaned back in my chair, causing the expensive black leather to creak, and smiled.

"I expected nothing less, Mr. Ford. I'm familiar enough with your internal policies to know that you wouldn't have allowed me to cash out my account before now. However, now that I've met the relevant criteria, I'd like to proceed."

I'd paid some very unsavory contacts a total of nearly two hundred thousand dollars to find out exactly how long my money needed to sit in Mr. Ford's bank before I could liquidate it, and I hadn't waited a day longer than I had to before arriving to start the process of moving it yet again.

Most governments had a decided interest in knowing whenever anyone opened or closed a large account, but even now there were a few countries where the banking laws were strong on privacy and weak on regulation. I'd moved the money I'd stolen from Kaleb—stolen from my father—more than a dozen times since I'd left Sanctuary.

Kaleb had kept the money in a variety of accounts, all of which I'd moved into an offshore account that Donovan had set up for me years ago. If I'd been up against someone with less resources, that probably would have been enough to shield me, but Kaleb still had billions, maybe even tens of billions in assets and he wasn't the kind of guy to confine himself to strictly legal methods of getting what he wanted.

I'd bounced the money around to accounts in the Middle East, Hong Kong, and Singapore every few days before finally deciding to make the switch here in the Cayman Islands. Some of the countries my money had passed through were very hostile to the U.S. government, so Kaleb's contacts in the Justice and State departments wouldn't be enough to get him access to the records he'd need to track the money down, but I still felt like the clock was ticking.

Getting people inside of the bank's computer systems would take time, even for Kaleb, but he had access to some of the best hackers in the world, and if that didn't work then he'd eventually get someone inside the buildings. It ultimately wouldn't matter if he did it by hiring someone to pose as a new employee, by bribing a VP somewhere, or by old fashioned breaking and entering. It was just a matter of time before Kaleb followed the electronic trail that my funds transfers were leaving.

I needed this money to fight the war that I'd committed to when Kaleb had tried to sell off my sister Rachel to one of his goons. The only way to make sure the money would be safe was to move it without using electronic transfers.

"Mr. Ford?"

Apparently the stress was getting to him even more than I'd realized. He'd just spent the last thirty seconds staring off into space.

"I'm sorry, what was that?"

"I'd like to go ahead with the closure of my account here."

"Are you sure? We would really like to keep your business, Mr. Peterson. You have a significant balance in your account. Possibly we can arrange to put you in a better account. I'm sure we have something with a better yield than what you're getting right now."

I shook my head. "I'm afraid not."

"Very well. You indicated that you'd like to close out your account by purchasing bearer bonds?"

He didn't actually wait for my response; it was just more conversational filler. He knew I was probably doing something illegal, but I'd met all of the bank's requirements so there wasn't anything he could really do to stop me. Besides, he was about to make a ridiculous amount of money off of me.

"We don't actually have enough bearer bonds on hand to cash out the full value of your account..."

"That's fine, I'd like to proceed with purchasing all of the bonds you have on hand. I can always come back tomorrow to redeem the rest of the balance."

I half expected him to tell me that tomorrow was too soon, but apparently he'd pushed me as far as he was comfortable pushing. There weren't as many bearer bonds being issued these days precisely because they were so ideal for money laundering, but there were still trillions of dollars' worth out there, and hundreds of billions of it circulated between the banks here in the Caymans.

Mr. Ford would get ahold of the debt instruments I needed, and he'd do so by purchasing them from at least half a dozen different banks later on in the day so that he'd be less likely to know which bank I'd taken the bonds to. What he didn't know couldn't be pulled out of him on a witness stand at some later date.

"Very good. Have you made your own security arrangements, or would you like us to assist you there?"

"I've made my own arrangements."

He nodded absently as he typed something into the terminal positioned to one side of his desk. "Very good. When should I tell my people to expect the armored car?"

"That won't be necessary. I just need the bonds; I'll take care of everything else."

Mr. Ford's eyes practically popped out of his head. "I know it's not my place to tell you how to secure your wealth, but you must admit that simply walking out the front door with...that amount of money is irresponsible."

I fought down a smile at how careful he was being to avoid actually saying how much money we were dealing with.

"You're right, Mr. Ford, it's not your place. My people are very, very good. As long as there's no leak on your end of things, there won't be any issues."

I was momentarily grateful that the bank's policies prohibited the presence of non-account holders in meetings like this. Jasmin, James and Jess were incredibly dangerous, but they didn't look it and I wasn't sure that Mr. Ford would have agreed to let me walk out the door with nothing more than a trio of teenagers to guard that kind of money. That or *he* would have decided to see if he could arrange to steal the money.

He wavered for a moment, but I knew how to deal with these kinds of concerns. "Your bank's responsibility ends the moment you hand me the debt certificates, Mr. Ford, I'm well aware of that. I'll even sign something to that effect if needs be, but one way or another I will be closing out my account here over the next two days. If I have to, I'll wire the funds to another bank, one that will follow my instructions without all of these questions."

It was a bluff, a small one at least. I would happily wire the money to another bank if I had to, but my contacts had said that Mr. Ford was easier to deal with than most of the rest of his contemporaries at the other banks. If I had to wire the funds elsewhere I'd be forced to fly to Hong Kong or somewhere similar, and that would take time I didn't have.

"Very well, I'll have my secretary draw something up. There will, of course, be a small fee charged by the bank for our role in obtaining the bearer bonds."

"You can have a quarter of a percent."

That sealed the deal. It was only slightly more than my contacts had indicated was the going rate for something like this, but it would amount to tens of millions of dollars, tens of millions of dollars of which he would get a small but significant cut. Our complicated dance was now done and all that remained was the actual transfer.

"Very well, if you'll please follow me to the vault, we can proceed—unless your people need more time to complete their arrangements?"

"No, we're ready to go."

Two days ago I wouldn't have known how much security to expect, but my contacts had filled me in on that as well. Mr. Ford couldn't get access to the vault by himself any more than I could, so we stopped off at both the branch manager and the assistant manager's offices and collected them before heading to the back of the building.

I caught a glimpse of James and the rest waiting in the lobby, but they didn't acknowledge my presence any more than I acknowledged theirs. As we passed through a large, metal door I felt an unfamiliar sense of pressure that nearly made me stumble, but Mr. Ford and the others didn't seem to notice my clumsiness.

The pressure hadn't been completely unanticipated, but it still wasn't a welcome development. Getting the money to the Cayman First National Bank was going to be more complicated than I'd hoped.

The Deutsche Bank vault here was no fewer than three stories underground, but that wasn't a surprise to me either. My contacts had been *very* well-informed. We passed through four security checkpoints and were forced to shed all of the metal in our pockets before we finally came to our destination, or rather *my* destination.

A pair of very competent security guards showed me to a tiny room that had more than six inches of Plexiglas positioned between me and the actual vault. I watched as Mr. Ford and the others went through a series of biometric checks before being allowed past the final checkpoint and into the vault. Once they were inside, I moved over to the pair of old-fashioned binoculars that had been left in the room precisely so that I could watch what happened next.

Mr. Ford and the others opened up the vault and then used a combination of keys and their fingerprints to unlock a heavy steel drawer that functioned as a kind of mini-vault inside of the main vault.

Once all three of the bank employees had done their part, the drawer slid out and they started pulling out bearer bonds that each had a face value of fifty million euros. I kept a silent count as they pulled out fifteen separate certificates and then counted again as they moved on to bearer bonds in smaller denominations.

By the time the vault had been emptied, they had pulled out nearly a billion euros' worth of bonds, and the assistant manager's hands had started shaking slightly. It was an almost unimaginable amount of wealth, but they were going to have to have many times that amount on hand tomorrow in order to fully close out my account.

I didn't actually expect any of the bank employees to try anything funny with the certificates, but I kept an eye on them regardless as Mr. Ford and the branch manager walked the bonds out of the vault. The assistant manager was left to close the drawer that had been holding the certificates. Under normal circumstances the other two probably wouldn't have left him to lock up by himself, but there wasn't anything of value in the drawer now.

One of the security guards buzzed the door to my room open, which was more of a relief than I let on. The room had been furnished with a comfortable chair and a small table, but my beast could recognize a cage and he hadn't liked being trapped inside such a small space. We probably could have transformed into our hulking hybrid form and shattered the locking mechanism on the door if push had come to shove, but neither of us had been completely sure of that.

Mr. Ford and the branch manager met me just past the final security checkpoint and then Mr. Ford and I walked down the hall side by side so that I could continue to keep an eye on the bonds he was carrying. It took only a few minutes to go back through the security check points in reverse order, but we stopped before exiting the last one and Mr. Ford led me into a small room that had just enough room to seat all four of us around a table that was empty but for a couple of sheets of paper and a dumb terminal on the far end.

I did my best not to fidget, but my beast was still riled up, and being confined once again inside of a small room with three other people wasn't doing anything to calm him down. The others were probably just assuming I was nervous at having so much of my wealth concentrated in a few frail pieces of paper, but I still couldn't afford to seem too uneasy. I abandoned my attempts at placating my beast and instead just shoved him back into the tiny corner of my mind where he spent most of his time.

My beast roared in protest and threw himself at the metaphysical bars of his cage, but I was a dominant, I ruled my beast, he didn't rule me. Saying you were dominant was a bold, uncompromising statement, but things weren't always as cut and dried as that, sometimes it was closer than I liked to admit.

I took a couple of deep, calming breaths, and then turned my attention back to Mr. Ford who was waiting on me to begin a final count of the certificates. Someone had delivered the liability release to the room while we'd been down in the vault, so once Mr. Ford was done counting the bonds, I signed the release and accepted the stack of paper that had been my whole purpose in traveling to the Cayman Islands.

"And now if you'll sign here, accepting receipt of the bonds, I'll counter-sign and then we'll update the balance in your account."

A few seconds later the paperwork was all done and we were all standing to leave.

"Your backpack and briefcase should be right where you left them, Mr. Peterson. If you'll come right this way, please."

I nodded and followed Mr. Ford across the hall. It was almost amusing how much more relaxed he was now that the bonds were safely in my custody. He'd done his part, he'd earned his commission, and now he could safely focus on the next step, that of buying up enough additional bearer bonds to finish our transaction tomorrow.

Mr. Ford showed me into the small, windowless room where I'd left my backpack and the heavy steel briefcase that I'd brought into the bank, and then closed the door. I spared a moment to wonder if he'd wait outside for me, and then opened up the briefcase and fished out the handcuffs and key that were a vital part of my plan.

The debt certificates went into a rigid plastic case, which I stuffed into the backpack. I locked the briefcase, handcuffed it to my left wrist, and then slung the backpack over my right shoulder.

As I stood back up to leave, I felt the same sense of pressure that I'd felt on the way in. It was even stronger this time, strong enough that I dropped back into the chair as my legs collapsed underneath me. I'd been told that no two people experienced a mental invasion in quite the same way, but for me it felt like someone was pulling my mind out through a keyhole in my skull.

I loosened the chains I'd been using to restrain my beast, and smiled as he charged out to do battle with the alien presence that was trying to find out who I was and where I was taking the money. The flare of power from my beast was only a shade less than would have been required to shift my body into one of my alternate forms, but this time the energy was directed elsewhere.

The vampire—it had to be a vampire—pushed harder and suddenly the keyhole was replaced with two burning knives that were slowly cutting their way through my mind. My beast attacked one of the daggers, shattering it into millions of pieces while I focused on pushing the other one out of my mind.

It was like trying to lift an SUV using nothing but my fingertips, but I refused to let the vampire beat me. For a second it seemed as though my beast was going to be able to come help me, but then he was distracted by another attack.

My physical muscles clenched tight as my body responded to the enormous mental effort I was exerting, but I wasn't making any headway. I needed to shift the battle to something that favored me rather than something that favored my enemy.

I could feel the vampire, could almost see the black ribbon of light that connected us as it bored through the wall to my right. It was a small thing, but everything I'd ever heard about vampires indicated that they had a harder time working as the distance between them and their target increased. The room was too small to allow me to put much distance between us, but I let myself slide out of the chair and started crawling towards the door.

The effort of moving even just a few feet left me shaking and weak, but it was enough to allow my beast to get the upper hand in its battle and come help me in mine. We pushed the dagger up out of my mind, *our* mind, and I forced the outer layer of my psyche to harden, transforming it into an opaque bubble that was less susceptible to invasion.

I knew the vampire didn't have long to finish ransacking my mind. Even a very powerful, very old mentalist would have to be motionless, probably with their eyes closed, in order to sustain such an effort across any kind of distance. I just needed to hold out for another minute or two.

"Mr. Peterson, are you okay?"

Mr. Ford must have heard the briefcase hit the floor from outside the door. I didn't want him in here, didn't want him to see me when I was vulnerable like this, but I didn't know if I had enough energy left over to respond to him.

The vampire launched another attack, and this one wasn't like the others. The distance was probably still working in my favor, but even so the attack had so much strength behind it that it shattered my outer defenses. I tried to heal the fracture he'd made in my mind, but before I could even begin another rod of fire stabbed into my mind.

This one was different—it didn't move, didn't try to read my thoughts, it just turned my own mind against me. Dozens, maybe even hundreds of tiny creatures skittered away from the point of impact, semi-intelligent constructs that had been created out of the very stuff that made me who I was.

My beast responded with the kind of blinding speed that we usually only had after shifting into something without all of the weaknesses inherent in normal human bodies. The constructs died singly and in pairs, ripped apart by metaphysical claws, crushed by insubstantial fangs, but it wasn't enough. None of the vampire's creations were even remotely a match for my beast, but there were just too many of them.

Those my beast destroyed melted away to be reabsorbed back into my being, strengthening me, but it wasn't enough, not when faced with the dozens that were being birthed each second. My strength was leaking away, turned against me, and suddenly I was the one time was working against.

I rolled myself over, blocking the door with my body, and joined my beast shattering the many-legged forms moving through my mind. Together we seemed to be stemming the tide of new creatures, but we weren't making any headway with regards to stopping the ones that had already been created.

I saw two returning from the furthest reaches of my mind, mandibles clasped around a glowing packet of memory, and jumped towards them. I landed on the first one, crushing it under my weight, and then tore the second one in half, but I could see others returning. There wasn't any way that I was going to be able to stop all of them; at least some of them were going to make it back to the vampire with the information they'd gleaned.

Instead of trying to fight them one at a time, I left my beast to continue that battle and moved to the outermost edge of my mind. The molten spike that had breached the shell around my mind was thickest at the point of impact, but that was where I needed to attack.

It took the barest fraction of a second to gather my strength and then I reached out towards the vampire's presence in my mind. It burned in ways I didn't know I could be hurt. Just getting a single mental finger on the spike caused enough pain to nearly make me back down, but I refused to be stopped.

I was still fighting the battle on the vampire's terms. It was the same thing I always did; it was the reason that Kaleb and Brandon had dominated my life for seventeen years. There was too much at stake this time though—a vampire who was this powerful would have contacts with other vampires, vampires who couldn't be allowed to know that my species existed.

I stopped resisting the pain and instead drank it down. My enemy was trying to use heat and fire against me, but there was one thing that fire couldn't harm. *I* became fire—not all of me, I couldn't do that even inside the refuge of my own mind without losing my identity—but everything from the shoulders down of my psychic body transformed into a living blaze.

I reached out mental hands that burned with the intense white of a blast furnace, and grabbed hold of the glowing metal nail before me. The vampire tried to change the terms of the fight once again, tried to cool the spike and turn it into something that would quench my blaze, but he wasn't just working against me now, he was working against the energy and effort he'd already expended.

In the split second between when I grabbed the spike and when the vampire reacted, I sent the temperature of the spike up thousands of degrees. A wave of chill, the icy cold of a perfect void, traveled down the vampire's probe towards me, but it was too late.

We were too closely matched for him to stop me and I'd already destroyed the structural integrity of the spike. The spot I was holding onto stretched and pulled like taffy, and my beast began to win his fight with the army of invaders.

The probe went both ways. It allowed the vampire to access my mind, but it also allowed me glimpses into his. The vampire panicked. He was old, centuries at least, maybe even more. It had doubtlessly been hundreds of years since he'd been up against someone strong enough to stand him off, even at a distance like this, but that was nothing compared to the sheer terror of knowing that someone was touching his mind.

The cold doubled and then doubled again. Frost started to form on my legs and torso as the heat was sucked out of the spike. I'd only thought we were well-matched. He had reserves of power and energy that I could only dream of, but something inside me still stubbornly refused to quit. I wrapped my arms even tighter around the spike, and as the fire they were made of started to flicker, I wrenched against the spike with every ounce of strength I had left.

Hot metal was flexible. I'd heated it up to the point where it had stretched, becoming narrow. Cold metal was brittle and I hit with enough force that the thin, attenuated section couldn't hold. The vampire's probe shattered and, aided by my beast, I began to absorb the creatures and the probe both.

I gasped, and realized that somewhere along the line I'd stopped breathing. I half expected another attack, but the sound of Mr. Ford trying the doorknob reminded me that I had other, equally pressing concerns.

"I'm fine, Mr. Ford, I just need a minute. I'm still a little jet-lagged and tripped as I was trying to pack everything back up."

"Very well, Mr. Peterson. I'm just outside of the door if you need anything."

I pulled myself back to my feet, zipped the backpack up, and turned back to the door.

Chapter 2

Jasmin Bianchi
Deutsche Bank, Cayman Office
George Town, The Cayman Islands

Alec looked like he'd been through hell as he came back out into the main part of the bank and walked towards us across the polished granite floor. The humans around us probably couldn't see the difference, but for someone who could put the visual clues together with the changes in his scent, it was obvious that he'd run into complications.

"Are you okay, Alec?"

He nodded as he handed Jessica the black backpack he'd been carrying.

"I got what I needed. I want a diamond formation, Jessica takes point."

My beast was thankfully silent. The question of who was dominant to whom had been settled between us years ago, but that didn't mean that my beast was always thrilled at the fact that we were submissive to him. Lately things had been even worse than normal in that area.

It wasn't that Alec was a bad alpha; he was actually one of the fairest hybrids I knew. It was more that my beast still seemed to think that we should be competing in a higher weight class than we were actually equipped for.

James didn't seem upset about being ordered around, but then again he had a lot of other stuff to worry about these days. Chief among his concerns was what would happen to his mother if we weren't around, but more than that, he'd lost some of his swagger after Vincent had nearly beaten him to death during our escape from Sanctuary.

The old James hadn't been very prone to challenging Alec, but the new one was even less so. James' beast seemed to understand that we were in the middle of a war now. You could posture and fight for your place inside of the pack all you wanted during peacetime, but once everyone's lives were on the line even our beasts mostly understood that we had to work together if we were going to have even a tiny chance of surviving.

I hadn't even bothered to see if Jess resented being ordered to carry Alec's backpack. Jess was submissive; she always had been and likely always would be. She wasn't worth much in a fight, but even a pack as small as ours needed someone to serve as a pressure relief valve. Jess being around meant that she got bossed around instead of Alec ordering James or me around on a constant basis. That made life a lot easier for everyone, except maybe for Jess.

We fell into the loose diamond formation that Alec had asked for as we exited the bank. Jess being in the front meant that she was the one most likely to trip any ambushes, which was good since she was the one that we could most afford to have injured in the opening seconds of any fight, but she didn't know where we were headed any more than I did.

"Turn left and keep the speed casual."

Alec's order was so quiet that only our unnaturally keen hearing allowed us to catch it. It was yet another benefit of being a shape shifter, a valuable one considering how much effort we had to go to in order to keep our existence secret from the humans. It was nice to be able to talk to each other and have people standing next to us not know what was going on.

Jess set out at a slow walk down the sun-drenched sidewalk. It was all I could do to stop myself from staring at the metal briefcase handcuffed to Alec's wrist. He hadn't actually ever come clean with regards to just how much money he'd stolen from his dad, but I knew it was several billion at least. I wasn't sure I could have calmly walked down a busy street with that much money dangling out as a lure to anyone who felt like trying to improve their position in life by way of a good old fashioned mugging.

"Cross the street at the next corner. Go into that parking garage up ahead."

James cleared his throat. "Alec, I think we've got someone following us."

"Yeah, I saw them two blocks ago. The black van, right?"

"If you saw them, then why are you leading us into a mostly abandoned parking structure? That's practically asking to be attacked."

My response had slipped out with more of an edge than I'd meant for it to have. Despite what my beast sometimes liked to think, I knew I wasn't any kind of match for Alec, but apparently I was feeling some pre-game jitters. I'd been up against vampires, jaguars, and even a werewolf, but I'd never faced off with a van full of humans.

Normal humans weren't usually much of a threat, but if they were as heavily armed as I was suspecting, then they'd still be dangerous. A semiautomatic shotgun didn't need a direct hit to knock a wolf out of the fight. Alec and James could generally shake off a single bullet or a load of buckshot, but we wolves were less sturdy. Besides, being able to withstand one shot wasn't worth a whole lot if someone shot you repeatedly before you could close with them.

"Someone tried to read my mind back in the bank. I'm betting it was one of the bank employees."

"I thought that only two people in the entire bank had access to your account information."

Luckily Alec seemed more amused by my nerves than anything else. It was nice when my big mouth didn't land me in more hot water for a change.

"That's right, there are only two people with that kind of access, but I'm sure every bank employee knows that something big is going on when the three most senior people in the office all take a client down to the vault."

Jess looked even more scared than I was as she led us across the road, but James just nodded in understanding. "So once they know that they've got a potential target, they just pull the information they need out of the client's mind."

"Yeah, or failing that they could probably get what they need out of Mr. Ford or one of the other two."

I wanted to lick my lips, but that was a nervous tic that I'd worked hard to conquer. I wasn't about to give into that particular idiosyncrasy now. I looked over at the black van as I followed Alec across the road, but I kept the gesture relaxed.

"So we're probably dealing with more vampires. The worst case would be what, eight or nine of them?"

Alec reached forward and steered Jessica slightly off to one side as we all made it up onto the sidewalk.

"Yeah, but I don't expect them to be quite that paranoid. Unless the ringleader got more out of my mind than I think he did, they won't know that we're anything other than normal kids. Hopefully there won't be more than four or five of them."

James actually perked up a little at the prospect of a fight. "What about the mentalist, do you think we're going to be up against him too? What if he's not even the one in charge of this little field trip?"

"I suspect that the mentalist will have a hard time getting away from his desk at the bank. Not only will he have all of the normal workload that you'd expect from a bank employee, he'll want to avoid doing anything that might link him to robberies of the bank's customers."

We were less than fifty yards away from the above-ground parking garage, which meant that we were almost to the end of the row of banks, but the fact that Alec had crossed over to the other side of the street told me that he wasn't planning on slipping inside a bank and losing our pursuers that way.

"Are you sure you want to do this, Alec? Even without the mentalist, we could be up against some really, really old vampires."

He looked at me for a couple of seconds before nodding. It wasn't a good look, it was a look that said he was starting to wonder if I'd lost my nerve.

"We don't have any good options at this point, but I don't want these guys giving us problems tomorrow. This is only part of the shipment, the one tomorrow is even more important. Besides, I can't afford to leave witnesses that Kaleb could use to track the money to the new bank."

I nodded, but it wasn't just any nod. I put everything I had into making it as unconcerned and reassuring as I could. We all knew that our odds of surviving the next year were practically zero, but even so I was still safer with our little pack than I would be hiding somewhere by myself. There was more than just Kaleb and the Coun'hij to worry about.

"We're almost there. As soon as we turn into the parking garage I want everyone to sprint to the nearest set of stairs. We need to lure them out of the van, but we also need to spread them out enough that we can pick them off a few at a time."

Everyone acknowledged the order with sub vocalizations of their own, and then it was time to run. There was no sign of any humans on the first floor of the structure, so we sprinted, covering the fifty yards to the enclosed stairwell in just under five seconds. It was fast enough to set a new world record, but more importantly it got us to the stairwell before the van that was following us pulled into the garage.

"James, you're bait, make sure they see you. Everyone else up to the second floor pronto."

I took the stairs three at a time and still lagged behind Alec. I was faster and stronger than any normal human, but Alec's legs were longer.

"Jess, you stay back as much as possible and try to stay in human form. Whatever you do, don't lose that backpack."

I opened my mouth to ask Alec what he meant, but he'd already pulled a key out of his pocket and undone the handcuffs that had secured his briefcase to his wrist.

"It was a ruse the entire time?"

I said it in a low hiss, something less even than a whisper, but it still earned me a dirty look from Alec as he walked over to a nearby Toyota sedan and set the briefcase on the hood. He was right. Vampires didn't seem to hear as well as us wolves, but still it was foolish to risk someone overhearing.

Jess looked back and forth between us with a nervous energy that told me she was profoundly uncomfortable now that she knew she was the one carrying the money. I didn't blame her. The only thing worse than going into a fight against a superior number of vampires was going into that same fight in human form.

The heavy metal door down on the first story clanged shut at the same time that James' footsteps started up the stairwell. I did a quick visual circuit of our level to confirm that there wasn't anyone around. The buildings that butted up against the back and sides of the garage were windowless monstrosities, so we'd be able to shift forms without worrying about who would see, but that didn't completely offset the rising tension tying me up in knots.

A second later I heard a squeal of overworked rubber as the van arrived at the door that James had just vacated. Alec moved closer to the concrete half-wall that formed the outside edge of the building, but I could hear the vampires just fine from where I was standing.

One of the van doors opened with a click and two sets of footsteps hurried across the concrete. "You two secure the two stairwells here on the ground floor, we can't afford to let these kids get away, not with a billion euros at stake."

As the van started back into motion, Alec completed his survey of our little section of the parking garage and decided on a plan.

"Jess, stand over there next to the Hummer so that they don't see you until they've driven past us. James, take the outside wall. Shift into hybrid form and then just sink your claws in deep enough to hang on the outside of the building. I'll hide behind a car up by where I left the briefcase. With any luck they'll see the briefcase at the same time that they see Jess."

It was a plan, I wasn't sure it was a good plan, but it did provide us with the element of surprise.

"What about me, Alec? What do you want me to do?"

"I need you to make sure none of the vampires get away. Hide next to the edge of the building, and then as soon as we know that we're not too badly outnumbered, jump down to the first floor and take out the two vampires they left behind to bottle us up. They'll probably be spread out between the two doors."

"Okay, I can do that."

I could hear the van's engine, laboring to pull its weight up the incline leading to the second level, but that didn't matter. It took only a couple of seconds for us all to take our positions. James had already stripped off his clothes while Alec had been explaining the plan. He shifted forms in a rush of power that was remarkably similar to what happened on the physical plane. The transformation always took place too quickly to see exactly what happened, but just like always, I got the impression that James' body exploded outward and then instantly contracted back down to his hybrid form.

James covered the distance to the outside wall in two long steps and then reached up and pulled himself out of sight, hanging from the outside of the building by nothing more than his claws and talons.

Alec likewise shed his clothes as he moved to his position, and as he ducked down between two cars another burst of power signaled that he'd shifted forms. The van was closer now and I stepped behind one of the huge cement pillars by the stairwell a split second before it rounded the last corner that had been stopping the vampires from being able to see us.

Time stretched and pulled, behaving oddly. I'd risked my life dozens, maybe hundreds of times before, but this time felt different. My pulse stuttered, speeding up and slowing down, but I couldn't tell whether that was what it was actually doing or if my time sense was just off.

Each heartbeat slammed against my chest, echoing in my ears as the van got closer. I prepared to slide around to the other side of the pillar I was hiding behind. Timing was everything, if I moved too soon or too late then they'd see me and I would ruin the ambush.

I made my move as the van passed my position, settling back against the other side of the pillar, and then suddenly the van slid to a stop.

"Samuels, go get the girl, Fiver and I will grab the briefcase."

I'd heard two doors open, not three. That meant that the driver was still inside the van. Alec and James were outnumbered at least four to two.

I looked down and realized that I'd also pulled my clothes off sometime in the last minute or two. My shirt, pants and shoes were all balled up in my left hand.

We were going to have to risk the two downstairs getting away. It was too dangerous for Alec and James to take on four vampires by themselves. I took a deep breath and started to loosen the chains on my beast as I looked around the pillar.

The first vampire was almost to the silver briefcase when Alec appeared as if by magic from behind the car that had been sheltering him. The vampire tried to get his weapon out, tried to step back out of the range of Alec's claws, but he wasn't up against a normal human. Reflexes that would have dealt with almost any other opponent weren't enough to save him from Alec.

Vampires are so fast that most normal humans wouldn't have even been able to follow the vampire's dodge let alone compensate for it, but Alec was faster still. The claws on Alec's right hand took the vampire through the neck, and the bloodsucker collapsed to the ground in a spray of blood.

James abandoned his perch on the outside of the building, dropping down onto the concrete floor with enough force that I could feel the tremors underneath my bare feet. James' target, the vampire who had been headed towards Jess, already had his weapon out, but James covered the ground between them too quickly for him to set himself.

The vampire sliced at James with a curved Japanese samurai sword, but James slapped the weapon away and sank his claws into the vampire's chest at the same time that Alec stepped forward to engage his second opponent.

"Jas, move!"

Alec's yell startled me into motion and I realized that I'd allowed myself to become so caught up in the fight that I'd frozen in place, not going to help the boys and likewise not fulfilling my original assignment.

I turned away from Alec and the others and sprinted towards the edge of the parking garage. It only took me three steps to get up to full speed and then I threw myself over the half wall and out into empty space. The ground was only twenty feet below, but that was far enough to break my legs if I didn't handle things just right. I was sturdier than a normal human, but unlike Alec and James, I couldn't shift into hybrid form at the last moment and absorb that kind of impact without risk.

Luckily I managed to generate enough momentum to hit the wall of the building next to the garage. I had a second as the rough brick tore my feet to shreds to wish that I'd left my shoes on, and then I pushed off of the wall, throwing myself into a backflip. It was like something you'd see in a movie. I'd only tried stuff like that a couple of times before and if I'd been thinking clearly I probably wouldn't have tried such a chancy maneuver, but it worked. My collision with the brick wall slowed me down and allowed me to angle my trajectory so that I landed back inside of the parking garage, now on the *first* floor.

I still hit hard enough that I had to roll to bleed off some of the force of my landing, but I shifted to my wolf form before I completed the second full rotation. The transformation tore through me with the familiar shadow of pain—a kind of half-agony that was over before my body could fully register what was going on.

The closest vampire had been leaning against the concrete wall that encased the stairwell. It wasn't a bad spot tactically speaking. Nobody would be able to sneak up on him and it allowed him to watch as much of the first floor as possible, but he shouldn't have leaned against the wall like that. Under normal circumstances he probably would have seen or heard any threats approaching with plenty of time to ready himself, but he obviously hadn't anticipated someone dropping down from the second story and I was on him as he was still pushing himself away from the wall.

He was fast, faster even than the vampires from up above, and his instincts were good. He didn't waste time trying to get at the longer weapon I was pretty sure he had concealed underneath his shirt. Instead he went straight for the dagger up his left sleeve, but even that wasn't something he could get into action fast enough, at least I didn't *think* he'd be able to get it out fast enough.

AMBUSHED

The truth was I wasn't positive, but it was too late to do anything about it one way or the other, I was already airborne, already arrowing towards his throat. The collision as I knocked him back into the concrete behind him, my jaws closing around his throat, was the most welcome thing I'd felt in a long time because it meant that I'd beaten him to the draw.

Being knocked back into the wall should have messed up his draw, but all of the stories agreed that vampires were tougher than normal humans, so I didn't leave anything to chance. As soon as my feet touched down I planted and whipped him to the right as hard as I could.

The violence of the action probably would have broken the neck of a normal person, or barring that ripped out their throat, but my opponent managed to get his left hand up and grab a handful of fur around my neck. He couldn't kill me with such a weak hold, but it was enough to let him offset some of the force as I whipped him back the other direction.

It also let me feel that there wasn't anything in his wrist sheath anymore, and I hadn't heard the clatter of metal on concrete so that meant that he still had ahold of his knife. I slammed him back into the wall hard enough that *I* practically saw stars, but I wasn't rewarded with the sound I was after.

The vampire tried to get his feet underneath him at the same time that his left arm tensed up, and I desperately tried to switch direction again. I threw him to the right again, mustering every bit of strength I had, but all I managed to do was throw off his aim a little.

Instead of sinking home between my ribs, the knife skipped off the large bone in my shoulder. It hurt, but it wasn't immediately life-threatening. A part of me debated releasing his neck and trying for a better hold, but that went against thousands of years of instincts, instincts that it turned out were right in this case.

The snap as his legs shattered against the bumper of an old Dodge pickup truck was music to my ears. The pain was too much for him and he dropped his knife at the same time that he relaxed his grip on my neck. A second later his neck snapped and I dropped his lifeless body to the ground.

The entire fight had taken no more than two seconds. The other vampire had drawn his sword, a short stabbing weapon, and headed towards me, but he was still more than a dozen yards away.

A multitude of sounds washed over me as I started towards the second vampire, angling myself so that by the time we met I'd have plenty of room. Up on the second level weapons clashed against hybrid claws and metal crunched as someone was thrown into a car with enough force to crumple the hood. That was probably a good sign. None of the vampires could possibly be strong enough to throw a hybrid like that and

Jess was probably fast enough to avoid coming to grips with anyone she didn't want to fight.

Down here, on the first level I could hear the steady drip of my blood onto the concrete floor. It served as a kind of morbid counterpoint to our paired footsteps as we slowly closed with each other. If I'd been a normal human I would have been worried about leaving so much blood at the scene of a double homicide, but shape shifter blood wasn't stable in the same way that human blood was.

We can benefit from human blood, I've had plenty of transfusions of human blood, but our own blood breaks down incredibly quickly once it leaves our body. Unless someone arrived to take samples of the blood on the pavement in the next fifteen minutes, it was going to be virtually impossible for them to get any usable DNA out of it.

The vampire took another step towards me and I forced my mind back to the situation at hand. My new opponent was obviously nervous. I'd hoped he might think that I'd merely been lucky in taking down his friend, but he wasn't acting the least bit over-confident. He feinted with his sword, a lightning-fast jab that I had to honor as potentially being a real attack.

I twisted to one side as the blade passed within inches of me. I snapped at his arm and apparently I was even faster than he'd expected because he almost didn't get out of the way in time. I still got a piece of him but I didn't get a good enough grip to turn it into anything useful. I felt a slight tug against my fangs and then they tore through the muscle of his arm and he was spinning away from me.

I expected the vampire to renew his attack, but he backed away, buying himself room to analyze what had just happened. That was a very bad sign. Normally I would have said that the waiting game would favor me. He was injured and the blood oozing out of his arm would eventually make its way down to his hand and interfere with his grip. That all went out the window though if I was fighting someone who was good enough to adjust his tactics on the fly.

It was unlikely—most people couldn't do much more than regurgitate the blocks and strikes that they'd had drilled into them—but every once in a while you ran into a true weapons master, someone who understood how to improvise, someone capable of creating an entirely new method of fighting if given enough time and a compelling reason to do so.

I couldn't take that chance. Besides, Alec and James might not survive without my help. I needed to finish off this fight now.

I moved towards the vampire and then planted and changed direction at the last second. His blade missed me again, but this time I felt it disturb the hair on my back. He was getting closer and my jaws snapped shut on nothing more than air this time.

I charged him, relying on speed to close before he could recover, but I almost wasn't fast enough. I ducked down as his sword darted towards me again. This time it skittered off of one of my ribs, tearing a long, bloody furrow across my back.

If the tip of his blade had been angled just a couple of degrees further down he would have impaled me, but it hadn't been and I crashed into him with enough speed to knock him over. He tried to roll back to his feet, but I grabbed hold of his lower leg and whipped him to the side.

There wasn't anything solid close enough to slam him into, which meant that it was only a matter of time before he recovered enough to skewer me. He hit the concrete floor hard, but he kept his chin tucked so that he didn't lead with his head. I heaved, whipping him back the other direction, but he was heavy and the concrete where we were standing was smoother than where I'd fought the first vampire.

My front legs started to slip out from underneath me, and I had to let go in order to stop from being knocked over. It proved to be for the better though because a second later his sword stabbed down through the space where I'd been standing.

He was bleeding from two places now, just like me, but none of our wounds were serious enough to affect the balance of the fight, in the timeframe that we were dealing with. He rolled back to his feet as I started circling him.

I needed an opening, but if anything I seemed to be losing ground to him. He was getting better and better at anticipating my attacks. I feinted to the left and then writhed away as his sword licked out again. He obviously expected me to grab his arm again, but instead I launched myself up over the top of his blade. He was good, but he'd let his weight shift too far forward in an attempt to counter another of the peripheral, low attacks that I'd been using until now.

My aim was true and a split second later, my jaws closed around his throat. Alec was the martial artist, he was the one that had told me that any punch was supposed to stop two inches behind its true target. Some things didn't transfer between fighting as a human and fighting as a wolf, but that did.

I didn't jump with the aim of just getting my fangs on the vampire's throat and then dropping straight down, I jumped with enough force to carry myself well past him. I hadn't been able to do that with the first vampire because of the wall behind him, but I wasn't under that kind of restraint this time. He was dead before he hit the ground.

Chapter 3

Alec Graves
George Town Banking Sector
George Town, The Cayman Islands

It was done. The first batch of cash had been deposited at the Cayman National Bank.

Everyone but Jess had been bleeding from at least a couple of spots, but we'd turned James' shirt into a set of improvised bandages and then gone into a fast food restaurant a few blocks over and taken turns cleaning up in the bathroom.

I would have donated my shirt to the cause as well, but I didn't want to draw any more attention to myself than I absolutely had to when it came time to deposit a billion dollars into the account I'd just finished setting up the day before.

Planning, or possibly luck, had won out and nobody had given me any problems when I'd asked to see the branch manager. Apparently my contacts hadn't been kidding when they said that the Cayman banks were used to having people in jeans and a t-shirt show up out of the blue and make extremely large deposits.

James and the girls had waited just outside of the bank as I was conducted back to a private room. Once I pulled out the first fifty-million-euro bond I was promptly taken down to the vault, and fifteen minutes later the bonds were the bank's problem rather than mine.

It was obvious that Jasmin wanted to go back to our hotel and lick her wounds. It was hard to say exactly what was going on with her, but she'd definitely lost some of her edge.

It was bad timing. I would have liked to give Jasmin a few weeks to unwind. She deserved at least that after everything we'd been through over the last month, but unfortunately that wasn't an option right now. Instead of letting her go back to the hotel, I'd ordered her and everyone else back to the Deutsche Bank branch while I went back to the hotel to get our rental car.

Jasmin had been almost ready to rebel when I gave her the order, but she knew I was right. We couldn't afford to leave an old, extremely powerful vampire mentalist in place at the bank. Not if we wanted to be able to make the next money transfer safely, not if we wanted to make sure that the vampire population at large didn't find out about us.

AMBUSHED

I'd been ready to try and scent-track the mentalist through the city, but we got lucky. James and the rest checked the front and back doors and the secure loading dock that was used whenever the bank needed to physically move anything high-value. There wasn't any trace of the vampire having left the bank while we were dealing with his lackeys. He could have still left via the loading dock, assuming that he was in a vehicle at the time, but the odds against that were pretty heavy—unless the vampire had gotten more out of my mind than I'd thought.

I hadn't been able to smell the vampire while I'd been in the bank, so I was pretty sure that our vampire worked in the back of the bank somewhere. My money was that he'd eventually leave via the back door, but we wouldn't know for sure until he actually exited the building. A brief storm had swept through the city a little while before I'd gone to the bank the first time around, so there weren't any old scent trails that we could follow back to the vampire's apartment.

I'd always wanted to be the one calling the shots, but now that I was out from under Kaleb's thumb I was finding that I didn't like how big the stakes had gotten. There wasn't any two ways about it, the vampire who had invaded my mind needed to die, but I didn't like the fact that bringing him down might cost me the life of one or more of my friends.

It was nearly six p.m. before James broke the silence on our four-way conference call. "He just left the building, guys."

"You're sure it's him, James? We can't afford to follow the wrong guy."

"Yeah, I'm downwind of him and he smells old, older than any of the other vampires I've ever run into. He's either our guy or there's more than one vampire holed up inside of the bank."

"Okay, you all know the drill. Stay far enough away that he can't scan you with his power. We need to anticipate his route enough that we can keep eyes on him at all times."

I turned the rental car on and started watching the alleyway to the back of the bank out of my side view mirror. It wasn't surprising that our target hadn't come around to the front of the building, but it did make things more difficult.

I dropped the car into gear. "I'm in motion, I'll head to the road just north of us and take station on the east corner. Jasmin, can you see him?"

Jasmin had snuck onto the roof of the building next door to the bank.

"Yeah, I can see him; he's headed north. James, keep moving south. Jess, if you hurry you should have time to reposition to the corner on the west."

I'd forgotten how much I hated driving inside of cities. I didn't have time to screw around and I now had enough money to replace the rental car several times over, so I drove aggressively and ended up trading paint with a couple of cabs before I managed to get into position.

Jasmin's voice in my Bluetooth earpiece was a constant reminder of just how little leeway I had.

"He's headed your direction, Alec, are you there yet?"

"No, but I'm just about there, is there anywhere to park once I get there?"

"Not really, you might have to ditch the car."

I took a deep breath to stop myself from grinding my teeth. Abandoning the car wasn't feasible, not until we were positive that he wasn't going to jump into a car of his own after just a block or two of walking.

The light ahead of me turned yellow and I gunned the engine to get through before cross traffic started moving.

"Okay, I'm here, can someone tell me what I'm looking for?"

I wasn't actually quite there, but I was close enough that I might be able to spot him if he was already at the corner.

"Slacks, a white collared shirt, not much skin showing..."

"And huge sunglasses?"

My interruption didn't even make Jasmin lose a beat. "Yeah, that's the guy. He must be pretty old if the sun is bothering him that much."

I watched the vampire cross the road and continue east. I was in the turning lane with a red light. A cab behind me honked, obviously unhappy that I hadn't turned right when there was a break in the traffic, but I ignored the growing line behind me. The longer I stayed here, the better.

The vampire was walking at a good clip, but not fast enough to make me think he knew he was being followed. He probably just wanted to get inside so he wasn't exposed to the sun. The really old vampires sunburned easier than most people and they often had a hard time getting their eyes to adjust to the light.

My light turned green to a chorus of honks and I turned right onto the road the vampire was walking along.

"James, how close are you? I can see a place to ditch the car if I have to, but I'd rather not do it unless you are close enough to pick it up right afterwards."

Jasmin muttered a profanity. "James, you've got to unmute your earpiece. Nobody can hear you."

"Sorry, I turned it off so the sound of the wind didn't drown the rest of you out. I'm headed north right now, Alec. If you need to ditch the car you can go for it, I should be able to get there before anyone drives off with it."

I pulled up next to the open spot and pushed the computer-assisted parallel-park button as I watched the vampire out of my rear-view mirror.

"I've got eyes on him. Jasmin, you can relocate if you want; I can't imagine that you'll be able to see him from up there for very much longer."

Jess cut in before Jasmin could respond. "I moved up one street to the north, the foot traffic is pretty bad on this one, but I think I'm gaining on him. Do you guys want me to stop at Coral Avenue or should I keep on and stop at the next one?"

I hadn't been paying enough attention to the street signs. Everything about this operation felt thrown together. I quickly checked the name of the street in front of me. "Yeah, wait on Coral, I'll let you know if he turns and heads your direction."

The next fifteen minutes were stressful. I had to ditch the car when the vampire turned south on Coral, but James made it to the vehicle before anything happened to it. It seemed impossible that the vampire wasn't worried. The fact that his people hadn't checked in after trying to mug us should have had him spooked, but I was pretty sure that he would have lost us if he'd been trying to do so. It was all we could do to keep him in sight.

James stayed with the car while Jasmin, Jess and I bracketed the target. The only thing that allowed us to get away with it was the fact that we were so much faster and had so much more endurance than normal humans.

As long as the vampire kept moving in a straight line things weren't too bad, but every time he changed directions it forced one of us to swing around wide, racing down an alternate set of roads to get into position so that we could maintain a perimeter around him.

The vampire finally disappeared inside of a large, fifty-story residential building and I sighed in relief.

"My bet is that this is where he lives, but stay alert and make sure that he doesn't slip out the back."

I waited a couple of minutes and then followed our target inside to confirm it was his actual home. I knew we'd found the right place before I'd even taken my second step inside. The stench of vampire was thick; it was layered over every other scent in the lobby the way that only happened when someone passed through a place multiple times per day.

I stepped back outside and walked over to the small café where everyone else was waiting for me. Once I was safely under the canopy, and therefore hidden from view, I waved the other three over.

"It's the right place, there's no doubt about it. We'll need to stay here and watch in shifts, at least two of us at all times, to make sure that he doesn't leave, but once it gets dark and things calm down we're going to go in and take him out."

Jasmin nodded, but she didn't look very happy at the idea of going up against a vampire old enough to do the things that I'd described earlier.

"You're sure this is the smart thing to be doing, Alec? This guy could be incredibly dangerous."

"Yeah, I'm sure. It's not just a matter of needing to get the rest of the money out, either.

I'm not going to go down in history as the one who let the vampires find out about us. Even if he's as powerful as I think he is, he still won't be able to stand off all four of us."

Jasmin and I took the last shift, me because I wanted to keep an eye out for any problematic developments, her because I didn't want to stick James with her in her current state.

James and Jess showed up a few minutes before three a.m. It was late enough that I was starting to think longingly of my pillow, but I knew that waiting until then to attack was the prudent thing to do. Vampires supposedly needed just as much sleep as humans, and this vampire was still maintaining his cover at the bank, so attacking this late almost guaranteed that we'd catch him asleep in his bed.

Jess handed me a thin black roll of cloth. I unrolled it enough to confirm it was a ski mask just like I'd requested, and then stuffed it in my pocket.

"Were they hard to find?"

James grinned and shook his head. "Considering that it never snows here it was ridiculously easy to find them. This place has a very robust criminal side to it."

"Yeah, well, the street thugs are probably just taking their lead from the bankers."

Jasmin accepted her ski mask and nervously played with it as I stood and stretched. "Okay, we do this just like we discussed. Try not to kill the lobby clerk, but make sure he's down for the count. Once we find the vampire's apartment we go in hard and fast so that we've got our claws inside of him before he's had a chance to realize anything is going on."

I waited while everyone nodded and then led the way back towards the vampire's building. I'd spent the day looking for cameras on the street, so I knew exactly where we needed to hood up. The ski mask slipped over my face without any fuss and then we were stepping inside of the lobby.

The desk clerk was fiddling with something on his computer monitor and didn't look up until we were less than ten feet from him. His hand darted towards the phone as soon as he saw me, but he never even had a chance. I crossed the distance between us in two quick bounds and slammed his head into his mahogany desk. I checked his breathing and his pulse and then followed James over to the elevator where he was busy dismantling the security camera that had recorded our entrance.

Jess had shed her clothes while I was taking care of the desk clerk. Once James signaled that the camera was out of commission, she took off her mask, handed Jasmin her clothes and her earpiece, dropped down onto all fours as the elevator arrived and then darted inside and sniffed the buttons on the panel. I stuck my head inside of the elevator, but the stench of vampire was too overpowering for me to pick out anything.

Jess sneezed a couple of times and then staggered back out and shifted to two legs, adjusting her ha'bit as she leaned against the wall. "I think he's on the twenty-fifth floor."

I handed her phone back to her. "Okay, good work. Stay here with an open line and make sure he doesn't leave without us realizing it. Don't engage him. If he shows up make a run for it. If you can circle back around this way we'll try to set up an ambush of some kind."

"Okay, hopefully it doesn't come to that."

I turned back to James who was shooting the stainless steel elevator a distasteful look. "I take it you'd rather take the stairs?"

"Yeah, as bad as that's going to suck, I'd rather not spend any more time surrounded by that stink than I have to."

It was almost enough to draw a chuckle out of me, but I just waved him towards the stairs. "You've got point, I'll take tail."

It wasn't the right formation. Jasmin should have been point, but she was so jittery that I didn't have any choice but to put her in the middle.

I turned my phone on and slipped my earpiece in as we started upwards. Jess answered on the first ring.

"I assume we're going to want to ditch our phones as soon as we're done here?"

"Yeah, that goes without saying, but I appreciate the reminder."

We took the stairs two at a time, reining ourselves back a little to make sure that we didn't arrive at the twenty-fifth floor winded. Even so, it only took a few minutes to make it to the floor in question and the three of us exited the stairwell moving with well-practiced silence.

The scent trail led from the elevator around to the right. We followed it until we arrived at a single door that had to belong to the vampire. James started to move forward as if to crash through the door, but then stopped and put his ear up to the cool metal.

He waved me over before I could ask him what was going on and as I got closer I realized that the door hadn't been soundproofed very well.

"...I pay you for results, not excuses. No, if I had any clue where they'd gone I wouldn't need you. All I can figure is that they decided to try and make a run for it after they saw how much those kids were carrying."

There was silence for a couple of seconds while the vampire listened to whoever was on the other end of the line and a smile crept out onto my face. It was ironic that the vampires' own nature was working against them like this. If their boss had even a shred of faith in their loyalty he would have made a run for it himself after they failed to report back to him. Instead he'd just assumed that they'd taken the money and run.

"No, they haven't taken a plane. I've got normals in place watching all of the outbound flights. They have to be trying to make it out by boat...no, they wouldn't just go to ground, not for more than a day or so, at least. Any longer than that and their conditioning would start pushing them back to me."

My smile started to fade as I realized that the phone call was a double-edged sword. It meant that we knew he didn't suspect us of having been the reason his people had disappeared, but it also made our attack less likely to succeed. We couldn't go through the door right now and risk him saying something to whomever he was talking to, but by the same measure we couldn't just wait outside of his door indefinitely.

I stepped away from the door and walked back down the hall, making sure that I was far enough that the vampire wouldn't be able to hear me.

"Jess, we need you up here. Grab the desk clerk and take the elevator. Maybe if someone shows up they'll just think he's using the bathroom or something. It's not much, but we need every edge we can get right now."

I waved Jasmin back to the elevator to help Jess with the doorman and then rejoined James at the door.

"...I don't care, just make it happen. I want a status update in four hours."

There was a muffled impact that I was pretty sure was his phone hitting the sofa, and then what sounded like bare feet moving across tile.

James looked at me expectantly, but I was still trying to make a decision when Jasmin and Jess arrived. I'd put on a confident front for the others, but I was worried about going up against this particular vampire.

In a lot of ways mentalists were the most dangerous vampires to tangle with, and this one had nearly overpowered me from several feet away. I'd been sure we could take him if we had surprise on our side and caught him half asleep. I wasn't as sure we could take him in a standup fight, at least not without losing someone from our side.

Jasmin and Jess quietly lowered the doorman down onto the carpet and I finally decided that we had to move now or risk having the building surrounded by police at some point in the next hour or so once people realized that the doorman was missing.

I double-checked to make sure that there wasn't a security camera in this hall, and then ripped my ski mask off, shed my clothes, and unleashed my beast.

The transformation swept through me and took most of my worries with it. Part of that was the fact that I'd already made my decision and it didn't do any good to second-guess a plan once I was committed to it, but mostly it was the fact that my beast was looking forward to this particular fight.

My beast saw things as being much more black and white than most people did. For him vampires were bad, they were dangerous and they preyed on the humans that legends said we'd been created to protect. As far as my beast—my wolf—was concerned, the only good enemy was a dead enemy and he couldn't wait to make sure that this particular vampire would never again pose a danger to us.

It was a heady, addictive feeling, but it wasn't my first time dealing with it. I forced my beast back into a corner of my mind, not far enough back to trigger a transformation into human form, but far enough that there wasn't any question who was in charge. I was going to fight this vampire, but I was going to do it on my terms, fully aware and calculating.

My transformation was the signal that the others had been waiting for and they all followed suit in a multi-pointed surge of power. A few seconds later everyone was ready and I charged forward, throwing all of my considerable bulk against the door.

The vampire had chosen well. The door was well-constructed and the locking mechanism held despite the titanic forces I unleashed upon it, but the hinges gave way and I stumbled into the apartment as the door went flying into a wet bar only a few feet inside of the entryway.

James was less than half a step behind me with the girls mere inches behind him. We must have made for a fearsome sight, but the vampire reacted with the kind of smooth reflexes that were inevitable after centuries of infighting against other vampires.

We'd managed to catch him by surprise, but I hadn't counted on the apartment being quite so big. Our massive hybrid legs devoured nearly ten feet with each stride when we were running like this, but even so it took us too long to reach him.

He held his hand out and a sword flew across the room towards him, arriving a split second before I did. I slashed at his neck, but he knocked my claws to one side and probably would have taken my head off at the neck if James hadn't followed up my attack with one of his own.

The telekinesis was a bad sign. Most vampires had only one supernatural ability. The fact that this one was enough of a telekinetic to grab his sword like that meant that he was probably even older than I'd expected.

Jasmin nipped at the back of his leg, but was forced away as his blade nearly sliced off her front paw. Jess tried for an arm and got an elbow to the side of her head that sent her sprawling. The vampire ducked under my next attack without even looking at me, and I suddenly realized that he must already be inside of our heads.

"He's reading your minds, don't overcommit!"

AMBUSHED

The fight ground to a halt between one second and the next as James, Jasmin and Jess all took a step backwards and turned most of their attention inward in an attempt to push the vampire out of their minds.

Their actions were understandable, but it was a mistake. I unleashed my beast, pointing him at the clear, almost invisible tendrils invading our mind, and grabbed a nearby chair. The improvised projectile spun as it left my hands, blurring towards our opponent.

I nearly got him. He slapped the metal projectile to one side at the last moment with a blast of telekinetic power that sent it into the floor-to-ceiling window behind him, but his response was delayed. I was already moving towards him, trying to capitalize on his distraction, but that didn't stop me from worrying.

My worry proved justified a split second later when Jasmin threw herself at James.

I tried to take the vampire's head off with the claws on my right hand, but even as he ducked away and slashed at my leg with the curved edge of his sword, I had visions of him taking all four of us over at the same time.

James managed to interpose his elbow between Jasmin and his throat, but it was a close thing. A heartbeat later Jess sailed through the air and wrapped her jaws around the back of Jasmin's neck. It was a killing hold, but it didn't have to be. From there Jess could hold onto Jasmin and for the most part control her.

Almost as soon as Jess got ahold of Jasmin, James took a swipe at Jess. I yelled out a warning as I grabbed two more chairs and threw them at the vampire, but if Jess hadn't been paying attention she still would have been killed. She released Jasmin and darted to the side, getting just far enough away that she was able to roll with the force of James' blow. She came up bleeding, but still alive, which was more than I'd had any right to hope.

Jasmin nipped at James, apparently having been released as soon as the vampire had taken James over, but the momentum of the fight had shifted away from us. All four of us had been hard-pressed to keep the bloodsucker occupied. Now that he was turning us against each other there didn't seem to be much hope of winning.

Amazingly, one of the chairs I'd just thrown clipped the vampire in the shoulder before ricocheting off and hitting the window behind him. He stepped out of the path of the third chair, and the cracks on the window behind him doubled in size.

I had managed to hit him though, and that meant he couldn't take one of us over and stay inside our minds well enough to anticipate our every action at the same time.

Jasmin yelped in pain as James connected with his claws, but I was too far away to stop

James, and if I let myself get distracted it would leave the vampire free to do whatever he wanted. I heard movement off to my left and charged forward just in time to avoid a large knife that leapt off of the kitchen counter, powered by a telekinetic push.

There wasn't any way to get all of us out of this particular fight alive. I'd gotten us in over our heads, which meant that I needed to be the one to save them.

My dodge of the knife hadn't just been a single step forward. That's probably all it would have taken to avoid being impaled, but I'd dashed towards the vampire at a full sprint. The distance between us wasn't sufficient to get up to full speed, but I came close and the vampire obviously hadn't been expecting that.

The smart thing would have been to avoid overcommitting. You had to commit your bodyweight to any given attack when you were fighting another hybrid or a werewolf because they were too big for anything less, but that wasn't how you fought a wolf.

For those kinds of fights you kept your weight balanced so that you could change directions on a dime and used your claws in lightning-quick attacks to keep your enemy off balance. Fighting a vampire was a lot more like fighting a wolf than anything else and that went doubly so when it came to fighting a vampire who might or might not be inside of your head at any given time.

I ignored all of the rules of smart fighting and threw myself at the monster currently inside of my friend's mind. The katana darted in from my left side, but the sheer stupidity of my attack succeeded in catching the vampire off guard. He started to hold his ground just like he would have done against a human, but even if he'd cut me in half that still wouldn't have been enough to stop me from colliding with him.

At the last second he tried to move to the side, which robbed his blow of most of its power. My claws deflected the blade up into the meaty part of my side, and then my right hand grabbed him.

We were going to hit the glass hard.

Maybe the glass would have held if it hadn't been compromised already by the chairs that had cracked it, but more than likely we still would have shattered it. I pushed the vampire ahead of me and felt him trying to break into my mind in the split second before he hit the window.

It was the last effort of a desperate man, but even as dark threads of thought breached my defenses I knew he was too late. Even if I'd been trying to stop us from hurtling out into space I wouldn't have been able to.

I heard footsteps, James' heavy hybrid thumps and the lighter ones from the two girls and wondered whether or not one of them was still being controlled by the vampire, but that didn't matter either. Even another hybrid couldn't stop me now, there was simply too much mass moving at too great of a speed.

The glass bowed as the back of the vampire's head hit it, and then it shattered. I had so much adrenaline in my system that it all happened in slow motion. One moment I was looking at a single pane of glass, spiderwebbed with cracks, and then tens of thousands of pieces shivered in the air as the vampire cut through them in a spray of red.

The vampire was all of the way out of the building now, but he let go of his sword and was trying to grab hold of my arm. It didn't matter, nothing mattered anymore, but I didn't want to fall to my death connected to a parasite who had killed thousands of people to preserve his unnatural existence.

I shifted forms, and the vampire's hands closed on empty air, my human fingertips now ending nearly a foot sooner than they had as a hybrid. The vampire finally realized that there wasn't anything he could do to save himself and I saw a level of terror on his face that I hope to never see again.

Popular culture glorifies vampires and portrays them as powerful beings who survive for centuries based off of willpower, but at that moment I saw the truth. He'd survived for centuries, but it hadn't been because of a drive to achieve some kind of master plan. He'd survived because he'd been terrified of dying.

I closed my eyes as gravity started to take hold of me. Things had happened so quickly that I couldn't have traveled more than a few inches, a foot at most, out of the building, but I had nothing to push against, no way of reversing my course.

I had a moment to hope that my death wouldn't hit Rachel too hard, hidden away back in the States against her will because I hadn't wanted to expose her to danger, and then my leg was practically ripped from my body.

The pain nearly made me black out. It wasn't just the sudden deceleration. James tried not to tear me up too badly, but he'd been most concerned with stopping me, so he'd sunk all five claws into my leg nearly down to the bone.

My course reversed with a suddenness that would have been impossible with anything less than the massive, preternaturally strong muscles of a hybrid powering the change, and then I was sliding across the floor.

I looked up to see James stagger back from the broken window. The claws on his right hand were painted red with my blood, and he'd left deep gouges in the metal of the structural steel beam he'd been holding onto.

James met my eye for a second before falling to the ground and shifting back to human form. I'd had no idea just how outmatched we were when we'd set out earlier that evening, but somehow we'd all survived. We'd just burned up all of our luck for at least the next couple of decades.

Chapter 4

Adriana Paige
The Premier Pillow Motel
North Platte, Nebraska

I opened the door to our motel room, which turned out to be furnished all in browns that hadn't seen an update since before I'd been born, and then turned and watched as Taggart maneuvered our suitcases through the door with an ease that contradicted his apparent age. He looked like a sixty-year-old Native American man who would have a hard time withstanding a strong gust of wind, but in truth he was both older and stronger than he looked.

I'd tried several times to get him to let me carry my own luggage, but Taggart was old-fashioned. Not old-fashioned like some people I'd known who had latched onto something they'd read about for some reason or another. He was old fashioned in that he still clung to ways of behaving that he'd grown up with, protocol and etiquette that had mostly died out a couple hundred years ago.

As much as I wanted to, I'd never quite been able to bring myself to ask Taggart how old he was—it didn't seem polite—but from some of the stuff he'd let drop I was pretty sure that he'd been around when the United States had been founded. In addition to being incredibly strong, shape shifters apparently lived for a lot longer than normal humans.

"You know it would look a lot more normal for me to get my own luggage, don't you? Even if we ignore the fact that girls have been carrying their own stuff for decades, you don't look like you should be able to casually swing a couple hundred pounds over your shoulder. That's the kind of thing that people remember."

Taggart looked up at me with a hint of fire in his eyes. It took a moment for him to force the anger back down, but I was getting used to that.

"There are some things I'm prepared to abandon in the name of expediency, Adriana, but I learned a long time ago that if you don't hold to at least a few core principles then you're liable to be blown completely off course when you least expect it."

It was another clue. Taggart had saved my life. He'd rescued my sister Cindi and me from an honest-to-goodness vampire and in the process he'd saved Tristan, the star quarterback Cindi had been crushing on. I was incredibly grateful that he'd risked so much to help me, but that didn't mean that I completely understood him.

Taggart wasn't always the safest person to be around. I'd first met him in a dream shortly after I'd realized that my dreams weren't like everyone else's.

It seemed impossible, but I could reach out to people while I was asleep, share their dreams and interact with them while they were at their most unguarded. I'd initially thought that I was the only person who could do what I did, but it turned out there was at least one more, Taggart, although even he didn't seem to have exactly the same gift as me.

Our first two encounters had been terrifying. Part of that had been because neither of us had been sure we could trust each other, but that had only been a small part of the reason. Mostly it had been the fact that Taggart's beast, the otherworld energy that allowed him to change shapes, was always just a second or two away from trying to take control away from the man I'd just spent the last several days driving cross-country with.

Taggart had explained the basics of his condition in a few brief sentences during our first full day together, but he'd been less expansive when it came to the details and causes. Mostly he'd focused on what I needed to do to help defuse the situation if his beast got too close to the surface. It mostly centered on not escalating things. Don't look him in the eyes, try to take up less space, talk softly.

It was more or less what I'd always imagined you'd find in a Boy Scout book in the section about dealing with dangerous animals. I'd spent my first day alone with Taggart wondering if I should be trying to make a run for it, but little by little I started to see the other parts of him, the less scary ones.

He held onto his manners because they were one more link in the chain he used to keep himself under control. He didn't always succeed, but it was obvious to me that he really was giving it his best. Someone else might have dismissed his efforts, might have said that he was just another kind of addict, but I didn't. I didn't understand his beast, but it was obvious to me that there was something else there, something inside of him that had its own set of priorities, something that was as strong-willed as any other person I'd ever met.

Taggart's manners weren't just odd because they were so anachronistic, they were odd because they didn't come from any one time period. They were an eclectic collection of things that he'd managed to hold onto despite the long years that had worn away at him. I didn't know how long he'd been on the run, but I'd been doing it for less than a month so far and it was already changing me in ways I hadn't anticipated.

"Do most shape shifters wander around on their own like this?"

The question slipped out of me without conscious decision. It wasn't the smartest thing to do, not so soon after he'd had to force his beast down from a perceived slight, but Taggart seemed to have himself well in hand now.

"No, Adriana, most of my kind live very different lives than I do. We're social by nature. Humans are inherently that way, but there's an extra degree of that for us. We form packs because they offer us a place in the world, they let us know where we fit into the dominance hierarchy and they offer protection for the strong and the weak alike."

"From vampires?"

"Yes…and other things."

"Like what?"

He studied me for several seconds and then shook his head. "You're already dealing with nightmares, I don't think that it's wise to add to your worries right now. Later, once you've had a chance to see how drastically your world has changed, I'll tell you more about the dangers most people never encounter."

I wanted to argue with him, wanted to tell him that I was ready to hear everything, but he was right. I hadn't slept very well ever since Jackson had tried to kill me. For a normal person nightmares were unpleasant enough, for a dream walker they could be deadly.

As long as I realized I was dreaming there wasn't much to be concerned about, but I was generally more present in my dreams than a normal person was. I didn't understand how—I wasn't sure that even Taggart really understood how it happened—but that meant that I could be injured while dreaming.

For Taggart, any injury was potentially problematic because anything that happened to him physically during a dream was carried back into the waking world. Things didn't work quite like that for me.

So far it seemed like broken bones and the like weren't a big deal, they usually just meant that I'd spend the next day or two dealing with an odd phantom pain while I was awake. The big question was what would happen if I was seriously injured. There was a remote possibility that something life-threatening would just result in me spending several days in bed suffering in extreme pain, but Taggart and I were pretty unanimous in the belief that if I got hurt badly enough inside the dream it would be just as fatal for me as those kinds of injuries would be for him.

It was a sobering possibility. Taggart was more experienced than I was inside of the dream and he was naturally stronger and harder to kill as a result of being a shape shifter, but even so we'd lost several days of travel time not too long after he'd found me. He'd tangled with someone or something in a dream that had nearly gotten the better of him. It had been a chilling lesson in just how deep the waters I was now swimming in were.

"Okay, you're right."

Taggart nodded and turned away as if to unzip his suitcase, but I wasn't done with him yet. If he was in the mood to talk then I wanted to get as much out of him as possible.

"Why did you leave your pack then? Is it because of Kaleb and the rest of the...Coun'hij?"

"I've been on my own for more than two hundred years. Kaleb is practically a child. He's been part of the Coun'hij for less than two decades. No, he didn't have anything to do with my exile."

I waited for several seconds, hoping that he'd choose to tell me, but growing more nervous with each heartbeat. I wanted to know, but I also didn't want to push and cause problems between us.

"You don't have to tell me if you don't want to. There's just so much I don't understand."

Taggart sighed and then sat down on his bed. He looked even older when he was hunched over like that. I'd seen his hybrid form. It was still huge and unbowed despite the silver mixed in with his fur. It was hard sometimes to view the two forms as being the same person.

"I'm by myself because I couldn't be trusted to control my beast. I hurt some people when I wasn't much older than you, and my pack drove me away."

"I'm so sorry."

I wasn't sure it was the right thing to say, but then again I spent most of my time these days uncertain of how I was supposed to be responding to things. Taggart had said he'd *hurt* people, he hadn't said that he'd *killed* anyone, but even if he had, I could tell that he was sorry for what had happened.

"Don't be, Adriana. It was no less than I deserved. I was as bad as the men and women I've spent so many years fighting. I was completely sure of myself, confident that whatever I wanted was right simply because I wanted it."

"I'm not saying it's right, but that's not that uncommon for a seventeen-year-old. Most of us tend to be pretty self-centered."

Taggart shook his head, refusing to meet my eyes. "Most seventeen-year-olds aren't killing machines who weigh four or five hundred pounds. It was worse than that, I was addicted to the thrill of the fight. My alpha had told me repeatedly that I needed to call my beast to heel, that I needed to control it rather than letting it control me, but I refused to listen. I thought my beast made me strong."

He stood and walked over to the window, still refusing to look at me, still determined to put as much distance between us as he could.

"He was right. There was a girl and another boy who was competing with me for her affections. Things were different back then.

There were places where we weren't completely in hiding. They were both humans, but they knew what I was. The boy thought I should stick to my own kind, that I shouldn't be chasing after a human, that I wasn't *safe* for her to be around."

"What happened?"

"We got into an argument and I lost control of myself. It had happened before against other hybrids, but that was the first time I'd given into my beast when facing off against someone who couldn't possibly stand up to me."

"I'm sorry. I know you said I shouldn't be, but I am."

Taggart shrugged. "I tried after that. My pack kept me imprisoned until they knew whether…well, until they knew whether I was a murderer, but I knew I was probably going to be exiled, turned into one of the dispossessed. I tried to control myself, tried to master my beast in the hopes that they would recant and let me stay, but it was so hard."

Taggart, the terrifying apparition that other shape shifters called Dream Stealer, rested his forehead against the cool glass of the window and I realized for the first time that his stooped back wasn't from age as much as it was from what he'd been through.

"It seemed so much harder for me than for the others my age. It wasn't until later, after I'd been exiled, that my ability manifested. Sometimes I want to blame everything that happened on my ability, but that is just another way of trying to shirk my guilt."

"An ability means that you have a stronger beast?"

"Nobody knows for sure. It's true that the weaker of my kind seem to struggle much less with their beasts. Some of the weakest wolves claim to not even believe that the rest of us have a distinct entity inside of us, but there are aberrations even to that, wolves who struggle like I did to control themselves. More importantly, there are powerful hybrids, individuals with legendary gifts, who don't seem to have any problem mastering their beasts."

"So since they can do it you feel like you should have been able to?"

"It's more than just a feeling, Adriana. I've spent nearly two centuries trying to learn how to control my inner nature, trying to replace savagery with something higher. I've made some progress, maybe—no, certainly—less than I should have, but I've made progress. I'm damned by my own success. My accomplishment since then has only proven that I could have done better back then if I'd really wanted to."

I opened my mouth wanting to say something comforting, but he cut me off.

"That's not important other than making sure you know what you're getting into. I'll do my very best not to harm you, but I can't make any promises."

I knew I should be scared, but somehow hearing the story of how he got like this, the reason he'd spent two hundred years alone and on the run, reinforced something I'd known all along. He wasn't going to hurt me. I needed to do my absolute best to make it easier for him, but when push came to shove, I knew he didn't want to hurt me. I'd seen him do incredible things inside of the dream, things that had taken an almost inconceivable force of will, and I refused to believe even his beast was stronger than the man I'd seen, the one who'd saved me and two of the most important people in my life.

"I understand, but I want to continue training with you. I need to master my power or I'll end up dead anyways."

Taggart sighed and then pulled out the two bags of fast food that we'd picked up right before stopping at the motel.

"Okay, then you're going to need to eat up. We're still burning off the calories as fast as you're taking them in."

I sighed as I accepted the two cheeseburgers he pulled out of the bag. I'd always assumed anyone who'd been alive for more than two hundred years would be rich, but apparently Taggart's resources weren't unlimited. I guess all of that running had precluded staying in one place long enough to earn any kind of substantial nest egg.

He was too principled to turn to theft, although he'd been quick to liquidate everything he could get his hands on from the two vampires he'd killed in Minnesota, so he was very careful about how he spent his money. It took a lot of calories to stoke his shape shifter metabolism and my dream walking ability likewise consumed all of the energy I could feed it, so we tended towards greasy, fatty foods.

I knew I couldn't survive on fast food forever, but this was only temporary. Besides, he was right, there was no way I could consume enough calories eating salad—my ability simply used up too much energy.

Since Taggart had put me on a steady diet of cheeseburgers and fries, my weight had finally stabilized for the first time in months. I was still as skinny as any of the girls on my cheerleading squad back home, but at least I wasn't still losing weight.

It was still light outside, but I stifled three separate yawns by the time I made it through the mountain of food in front of me. Dream walking was hard work and I never felt quite rested after the nights I spent in other people's dreams, which was nearly every night since I'd met Taggart.

"Why is it that you don't seem to lose weight like I do as a result of dream walking?"

Taggart pondered the question for nearly a full minute before shaking his head. "Honestly, I don't know, but it explains some things that I'd always wondered about."

"What do you mean?"

"You're not the first human I've run into who had an ability of some kind or another. It's rare, but it happens. Usually it's clairvoyance or some kind of precognition. Stuff that doesn't actually affect the material world."

Taggart folded up the foil wrapper that had been around his second hamburger and shrugged.

"Shape shifters, on the other hand, frequently have abilities that have physical manifestations of some kind or another. I always wondered at that, but now I'm pretty sure humans don't get that kind of gift because it takes a lot more energy to power something like that than dream walking or another similar ability. I think humans have to power their gifts out of the energy reserves they have physically present in their bodies."

"But you don't?"

"It doesn't appear like it. Even our ability to shift forms, instantly adding more than a hundred pounds of bone and muscle, would be impossible if we weren't getting fed from some kind of external power source."

I thought about that for a couple of seconds before nodding. "That makes a lot of sense, I mean for something that I don't understand in the slightest. Part of me thinks I should feel ripped off because I didn't get a bigger, more powerful ability, but the truth is I'm already in over my head as it is."

Taggart frowned at me. "Don't sell your gift short, Adriana. It's not as flashy or straightforward as being able to electrocute someone, but wars are usually won because of information and you and I are ideally placed to find out things that nobody else could learn. That's actually what I need to do tonight."

I couldn't decide whether to be disappointed or relieved. Most nights Taggart trained me by either joining me inside of my dreams or having me join him inside of his, but occasionally he took the night off from training me so he could tend to the network of informants and spies he'd spent the last several decades putting together.

Apparently my indecision made it onto my face. Taggart gave me a rare smile and then pointed to the bed on my side of the room. "This doesn't mean you get the night off. I want you to try and come with me to meet my informant tonight. You're getting good enough inside of the dream that I think it's time for you to start doing some of your learning on the job."

I tried to look confident, but the last time I'd run into anyone other than Taggart in a dream I'd nearly died.

Chapter 5

Adriana Paige
The Premier Pillow Motel
North Platte, Nebraska

Taggart always dropped off to sleep as soon as his head hit the pillow, but it wasn't that easy for me this time. I was just as tired as always, but I was nervous enough that it took me a few minutes to finally transition to sleep.

That meant that I had even more time than normal to worry. Before he'd gone to sleep, Taggart had shown me a picture of his informant, someone name Eric, and then rattled off a handful of facts about him like his date of birth and parents' names.

That was how Taggart made his way into someone else's dream. Making the initial connection seemed pretty hit-and-miss, but once Taggart had visited someone else's dreams, he could almost always return to them. Whether it was the first trip or the hundredth, Taggart always accomplished it by visualizing his target and remembering some of the things that made them unique.

I'd had his method of making first contact drilled into me a dozen times already, but each time I'd tried to make contact with one of his people I'd failed. The failure itself wasn't unusual, but I should have had a success by now. It rarely took Taggart more than a month to contact someone for the first time. I wasn't up to a month straight of trying yet, but I couldn't get away from the feeling that I wasn't getting any closer to success.

Even as worried as I was, it only took another ten minutes before I nodded off. Apparently I was even more exhausted than I realized.

I transitioned into my own dream after what felt like no time at all, and found myself inside of my bedroom back in Minnesota. I'd been dreaming about home a lot. I was getting better at remembering my dreams lately even after I woke up, so I had a unique view into what was going on inside of my subconscious.

I was homesick. It wasn't like that was any kind of surprise or anything, but it didn't make being away from my family any easier. I hadn't even been able to call them. I understood why, but that also didn't make things any easier.

Taggart was being hunted by the Coun'hij, the shape shifter ruling council, and I was probably being hunted by more of the vampires who had nearly killed me back in Minnesota. Illegal phone taps and traces were nothing to people like that. As long as I cut off all contact with my family they would probably be safe, but if I were stupid enough to call home it would put them, and me, in danger.

I couldn't change the fact that I was homesick, but I could choose not to dwell on it. I changed the bedspread on the bottom bunk to a fluorescent orange that Cindi never would have chosen for her bed and some of the tension between my shoulder blades disappeared. It had been easy to make that small change to the dream, which meant that I really was inside of my own dream rather than having accidentally wandered into someone else's dream again. That meant I was safe, as long as I didn't pull someone else inside of my dream with me.

Well, that wasn't quite guaranteed either, but I was fairly sure that there weren't any powerful vampire mentalists crouched outside of our room. Vampires were a lot more common than I ever would have believed, but not as much so once you crossed the Mississippi. Apparently the shape shifters made it a point to try and keep the vampires confined to the more urbanized eastern section of the United States.

Safe was good. Good except for the fact that I was supposed to be trying to get out of my dream and into someone else's. It was tempting just not to try. I was exhausted and scared, and it would probably be good for me to take a night off from dream walking, but if I was going to make that argument I probably should have made it before I went to sleep.

I couldn't lie to Taggart. I'd tried a little white lie not long after we'd left Minnesota and he'd caught me instantly. Apparently being a shape shifter turned you into some kind of human lie detector. It was possible to lie to a shape shifter and get away with it, but I wasn't a complete psychopath, so I wasn't going to manage it anytime soon.

All of which pretty much meant that I was going to have to try and make it into Eric's dream. I hadn't told Taggart beforehand that I needed the night off, so he was counting on me being there, or at least doing my best to be there at the meet. Besides, he was right. A certain amount of learning to dream walk was just going to come down to getting out and dream walking.

To be fair though, I had expected things to be a lot less trial and error now that I was working with Taggart. It only made sense that one dream walker should be able to shorten the learning curve for another, but so far that hadn't really been the case. Taggart had warned me about that, but I hadn't realized until we'd been working together for a few days just how different our abilities were.

AMBUSHED

We could both dream walk, but he seemed to be a lot stronger inside of the dream than I was. Even when we were in *my* dream sometimes I couldn't stop him from changing our environment. When we were inside of his dream I couldn't even come close to holding my own.

I'd initially thought that had to do with the fact that he was a lot older and more experienced, but there were other differences, the biggest one being that I was able to pull other people into my dreams against their will.

It sounded like a small thing, but Taggart, the infamous Dream Stealer, hadn't ever managed it. More amazingly, I was able to pull people into the dream strongly enough that they could even die there. That wasn't supposed to be possible. Dream walkers are vulnerable whether in their own dreams or in someone else's, but non-dream walkers are supposed to be safe.

It was possible to torture someone and make the experience traumatic enough they would remember it when they woke up. It was even possible to cause them phantom pain the next day, but it wasn't possible to kill them. Except I could.

That was how Taggart and I had killed one of the vampires who had been after me back home. Taggart was practically jumping up and down at the possibilities, but I wasn't so sure how I felt about being the perfect assassin.

As a general rule I wasn't interested in killing anyone, but I'd had a rather pointed lesson in the fact that there were...well, I guess you still called them people...out there who were truly evil. I've never been a fan of those tricky philosophical questions, but if there was a modern-day Hitler out there killing a lot of innocent people and I had the ability to sneak into their dreams and kill them no matter how well-protected they might be in the real world, didn't I have a duty to prevent even more innocents from being killed?

Luckily it wasn't something that I had to decide right away. Taggart might have some flaws, but he wasn't going to force me to kill people. For now I just needed to learn how to control my abilities enough that I wasn't always showing up inside of the dreams of every nearby shape shifter or vampire. That was a good way to draw the kind of unwanted attention that could end up with me being dead.

I sighed and climbed up to the top bunk. If I was going to do this I figured I might as well get comfortable and I couldn't think of anything more comfortable than my old bed.

For all that there were some serious differences in how our abilities worked, Taggart's description of making initial contact with someone matched up exactly with what I remembered from the time I'd pulled him into my dream. It was like your mind sent out thousands of tiny threads, racing away at incredible speeds.

Once one of the threads found the person you were looking for, you reabsorbed all of the other threads and then strengthened the remaining thread enough that you could pull yourself to them. Or if you were me, you sometimes pulled them to you.

I slowed down my breathing—apparently even in my dreams I still needed to breathe—and focused on the image Taggart had shown me. I cleared away all of the emotions that Taggart said were nothing more than a distraction and started pushing tendrils of energy out of myself. I was getting better at that part, but although they left, they didn't seem to really be going anywhere.

It was frustrating, and not just because I couldn't explain it. I'd never realized before I started working with Taggart just how hard it was to describe a *feeling*. Sure, we talk about feelings all the time, especially us girls, but how do you really know that the feeling you're describing is the same feeling that someone else is experiencing?

It didn't seem like what was going on now was the same as the time I'd consciously pulled Taggart into my dream, but the last time I'd tried to explain that, he'd told me that once the threads started spinning out of him that he either found his target or he didn't, there wasn't any way to mess things up once you got to that point.

The surge of frustration triggered a reflexive effort to clear my mind once again, but I stopped before I even really got started. Taggart was big on being a blank slate when he was working, but nearly every single time I'd accomplished anything big strong emotions had been fueling me during the experience.

Acting more on a hunch than anything else, I let the frustration stay and added in half a dozen other emotions. Respect, dependence, a slight dose of fear, all of the emotions that I'd come to associate with Taggart went into the mix and then rather than just letting the filaments spool out slowly on their own, I *pushed* in the odd way that I'd learned made things happen for me inside the dream.

They shot away from me with exactly the speed and urgency that I'd been looking for, the speed that, up until now, had been missing. My strength poured out of me in step with the movement of the threads and I felt a familiar sense of worry at how quickly it was fading.

Taggart was convinced that a failed attempt to find a specific individual was of no long-term consequence. He'd told me several times that the only result of a failure would be that I would exhaust my strength and then simply lapse back into a normal, dreamless sleep.

I wanted to believe him. Certainly my limited experience so far had seemed to support that idea, but the sheer pace at which I was spending energy this time was alarming.

A combination of worry and fear spiked inside of me. The rising tide of emotion threatened to destabilize the mixture I'd whipped up intentionally, the feelings that made me think of Taggart, but I managed to hold on for just long enough for one of the threads to connect with something that *felt* like what I was looking for.

Just as I remembered happening before, the rest of the threads came whipping back towards me, melting back into my body and providing me with the strength I needed to thicken up the thread that had found Taggart.

For a single heartbeat everything balanced on the edge of a knife. I didn't want to go forward, didn't want to take the risk that I hadn't actually found Taggart, but I knew I had to act right then or I would lose my chance.

The thread reached some kind of critical mass and started to unravel, but I pushed off against my surroundings at the same time that I pulled on the line between the two of us. There was an odd catch, as if for a moment the universe wasn't sure whether to pull him towards me or send me hurtling towards him, but then I accelerated at an impossible speed.

I couldn't have said whether the trip took hours or was over in an instant. My head felt full, like I'd had hours of thoughts impossibly compressed into a fraction of a second, and then I was there.

I'd been moving faster than I'd ever moved before, but I arrived without stumbling, without even a whisper of sound to betray the fact that Taggart and Eric weren't alone anymore. We were standing in the middle of a featureless white plain. Eric was facing away from me, looking at Taggart, and didn't give any indication that he'd noticed any kind of change in his surroundings.

I knew I was looking at Taggart because I could see a shimmer where he'd altered his features, but if not for that I'd never have recognized him. He looked like an eighth-century Irishman. He had red hair, a full beard and looked like he could crack rocks with his bare hands.

Taggart hadn't given me any kind of instructions on what to do once I arrived—probably because he hadn't actually expected me to be successful—so I simply shifted my clothes and body, making them clear and thereby rendering myself invisible.

It wasn't perfect. Looking down at myself I could see the same distortion in the air that had clued me in to the fact that Taggart had changed his appearance. Eric probably wouldn't be able to see the difference, but I knew that Taggart saw the same shimmer in the air as I did when someone changed their appearance.

"What do you know, Eric?"

"I told you—nothing is happening right now. No news is good news, right?"

Taggart didn't look happy, in fact he looked like he was starting to lose the tiniest bit of control over his beast. I circled around, moving slowly so as not to make any sound. Even so, it only took me a couple of seconds to get far enough to the side to see that Eric understood just how thin the ice he was standing on was.

"Don't play with me, Eric. You were the one who approached me. In the last five years there hasn't been a single time when you didn't have something to report, some new development or rumor."

"There's nothing—I swear it!"

Taggart grabbed him by the throat. "I can make your life misery incarnate. Imagine going to sleep every night worried about what would be waiting for you here. Do you know how often you have to torture someone to drive them insane? It varies from person to person, but I don't think it would take much to send you over the edge. If you want out then just say so, but don't waste my time, don't try to play me. I won't be mocked."

Eric shifted forms, becoming a hybrid in an explosion of flesh and power that knocked Taggart away. Taggart responded in kind, transforming into a hybrid before he'd even finished rolling back to his feet. My heart shot up to my throat as the two hybrids circled.

"I've wanted out for years now, but you're never going to let me go. If I stop helping you, then in your mind I'm no better than any other Coun'hij enforcer. You'll still come here and spy on my dreams, you'll report everything you learn to Agony, and one day I'll turn around and find him waiting for me. I'm good, but I'm no match for Agony."

Taggart's voice came out low and savage. "We're at war, Eric. You have to choose a side. I'll respect your choice, but that doesn't mean that you get to sit out the fighting."

There was an edge of hysteria to Eric's laugh. "I never had a choice. Once you picked me, once you managed to make contact with me, it was only a matter of time before I was going to end up dead. I've been playing a losing hand ever since then. I tried to convince myself that I was doing something good by helping you, that I was honoring Audrey's memory, but the truth is that I've been scared every moment of every day since you found me."

"You always have a choice, Eric. It's not my fault that you're too craven to make the choice that you wanted to, not now, not five years ago, not twenty years ago. That's on you."

"Yeah, well, the joke's on you. Dream Stealer, the master manipulator, the man who is better than anyone else at turning people and corrupting them. You pushed me too far, the fear got to be too much and I couldn't manage to avoid suspicion anymore. They know."

The fear that I was about to witness a massive fight was replaced by a certainty that Taggart and I had just walked into a trap.

Taggart apparently felt the same way. He dodged to the right a split second before another hybrid appeared out of thin air and tried to rip his heart out of his chest.

Everything happened so quickly that my head spun. I shouldn't have been able to follow it all. Shape shifters fought with such blinding speed that humans had no hope of keeping up with the lightning-fast exchanges, but somehow I was able to see what was going on.

The new hybrid, a hulking, red-furred monstrosity, missed his initial attack, but pivoted on one foot and caught Taggart in the shoulder, scoring what looked like a shallow set of slices in the muscle there. Eric took advantage of Taggart's apparent preoccupation with the newcomer to try and charge him from behind, only to run into a featureless black slab of rock that materialized out of thin air between one heartbeat and the next.

As Eric reeled drunkenly away from the rock wall, it disappeared and Taggart attacked the red hybrid. I'd always thought that Taggart was impossibly huge in his hybrid form, but he gave up an inch or two in height and even more than that in reach to this newcomer.

I was pretty sure that in a purely physical confrontation that Taggart was going to come out second place, but the red hybrid wasn't just up against Taggart, he was up against Dream Stealer, the man who'd spent two centuries inside of people's dreams. The red hybrid dodged to one side, but his attempted evasion was cut short as thick, cable-like plants wrapped themselves around his legs.

That would have sent me crashing to the ground, but the new hybrid not only kept his feet, he managed to get his claws up and deflect most of Taggart's attack away from him. He still ended up with some deep gashes across the side of his chest, but based on his expression it wasn't anything life threatening.

"You're new. I didn't know that the Coun'hij had started another recruiting drive."

Even as Taggart spoke, another set of vines appeared, this time wrapping themselves around Eric's neck, but the new hybrid made no effort to go help his supposed ally.

"They brought me in specially, just to deal with you."

The two hybrids blurred towards each other again and when they staggered back apart they were each bleeding from new wounds. I was pretty sure that Taggart had hardened his skin at the last second to stop one of the attacks from striking home. The plants were gone from around Eric's neck, and the wound across his stomach didn't seem to be bleeding as much as it should have been.

"Should I be flattered? I thought the Coun'hij had finally realized that every time they bring someone new in there is a chance that they are bringing one of my agents into their inner circle. If I've got them nervous enough to start recruiting again, it's only a matter of time before they make an even bigger mistake."

The bigger hybrid bared his fangs in something that couldn't really be called a smile. "Let's just say that other developments necessitated a more proactive stance where you're concerned. Alec Graves' recent rebellion against his father means that the Coun'hij ran out of room on their dance card, so they've decided to eliminate some of their old partners. Your name was towards the top of the list."

More blood spattered the ground as both hybrids tried once again to get past each other's guards. Eric was slowly pulling himself back to his feet, but I was having a hard time concentrating on the fight.

Alec Graves was the biggest remaining point of contention between Taggart and me. The single dream that I'd shared with Alec remained etched in my memory as the one and only time I'd felt truly safe during the weeks leading up to my rescue by Taggart.

There hadn't been much to the dream—a few minutes' worth of talking followed up by an epic kiss. Alec hadn't even been able to offer me any protection, but his advice had been what had ultimately caused me to trust Taggart enough to call on him for help.

Even so, interacting with Alec had changed me in ways that I couldn't really explain. It was like I'd spent my entire life in darkness. I hadn't known what I'd been missing, but I'd still been unable to escape the nagging suspicion that there was something more to the world.

Meeting Alec had flipped on a light. I couldn't go back to a life of blindness after that. Taggart didn't trust Alec because he thought anyone related to Kaleb Graves had to be a worthless snake, but I knew that Alec and I were meant to be together. It didn't make any sense, especially for someone who didn't believe in soul mates, but that didn't change the fact that I knew it was true. If Alec had really run away from home and was working against his father then Taggart would eventually relax his prohibition against me trying to make contact with Alec again.

In the grand scheme of things maybe it wasn't that important, especially not with the fight that was currently raging just a few yards away from me, but it was incredibly important to me.

As much as I wanted to dwell on the possibilities that being able to talk to Alec again raised, I forced my attention back to what was going on around me as Taggart slapped the other hybrid's hand out wide to one side and raked his own claws down the inside of the other man's arm.

The red hybrid seemed to be bleeding from more places than Taggart now, but Eric was creeping stealthily forward in an effort to surprise Taggart and end the fight in one fell swoop. I couldn't afford to continue to just sit the fight out, not if I wanted Taggart to have a chance of surviving.

Shape shifter hearing was acute, but I changed my features, invisible though they were, and visualized myself as being nearly weightless. I pushed that change into effect as I started running towards Eric. He was moving slowly enough that it took only a couple of seconds to make it over to him and then I was left with the question of how to go about disabling the tower of muscle and bone that was a hybrid.

I didn't realize that I'd made a conscious decision until a shiny aluminum bat materialized in my right hand. It was exactly the same as the bat that Tristan had used to try and stop Jackson. There were probably better choices as far as possible weapons went, but it had materialized without the invisibility that had been protecting me, so my cover had just been blown. I didn't have time to mess around. Besides, the bat felt good in my hand.

The red hybrid yelled out a warning as I wound up for a swing at Eric's leg. Whatever change I'd gone through that allowed me to follow the blindingly fast motions of a hybrid fight hadn't done anything to actually speed up my muscles and bones.

I could tell that I wasn't going to be fast enough. Eric was already spinning around, and my arms were taking too long to accelerate the heavy aluminum bat. Only it didn't *have* to be heavy. I'd never had much luck changing my own strength inside of the dream, but the weight of the bat was another matter entirely.

A concentrated burst of thought was all that was needed to make the bat nearly feather-light. I nearly overbalanced as muscles that had been straining against the momentum of a nearly motionless bat suddenly whipped the length of aluminum through an arc faster than any major league player had ever managed.

Just before the bat connected with Eric's knee I realized that the blow wouldn't actually hurt unless the bat was heavy. Even with my enhanced reflexes and time sense, I almost didn't have enough time to make the needed change. I imagined the bat regaining its former mass, but I was more focused on the concept of *heavy* than an actual defined amount of weight.

I over-compensated. The bat went from weighing less than three pounds to something in the neighborhood of a hundred and fifty pounds. I had no prayer of holding onto it at that point, but it didn't matter because the bat retained its original velocity.

It crunched into Eric's knee with enough force to shatter the spine of a rhinoceros. The bat tore itself free of my hands and nearly knocked me down in the process, but it laid Eric out flat. I stumbled backwards, trying to make sure I was out of range of the deadly claws that flailed towards me.

I wanted to be sick. I'd helped kill Pamela, but I hadn't been the one doing the damage to her, that had been Taggart. I told myself that it wasn't real, that Eric would wake up in a few hours with nothing more than a dull pain in his knee, and forced myself not to throw up. I didn't have time to be squeamish.

The red hybrid darted towards me, no doubt intending on killing me quickly so that he could return his attention to Taggart, but he made it less than a full step before Taggart grabbed his arm and swung him around, hurling him headfirst into another pillar of stone that appeared between one heartbeat and the next.

"Hold them here!"

Taggart was fearsome in his hybrid form, blood dripping from his wounds, his claws painted the same gory red, but I found myself shaking my head.

"I'm sorry, I can't do it."

An invisible, metaphysical wind tore across the white plain where we were standing. It would have scared me, but I'd felt it before. Taggart was holding both Eric and the other hybrid here in the dream, but he couldn't keep them here indefinitely. The best he could do was prolong their stay, only I could pull them into the dream completely enough for him to kill them.

He apparently misunderstood my refusal.

"Fine, just hold the red one here. We can always come back and deal with Eric later, the red one is more dangerous anyway."

I shook my head as I slowly backed away from all three of them. He thought I just couldn't hold two of them there at one time. If I'd been able to get away with lying to him maybe I would have claimed that I couldn't hold someone inside of their own dream, that it only worked inside of my dream, but he would have known immediately that it was a lie.

Besides, it wouldn't have changed anything in the long run, it just would have meant that he'd have wanted me to pull them into my dreams, one at a time, and kill them tomorrow or next week, or next month.

"It's not that I'm unable, Ta...Dream Stealer. It's that I won't do it. Not now, not like this."

I threw myself out of the dream. I'd half expected Taggart to keep me there too, but he let me leave. It didn't matter though. I'd saved myself from watching him torture them, but that wouldn't protect me from his rage once he woke back up.

Chapter 6

Jasmin Bianchi
Two Pines Private Airport
Atlanta, Georgia

Alec hadn't confronted me about the fact that I was losing my nerve yet, but it was only a matter of time. After the fight with the vampire mentalist I'd managed to keep the shakes from setting in until we made it back to the hotel and I was safely alone in my room, but it had been a close thing.

I'd been scared a lot lately, but having that *thing* wear my body like a glove had been the worst yet. I'd been fine, fighting as best as I could against an enemy that could read my plans as fast as I could come up with them, and then between one instant and the next I'd been nothing more than a passenger inside of my own head.

Alec and James had both indicated that for them the mental contact had gone both ways. They'd gotten bits and pieces, memories and thoughts from the vampire, but it hadn't been like that for me. All I'd gotten from the vampire was an incredible sense of wrongness, a dark decay that could only be described as evil.

I pulled my crap together enough to go back out with everyone the next day, but it was a good thing that we didn't run into any problems with the second delivery. James, Jess and I once again waited in the swanky bank lobby while Alec went down to the vault and took delivery of an obscene amount of wealth.

This time at least we got to listen to a new round of rumors while we cooled our heels. Being a shape shifter meant that we could hear whispered conversations from a lot further away than a human, and every person I could hear had been talking about the sheer number of armored cars that had visited the bank that morning.

The line employees hadn't known what was inside the cars, but everyone had known that *something* was up. Apparently the VP Alec was working with was worth whatever the bank was paying him though, because by the time we'd arrived he'd already taken four other people down to the vault.

Decoys, brought in for the express purpose of making sure that nobody could say for certain that Alec was the recipient of the dragon's hoard that had been shipped in from the rest of the banks on the island.

I'd actually been more than a little surprised that there had been enough bearer bonds on the entire island to cash Alec out, but then again maybe there hadn't been. Maybe one or more of the banks had issued an entirely new round of debt just to make sure that they got in on the fees Alec was ponying up to break the electronic trail of what had happened to Kaleb's money.

I thought I was going to lose it again between when we left Deutsche Bank and when we arrived at the Cayman National Bank. I probably would have if we'd been jumped again, but we weren't and I didn't.

I expected Alec to order us back onto a charter plane as soon as we finished up at the second bank, but he led us back to the hotel and left us twiddling our thumbs there for two more days. You would have thought that two days of downtime would have helped me put myself back together a little, but the waiting was almost as bad as the fighting had been, and it wasn't just that way for me. I was pretty sure I was seeing the same signs of stress in James and Jess.

None of us came right out and said it, but we all knew that Kaleb was looking for us and there were only so many places you could go if you wanted to launder billions of dollars' worth of stolen money. When you threw in the fact that we'd been involved in not just one, but two, sets of homicides since we'd arrived on the island, it felt like we were running on borrowed time.

When Alec finally showed up and told us that he'd arranged a charter flight back to the States, I hoped my stress level would start going down, but I spent the whole flight fidgeting in my seat. I probably would have given Alec a piece of my mind, but he'd found four more people from the island and lured them onto the plane on the pretext of them having won some kind of trip to the mainland.

It didn't seem very wise to air all of our dirty laundry in front of a bunch of humans, so I refrained. That and the plane wasn't big enough to deal with Alec in hybrid form, which is what might have happened if I'd unloaded on him.

Exiting a chartered flight is pretty much just like arriving on a private jet. You walk down the stairs onto the tarmac, grab the luggage that is lined up waiting for you, and walk to your car.

Depending on how rich you are and the size of the airport in question, your vehicle might be less than twenty yards away or it might be a five- or six-minute walk away, but either way you could be on your way while the commercial passengers were still waiting for the fasten seatbelts light to turn off.

Usually it's the best possible way to travel, but my spider sense started tingling as soon as we got out of the plane. Alec had a white SUV waiting for us, but there was another SUV, a black one, idling just outside of the gate onto the tarmac.

Alec didn't seem to notice. He was busy shaking hands with the four shills who'd shared the flight with us. I grabbed his arm to get his attention, but he reached down and removed my hand without looking at me.

"Act natural, Jas. Trust me, you do not want to blow things right now."

"Are you out of your frickin' mind, Alec? We got lucky with that mentalist, hell, we got lucky with his minions earlier that day too. That SUV could be chock full of hybrids who are waiting to follow us to whatever hotel you've got lined up for us. Even the best case scenario, that there are only one or two guys watching us right now, is still bad because now they know where we are and it's going to be that much harder to disappear again."

Alec finally looked at me. He had a casual-looking smile on his face, but I could feel his anger bubbling just beneath the surface. He was wearing sunglasses, but I would have bet any amount of money that his eyes had turned a paler shade of blue, the color of his beast rather than the color of the human that was normally in the driver seat inside his head.

"I gave you an order. Smile and then go get your luggage like you don't have a care in the world. You're above your pay grade on this one."

I wanted to flip him off, or shift and go for his throat right there in plain view of everyone, but the first idea was bad and the second one was even worse. I pasted a sarcastic smile across my face and then turned and stalked off towards my bag.

It took all of two minutes for us to pile into the SUV with James and Alec in the front and Jess and I in the back seat. Our windows were heavily tinted, so I watched the other SUV as we pulled out onto the main road.

Whoever was driving it was good. They waited until we were quite a ways ahead before they pulled out and followed us. They kept two cars between us at all times, but I still caught occasional glimpses that confirmed my fear that they were following us.

I managed to bite my tongue for nearly ten minutes before I couldn't stand it anymore.

"Alec, you can tell me to shut up all you want, but it isn't going to make that SUV from the airport go away. We've got a serious problem on our hands."

Alec looked like he wanted to bite my head off, but he took a deep breath and pointed out our exit for James before turning back to look at me.

"I tried telling you to shut up already, but it didn't work the first time so I don't suppose yelling at you again is going to make any difference. You're right, that SUV is following us and it's probably full of either Kaleb's people or maybe Coun'hij enforcers if Kaleb has finally come clean with the Coun'hij about the fact that we're in open rebellion against him. Either way, there's a reasonable chance that we're screwed, but you telling me that we've got a problem when I already know about it isn't going to solve the problem. *Please* shut up and let me concentrate. The only way to get out of a situation like this with our skins intact is for me to outthink whoever is back there."

I felt the shakes threatening to return. I wanted to scream at Alec, to tell him he was the alpha and it was his responsibility to make sure that we didn't get outmaneuvered like this, but I gritted my teeth and looked away from him. If I started yelling at him I was virtually guaranteed to lose control in other ways, and none of us could afford for me to have a breakdown right now.

The rest of the trip took less than five minutes with Alec navigating and James driving, but it wasn't until the very end that I surfaced enough from my internal battle to realize that something wasn't right. Alec's words weren't matching up with his actions. He didn't seem like someone who was worried.

As far as alphas went, Alec was pretty standup. Any dominant was going to treat you like crap from time to time simply because their beast wanted to push your nose in the fact that you were subordinate to them, but Alec usually kept that kind of stuff to a minimum.

We'd been through a lot together already and Alec valued loyalty too much to treat me like dirt without a good reason. Besides, his instructions to James were coming too smoothly. He wasn't choosing our route on the fly; he was following a preplanned route.

A second later we pulled into what had to be the largest parking garage in the city. We started down and with every level we descended the tension inside of our SUV ratcheted up a little tighter. I counted seven levels before Alec sat up in his seat and pointed at a line of orange cones to our right.

"Run over the cones."

The cones were placed in a curved line to guide the traffic down to the next level and there were a couple of signs indicating that there was some kind of construction going on, but James didn't even hesitate. He turned the wheel hard to the right and mowed over three of the cones, crushing them under our tires.

"Go on to the very back. There, pull into a space behind that Escalade and kill the engine."

It wasn't a very good plan. Alec seemed to be hoping that the guys who'd been following us wouldn't notice the crushed cones, or if they did that they wouldn't pick our SUV out of the line of six cars we were parked next to. It wasn't bad considering how little time he'd had to plan, but it was a slim hope to be risking our lives on.

Fifteen seconds after our engine died, the black SUV that had been following us pulled into view. I hadn't gotten a good look at the plate back at the airport, but I knew it was the same one. There was simply no way that a different black GMC had decided to drive over the cones and come our direction.

My suspicions were confirmed when the other vehicle coasted to a stop and all of the doors opened up simultaneously. The five guys who got out weren't anyone I recognized, but they were the kind of big bruisers who seemed a fixture of Coun'hij operations.

"They aren't from our pack, I mean the Sanctuary pack. I'm kind of surprised, I thought Kaleb would try and keep our disappearance a secret for longer than this. It must have really hurt his position inside of the Coun'hij to admit that he'd lost control of his own son and needed help hunting us down."

My voice came out calm, disinterested even, but inside I still felt like I was going to go to pieces at any minute. I knew I wasn't fooling anyone. Alec and the rest could hear my heart racing, could probably smell the perspiration trickling down the back of my neck.

Alec looked back at me and I expected him to tell me to stop freaking out, but he just grunted. "Yeah, I expect he's lost some pull as a result. I'm not entirely sure that's something to be celebrating. As bad as Kaleb is, there are others on the Coun'hij who are worse. Okay, everyone out."

It was pretty much the same as ordering us all to jump out of an airplane without a parachute, but we all piled out of the SUV and lined up opposite the Coun'hij enforcers.

"We're here to take you in, Graves. Your daddy still has enough influence to make sure you aren't executed out of hand, but we've got more flexibility when it comes to your friends. Resist and we'll kill all of them, really piss us off and we'll kill you too and just tell Kaleb to go screw himself."

I looked over at Alec. Taking your eyes off of a group of thugs who'd just threatened to kill you wasn't exactly the smartest thing to be doing, but he was my alpha, he was the one who got to decide whether or not I was about to die. Alec examined the five guys facing us and then smiled.

"I'll make you a counter-offer. Surrender now and I'll let the five of you live long enough to have a fair hearing. If you're not guilty of the disgusting excesses most of your fellows are so fond of, I'll even give you a chance to swear allegiance to me."

I looked at Jess out of the corner of my eye and she looked terrified. Her breathing was coming nearly as fast as mine, and James was shifting back and forth from foot to foot, but apparently none of us were stupid enough to think that turning ourselves in would guarantee us any kind of safety.

We'd made our bed when we'd helped Rachel escape and there wasn't anything we could do about it now. I wasn't exactly sorry I'd helped save Rachel. I would have done it again if faced with the choice, even knowing how things were going to end up, but I'd hoped that we'd have a longer run than this.

One of the Coun'hij enforcers, a massive guy with a neck like an ox and at least a dozen different facial piercings, started laughing. The rest of them joined in over the next couple of seconds, but Alec's voice cut through all of that like it didn't matter.

"Very well, don't say I didn't give you a chance."

A maroon van thirty yards behind the Coun'hij guys opened up and seven people exited it in short order and shook out into a loose line. Even if I hadn't recognized them I still would have known that they were shape shifters. They were all wearing ha'bits and they all moved with the easy grace of someone whose balance and reflexes were literally superhuman.

It was Jack, the squad leader we'd worked with in St. Louis, and his entire group. He was the only hybrid, but that meant we had three hybrids and eight wolves against their five hybrids. They didn't stand a chance.

I looked over at Alec and saw that he'd kicked off his shoes. "I'd offer to make introductions, but there really isn't any point."

The enforcers all shifted at the same time, flaring power like a single metaphysical supernova, but Alec and the rest of us shifted a split second later and Jack's people were only a heartbeat behind us. The next three or four seconds would determine the course of the fight and we all knew it.

The five hybrids had three choices. If they stayed where they were and waited for all of us to come to them then they'd lose. They might hurt a few of us, maybe even kill a couple of us, but they would lose, the odds were just too far against them. If they'd had someone with some kind of useful ability like Brandon or Kaleb with them, then it would have been a whole different matchup, but they didn't, not based on the way Alec had been looking them over.

He'd been checking them against the files he carried around in his head, the files that listed every really dangerous hybrid in North America along with their picture and a description of their power. Alec could bluff, but I knew that smile. He'd smiled because he knew we were up against five normal hybrids.

Since the first option was out that meant that the hybrids all either needed to charge the four of us or they needed to charge Jack's people. If they charged us then there was a chance they could kill us before Jack's people arrived and then they'd be able to turn on Jack and the others and probably beat them too.

It was a workable option, but my money had been on them going the other direction. By charging Jack they would be up against only one hybrid, but the other four hybrids would be up against six wolves. The odds were still in their favor with that kind of matchup, but it wasn't as good as three hybrids against two wolves.

No, the real reason to go after Jack's people rather than us was that it gave them a chance to break free of the ambush. It gave them room to move and the psychological reassurance of not being trapped anymore.

I ended up being right. All five of the enforcers shifted to wolf form and bolted towards Jack and the others. Wolves were faster than hybrids in a long race, which was why Alec and James had likewise shifted to wolf form. It was a race and the stakes were life and death for all sixteen of us.

My earlier jitters had disappeared as soon as Jack and the others showed up. I tore across the concrete with reckless abandon, Alec hot on my heels, James and Jess a couple of yards back. Alec was strong and he was fast, faster than most wolves, but this was the kind of fight I'd been born for. Nobody else in the Sanctuary pack was as fast on four legs as I was.

I was gaining on the five Coun'hij wolves, but even I couldn't make it to them before they reached Jack and the others. To an uninformed eye, the five lithe shapes running towards Jack's massive hybrid form didn't seem like a threat, but this was actually the trickiest part of the whole ambush.

If Jack and the others just scattered then the enforcers would get away. Not all of them certainly, I'd be able to run one of them down and Alec might be able to catch another of them, but at least some of them would get away.

If we'd been out in the wilderness that wouldn't have been the case, but we didn't have forever to run them down, eventually we'd be out in full view of the public, at which point things would get a lot more dicey. Jack might have one or two people who were fast enough to catch an enforcer, those of us who only fought on four legs tended to be faster than the hybrids even when they were in wolf form, but if even one enforcer got away, then Jack's role in rescuing us would make it back to Kaleb and the rest of the Coun'hij.

I was pretty sure that Jack didn't want that to happen, but if he and the others stood their ground then they risked having the hybrids shift forms at the last instant and crash into their line as hybrids instead of as wolves. There was no way that six wolves and a hybrid could possibly stop more than a ton of determined hybrids who were already moving at full speed, it was suicide to even try.

All of which explained my shock when Jack refused to back down in the face of the oncoming enforcers. His wolves melted away, getting out of the way, but Jack simply set himself as if to stop the charge singlehandedly.

Jack had treated us well when we'd been in St. Louis and he'd risked a hell of a lot in coming here to bail us out. I liked Jack, at least as much as any wolf could like a hybrid. I reached inside and came up with a little more speed, but it wasn't going to be enough, nobody could possibly get there in time.

It was a sacrificial play, but it was one that the enforcers had to honor. If they just charged past as wolves then they were going to get hurt. Wolves are fast, but hybrids are practically purpose-built for killing fast things. Jack couldn't chase them down, but he'd get claws into two of them, he'd probably kill them before they even hit the ground, and then the other three would be faced with even worse odds when it came to trying to escape.

They might be able to outrun one or two wolves apiece, but there wasn't much chance they'd be able to get away from three of us. That meant that at least two or three of the hybrids were going to have to shift form and hit Jack as hybrids rather than as wolves. They'd mow him over like he wasn't even there, but that would slow them down, which meant that the four of us would be that much closer to them when they tried to make a break for it.

It wasn't much to trade your life for, but it was the best option that Jack had available to him. The mechanics of the situation were stark and merciless. We all knew them and we were all ready to play our part. I jumped lengthwise over a Ford sedan and slid past a concrete column so close that I felt my fur brush it.

My feet just about came out from underneath me as my pads landed on a strip of dry paint that was slightly slicker than the unpainted concrete, and I had to look down to make sure that my next step wouldn't put me on more paint. I looked back up just in time to see three of the enforcers shift forms a split second before they collided with Jack.

Only there wasn't any collision. Instead of just throwing himself forward to try and offset their momentum, Jack leaped straight up, just managing to clear the center hybrid as the three of them flashed past him.

It was a masterful display of strength and timing. Hybrids are strong, but they are also massively heavy. The three Coun'hij hybrids who had been charging him had been running full speed, so they'd been leaning forward, but in order to get high enough up to clear the reach of their claws he'd still had to jump nearly seven feet straight up. Some parking garages didn't even have tall enough ceilings for him to do what he'd just done, but this one did and as he came back down he managed to turn slightly in the air and get a single toe talon into the back of the center hybrid.

Jack's people sprang into action even before the center hybrid crashed into the ground. Two wolves, presumably his fastest, streaked after the two enforcers who had stayed in wolf form, while the other four attacked the two hybrids who were still on their feet.

The melee was a blurring mess of blood, claws and fur that couldn't last for very long. Hybrid-on-hybrid combat is plenty brutal; hybrid-versus-wolf combat tends to end even more abruptly. Either the wolves manage to slip past the hybrid's defenses and get a killing hold on their neck or we die. We aren't sturdy enough to trade blows with them like another hybrid.

A two-to-one matchup was a fight in which the wolves *could* come out on top, but it was by no means guaranteed. Luckily Jack's wolves didn't need to last for very long because I was almost there.

The hybrid on the far left of the fight stumbled, but it was a feint to try and lure one of his opponents into a bad attack. It worked and I saw a gray form plant and throw itself at the hybrid from the side. The hybrid recovered with preternatural quickness and spun around, claws flashing to rip the wolf out of the air.

It was the perfect play on the hybrid's part and it was a major screwup for the wolf. The hybrid had chosen an instant in which the second wolf was off balance and unable to attack, but that shouldn't have been an issue because the gray wolf should have known that time was on his side for once. All he'd needed to do was distract the hybrid long enough for Alec and James to arrive, but he'd tried to push the issue and it was probably going to cost him his life.

The one mistake that the *hybrid* made was not realizing just how close I was or just how much faster I was than any normal wolf. I didn't plant, the concrete was too slick for that, but I put a little extra force into my next bound.

The hybrid's attack had turned him so that his right flank was towards me. It wasn't a perfect setup like an attack from directly behind would have been, but it was close enough. The air clawed at me, trying to slow me down, but I still hit the hybrid at more than thirty miles per hour.

I'm only something like a hundred and twenty pounds in human form, but I push almost two hundred when I'm a wolf. My jaws clamped onto his neck and then I felt the familiar wrench of deceleration as all of my kinetic energy was shifted to him over the course of a few fractions of a second.

We wolves look a lot like real wolves, albeit much bigger than a normal wolf, but there are differences if you know what you're looking for. The biggest is just how much more muscle we have around our neck and shoulders relative to the rest of our body.

Real wolves are strong—they have to be to bring down elk that are several times their weight—but they are dealing with prey animals. Granted, they are relatively dangerous prey animals, but that's not quite the same thing as trying to snap the neck of something like a hybrid. There's no such thing as an apex predator in the supernatural world, but hybrids came close.

I spun around, my jaws still anchored on the enforcer's neck even as my back legs slipped over his shoulders and slid down his left arm. Hybrid necks are incredibly well-muscled and those muscles are full of the same kind of unnatural vitality that makes me so strong and fast, but any physical construct has its limits and I'd exceeded those limits.

The hybrid's neck cracked and he dropped bonelessly to the ground.

I'd achieved the perfect kill, something that some wolves said wasn't even possible, but then again it might not have been possible without the special advantages that my bloodline bestowed upon me.

The entire attack had taken barely more than a second. I let go of the hybrid's neck, hit the ground, rolled through two full revolutions to bleed off the rest of my momentum, and scrambled back to my feet just in time to see Alec change forms and throw himself at the enforcer on the far side of the fight.

"Jess, James, help the runners!"

Alec's command cut through the air a split second before he collided with the other hybrid. The impact was nothing less than titanic. The enforcer saw him coming and tried to sink his claws into Alec's chest, but Alec knocked the deadly claws high and to the left as he dropped his shoulder and hit the other hybrid with enough force to knock both of them off their feet.

The wolves who had been harrying at the hybrid's flanks, dodged out of the way with yelps of surprise and then spun back around and latched onto the enforcer's wrists before he'd even had a chance to come back down from his first bounce.

The second enforcer was as good as dead. Alec was no slouch in a fight and probably could have given any of the hybrids a run for their money even without help, but with a pair of wolves in the mix it was just a matter of time before Alec came out on top.

Jack and the third hybrid were still trading blows. They were both bleeding from half a dozen different places, but he seemed to be holding his own, so I charged after James and Jess.

The gray wolf I'd figured for a goner had been bleeding profusely, but he'd still been walking under his own power. Even if he couldn't help Jack out, the other wolf who had been fighting the hybrid I'd just killed should be enough to tip the balance. Besides, I wanted those other two hybrids and I was faster than Jess and James.

The air had a cold, mechanical smell to it and the huge fans that kept carbon monoxide from killing everyone made it harder to follow the scent trail, but my nose was so sensitive that it didn't matter. Nothing less than a torrential downpour could have eliminated the scent markers left by six moonborn in full flight.

I had a lot of ground to make up, but my earlier jitters were so far gone that they might as well have never even occurred. Nobody else was as well-suited to chasing down a fleeing hybrid as I was. The trail unsurprisingly led back up towards the surface rather than deeper underground, but I'd half expected for the two of them to split up.

One of them could have retraced the route we'd used originally to get down here. They would have been going against the flow of traffic, but it would have doubled their chances of getting away.

I came around a corner a second later and saw why they'd chosen to stick together. One of the enforcers had shifted into hybrid form and stayed behind to deal with Jack's wolves. It was too bad that one of the wolves hadn't been able to slip by and continue after the other enforcer, but the hybrid had picked his spot well. He had the ramp pretty much blocked off.

James and Jess were only a dozen yards ahead of me. I had a second to hope that James would be smart enough to make a hole for me and then he shifted forms and crashed into the hybrid.

Alec's attack had been dangerous. He'd charged full-speed into another hybrid from the side and if his timing had been even a little off he would have missed his block and been killed. James' attack was nothing short of reckless. He didn't charge in from the side, he charged the enforcer from the front. It was virtually guaranteed that he wouldn't be able to block attacks from both of the other hybrid's hands at that speed, but it was exactly what I needed.

One of Jack's wolves grabbed the enforcer's right wrist in her jaws at the same time that the other locked onto the hybrid's left leg, and then James barreled into him, sending all four of them skidding across the concrete.

I sailed over the entire mess in one giant leap and reacquired the scent trail of the last enforcer. My lungs were burning now. The ground was blurring away underneath me, but that was only part of the problem. I wasn't just racing across level ground, I was going up at a rate that would have left a professional marathoner sobbing on the side of the road.

Under normal circumstances I would have just cut back my speed, but that wasn't an option right now. I had to catch the enforcer ahead of me or Jack's people were all in just as much trouble as we were. At least the hybrid I was chasing had to be suffering as much as I was.

I jumped over a curb and leaned over hard so that I could make the next corner without slowing down. The real problem was that this kind of chase didn't play to my strengths. I was fast, but speed wasn't just about strength and endurance, it was also about agility. In a normal run there was plenty of dodging around trees and the like. It was avoiding the obstacles that tended to slow down the hybrids in wolf form so much, but that was exactly what was missing right now. This had turned into a brutal competition to see whose endurance gave out first.

The scent trail had seemed like it was getting closer for the last few seconds, but I wasn't sure it was anything more than wishful thinking until I hit the third floor and was able to hear him up ahead of me. Someone, probably Jess, was behind me too, but they were losing ground on us; if—no, when—I ran the enforcer down I was going to have at least several seconds where I'd be by myself, seconds where he would push the engagement and try to kill me before help could arrive.

Lactic acid buildup was becoming a problem. Not only was I gasping for air now, my muscles were burning. I didn't have much more time before my body simply refused to continue moving.

We'd made it nearly back up to ground level without anyone seeing us, but our luck ran out on the second floor. I arrived just as a red Mazda bounced off of the enforcer's massive hybrid body before the driver slammed on the brakes and brought the car to a screeching halt.

The only thing I could come up with was that the car had taken my opponent by surprise and he'd been too far off balance already to avoid it so he'd just shifted forms to at least give himself the benefit of being hit while he was in the form best suited to take that kind of punishment.

The driver must have nearly had a heart attack, but she seemed to have only clipped him. Most of his injuries seemed to be from colliding with the concrete wall before he went cartwheeling away and back into the car a second time.

I didn't need to kill the hybrid I was facing, I just needed to keep him occupied long enough for James and the others to arrive. I slowed down, stopping a few feet outside of attack range as the Mazda's driver started screaming.

I couldn't blame her, I would have been just as freaked out in her position, but it was the wrong thing to do. The enforcer was already back on his feet and it was no effort at all for him to drive his fist through the driver-side window and impale her with his claws.

My hackles pulled back as a deep growl worked its way out of my chest. The woman had been a problem, but she could have been dealt with. The Coun'hij had special teams specifically tasked with making sure witnesses didn't make any waves for us shape shifters. She hadn't needed to die, Oblivion could have been brought in to wipe her mind, but the enforcer was having a bad day and wanted to take some of his frustration out on someone else, someone who couldn't fight back.

AMBUSHED

We stood there for one impossibly long second, both growling at each other, and then he attacked. I'd been expecting his move, and while I was tired and slower than usual, the same was true of him. I dodged to the right and moved into his attack, ripping a chunk of flesh out of his leg as I went past.

It was a small victory. More than anything I wanted to go for another kill shot like I'd done to the hybrid I'd taken down just minutes before. Every instinct inside of me screamed that fighting on the hybrid's terms was suicide, but I forced all of that to one side and leaped over the next attack, a claw swipe that was moving so fast that I almost couldn't even see where his claws ended.

I didn't try to bite him this time, I was just relieved not to be opened up from muzzle to tail. It was a close thing, he was exhausted and banged up, but he was faster with his hands than I expected. I jumped over his claws, but then he reversed his hand and tried to tag me while I was still in the air and unable to change direction. He would have succeeded, but his collision with the wall seemed to have messed up his shoulder.

I landed and sprang away again, trying to lure him deeper into the parking garage, praying the whole time that there weren't any other humans where they could see us. Two giant wolves fighting were conspicuous enough, once you threw a hybrid into the mix nobody was going to believe that they'd seen anything but what they'd actually seen.

He took two steps after me and almost tagged me again. His talons got better traction, cutting into the concrete like they did, but that was only good for short bursts of speed. His claws missed my tail by less than an inch and then he stopped chasing me.

I spun back around and moved towards him, thinking that he was going to turn and make a run for it, but he simply picked up a heavy metal sign and threw it at me. He threw it like a boomerang, end over end, which made it even harder to dodge.

I darted to the right, but it ricocheted off of a wall and grazed my left side. Breathing was agony. He'd cracked at least a couple of ribs and I was bleeding for the first time in the fight so far.

If he took off now I was screwed. I couldn't possibly hope to catch up, and while our fight hadn't been exactly restful, he wasn't gasping for air anymore, which meant that he'd be able to outrun Jess and whoever else I could hear approaching.

I was so outmatched at this point that it wasn't funny, but I didn't think about that. Instead I bluffed. I started creeping towards him, growling the whole way and doing my best not to let him see the stabbing pain that made me want to flinch with each breath.

I must have been more convincing than I thought, that or he was just too caught up in the fight to realize he was going to kill me but lose the war. He moved towards me, and while there was a slight hitch to his stride from the chunk of muscle that I'd ripped off of him, he was obviously in a lot better shape than I was.

I put a concrete pillar between the two of us, ducking behind it to avoid his first attack, and then tried to dart in and savage his legs again. I almost succeeded. I came within inches of landing another bite, but he connected with a backfist at the last second that sent me flying.

My ears were ringing and I was seeing stars when I landed, but I staggered gamely back to my feet and saw the most beautiful sight I'd seen since Jack and his people had climbed out of their van. Jess came sliding around the corner. She was gasping and soaked in sweat, but she was here, which meant that there was a chance I wasn't going to die after all.

I expected the enforcer to turn and run. He had to know how badly I was hurt after I'd failed to get away from his last attack, but he didn't. It took me a couple of seconds to realize that he'd knocked me towards the direction of the exit. I was now between him and freedom.

He couldn't risk turning his back on Jess to rush me as a hybrid, but if he shifted back to wolf form he would be fighting me on my home turf. I might be bruised, broken and bloody, but

I'd still put money on myself against some arrogant jerk of a hybrid who probably hadn't fought in his wolf form since he'd manifested a third shape.

Even better, I could hear more feet running our direction. James or the other wolves were now only seconds away. I'd done it, I'd stalled him for long enough, now I just needed to keep myself alive long enough for everyone else to pull him down.

He correctly fingered me as the weak link, so he came for me. I should have moved to meet him, or barring that at least tried to put some more distance between us. My own blood made the floor extra slippery.

I tried to dodge again, but I just didn't have the traction. He would have ripped me in half, but Jess threw herself into the fight at precisely the right time and latched onto his right wrist. She threw his aim off just enough that I escaped with three inch-deep slices in my left side rather than being killed.

Even a hundred-and-eighty pound wolf hanging from their wrist doesn't do much more than slow most hybrids down. The hybrid tried to spin back the other direction and catch me with his left hand, but by then I'd moved far enough away from the pool of blood that I was able to dodge.

As soon as his claws had sliced past me I reversed direction and got my own piece of his left arm. I wasn't much of an impediment, and I dropped away after just a second, but it was enough to let Jess get away from him without getting disemboweled.

Jess and I spread out, circling our foe, daring him to commit to one of us so that the other could go for something more vulnerable, but we never got a chance to start into him because one of Jack's wolves arrived a second later. By the time that James and the last wolf finally arrived, there wasn't much left to do but wait for the hybrid to finish bleeding out.

The run back down to Alec and the others was a complete nightmare. Every step hurt and I left a trail of blood that was going to eventually lead the police right to us, but there wasn't anything I could do about that. I'd be even slower as a human and I'd still be bleeding all over everything.

Jack and Alec ended up meeting us halfway down with both vehicles and the rest of our people. I collapsed into the SUV as Alec waved James into the driver's seat and slapped gauze over the worst of my wounds.

"Find us a parking place somewhere on the second floor, James, while I get Jasmin stabilized."

James grunted and then once Jess was inside, got us back into motion. I was pretty sure that I was starting to go loopy from blood loss, but I couldn't make myself care.

"You knew. You knew that Kaleb would have people waiting for us when we got off of the plane and you set this whole thing up."

Alec nodded. "Yeah, I knew it was going to be an issue even before we flew down to the Caymans. I didn't have a solution in place when we left, but I spent a good chunk of the time we were down there trying to come up with some way to get back stateside without getting all four of us killed."

"Jack. That was brilliant, I never would have thought of recruiting him."

There were already some pretty massive gashes in my ha'bit, but Alec tore them even wider. Jess kept direct pressure on my right side while Alec started taping up the more dangerous gashes between the ribs on my left side.

"You were out on patrol for a good chunk of the time that we were in St. Louis, but I got to spend a few minutes talking to him once I woke up the next day. I knew that he was furious at Kaleb over his son's death, so I figured it was worth a shot. That's why we stayed longer than you were expecting in the Caymans. Jack and his people came over to scout out what we were likely to see in the way of opposition when we landed."

Alec moved over to my other side and I hissed in pain as he pushed on the cracked ribs. "I'm sorry."

"Don't be. I know the drill. You have to make sure that they are only fractured and not broken."

"No, not for that. I'm sorry that I couldn't tell you what was going on. That was Jack's condition for coming and helping. He trusted me, and he believed that I thought you were all trustworthy, but he wasn't ready to risk his people's lives on that. I had to promise that I wouldn't tell any of you what was going on."

"Because if we'd been double agents then we could have ruined everything by letting Kaleb know that he needed to increase the size of his welcoming party."

"Yeah, that about sums it up."

"So what now? Jack still isn't going to trust any of us, and now he's got to worry about the fact that we'll leak the fact that he helped to Kaleb."

Alec shook his head at me. "I don't think that's going to be an issue. All three of you practically killed yourselves running down those last two hybrids. If any of you were working for the other team you would have let that last guy get away. If James had picked even a slightly more cautious way of engaging the one who was running interference then you never would have caught the last guy, and Jess could have very easily gotten you killed once she met up with you."

It took a couple of minutes for that to process through my pain-dulled mind. "I guess you're right. Jack's still got to worry about us getting captured and tortured, but he's probably safe other than that. Unless the Coun'hij is playing an even longer game and they are hoping to use you to flush out all of the rebellious elements so that they can take care of the undesirables once and for all."

"I know, but Jack's already thought of that too. If he really thought that Kaleb and the others were trying to do that then he never would have agreed to talk to me in the first place."

"I guess you're right. I'm sorry too, Alec. I don't mean to be losing my edge, I just can't seem to help it."

"Don't worry about that, you did exactly what needed doing and you did a spectacular job of it, Jas. I know no matter how bad things get that I can count on you, on all of you."

He pulled out a syringe and injected me with a general anesthetic. It wasn't enough to put me out, there weren't a large number of things that would do that to a shape shifter, but it took away the pain and left me floating in a pool of relaxation.

"Alec."

"Yeah?"

"Can we go find Rachel now?"

"Sure thing. She'll be excited to see you too."

I was just enough with it to notice as Jack walked up to our vehicle and let himself inside.

"Alec, I hate to be the bearer of bad news, but we've got a massive problem."

Chapter 7

Adriana Paige
The Premier Pillow Motel
North Platte, Nebraska

I'd fled Eric's dream sure that I was going to wake to find Taggart's beast in control, but I'd fled anyway rather than be forced to kill another person with my gift. My fears were so embedded in my subconscious mind that I was extremely disoriented when I woke up the next morning.

I just lay there motionless for nearly a minute while I tried to process what was wrong. Eventually I realized that I wasn't disoriented because of *where* I was waking up, I was thrown off because of *how* I was waking up.

Taggart wasn't yelling or stalking around the tiny room like a caged predator, he was sitting on his bed writing in a plain leather-bound journal. Not only that, I wasn't getting any of the usual signs that alerted me to the fact that he was having a hard time controlling his beast. There was no unearthly hum of power in the air, his eyes were even their normal tired green rather than the hot yellow of his beast.

He looked over at me and gave me a sad smile as soon as he felt my gaze. "I'm sorry, Adriana. I owe you an apology. When I agreed to train you I vowed that you'd be able to choose your own targets or no targets at all. I didn't mean to break that promise last night. I can't change the fact that you're a weapon, neither of us can, but you at least deserve to decide how you'll use your power."

Even despite all of the clues to the contrary, I'd still been ready to stand up to him and defend my actions. I'd been ready for a yelling match; this was so far different than my expectations that it nearly brought me to tears.

"I'm sorry, Taggart. I just couldn't do it. Maybe Eric and that other guy were both deserving of death, but I just couldn't be the one to make it happen. We'd beaten them, it wasn't like last time when Pamela was just outside of my house. I wasn't in danger this time, not by then."

Taggart sighed. "I understand. You haven't had a chance to see for yourself what the Coun'hij has been responsible for, but that's just the way that things have to be for now. Once you have control of your nightmares, maybe I'll be able to change your mind. I'm just glad that you chose to intervene on my behalf during the fight. It probably would have gone very badly for me if you hadn't."

I nodded uncomfortably. "To be honest, the deeper I get into all of this, the more worried I am about everything. I don't know anything about your world and I'm worried I'll end up doing things that I'll come to regret."

"Believe it or not, I understand what you're going through, Adriana, at least to some extent. Initially my exile wasn't of my own choice. I spent a lot of years in isolation, but eventually I was contacted by the Coun'hij. I'd tried to keep my abilities quiet, but they'd figured out that there was more to some of their dreams than pure chance. They didn't know who I was, but they invited me to join them, on any terms that I cared to name."

I was having a hard time believing what I was hearing. Taggart had told me again and again, ever since we'd met, that the Coun'hij couldn't be trusted. I'd never even suspected that his knowledge might have come from having worked with them, from having committed the kinds of atrocities that he was always hinting that they routinely turned to in order to keep control of the other shape shifters, in order to keep the existence of Taggart's people a secret.

"They weren't as bad back then, Adriana. I know that sounds like a cheap justification, but it's the truth. Oh, there were signs, things that were distasteful, instances where someone went too far, but their goals were worthy goals. They were the ones who kept the chaos and corruption south of our border from boiling up into our homeland. They were the ones who were hunting down the vampires and the werewolves. The only reason that we hadn't been wiped out by the humans decades ago was that they had kept our existence a secret."

"What happened?"

He refused to meet my eyes. "I had nearly accepted...no, that's not true, I *had* accepted their offer. I was working with them. Not in any big ways, but in a multitude of smaller things. I kept an eye on some of the more dangerous figures south of the border and I was responsible for gathering intelligence about vampires in Los Angeles and Chicago. My work was key to identifying a network of more than fifty vampires that Ulrich and the rest of the Chicago pack destroyed over the course of a single night. Just that one raid saved the lives of hundreds, possibly even thousands of humans who otherwise would have been killed in Chicago each year."

"You're right, that sounds like an admirable goal to me."

"I spent nearly ten years as a de facto member of the Coun'hij. The first eight years was a heady time. You know how hard it is for me to form new dream connections with individuals. I didn't bother forming connections with most of the Coun'hij. Some of them operated in a cloak of secrecy just like I'd been doing, but mostly that was just because there was always someone else who I needed to make contact with. Vampires and jaguars mostly, but by the end I was being used more and more against my own kind."

"They started cracking down on dissident elements?" I wasn't a history genius or anything, but I'd seen enough documentaries on what had happened in Nazi Germany and other totalitarian regimes to have an idea of how governments went from being the good guys to the bad guys.

"Yes. There was always a reason. Mostly I was being used against rogue dispossessed, people like me who were considered too dangerous not to keep tabs on. Some of them had extreme abilities, the kinds of things that could be used to wipe out a small town all by themselves. It was hard to disagree with the need to make sure that they weren't becoming unstable."

Taggart dropped his head into his hands. "Some of them were complete monsters. I found proof that they'd done terrible things, things that deserved execution, but I later found out that the Coun'hij was recruiting them, just like they'd recruited me. They cared more about securing their power than they did about justice or protecting the humans who were being caught in the crossfire."

"So you left?"

"No, not at first. I still thought that I could help with the good stuff and not get caught up with the bad. My contact with the Coun'hij was surprisingly understanding. I didn't come right out and tell him that I wouldn't continue to spy on the dispossessed for him or that I wasn't going to continue to gather intelligence on the various unaligned packs, but he saw the pattern. When I was given an assignment to establish a connection with one of the jaguars I could usually manage it within a month. When I got an assignment I didn't want to do, I just never managed to establish contact.

"I made it another year and a half like that, picking and choosing assignments, telling myself that I had to work with the Coun'hij because nobody else had the resources it would take to deal with the biggest problems out there. I was miserable, but I was fighting the best way I knew how. I might have still been doing the exact same thing today except I screwed up and my contact was able to figure out my real identity."

A wave of sympathetic terror ran through me. Our anonymity was our greatest defense. Even before I'd really understood anything about my ability, I'd instinctively understood that as long as nobody knew who I really was that I'd be safe.

"What happened?"

"My contact turned out to be a much better person than I'd realized. I'd spent the entire ten years I was working with him thinking he was just like all of the rest of the Coun'hij. I thought that he didn't give me static over my refusal to spy on the dispossessed because the Coun'hij, as a group, had decided that it wasn't worth forcing the issue and risking the possibility that I'd just walk away."

"They were mad, and he was running interference for you?"

"Yes. I think he saw something of me inside himself. He was—he is—younger than me, but he'd spent some time as one of the dispossessed too before joining up with the Coun'hij. The next time I saw him he told me that he knew who I was, and that the Coun'hij wouldn't allow him to keep that secret for long once they realized he'd figured it out. He said that I needed to go to ground, to disappear for a few years and after that I needed to make sure I had even less contact with other shape shifters than I'd been having."

"That doesn't sound like enough. You've said again and again that if the Coun'hij actually knows who it is they are after that they can find anyone. They can hack the facial recognition software at airports and train stations, they are unstoppable."

"Yes, I told you that because that's exactly what he told me, that I wouldn't be safe once they knew what I really looked like. Then told me that I'd been right all along. He said that he'd spent so long thinking that the ends justified the means that he'd almost convinced himself, but in obtaining our end we'd become the very thing we'd been fighting against. He slipped away from the Coun'hij's secret base that very night and has been on the run ever since."

"He ran away to keep your secret safe."

The sheer scope of what Taggart was implying boggled my mind. I'd been struggling to comprehend what it must be like to live on the run for years because you had no other choice. It seemed impossible to believe that someone would choose that life on behalf of someone else.

Taggart finally met my gaze and nodded. "Indeed he did. He told me at the time that he didn't expect to last long, maybe a decade or two, but at least he'd buy me that much longer before the Coun'hij came looking for me armed with the knowledge of who I really was. He was wrong though, he's made it longer than anyone else believed possible.

"They've been looking for him this entire time, but he's become a ghost, slipping through the cracks in our society even as he became a symbol for everyone who wants to see the Coun'hij overthrown."

"Why are you telling me this?"

"For a lot of reasons. You deserve to know the truth about me, you deserve to know that my history is nearly as dark as that of the people I'm trying to fight, but that isn't the only reason. I'm also telling you because it's the perfect example of what I need to be doing with you. I knew I could trust my friend on the Coun'hij because he was willing to allow me to make my own choices, even when those choices meant extra risk for him.

"I would never have even thought to ask for such a sacrifice from him, but the fact that he was willing to make it for me told me all I needed to know. It told me that he was someone I could trust with my life and, even more importantly, someone I could trust with my honor."

"There's more, isn't there?"

I couldn't have said how I knew, but I did. Taggart was about to deliver some kind of terrible news, something that was going to change everything for us.

"I visited another contact last night after the fiasco with Eric, and I learned something important. My friend has finally been captured after all these years. His name is Agony and the Coun'hij has him. I'm going to do whatever I can to free him, which means that I'm going to be putting myself back in the crosshairs again. I won't compel you to help, I'll respect your decision to get as far away from me as you can if that's what you want to do, but I have no choice but to at least ask for your help.

"I can't do this by myself, but I have to try. The only question is how much, if at all, you'll be willing to aid me."

Chapter 8

Adriana Paige
Marauder's Gas Station
Central Wyoming

My mind had been spinning non-stop ever since Taggart had told me that his friend Agony was in trouble. Taggart had helped me when I needed it, and a part of me wanted to respond in kind, but in a lot of ways his story had just reinforced my fears. I was in the middle of an impossibly complex situation and I could only come up with one possible way to figure out how far I could trust Taggart.

I already trusted him with my life, but I still didn't know if I could trust him to tell me who lived and who died. I needed to know if I trusted him enough to kill for him.

I needed another source of information, a source as close to unbiased as possible, or at least one who didn't have a vested interest in working *with* Taggart, but I didn't know very many shape shifters. Taggart, Eric, the red hybrid...and Alec Graves, the one person Taggart was almost desperate to keep me from talking to.

We'd gotten a late start, but we'd still been driving for long enough that I desperately wanted a chance to stretch my legs. Luckily, the fuel gauge was down to just over a quarter of a tank, so a break couldn't be too far away.

Taggart said that we were headed to Montana. He apparently had a cabin up there in some remote corner of the state. It wasn't the perfect location when it came to dream walking. Distance mattered when it came to our ability, just like it mattered with most other things. Reaching someone on the East Coast would be difficult, as would contacting someone all of the way down in Arizona or in Mexico, but Taggart said that the extra fatigue involved was more than offset by the fact that we'd be safe up there.

Safety sounded good to me. There was a chance that the Coun'hij already knew Taggart's name and were slowly looking through every video feed in the United States in the hope of finding him. It would take a lot of computing power to go through weeks and weeks of video feed, but eventually they were bound to find a hit of some kind or another. Nobody could hope to make it through even a single month without being caught on a video camera of some kind at least a couple of times.

The real question was whether the Coun'hij would hack into the right video feeds. They already routinely scanned the feeds from airports and train stations simply because it was a good way to keep tabs on known vampires. There were so many people on those feeds that it was a great return on their hacking investment.

Breaking into the computer systems that supported some backwater gas station was another matter entirely, as they mostly just recorded an unchanging view of the gas station in question. All we could do was try to avoid high-population areas and hope that any hits the Coun'hij did manage to get would be too old and too scattered to be useful.

I'd just about worked up the nerve to tell Taggart that I was going to start trying to contact Alec when we drove past a sign that said we were approaching the last gas station for the next eighty miles.

Taggart frowned. "I guess that settles it, we'll have to stop."

I bit back a sigh of relief, but I shouldn't have even bothered, Taggart of course heard the nascent sigh.

"That really settles it then. We'll stop so you can get out and walk around. Hopefully this gas station is large enough that we can pick up something more than just a couple of candy bars for dinner. I'm starving and you still need to put on more weight so you don't blow away after the next time you dream walk."

I stuck out my tongue at him and then leaned back in my seat. Taggart's current ride was an eight-year-old Honda. The air and heat worked, as did the radio, but that was where the amenities ended. The one thing it did have though was a very, very comfortable set of seats. Apparently when you spent as much time on the road as Taggart did you figured out which cars would leave you still able to walk after fifteen hours behind the wheel.

"Will we make it to Montana tonight?"

Taggart shook his head as he slowed down and pulled up next to the pump. "I doubt it. If we really had to make it there I could probably manage to drive straight through, or we could maybe swap off and I could grab an hour or so of sleep while you keep us going, but I think it's more important not to miss a night of dream walking than it is to make it to my cabin tonight."

That made a lot of sense. I'd already realized that Taggart viewed his nights as a kind of non-renewable resource. He made a difference when he was sleeping and therefore he tried very hard to make sure that his sleep schedule didn't get out of sync with the rest of North America.

"I'm serious about you eating more, Adriana. The limiting factor on how much I can get done in a given night is fact that we shape shifters don't require as much sleep as you humans. I'm lucky if I can stretch it to four or five hours most nights. It's enough to visit a couple of people, but it still means that a lot of things happen with a kind of frustrating slowness that you've luckily never had to deal with."

I knew where he was going with this and he was right, but that didn't mean that I wanted to hear it. I'd been eating enough lately that I'd put on a few more pounds, but part of me was still worried that if I upped my caloric intake even more that I'd balloon up to twice my old size.

I liked to think that I wasn't as shallow as most people, but the truth was that I liked being skinny. I liked guys looking at me with the kind of appreciation that had once been reserved only for Cindi, and I liked the fact that I looked *good* in my clothes now.

"I know, my limiting factor isn't how long I can sleep, it's how much fat I can pack onto my body."

Taggart frowned at me as he reached down to pop open the little door on the gas tank. "I'm not trying to say you should become unhealthy, Adriana. Believe it or not, I remember what it was like to be seventeen. The definition of physical perfection has changed a lot since then, but the way we feel when we do or don't achieve that standard hasn't changed. You don't need to add back a lot of weight, but you need more of a margin of safety than you have right now."

"Right, or my heart could stop mid-dream."

Taggart's eyes got a little bigger and I realized that he'd never thought in those terms. "Actually, I was thinking that you needed to have the physical reserves to go on an extra dream walk or two if something terrible happened and you needed to redouble your efforts for a single night."

"Yeah, that's what I meant. That's a way better reason, my most paranoid sensei."

That earned me an eye roll and then Taggart opened his door and started to get out. I was reaching for my door release when Taggart reached over and grabbed my arm. There was a smile on his face, but I could see the tension around his eyes, the wrinkles that only showed up when he was really worried.

"Change of plans, Adriana. You're going to need to stay in the car."

"What's going on?"

I was proud of the fact that I managed to keep my voice level and my expression steady.

"Vampires. I can smell them and it's strong enough that I don't think it was just someone passing through."

I could feel myself starting to shake, but I forced my upper body at least to stay mobile. The fight with Eric and the red hybrid had been pretty intense, but I'd never been in that much danger. The fight with Jackson and Pamela had been a whole different matter. I'd been terrified for what had seemed like hours and my nightmares hadn't mellowed out even weeks later. If there was a group of vampires here I was almost certainly going to die.

"We need to go, we need to get out of here."

Taggart reached over and rested his hand on my shoulder. "I know you're scared, but you need to act like nothing has changed. We don't have enough gas to make it to the next station, not without turning around and going back the way we came, and I'd rather not do that. I'll fill the car up and then we'll go."

I managed a nod, it was a choppy one, but under the circumstances it was the best I could manage. Taggart gave me another smile, this one more natural and less worried.

"Once I get out, go ahead and slide over into the driver's seat. That way we can get out of here more quickly. If push comes to shove leave me, drive two or three miles down the road and then pull off and kill the car. I'll shift to wolf form and come find you. Don't worry, I'm sure it won't come to that."

Taggart tossed me the keys and then climbed out of the car as he reached for his wallet. I undid my seatbelt and scrambled across to his seat. It wasn't until I was sitting behind the wheel that I realized why Taggart hadn't started pumping yet.

There wasn't a card reader at the pump. I didn't even know that it was possible to have a gas station anymore without a credit card reader at the pump. The urge to hyperventilate was almost overpowering. I would have gotten back into the car and headed back towards the interstate, but Taggart simply pushed the call button and bent forward to speak into it as the speaker crackled to life.

Neither the attendant nor Taggart was loud enough to hear through the windows, but a second later Taggart was sticking the nozzle into our fuel tank and I felt the vibrations of pumping fuel shake the car. It couldn't have taken more than a couple of minutes to fill our tank, but the experience seemed to stretch out into hours.

I was in a cold sweat by the time that Taggart re-racked the dispenser and started towards the store to pay for the gas. I forced a smile across my face and fidgeted with the radio as though changing the station, but the truth was that I was checking my rear and side view mirrors on an almost constant basis.

It was the next best thing to impossible, but somehow I still missed it. One moment I was all by myself and then suddenly there was a tall, pale man standing just outside my car.

He was gaunt—not quite like a starvation victim, but close—and his eyes were a lifeless, dull brown. He was also holding a very big, very black handgun up against the passenger side window.

I slowly moved the keys towards the ignition, but he motioned with his head and the keys were ripped away from me by some kind of invisible force. As I watched, the lock on the passenger door disengaged and the man pulled open the door.

He was a vampire, he had to be a vampire, and I was completely outclassed. If we'd met inside of my dream I might have been able to fend him off, but not here, not in the real world where he was faster and stronger than me.

The vampire slid into the car, still pointing the gun at me, and stuck the keys in the ignition.

"Turn on the car."

"Why, where are you taking me?"

"Just shut up and do it. Don't even think about trying something stupid like you see in the movies. If you try and speed up and wreck us I'll just force the brake and the clutch in."

I turned on the car and double-checked that it was in first gear. "Okay, it's on, what now?"

"Pull around, there's a gravel road behind the service station. Follow it."

It wasn't much of a road. I wasn't sure whether that was a good thing or not. Surely the vampires wouldn't just kill me and dump my body right behind the gas station. If they did this all the time then eventually someone would realize that all the missing people had stopped here before disappearing.

Then again, maybe the police wouldn't be able to figure even that out. There hadn't been a credit card reader outside. If they made people pay with cash then there wouldn't be an electronic trail for the police to follow.

The gravel road ended almost as soon as it began and now we were inside of a kind of miniature gravel pit. It was big enough to hide a semi-truck and trailer, but not much more than that.

"What now?"

"You shut up and wait."

I was terrified, which precluded snapping back at him, but I decided if I survived long enough to fall asleep tonight that I was going to try and pull this vampire into my dreams. Maybe it would be wasted effort, maybe he'd still prove too strong for me to defeat, but if I could I was going to kill him.

I didn't necessarily want to become the weapon that Taggart already said I was, and this didn't change my concerns when it came to fighting the Coun'hij, or anyone else, on nothing more than Taggart's say-so, but this was different. This guy, this vampire, had just kidnapped me and he'd probably killed dozens, maybe even hundreds of people just over the last few years.

Unless proven otherwise, vampires were fair game. Sure, most predators killed to feed, but just because it was their nature didn't make it okay. You don't give a lion a pass when it starts hunting down children, you get a bunch of people with guns together and do your best to kill it before it strikes again.

"Do you have a name?"

"I told you to shut up." There wasn't any of the anger that I would have expected underlying his words, but he more than made up for it by shoving his gun up tight against my temple. The unyielding steel connected hard enough that I knew it was going to leave a bruise, and even worse, I was positive that his finger was still on the trigger.

I was half convinced that I was going to die, but at that moment the ground in front of us started moving. The vampire was obviously expecting it, but it served as enough of a distraction for him to withdraw his gun.

"Pull in there."

'There' proved to be a gigantic underground bunker that was completely undetectable when the garage door, a massive concrete slab whose outside surface had been covered with real live grass, was closed. It was the kind of thing that I'd always thought existed only in novels, but I couldn't argue with my own eyes as I slowly brought the car forward and into the enormous cavern.

There were cars parked along each side, but there wasn't any way to know for sure whether they belonged to the vampires or were vehicles they'd stolen from other travelers. Deeper inside the bunker we came to an open parking spot and my captor waved me into it.

For the briefest of moments I considered waiting until the vampire got out and then trying to back Taggart's car outside, but the vampire reached over and turned off the engine before pocketing the keys. I'd known all along that I didn't have much chance of escaping, but I could feel my options narrowing even more quickly as the vampire opened the passenger door.

"Get out, very slowly."

I complied and then marched, still at gunpoint, even further into the bunker. We passed what looked like a paint booth and a shop area that I figured was used for disassembling some of the cars for sale as parts.

When the screams started up I felt the tears that had been threatening to escape my eyes finally succeed. I probably would have started bawling right then, but the vampire behind me seemed just as disturbed by the screams as I was.

Another man—this one a short, bearded guy with a gut—stepped out of some kind of hallway. He reached up and pushed a large red button mounted on the wall next to the hallway. A second later the massive exterior door started to rumble down.

"What's going on up there, Pete?"

The newcomer shook his head. "I don't know, maybe someone couldn't bring themselves to wait before starting in on the old man."

"Paulo isn't going to like that, there's never as much blood to go around when that happens."

Pete shrugged. "Maybe we should just do the girl right here."

The first vampire casually backhanded Pete. There was enough force behind the blow that the fat man careened off of the wall, but the gun never even shook.

"You're lucky you're so good with cars, Pete. If you were anyone else you'd probably be dead by now. Paulo usually punishes disobedience much more strongly than he's done with you."

My captor's voice had changed slightly. I couldn't tell if it was because he was angry or for some other reason, but he had a faint accent now. I half expected Pete to be angry, but he just shrugged.

"The world isn't much different whether you're a vampire or a human, Benito. The best way to make sure that you don't go hungry is to develop a skill that someone else needs badly enough that they can't afford to treat you like dirt."

"You're not the only decent mechanic out there."

"Sure, but I'm one of the best. Paulo would have to look for a long time to replace me and, given how little he makes it out of the bunker these days, he doesn't exactly get much chance to scout out new talent."

I blinked and the gun was gone, replaced by a long, slender knife. Benito was fast, even for a vampire. He got the point of the knife up under

Pete's chin and had him backed up against the wall before Pete could back out of his way. I was able to follow what had happened, but there was no way I was going to overpower Benito. Even if I caught him off guard I still had zero chance of taking him out before he killed me.

"You would be well advised to show Paulo more respect. Our fortunes may be on the wane right now, but it's only a matter of time before we move back into one of the cities and Paulo rewards those who supported him in exile. Eventually we'll return to the old land where the real power lies and we'll be made princes."

I was desperately trying to find something in their conversation that I could use against them, but there just wasn't anything there that would allow someone my size to take down or outsmart a century-old vampire.

Pete opened his mouth, probably to say something calming, and then the screaming started back up. This time there couldn't be any doubt but that it wasn't Taggart. There were two voices and they both sounded different than the first one had.

Benito spun around and grabbed me, shoving me into Pete's arms before handing the other vampire the pistol that he'd concealed underneath his shirt.

"Watch the girl. If you feed on her I'll kill you myself."

It took only seconds for Benito to vanish into the near darkness up ahead and then it was just

Pete and I standing there in the shop, him with a gun, me with a sinking pit where my stomach should have been.

Taggart was obviously still alive. The first scream had been close enough to his voice that I hadn't been able to tell for sure, but neither of those last screams had been him. That was a good sign, but he was obviously outnumbered and the vampires knew their way around the bunker.

Jackson hadn't proved to be a match for Taggart, but then again Taggart had taken Jackson by surprise. I moved my hand slowly towards a large wrench that was lying on one edge of the workbench behind me, but Pete noticed and waved his gun at me.

"Just because I can't feed on you doesn't mean that I'm going to let you arm yourself. Step away from the workbench."

A new set of screams broke out, and metal struck against metal as someone tried to stop Taggart. A second later some kind of explosion went off. A hot wind swept down the tunnel towards us and it was strong enough to scatter some of the screws sitting on the workbench next to me.

There was a howl which I knew had to be from Taggart, but it wasn't a howl of rage, it was a howl of pain. My fingernails sliced into my palms and I realized for the first time just how tight my fists were. I needed to help him, needed to be more than just another bystander, more than just someone who had to be protected all of the time.

Taggart roared again, this time in anger, and there was a loud crash that seemed like it was just around the corner from us. Pete looked away for a split second; I grabbed the wrench I'd been eyeing and threw it at him with every ounce of force I could muster as I stepped to the side in an effort to get out of the line of fire.

Another wave of heat raced down the corridor and this time it was fierce enough to almost scorch my eyebrows. Pete ducked down a split second before the wrench would have taken him in the side of the head. He wasn't as fast as Benito, but he was still too fast for me to possibly beat him.

Pete blurred into motion, gun down at his side and one hand forward to grab me. I couldn't escape, so I didn't even try. I grabbed a screwdriver off of the table behind me and brought my hand up just as he reached me. I didn't stab him, he impaled himself on it.

My only mistake was not getting the point of my improvised weapon up high enough to do actual damage to him. I'd been worried that he would see it at the last second and dodge to one side, but by playing things safe I'd stabbed him in the stomach, which wasn't going to kill, at least not quickly.

Pete threw me against the wall and then pulled the bloody screwdriver out of his gut.

"You've got fight, I've got to give you that. You made a big mistake though. You just wasted your one chance to take me by surprise."

The screwdriver was up against my neck now with its point dimpling my skin. I was having a hard time breathing, but it wasn't fear. Or maybe it was fear, but it wasn't *just* fear. I was mad. Guys like Benito and Pete weren't any better than the bullies I'd dealt with back in Minnesota.

If I'd been strong enough or fast enough to provide any kind of threat to them they'd never have picked on me. They liked sure things; they were in it for the sadistic enjoyment rather than for the challenge.

"If you let me go then he might let you live. If you kill me then he'll make your death painful. They call him Dream Stealer."

"I don't care what they call him, he's not going to defeat Paulo. I might be new at this whole vampire thing, but I know scary when I see it. Paulo is one of the strongest pyrokinetics alive. He'll take care of your friend, it's just a matter of time."

"If he's so strong what is he doing out here in the middle of nowhere living on table scraps?"

"It doesn't matter how strong you are, to rule a city, even one here in the U.S., you need an army to keep everyone else in line. Benito's an ass, but he's not wrong about the fact that it's just a matter of time. Us Americans think that we're a big noise, but things are exactly the opposite in the vampire world. America is for the rejects, the vampires who aren't old and powerful enough to rule in Europe."

There was a crash like someone had thrown metal rods against a wall and then another scream, this time a vampire. I opened my mouth to tell Pete that his master was dead, but before I could get the words out a blast of fire shot out of the corridor.

If Pete hadn't moved towards me he would have died. I'd made a mistake in throwing the wrench at him and causing him to move into the alcove with all of the tools, but there hadn't been any way to know it at the time.

Pete grabbed the back of my neck and force-marched me out into the corridor. He still had the gun in his right hand and I could feel the handle of the screwdriver sandwiched between his hand and my neck, but I was too busy trying to keep from falling down to worry about that.

It was a risk to go back out into the corridor, but after Paulo's last blast of heat Pete apparently figured it was most important to get far enough away that the fringes of the next blast wouldn't start us on fire. We ducked around the paint booth less than a second before there was another crash. This time it sounded like someone had thrown an oil drum against a wall.

I was waiting for another jet of fire, but it didn't come. The quick, sharp sounds of steel on steel floated down the corridor and then everything went quiet. I hadn't noticed it before, but one of the attacks had knocked out most of the lights. The bunker had been fairly dark even before Taggart had started killing the vampires; now we had little more than the flicker of a couple of computer monitors to see by.

I heard the breathing even before I heard the footsteps, which was saying something because the footsteps were incredibly loud.

"I'm in here with another vampire, he's got a gun..."

Pete's hand on the back of my neck clamped down so tightly that I let out a hiss of pain. My outcry was answered by a low growl that seemed to come from everywhere. The sound reverberated through the darkness, giving me goose bumps before it finally died out.

"Let the girl go."

"I'm not an idiot, if I let the girl go then I'll have zero leverage."

Pete's voice cracked and I found myself laughing. I stopped myself before Pete could respond. He was terrified, breathing hard and eighty pounds overweight. Some vampire.

"No, your refusal to let her go just means that you're no different than the others I've killed already tonight."

The screwdriver dropped to the concrete; the gun was back, grinding against the side of my head in time to Pete's heartbeat.

"Sure, you can kill me, but I'll take her with me before I go."

"How many bullets do you have in that gun, bloodsucker?"

Taggart's voice was coming from the other direction now. Somehow he'd crossed in front of us without either of us being able to see him. I wouldn't have thought it was possible. My eyes were merely human, but I would have thought that Pete would be able to see even when it was this dark.

"Enough."

"Are you sure? It would be a shame to waste one of them on the girl and then realize that you needed one more to finish me off."

Taggart's breathing had been silent for nearly a minute, but now it returned, a deep, rasping sound that gave away his position.

Pete spun around and fired off three shots to our right. Two of them ricocheted away, but the third hit something softer than that. My heart climbed up into my throat as the breathing stopped, but it started back up a couple of seconds later from a different position.

The gun left my temple again and three more shots rang out. This time the gun wasn't as far away from my face and the ringing in my ears got even worse. I was looking the right direction this time and caught a flash of movement in the muzzle flash.

Taggart staggered as at least one of the bullets struck home and I realized that I couldn't afford to keep waiting. I spun to the right, bringing my right elbow up so that it was traveling towards Pete's throat as my left hand grabbed hold of his wrist in an attempt to control the gun.

My elbow struck home and it was like hitting a wooden door. There was some give there, but not as much as there should have been. Pete gagged, but he didn't go down and I could feel that the gun was still tracking towards Taggart.

The breathing had changed, there was a slow hiss to it like one of Taggart's lungs had been punctured, and he seemed to be struggling to hold his breath. I threw all of my weight against Pete's arm and jostled it just enough that his next three shots ricocheted off of the concrete walls.

"Duck, Adriana."

I let my knees buckle and gravity pulled me down, but it almost wasn't fast enough. Taggart's claws passed over my head, close enough that I felt the wind of their passage before they tore out Pete's throat.

It all happened so fast that it felt like the attack came out of nowhere, but Pete got one final round off, directly into the center of the dark form that had just saved my life yet again.

Chapter 9

Adriana Paige
Marauder's Gas Station
Central Wyoming

My ears were ringing so badly that for a couple of seconds I couldn't tell whether Taggart was still breathing. Some of the lights flickered back on; they weren't much, but it was just enough for me to make it over to Taggart. His chest was moving ever so slightly up and down.

I was dizzy and my entire body was shaking, but I forced myself back to my feet and found the red button that Pete had used to close the exterior door. I prayed that the power was still working enough to lift the heavy concrete slab and punched the button. The reassuring rumble that worked its way up through the soles of my feet a second later calmed some of my terror, but it was going to take more than just some dim sunlight to save Taggart.

A few seconds later I was back at Taggart's Honda and grabbing the battery-powered lantern and first-aid kit that he kept packed in the trunk of his car. When I made it back to Taggart I almost wished that I hadn't been able to find the lantern.

Taggart was bleeding from three different bullet holes. I couldn't remember for sure, but I'd only counted two impacts. Either my hearing had been too far gone by that point or one of the ricochets had hit him after skidding off of the wall.

There was another nick in his right ear that must have been the work of another bullet, and he had a variety of what looked like knife and stab wounds all over his arms and torso, but that wasn't the worst of it. Taggart was naked just like after every shift back to human form, but most of his skin had been burned away by Paulo's fire.

By every rule of human physiology I knew, Taggart should already be dead, but then again he wasn't really human. He just happened to look like one right now. I knelt motionless at his side, for several seconds as I tried to decide where even to start and then nearly jumped out of my own skin when Taggart's eyes snapped open and he grabbed my arm.

"Get the bleeding stopped. Don't worry about the bullets or any internal damage, you don't have the tools or the skills to do anything about them. Do that and then go back up to the store and get me food and water. It will have to be enough."

I shook my head, tears streaming down my dirty, soot-stained cheeks. "You're burned, you lost seventy or eighty percent of the skin on your entire body. You're going to have massive infections; I need to get you to a hospital. This isn't like last time—I'm scared."

Taggart coughed and my hearing was back enough that I could hear the air wheezing out of the bullet hole that had taken him in the lung.

"The skin will regrow and infections aren't as big of a problem for my kind. No hospital; it would be like sending Kaleb and the rest a postcard with my name and address on it. Have faith, Adri. I'll pull through."

I was shaking as I popped open the first-aid kit and started pulling out gauze, rubbing alcohol and butterfly bandages. Maybe he wasn't worried about infection, but I figured it couldn't hurt to try and disinfect as much as I could. I talked as I worked, not because I expected any kind of answer out of him, but because I needed a distraction from all of the blood and raw flesh.

"I think that's the first time that you've called me Adri. You always use my full name."

Taggart's smile was a pale shadow of his normal expression, but at least he was still with me enough to make an effort.

"I guess I figured that after saving your life for a second time I'd earned a bit more familiarity. I can go back to your full name if you'd like."

"No, it's fine. You're right, you've earned the privilege of calling me whatever you'd like."

Taggart's eyes started to flutter closed and I desperately searched for something else to say as I taped a square of gauze over the lung wound.

"How did you beat the pyromancer? Pete was convinced that nobody could beat Paulo. I thought for sure you were dead."

Taggart winced as my fingers pushed a little too hard. "I nearly didn't beat him. The first attack caught me by surprise and the corridors are so tight that I wasn't able to dodge very well. Once I knew what I was up against though it was mostly a matter of just staying out of his sight while I picked off the rest of his guys."

"I could tell that was what you were doing, but how did you beat him once all of his guys were gone?"

"I lured him back towards the two of you and then I threw a barrel of oil at him. I could smell it all the way back from the tunnel that led into the bunker from the store. Once he was coated in oil and it was on the walls and floor around him, then he didn't dare use his ability anymore. Once it was down to just him and me, steel against claws, the fight was over pretty quickly."

I shook my head in amazement. "I never would have thought of that."

"You might be surprised at what you can come up with when the alternative is being burned alive. Besides, you didn't do all that bad yourself. You managed to stab your captor with a screwdriver and you got an elbow in to his throat."

"It wasn't enough, without you I still would have been dead."

Taggart closed his eyes. "You're welcome, Adri."

I reached up and touched his ear, the one that had the bullet crease in it. "You almost died."

"I still might, but yes, that one was too close for comfort."

I wiped my cheeks against my right arm and then poured some rubbing alcohol into the biggest slash across his chest.

"You could have easily killed whoever they had in the shop and then made a run for it. Why did you come down here? For all you knew there were a dozen vampires as powerful as Paulo waiting to kill you as soon as you stuck your head into the bunker."

"I came down here because you didn't stand a chance on your own. The vampires would have drained you and had your corpse buried before sunrise. You needed my help. I'm an old man and you're still young. I might have another thirty years left in me, but you've got your whole life waiting for you."

I shook my head, splashing tears everywhere. "But the resistance needs you. Agony needs you. I'm worse than useless. I don't even know enough about the Coun'hij to feel comfortable killing them let alone enough to actually fight them effectively."

Taggart gripped my arm with a strength that was surprising considering just how much blood he'd lost.

"Agony would understand. We've done what we could, but our generation has failed. The future lies in your generation's hands. You'll find your way, Adri. I trust your judgment; you'll make mistakes along the way just like I did, but you're too good to remain in error for very long."

I taped a square of gauze over the last bullet hole and then started on the smaller wounds, the stuff that normally wouldn't have been worth worrying about, but which were more of a concern given how low his blood pressure must be.

"Thank you, Taggart, and not just for saving my life. It means a lot that you trust me. I'm going to reach out to Alec Graves via my dreams. I know you think he's dirty, but he's the only other person I know who can confirm what you've told me about the Coun'hij. I have to know."

"I knew it was only a matter of time. You were as timid as a dormouse for the first three or four days we were together, but even back then you almost couldn't bring yourself to back down when it came to Kaleb's boy."

Taggart went silent for so long that I almost thought he'd passed out, but after nearly a minute he nodded. "Do what you think you need to do. Find me some blankets so the concrete isn't sucking all of the heat out of me and then go up to the convenience store and lock up. We can use this place later so it's important to keep the cover intact for as long as possible."

Chapter 10

Adriana Paige
Marauder's Gas Station
Central Wyoming

The next few days were a blur of activity and boredom intermixed with moments of extreme terror and a near-constant worry about Taggart. I did as he asked even though walking through the blackened, bloody concrete corridors was one of the most terrifying things I'd ever had to do.

Intellectually I knew that Taggart would have warned me if anyone else had survived the fighting, but that wasn't as reassuring in the near darkness as I stepped over corpses and pools of blood.

It took me twenty minutes to explore the bunker from one end to the other. I found a large bunk area with four or five beds in it after only a couple of minutes, but I forced myself to explore the entire complex before going back and grabbing the bedding off of two of the bunks. I was worried about leaving Taggart alone on the cold concrete for so long, but I needed to see for myself that the bunker was empty.

The underground fortress was an odd mixture of Spartan utilitarianism and ridiculous luxury. There was a big kitchen and dining hall that looked like it was designed to feed twenty or twenty-five people at a time, and then off in Paulo's section of the bunker there was a small kitchen obviously designed for a personal chef.

The main armory ran heavily towards swords, axes and knives, but it did also have half a dozen handguns and twice that many rifles and shotguns in assorted shapes and sizes. I grabbed a small pistol, loaded it up and then stuffed it down the waistband of my pants. Paulo's personal armory had only a few weapons, all of which were exquisite-looking swords that were as slender and light as they were beautiful, but it also had a huge store of gold. Either Paulo had brought a lot of wealth with him across from Italy or robbing travelers was a lot more lucrative than I would have expected.

That theme was repeated over and over again as I worked my way through the dimly lit corridors. Paulo's men lived with only the basics in an almost military setup while Paulo himself had most of the creature comforts one could desire.

The one exception to that rule was an enormous area full of weights, machines and a tumbling mat that was large enough to do Olympic floor routines on. Apparently Paulo didn't think it a good idea to skimp on the tools his men needed to stay in fighting trim. Not that it had done them much good. I'd known that Taggart was deadly, and he'd had the element of surprise on his side, but it still boggled the mind that he'd been able to kill so many people so quickly.

There wasn't any kind of swimming pool, but most everything else I could think of was present and accounted for. There was even a sizable firing range, which was a surprise after seeing how few projectile weapons were inside the armory.

By the time I'd looked into every room and opened all of the closets I was starting to feel safe enough that I felt a little silly carrying the gun, but I didn't return it to the armory.

I found the tunnel up to the store towards the end of my exploration, but I didn't waste time going up it at that moment. I simply barred the door with the massive metal rod obviously intended for that purpose and hurried back to the bunk room to get the blankets for Taggart.

A few minutes later I had Taggart wrapped up with three quilts underneath him to serve as a cushion and insulation from the floor. I would have carried him into the master bedroom, but even in human form he was simply too heavy. It was all I could manage to roll him to one side so that I could get the blankets underneath him.

I closed the giant garage door and then headed back towards the tunnel leading up to the store. The store was empty when I arrived, which was a good thing because it gave me time to figure out how the latch on the back wall opened the hidden passage back down to the bunker.

The sun was starting to set, but there was still enough light to see that I was bloody and dirty, so I spent a few minutes in the bathroom cleaning up. I spent another half an hour up in the store figuring out how the pumps worked and then I locked up, grabbed a selection of the healthiest food on the shelves, and carried it back down to Taggart.

Taggart wasn't awake enough to choke down any of the food, so I ate, made myself a bed with some clean bedding from the closet next to the bunk room, and went to sleep. I half expected to enter a nightmare immediately, but my control seemed to be getting better.

I was tempted to go find Cindi, or maybe Tristan. After everything I'd been through in the last forty-eight hours I really wanted a hug and a chance to talk to someone who was a step removed from all of this violence and death, but I knew doing that would tire me out too much to find Alec, so I forced myself not to reach for either of them.

Besides, I wasn't sure how well Cindi would handle knowing just how close I'd come to dying, and seeing Tristan was a bad idea. I'd told Cindi that she had a green light to pursue him and I'd be sabotaging her efforts if I kept popping into his dreams.

Instead, I shifted my surroundings, which had been the bunker I'd gone to sleep in, to my room back in Minnesota and then I climbed up onto the top bunk and closed my eyes. Thinking of Alec was easier than almost anyone else. Even after all of these weeks, I still remembered exactly how he'd made me feel.

The thrill as he'd kissed me had been like nothing else I'd ever experienced, and it was the only time I'd really felt safe since I'd started dream walking. I took a couple of deep breaths and then entered the Zen-like state that allowed me to start spinning out filaments of myself, self-aware threads that knew enough to look for him.

I hadn't been able to stomach as many calories from the convenience store. There'd been too much sugar and not enough fat for my tastes, but I still figured I had enough energy stored up to make contact even if Alec was all the way across the country from me.

The filaments continued to spin away from me, draining strength and energy away from me at an alarming rate, but I just kept telling myself that there wasn't any reason to panic. I'd done this before and I'd never had any problems.

There wasn't any reason to believe that it was going to be any different this time around.

Except it was. The threads seemed to search forever without finding anything. I'd never used this much strength up without finding the person I was looking for. Some of the filaments even stopped moving out and away from me. They were moving to the side now, almost as if they had searched as far as they could and now were hoping to find Alec inside of the sphere of their reach.

I was shaking now, but I couldn't tell whether it was just in the dream or if it was happening in the real world and was just bad enough that it was echoing here too. Just as it seemed that I didn't have anything left to give, I felt an odd kind of click. It was odd not because I'd never felt it before, but because I'd never realized that was what I was feeling when the threads connected. Always before there had been other sensations that drowned out the click, but this time those other feelings were absent, or maybe just muted.

My subconscious took over, reeling in all of the other strands of consciousness that had been searching, reabsorbing the strength that they'd drawn out of me. My heartbeat steadied as my reserves started to fill back up, and then it was time to push enough energy down the remaining thread to firm it up so it could be used to pull him to me.

Part of me just wanted to go to him. It would be easier—it seemed to require a lot less out of me to go to someone else rather than pulling them into my dream—but at least some of Taggart's paranoia had rubbed off on me. Inside of Alec's dream I would be almost completely at his mercy, but inside of my dream things would be different. I got the feeling that Alec was strong-willed enough that he'd still be able to effect *some* changes on my dream, which wasn't a small thing when you combined it with the fact that he had all of a shape shifter's inherent strength and speed, but at least I'd have a chance.

I'd let my mind wander as I'd been feeding my filament power. It was a dangerous thing, but I'd only let my thoughts drift for a second which wasn't much longer than it would have taken even if I'd been paying attention. I reached for the cable that I'd been expecting the filament to have become, but it wasn't there.

I hadn't lost the connection, but the thread hadn't grown any thicker despite all of the energy it had pulled out of me. My reserves were already dangerously depleted, I might have enough inside of me to strengthen a normal connection to the point of usability, but there wasn't enough left to pull myself to Alec let alone enough to pull him to me.

I reached towards the glowing white filament with a heavy heart. The night was a waste, but there wasn't anything to do but try again tomorrow. It should have been the easiest thing in the world to snap the connection between Alec and me, but when I tried nothing happened.

The thread wasn't any thicker than it had been a second before, but was stretchy and refused to snap like it should have. The panic that had been present in the back of my mind ever since I'd gone to sleep burst out in full force.

I was going to die here in the dream, sucked dry by something I didn't understand, and there wasn't anything I could do about it. I was as good as dead, which meant that Taggart wouldn't make it either.

Chapter 11

Alec Graves
Club Pure Vertigo
Chicago, Illinois

Jack's news was worse than anything I'd expected. Agony had outsmarted Kaleb and the rest for decades. Agony had been running from the Coun'hij since before I'd been born. He'd been running from the Coun'hij since before Kaleb had even been on it. Agony was a living legend and his capture couldn't have come at a worse time.

I didn't have any illusions about the amount of power and influence my friends and I actually had. Two hybrids and a couple of wolves weren't a lot to throw against the awesome might of the Coun'hij. Luring Jack out into semi-active rebellion against Kaleb and the rest was a good start, but even so we were so outclassed it wasn't even funny.

AMBUSHED

Kaleb could send Brandon and a dozen hybrids to wipe all of us out and not even have to ask the rest of the Coun'hij for help. The Sanctuary pack all by itself outnumbered us by so much that we couldn't hope to win any kind of standup fight. Our only hope was to remain mobile, stay hidden and choose our battles carefully.

It wasn't a very reassuring position to be in. If something didn't change quickly I didn't expect us to last for long, but what we lacked in actual combat power was more than made up for by the symbol we represented.

We'd bearded the lion in its own den. Kaleb was one of the most powerful members of the Coun'hij and the Sanctuary pack was the largest single group of shape shifters in all of North America. Even with Kaleb having detached so much of his strength away fighting the jaguars and the vampires, most people wouldn't have thought that four teenagers could steal away Kaleb's own daughter.

Of course it had helped that Rachel had *wanted* to escape with us, but it had still been an incredible accomplishment. Even more amazing, I'd fought Brandon to a standstill in the process. I'd been armed with Kaleb's sword at the time, and Brandon had been seconds away from killing me, but that didn't change the fact that I'd come out on top in a fight against the single most dangerous hybrid in the world.

That would count for a lot with the right people. Almost as much as the fact that Kaleb's own son had rebelled against him.

That was where our real power rested. There was a chance that Jack and his people would just be the first rumbling in an avalanche of discontent. If I could continue to persuade others to come out against the Coun'hij then I could have an impact all out of proportion to what anyone was anticipating.

It was a long shot, but it had just become even longer if Agony had really been captured. I was a symbol, but I was a relatively new, untested player. Agony was a symbol that had stood the test of time for decades. If he wasn't in the picture anymore, then there were some people who would be less willing to act against Kaleb and the rest.

I'd been hoping that someone would be able to disprove Jack's news, but that hadn't stopped me from moving forward on the assumption that it was all true. James, Jasmin, Jess and I had started driving towards Chicago as soon as we'd been able to steal a clean car out of the parking garage where we'd ambushed the enforcers.

Jack had wanted to come with us. It had taken a lot of convincing, but in the end he'd agreed to proceed with the original plan we'd formulated before I'd gotten on the plane to fly back from the Caymans.

I didn't particularly trust Ulrich any more than Jack did, but I had debts to pay off. I couldn't afford to drag all of my people up to Chicago or I risked defaulting on the most important remaining obligation.

The North American packs were a motley bunch. They ranged from Jaclyn in Tucson who was a hairsbreadth away from open rebellion at any given moment to Onyx in New Orleans who practically worshiped the ground Kaleb walked on.

Between those two extremes there was a lot of room, but Ulrich was notable precisely because he was so good at walking the line between getting his people killed and becoming a vassal of the Coun'hij. It was a delicate balancing act at the best of times, but Ulrich had managed it with flying colors and he'd done so while controlling the second biggest pack in existence.

Most packs were either for the Coun'hij or against it, and once you crossed over to one side it was as though every force in the world aligned to try and push you further towards the extreme. Even a small pack had a hard enough time remaining neutral simply because everyone else on 'their' side of the issue was constantly trying to cement relations in preparation for the day when the tensions broke out into outright hostilities.

For a pack the size of Ulrich's it was all but impossible to remain neutral. Ulrich was effectively the biggest single unclaimed piece still on the board. If I had to guess, I would have said that him having remained neutral was the only thing that had stopped the Coun'hij from trying to destroy Jaclyn and the other more outspoken pack leaders. Kaleb and the rest were worried that if they attacked the more rebellious groups that it would result in Ulrich choosing against them.

The smart money all seemed to think that the Coun'hij would still come out on top, even in a fight where Ulrich came down on the side of the radicals. It was hard to bet against people like Puppeteer and Brandon regardless of how many bodies you had to throw at them.

Of course that wasn't the full story. Ulrich would have loved for his pack to look like a single monolithic structure, but in reality he was dealing with a balancing act inside of his pack that was nearly as tricky as what he was doing with the Coun'hij.

Inside a pack as big as the Chicago pack even the factions had factions. The most outspoken group was headed by Ulrich's own son, Shawn Bishop. It added an interesting dynamic to things. Shawn wasn't the most powerful hybrid inside of the Chicago pack, but then again when it came to straight-up combat prowess neither was Ulrich.

Ulrich kept control of his pack by way of a complex web of personal loyalty from some of the more dangerous hybrids in Chicago, playing off the various factions against each other, and heavy use of the Bishop fortune. If something were to happen to Ulrich then Shawn was perfectly positioned to take over his father's pack, except for the fact that Shawn wanted to destroy the Coun'hij and reinstate the monarchy, presumably with Shawn in the top spot.

It meant that the Coun'hij had a vested interest in making sure that nothing happened to Ulrich, but by the same measure, Ulrich was fond of his only son. He'd made it very clear to Kaleb and the rest on more than one occasion that if Shawn was to suffer some kind of suspicious 'accident' the Chicago pack would all be on a first name basis with Jaclyn and the Tucson pack within hours.

With Agony captured, the situation had become even more complex. The Coun'hij would have their eyes on anyone they thought might be inclined to break Agony out.

Jaclyn and the other more militant packs would no doubt want to free Agony, but they would be the ones least in a position to actually do anything. I wanted Agony free, but the only way for that to happen would be if I could get help from a group of wolves and hybrids that the Coun'hij wasn't watching very closely.

The Chicago pack fit the bill perfectly, assuming that I could convince Shawn to defy his father once and for all, that or convince him to help me talk his dad into finally picking a side. Both options were risky, but it was past time for the Coun'hij to be pulled down, even if the cost was a civil war.

All of which explained how I ended up outside one of the hottest clubs in Chicago.

Shawn was apparently quite the social butterfly. Now I just needed to find him. Getting in hadn't been too difficult, but it had required a bit of planning.

There were only three ways to get into an exclusive club like this. Beauty, money or power. We opted to use all three.

James was dressed as a bodyguard, right down to the dark, severe suit and the earpiece. Jasmin and Jess were dressed in typical club wear, meaning that they weren't wearing a whole lot, but that every male we passed and some of the females couldn't seem to pry their eyes off of them.

All of which made it easy for me to blend in. Everyone saw me, but nobody really noticed me, they were too busy noticing the obvious trappings of wealth I was displaying so prominently. The night was cold enough that I could feel it through my jeans and tank top. I felt a little sorry for Jasmin and Jess, but at least they had our species' supercharged metabolism to offset the temperature. There were a lot of human girls standing in line who were wearing even less and they didn't have the same kind of genetic advantages.

We didn't wait in line, because really rich people, even when they're slumming, don't wait in lines. I walked up to the door, Jess and Jasmin on my arms, James exactly three feet behind me, and handed the doorman two one-hundred-dollar bills.

We were inside the club fifteen seconds later and navigating the hot press of bodies. The music and lights would have been an assault on the senses of normal humans; I couldn't even begin to understand why Shawn would choose to spend his free time in a place like this.

It only took me a couple of seconds to identify the entrance to the club within the main club. These places all seemed to be the same. The regular people waited outside trying to get inside, but once you got inside then you found out that all of the really important people were off in an area of their own.

We worked our way over to the velvet ropes and the very large bouncer who was stationed in front of them. Jasmin and Jess both swayed in time to the music, but Jess was doing a much better job blending in. Jasmin still looked like she was on a mission and just pretending to be having fun.

It still worked though. The expression on her face wasn't much different than what you might see from any other attractive woman who happened to be with someone solely because of his money. Some guys didn't care about the motivation of their companions, they just wanted someone attractive and submissive without having to worry too much about the reason the women were so compliant.

I palmed another couple of bills, but the bouncer saw us coming and was already shaking his head at me.

"The VIP club is already full, man."

"I can make it worth your while."

He snorted in amusement. "You and everyone else in here. Get lost."

James was already stepping forward. The bouncer reached forward to shove him back away from the ropes, but James easily sidestepped the push and grabbed the other man's arm.

A human would have put the bouncer in a wristlock or something else to apply their strength against their opponent's weakness. James didn't do that, he simply started squeezing.

Our human bodies weren't anywhere near as strong as a hybrid, but we were still much stronger than any human of an equivalent size. The bouncer tried to resist, tried to get his other arm in play, tried to get his bodyweight shifted around so that he could back James into the wall, but it was all fruitless.

James exerted such a crushing grip on the bouncer that the other man dropped down to one knee. It had to have been a humbling experience. A guy that big was used to dominating any physical confrontation, but he'd just been manhandled with ease by someone nearly an inch and a half shorter than him.

"You don't talk to Mr. Murphy that way. Nobody does. I'm going to give you one more chance to make things right and let Mr. Murphy and his dates inside."

"I could have you thrown out of the club in two seconds flat."

The bouncer's free hand had already started moving up to his mouth to call for help, but James just clamped down even harder so that the bouncer dropped to both knees.

"You could do that, but that would be a big mistake. Mr. Murphy is an upstanding citizen, he would never do anything to hurt you, but you can't say the same kind of thing about me. If you let us through then Mr. Murphy will hand you the two hundred dollars he approached you with a couple of seconds ago. If you get us kicked out of the club, then I'll follow you home one of these nights and the two of us will have a very unpleasant conversation."

"Okay, okay, you guys can go inside."

James just stood there for a second without letting go, driving home just how overmatched the bouncer had been.

"Jerome, please let the nice man go. You're causing a scene."

We hadn't actually come up with aliases for each other, but James let go of the bouncer without looking back at me.

"Yes, Mr. Murphy. I'm sorry, Mr. Murphy. I believe he'll let us by now."

I gave the bouncer my best apologetic smile, as if to say that there was only so much I could do to control a psychopath like Jerome, and then the girls and I followed James into the VIP area.

I knew Shawn would be in here somewhere, but finding him was going to be harder than I'd expected.

There was a very prominent bar just inside the door we'd entered by, and across the dance floor I could see a set of stairs that looked like they led up to some kind of private room for the club owner. I wasn't particularly eager to try and force my way past the two bouncers at the foot of the stairs—at least not until after we'd confirmed that Shawn wasn't in one of the huge private booths situated in long rows on either side of the dance floor.

In any other setting Jasmin and Jess would have been terribly conspicuous, but here they blended right in with the rest of the half-naked bodies, male and female, out on the dance floor. I pulled the two of them closer so that they could hear me despite the thrumming music.

"Go find Shawn for me, but try not to make it too obvious that you're looking for someone in particular. Pretend you're here looking for a sugar daddy."

Jasmin shot me a nasty look, but they both nodded and then glided onto the dance floor. They would dance for a minute or two and then start working their way down the two sets of booths.

I walked over to the bar and ordered a drink, not because alcohol actually did anything for shape shifters, but because it was the best way to blend in.

The bartender saw me looking at the booths and leaned in close enough to be heard when he brought my drink over.

"The booths with a red light are full. The booths with a green light are vacant or would welcome guests. If you decide to claim one of the booths, you'll find a call button inside. Push that and a waitress will come by and take your drink order."

I nodded my thanks and slipped him another hundred to cover the price of the drink and the information.

"Let's go find ourselves a booth, Jerome."

I headed towards one of the green lights and smiled when I found it empty.

"I don't think this place is anywhere near as full as our friend back at the rope tried to indicate it was."

James shrugged, but didn't sit down next to me. "He was probably just hoping to get another hundred bucks out of you."

I sighed and nodded. More than anything else, I suddenly wished we were back at the hotel where we'd left our luggage. I had half a dozen things that I needed to be doing. There were important plans that were sitting idle right now because I was here wasting time in a club, but all of the other things I was trying to accomplish might very well fall through if I couldn't find a way to save Agony.

"I'd ask you to sit down, but that probably wouldn't be very much in keeping with your cover."

"Yeah, I already thought of that." James paused for a second and then frowned. "There are two girls headed this direction, what do you want me to do with them?"

"Send them away, politely."

I hadn't scooted around all the way to the back of the booth, so I could still see out onto the dance floor.

The girl on the left was a blonde, the one on the right was a redhead, but neither of them looked like that was their original hair color. They were both young, probably barely old enough to buy alcohol, fit, and wearing the same kind of outfits as the rest of the girls inside the club.

James stepped forward to block the two of them, but rather than scaring them off, it backfired. The redhead took a quick, aggressive step forward, invading James' space. A real bodyguard, someone who was actually worried about the safety of his principal, would have straight-armed her.

James wasn't worried about my safety, not from a couple of human girls. Their clothing wasn't substantial enough to conceal a weapon bigger than a one-inch blade and they weren't vampires, but just because they were unarmed didn't necessarily mean they were *safe*.

There was a split-second pause as James started to straight-arm the redhead and then realized that he wasn't quite sure where to touch her. We shape shifters spent a lot of time trying to avoid casual skin-on-skin contact with humans, but the only parts of her that were covered were exactly the parts that polite society frowned on him touching.

The stutter to James' movements was barely perceptible, but it was just enough for the redhead to slip her arms around his neck and lean forward as if to kiss him. No wild animal likes to be trapped and the fact that she wasn't actually strong enough to restrain James didn't matter to his beast.

James reached up and pulled her arms apart, using his gentle but firm grip on her to push her back far enough that she wasn't rubbing up against him, but the damage was done. The skin-on-skin contact hadn't been enough to addict her to him, at least not unless she had a particularly addictive personality and the situation had been a lot more stressful for her than she'd let on, but she'd distracted James enough that her friend was able to slip into the booth with me.

"Buy me a drink and I'll tell you a secret."

There was a coy flirtatiousness to her tone that I hadn't had directed at me very often. The girls back home had been too scared of Kaleb and his plans for me to be that aggressive. It was intriguing, but that wasn't what made me wave James back.

She was gorgeous in an oversexed-beyond-her-years-way. No rich young man would kick her to the curb without at least talking to her for a few minutes. I couldn't let James get rid of her without potentially blowing my cover.

"Fine, I'll buy you a drink and you can tell me your secret, after which you should leave."

I found the panel on the wall that controlled the lights, flipped the switch to occupied, and pushed the call button.

"Oh, does that mean you're taken?"

Lying didn't come second nature to me yet. Maybe it never would, but I was starting to think that I was going to have to get a lot better at it if I expected to survive the next couple of decades. It was a mistake, but I temporized.

"Let's just say that there are a couple of very dangerous young ladies who aren't going to be happy to see you when they get back here."

"That wasn't a yes. Besides, I'm not afraid of a little competition, your friends aren't the only ones around here who are dangerous."

I was saved from answering by the arrival of our waitress. I slipped the waitress a pair of hundred-dollar bills and waved at my unwanted guest.

"The first one is for her, please get her whatever she wants until that runs out. The other one is for you."

The waitress flashed me a winning smile and then turned to the blonde.

"Scotch, neat."

Once we were alone again but for James, the girl turned back to me. "My name is Brindi."

"Hello, Brindi, are you always this determined?"

"Only when I see something I want."

She said it looking up at me through her lashes. It was an alluring combination of shy and bold that finally made me realize what had been tickling the back of my mind ever since I'd first seen her.

I'd known that there was something familiar about her, but I hadn't been able place it until then. She reminded me of the blonde from my dreams. It wasn't her face, although there was some resemblance there too. It was the way she held herself. Not all of the time, but half of her motions, the more reserved, shy ones were a perfect match for the girl from my dreams.

It had been weeks since I'd thought about the girl who had been haunting my dreams for years now. She'd been there as long as I could remember, but lately the dreams had changed, becoming more believable, more vivid. Recent events had been so overwhelming that I hadn't had a chance to dwell on anything but survival, but now that I'd been forcefully reminded of her, I felt a torrent of emotion.

Longing, loss, desire. It was all there with a strength that was nearly overpowering. That by itself would have given me pause, but there was something else there. It was less than a shadow of a fragment of a memory, but it was important. My mind picked at the sliver of experience, but it was slow reconstituting into something usable.

There had been a conversation, and after that a fight that I hadn't been sure I would survive. The conversation was too nebulous to remember, while the fight was vivid enough that I could almost remember the sequence of attacks and counters. Even so, I was positive that the conversation had been more important.

It had been important because of a...kiss? That couldn't be right, I'd never kissed anyone, never really felt the urge, at least not enough to risk it. Kaleb would have used any attachment on my part to anyone, in or out of the pack, as ruthlessly as he attacked any other perceived weaknesses.

Any recollection of a kiss had to be just an idle fantasy played out on the stage of some dream, but it didn't feel immaterial, it felt real, it felt important. I could almost feel *her* lips on mine, feel her trembling against me as she started breaking down the barriers of self-control that I'd spent a lifetime forging, barriers that kept my beast in check, barriers that were the only thing keeping her safe.

AMBUSHED

The kiss had been magical, life-changing even, but I'd been wrong, the kiss wasn't what was important. The kiss wasn't the reason that my subconscious had been picking at the memory for weeks now in an effort to bring it up to where I would remember. The kiss was only important because it had been with *her*, with...

Brindi's hands on mine shattered my entire train of thought into ten thousand pieces. It was gone, all of the feelings, the memory that I'd spent so long trying to reconstruct without even realizing it, the identity of the mystery girl who I'd kissed, it all went spinning away and even as I tried to grab ahold of *something*, the pieces all evaporated like hoarfrost before a desert sun.

Maybe I would have been able to retain enough to put some of the memory back together if not for the shock of realizing that I'd allowed myself to become so distracted that I hadn't seen Brindi reach out to touch me. No matter what else was going on inside of my mind, I shouldn't have allowed that to happen.

Her touching me was dangerous for her in ways that she didn't know enough to understand, but it was more than that. Letting someone I didn't know get that close to me wasn't the kind of thing that I could allow, not if I wanted to survive long enough to see the Coun'hij fall.

I moved my hands out from underneath Brindi's hands and then I slid a little to the side so that our shoulders weren't touching.

"I'm sorry, you're really quite attractive, but that isn't a good idea."

She pouted. Even her pout was a study in beauty. "I already told you that I'm not afraid of a challenge. Tell your bodyguard to keep those other girls away; they'll never even have to know."

I shook my head. "You need to leave. Go find your friend and the two of you can try again with someone else."

"I don't want someone else, I want you. Besides, my drink hasn't arrived. You wouldn't have your bodyguard throw me out before I'd had a chance to finish my drink, would you?"

I opened my mouth to tell her to leave, but something about her stopped me. It wasn't that she was gorgeous and I was suddenly feeling inexplicably lonely. It was that in that instant I realized that her curious mixture of brash self-confidence and shyness was less calculated than I'd originally thought.

It was an act, but it was the confidence that was a show. She was scared. Maybe that was too strong of a word. The club was too full of noise and bodies to get a very good read on her, but the less assertive part of her personality, the shy, withdrawn part, was the real Brindi.

"You're scared."

She gasped. Even that was perfectly understated. She was either a master actor or she really hadn't expected me to cue into that.

"How did you know that?"

"I'm...unusually observant. You could say it's a gift."

She wasn't satisfied with that explanation, but she obviously knew it was as much as she was going to get out of me.

"Okay, yeah, I'm scared. My ex-boyfriend is here tonight too. I didn't expect to see him here and I'm worried that he'll follow me home. After we broke up I moved to a new apartment so he couldn't hurt me."

My nostrils flared slightly as I tested the air. It was harder here with so many distractions, and I wished for a second that I could just shift to wolf form, but I could smell the lie rolling off of her. Her heartbeat spiked despite the fact that her face had stayed relatively composed.

"Let's try again, Brindi. This time lead with the truth or I'll have Jerome throw you out of my booth regardless of whether your drink has arrived."

Her eyes hardened and I could see her trying to figure out what she could get away with.

"Fine, the truth is I owe some people a lot of money. I came here tonight hoping for a ticket out of all of that."

"What about your friend, the redhead?"

"She's one of the people I owe money to. She's here to keep tabs on me and make sure I leave with the kind of guy they aimed me at."

"What's the end game?"

"I'm supposed to insert myself into your life, take an inventory of all of the valuables back at your place and then let them inside so they can rob you, after which I'll be free and clear."

My beast wanted her gone. Subterfuge was anathema to us. Some shape shifters obviously got over their beast's native straightforwardness, but I wasn't sure I ever wanted to be one of them. The animal inside me wanted to ensure that she couldn't hurt me, but the human part of me was curious at what could take someone down such a path so quickly.

"How did you get in debt to these people?"

"My parents died in a car wreck when I was seventeen and I…"

I cut her off with an angry wave. "This is your last warning. If you lie to me again you're gone."

"Fine, it was drugs. I'm into them for thirty thousand worth of cocaine. I ran away from my last foster home when I was seventeen and I've been selling drugs ever since. I use a little, but mostly I just deal. Some stuff happened and I ended up in trouble."

"So you turned to prostitution and theft?"

Her mouth tightened. "I don't have a lot of other options, not if I want to live to see next week. They gave me a week and last night was a bust, so I've only got six more nights to make something happen."

"So where does it end, Brindi? If you make your big score and get square with the redhead and the others you'll still be broke and scrambling to make rent."

I'd only thought she looked scared before, now she really looked terrified. It was fascinating though. A lot of people got mean when they were that afraid, that or they just seized up completely. She wasn't just waiting around for death to come after her, but it was obvious that she'd compartmentalized her life to an extreme degree. She didn't want to think about what came next because she knew things were almost certainly going to get worse.

"I don't know. Maybe I could leave the club with you and then make a run for it. If I find a new city and keep a low profile then they might never find me."

I stared at her for several seconds, debating.

"What would you do if you had the option to do anything in the world?"

She swallowed and then looked away from me. "I'd like to start over, for real. I'd like to have the kind of life most kids have. I can't go back and grow up in a normal family, but I'd like to pretend like that's where I came from. I'd like to go to college and just blow off the first year and a half trying to figure out what I wanted to do with the rest of my life. I'd like to worry about boys rather than drugs, and dating instead of grand larceny."

It was true. Every single word of it, which meant that I had a difficult decision in front of me. The money back in the First National Bank of Cayman was the next best thing to limitless, but I didn't have access to all of it right now. Banks here in the U.S. had to report any big money transfers, which meant that I had to be very careful still when it came to creating a money trail.

I'd brought several million in cash and negotiable instruments with me back on the plane, but it wouldn't last forever and once it ran out I was going to have to make another trip back to the Caymans. That was dangerous because Kaleb and the rest of the Coun'hij would be watching flights out from the mainland very closely and the next time they'd be waiting for me with a lot more than just five hybrids.

I already had other plans in the works, plans that should allow me to funnel some of the money into the U.S. without getting the attention of the IRS, but they would take some time to really get up and running. Until that happened, we were vulnerable. I didn't anticipate any big expenses, but then again I hadn't anticipated Agony being caught after all of this time and I didn't have any idea how much it was going to cost to get him free, even assuming we could.

Not only that, Brindi had made her own bed. It might not be completely her fault, but she could have chosen not to deal drugs. Was it right for me to help her and risk coming up short in my efforts to save thousands of children from growing up in a world where Kaleb and his cronies were going to use them as disposable commodities in the Coun'hij's wars?

"Okay, Brindi, I'm going to help you out. You've been mostly honest with me, and I do believe that you want the life you just described. There are stipulations though."

The cautious joy that had been shining from her face despite her best efforts died away as she tried to prepare herself for disappointment, for 'strings' that would be as bad or worse than anything she was currently dealing with.

"You can stay with me and I'll get you out of the club. I need to meet with someone here; you can sit in the booth with us, but you'll stay on the far end and you'll keep your mouth shut, both in the meeting and afterwards about anything you hear or see there. Once we're out of the club I'll give you the money you need to pay off the redhead and her friends plus a little extra to salve their pride at the fact that you're about to walk out on them and deprive them of a much bigger score."

"What's the catch?"

"You're never coming back here. You'll arrange for a dead drop so that the redhead can get the money and then you'll never have any contact with anyone from your old life. I'll get you a fake ID and you'll enroll in college and make something out of yourself. No partying, no dealing, nothing illegal. You need to be squeaky clean for the rest of your life."

"That's it?"

She didn't believe it. It really was too good to be true and she'd learned a fundamental lesson that most adults twice her age still didn't understand. There's no free lunch.

I was going to have to put a catch in there or she was never going to live up to her end of things.

"No, that's not it. From time to time you're going to move money around for me. You'll have some kind of business on the side, we can work out the details later—maybe photography. The money will come in, you'll move it to one of my accounts, and you'll take a very small cut for your time and effort. If you ever try and screw me then the consequences won't be pleasant."

"Okay, I'm in."

I held up a hand. "You also must stop trying to touch me, Jerome or any of the other people with me."

That earned me an odd look, but the waitress was back with Brindi's drink and Jasmin was only a couple of steps behind her. The waitress flashed me a three-hundred-watt smile as she asked if there was anything else we needed, but I simply held up my still-full drink and waved her away with a smile.

Jasmin didn't look happy to see Brindi. "Who is she?"

"Someone who's been very foolish up until now, but who we're going to help get a new start. Did you find him?"

Jasmin and Brindi exchanged mutually hostile stares and then Jasmin started working her way around the booth. I slid over, meeting her halfway and putting more distance between Brindi and me. Jasmin leaned in as though to whisper, which was a nice touch when it came to maintaining the illusion that we were just humans.

"I found Shawn. Jess is keeping an eye on his booth to make sure he doesn't send anyone out for help, but it's not like we can stop him from texting. He's expecting you now; you're going to want to move quickly so you can talk to him and get back out before more of the Chicago pack can show up and box us in."

"Okay, let's go."

We all stood up to leave, and Jasmin reflexively wrapped my arm around herself to keep our cover, which in turn caused Brindi to move up to my other side as though intending on hanging off of me as well.

"The deal was no touching."

"Yeah, but if I don't at least make an effort they are never going to buy it. I might not make it out of the club if they don't think we're together now."

"Grab our drinks, that gives you a reason for not throwing yourself at me. Once we arrive at the other booth you can set the drinks down and rub up against my back or chest, but no skin-on-skin contact."

Brindi shot me a high-powered smile as she turned back for our drinks, but I could tell she wasn't any more pleased about the situation than Jasmin was. Luckily Shawn's booth wasn't far away and once we arrived she behaved herself. The fact that there was a pair of particularly massive shape shifters posted just outside of Shawn's booth probably helped. Shawn's bodyguards were as dangerous-looking as they were big.

A couple of seconds later Jasmin, Jess, Brindi and I were all inside the booth. Shawn only had one other person inside the booth with him and she practically screamed shape shifter. Even to the eyes of my human form she still bled off energy and light the way that only really powerful hybrids could. That wasn't a guarantee that she had some kind of ability, but it was a pretty good sign and I decided to keep the table between us at all times.

Now that I had an idea of just how dangerous his bodyguard was, I looked Shawn over as I slid down the bench seat until I was nearly inside of arm's reach—for a hybrid.

In human form at least, Shawn wasn't anything special at first glance. It was hard to tell for sure inside of the dim lighting of the club, but he looked like he had short blond hair and a boyish cast to his features that would have made it hard to take him seriously if you didn't know who his father was.

That impression wasn't helped by the fact that he was built like the quintessential debate geek. So far he hadn't manifested any of the legendary Ulrich bulk and muscle; he looked like he would blow away if a strong wind came through the club. He was sitting down, so it was hard to be sure, but he didn't look like he was much over five-eight.

Even his power level didn't seem to be anything special. He glowed about as much as you would expect from a hybrid, but without the extra strength of the bodyguard next to him. It was still possible that he'd manifested a power that I hadn't heard about, but it wasn't very likely.

It wasn't until I got a good look at his eyes that I knew I was in the presence of Ulrich Bishop's heir. Shawn had the eyes of someone born into power. He didn't look arrogant, but there was an assurance there that people would do what he said, and a weight that said he carried more secrets than anyone our age should have to bear.

"Thank you for agreeing to talk to me, Shawn."

Shawn held up his cellphone. "It's hard to pass up a chance to talk to someone as infamous as you are right now. Just so you know, none of us texted, emailed, called or otherwise informed anyone else that you're here."

"I appreciate that."

Shawn's shrug implied it wasn't a big deal, but I knew his father would have been hard pressed not to turn me in if it had been Ulrich I'd approached instead of Shawn.

"So you're the one who wanted to talk, go ahead and talk."

"Agony has been captured."

"I hope you weren't expecting to surprise me with that little tidbit. That's practically ancient history at this point."

"No, I knew you'd be aware of his capture, and I suspect you understand exactly what it means to the resistance. I want to break him out, but I need help, a lot of help, preferably from a group that the Coun'hij isn't keeping too close of an eye on right now."

Shawn pursed his lips. "You're not the first one to approach me about this, Alec. It's no secret that I've got connections with people who would like to see your dad and the rest of the Coun'hij overthrown. Some people want me to convince my dad to jump into the situation with both feet, some people just want me to help arrange a meeting between likeminded parties, but so far I haven't helped any of my visitors out."

That wasn't the most promising start to the conversation, and the fact that Shawn's eyes kept sliding away from mine and drifting over to

Brindi was another sign that I didn't have his full attention.

"Why is that, Shawn? The word on the street is that you talk a good game, but you're not actually *doing* anything. Seems like maybe it's all just a bunch of hot air."

Shawn's metaphysical roar of power was strong enough to make my hair stand on end, but I forced myself not to respond in kind. The goal was to get his attention, to *really* get his attention, not start an actual dominance fight.

"You don't come into my city and question my commitment to *anything*, Graves. There are four of you and four of us, but I recognize the two girls, they are wolves. You wouldn't stand a chance against us."

I held my hands up. "No insult was intended, Shawn, but you have to admit that it's hard to believe you're really committed to the cause when you don't seem to be making any kind of difference. Agony's capture is a huge deal; it's one of those pivot points that could change everything."

Shawn could taste the truth of my statement—that I hadn't wanted to insult him—and that went a long way towards calming him down. He wasn't completely back to how he'd been, but that was okay, I didn't want him to go back to only listening to me with half an ear. He studied me over the rim of a glass of what looked like whiskey.

"All right, you've made your point. I actually agree with you, Alec. Agony being captured is as big a deal as we're likely to see in our lifetimes. The biggest question is whether anything we can do will make it better."

"What are you talking about? Of course we can make it better. Agony was captured just south of the Mexican border. It's only a matter of time before the Coun'hij decides to move him to somewhere more secure. Once he's in motion, his guards will be vulnerable."

Shawn sighed. "Let's just assume you're right. Let's assume that you can rescue him despite the fact that the Coun'hij currently have eyes on every pack that isn't already in their back pocket. Let's assume you're able to pull together a big enough force to take out whatever Kaleb and the rest have guarding the delivery, and let's just say that this isn't all a gigantic trap. What's the best-case scenario?"

"We rescue him."

"That's a lie and you know, it, Alec. That's the best-case scenario for Agony, but it's not what you're hoping to accomplish. The best-case scenario is that his rescue serves as a catalyst that causes our entire race to rise and overthrow the Coun'hij."

My beast didn't appreciate being called a liar. I stepped on it, forcing it back into a corner of my mind.

"It's all a question of timeframes, Shawn. In the short term I want to rescue Agony but obviously the long-term goal is to free our people."

"Right, well, here's the thing about revolutions. You only get one real attempt per generation. If you do this and everything doesn't go off perfectly, then thousands of our people are going to die and, at the end of it all, the Coun'hij will have an even stronger grip on whoever survives."

"If we're successful then…"

Shawn cut me off. "If you do everything perfectly then thousands of people are going to die and at the end there will be a power vacuum that will take another generation or two to shake out. The best-case scenario is that you get a lot of people killed and then we spend another six hundred years as a people trying to hammer out another system of governance which hopefully is better than what we've got right now."

"So the risks aren't worth it? Is that what you're trying to tell me? If so then your reputation as a firebrand is exaggerated."

"Honestly, I don't care what you think, Alec. You're coming from a position of not having any other choice. That's not the case for me. When I take over my pack, I'll have an actual possibility of sparking a revolution. It's a lot easier to throw everything to the wind when your actions only influence a few people."

My hands clenched into fists despite my best efforts. I'd come with the intention of keeping my cool. I'd even managed not to escalate things when I'd called him on the carpet for ignoring me, but his incessant barbs were becoming too much. There was too much truth to what he was saying for me to just shrug off his words.

"Where does that leave us?"

As Shawn opened his mouth to respond, the lights went off in the entire club simultaneously. It was one of the eeriest things I'd ever experienced. There was absolutely no natural light inside the club, but I could still see flickers of light emanating from the people around me. Shawn's bodyguard was on her feet, and I realized that I hadn't seen her move. I was actually tempted to say that she'd moved even before the lights had gone out.

Jess reached for her cellphone, but it died in her hands a second later. Shawn had his hands up and pointed in my direction; he was only a split second from shifting.

"It wasn't me, Shawn!"

"Crap, it wasn't me either."

Jasmin's voice cut through the bedlam as people started screaming.

"Werewolves?"

Shawn shook his head. "No the blackout is too complete. Someone physically cut the power to the building."

"What about the phones?"

There wasn't any need for me to interject anything; Jasmin was asking all of my questions.

"It's got to be some kind of EMP device. My dad has been funding research into a portable device that could knock out cellphones and cameras."

"Why on earth would you want to replicate the kind of devastation that werewolves cause?"

The question shot out of me before I had a chance to think. Shawn's response was quiet enough that I was pretty sure Brindi hadn't heard him, but he was obviously not happy at my tone.

"This isn't Utah, Alec. Our kind wasn't ever intended to live around this many humans. We needed a way to contain incidents when they happen. Things are a lot harder now that every individual walking down the street has a video recorder attached to their phone and the ability to post to YouTube."

The girl next to Shawn was already moving along the side of the booth, headed towards the dance floor with a speed that screamed she thought we were about to come under attack. Jess pushed Brindi out of the booth and Jasmin was only a split second behind them as Shawn and I both started moving too.

"That means that your pack is responsible for this?"

"It's not my pack, it's my dad's pack. Besides, it's not the whole pack or my people would have warned me, this is just the bootlickers."

"The bootlickers?"

"Yeah, the faction that wants my dad to cement our relations with the Coun'hij. We call them bootlickers, they call us traitors."

James and the two bodyguards Shawn had left at the doorway to the booth must have been able to hear enough to understand that Shawn and I weren't at each other's throats. All three of them had stepped a few feet away from the booth in an attempt to establish a perimeter.

My beast didn't want to take second place to anyone, but this was Shawn's hometown, so I let him exit before me and then it was my turn. I stepped out into what looked like a snapshot of hell.

It was still too dark to see anything inanimate, and the people who were stampeding towards the exit were just humans so they didn't give off as strong of a glow to my otherworld sight, but I could still make out enough to see that people had been trampled already. I took a step towards the dance floor and the worst of the injured, but Shawn grabbed my arm.

"They're here, I can smell them."

He pointed at more than a dozen figures approaching in three separate groups from both sides and the front. I bit back a curse as I realized that I should have noticed them myself. Their glow was much too bright for them to be humans.

"They're from your pack, what are the rules of engagement?"

"Would you just roll over and let them kill you if I told you to only use non-lethal strikes?"

"No, probably not."

Shawn gave me a sad smile that wasn't at all in keeping with his image as a revolutionary who was only moments away at any given time from shattering his father's pack into pieces.

"Do what you have to do. If you can disable them that would be great, but don't hesitate if it's you or them."

I felt a pair of trembling hands on my arm. Brindi had glued herself to my side.

"What's going on? Why are you guys all whispering?"

I reached over and pulled her hands off of me as I placed my other hand on the warm skin of her back and guided her into the booth.

"Stay here, Brindi. Go all of the way to the back of the booth and stay there until the lights either come on or I come get you. It's really important that you not see what happens next."

She tried to resist my gentle shove, but it was a passive kind of resistance which meant that she had no chance against my superior strength. I watched her disappear into the back of the booth and then turned around just in time to see the first set of transformations ripple through Shawn's people and my friends.

I threw open the cage where my beast spent most of his time and a blast of power ripped through me. There wasn't any reason to hold back, so I cut loose with the most intense blast of energy I was capable of.

It was…impressive…even to me. For a split second I almost thought I'd bluffed the other side into backing down. A couple of them took involuntary steps backwards, and even the boldest of them started moving with less confidence, but the four or five biggest guys stepped forward and the rest of them followed.

"Don't say you weren't warned."

The words rumbled up from my chest, deeper and harsher than my normal voice, and then I threw myself forward at the hybrid who had just replaced one of the closest men.

It was a confusing melee of fang and claw.

The Chicago shape shifters knew who was on each side of the fight, but the four of us from Sanctuary weren't as sure. It was still pitch black, and the lights each wolf and hybrid gave off weren't enough to identify someone. That meant my sense of smell was my best way to determine which guys were with Shawn. I hadn't gotten as good of a read on the two bodyguards and now it was too late. I simply concentrated on the hybrid I'd picked out before the lines merged and hoped for the best.

My enemy slashed at me with his right hand, but I knocked his claws down away from me and then stabbed my own claws into his shoulder. I probably could have finished the fight right then, but a whisper of sound brought me around just in time to deny the wolf that had been trying for a kill shot.

The angle was bad or I would have killed her while she was still in the air and unable to change direction. Instead I managed to hit her with my forearm hard enough to send her crashing into the booths behind me.

The hybrid I'd been fighting charged me, and I dug my talons into the floor, scraping against the concrete foundation as I tried to get out of his way. I was only partially successful. I got far enough to the side that he didn't hit me directly, but I couldn't make it far enough to avoid the wicked slash that ripped through my ribs on the left side of my chest.

He was looking for a contest of strength because if he could lock me up then even if I proved stronger it wouldn't matter once the wolf got back to her feet. I was younger than him and a lot less experienced, but I wasn't stupid.

Instead of resisting his charge, I pivoted in place, a growl ripping free of my throat as his claws moved around inside of me. I pinned his left arm in place as best I could to limit the damage, and used his shoulder as a fulcrum to throw him into the booths.

The hybrid hit with a titanic crash, but I couldn't follow up because the wolf threw herself at me. She was fast, not as fast as Jasmin, but still incredibly quick. She went from motionless to flying through the air at me without any telegraphing of her attack.

Against someone else, especially someone who was already bleeding from a dangerous set of wounds, it probably would have been enough, but I ducked down, denying her a clean shot at my throat as I reached up and sank my left-hand set of claws into her side. The easiest thing to do would have been to simply kill her right then. No wolf could hope to last long once a hybrid had hold of them, but instead I spun around and slammed her into the wreckage of the booth next to where we'd been sitting.

I'd aimed her at a length of steel that had been bolted horizontally into the wall and she hit with enough force to drive the rod completely through her. The metal had missed her heart, but it had gone through the ribs on her left side. Even a shape shifter wouldn't last for very long impaled on a piece of steel like that, but it was the best I could offer her. Either way, she wouldn't be going anywhere before the fight ended.

I crashed into the remnants of the booth behind her in an attempt to put the hybrid down before he could regain his feet, but I was half a second too slow. The hybrid launched a couple of lightning-fast swipes at my neck. I blocked the first one and stepped back far enough to dodge the second one, but that forced me out of the booth.

AMBUSHED

I probably should have kept him confined back inside of the debris, but I'd been able to see Brindi out of the corner of my eye. She was terrified, huddled up in a ball in an effort to make herself a smaller target, but if I'd stayed there, forcing the Chicago hybrid to fight constrained by all of that wreckage, there was just too much of a chance that she would have been hurt regardless of how small of a target she'd made of herself.

My opponent sprang forward, arms out wide to make sure that I couldn't dodge, so I did the last thing he was expecting and stepped into him. It was risky, nobody could guarantee who would come out on top of a collision like that, but I needed to finish him off quickly. We'd started out outnumbered by fifty percent, which meant that some of my friends were fighting a desperate, losing battle against two or even three opponents.

They needed my help and I couldn't afford to let this fight drag out. I stepped into him, but I darted slightly to the side at the last moment and slapped down his right arm.

He hit me like a wrecking ball, but I'd been prepared for that and my step to the side meant that at least some of his momentum was spun around me rather than simply smashing me backwards. I sank my jaws in the side of his neck while we were still airborne and then did my best to get a set of talons in each of his legs before we hit the ground.

I was only partially successful, his right leg was still free when we hit, but I managed to keep both of my arms in fairly close to my body so he was the one that hit first and that was the single most important thing I could have done. It takes an almost unimaginable amount of shearing force to break a hybrid's arm, but something snapped as I came down on top of his left arm.

His howl of rage was deafening, but I refused to loosen my grip on his neck. Instead I bit down harder, trying to get my fangs into something vital as we bounced and rolled out onto the dance floor. His left arm was useless, but he was much stronger than I'd expected him to be and I was having a hard time getting enough leverage to keep his right arm under control.

Our fight had devolved into a kind of slow-motion tug-of-war. I was trying to keep him from savaging my back while he was trying to stop me from snapping his neck.

I was losing control of his arm and I hadn't managed to get past the massive muscles of his neck. Rather than finishing him off so that I could go help my friends, I was locked into a fight I couldn't win. If someone else didn't break free and come help me it was only a matter of time before I was a dead man.

My right arm was pinned underneath the two of us. I tried to roll us over onto his back, but his legs were just too far apart and I couldn't budge him.

AMBUSHED

Footsteps approached from behind me and I tensed up in anticipation of the blow that was about to kill me. The fact that they were coming from behind me instead of from behind him was a bad sign, but then all of a sudden the pressure against my left hand weakened slightly. The change was so small that I almost thought I'd imagined it, but it was there. If he'd been just a hair stronger or if I'd had slightly worse leverage it wouldn't have made any difference, but it was making a difference.

We strained against each other and, with the help of whoever was behind me, I was able to push his arm up and away from my back. Even better, the further ahead I got it, the more the angles and forces involved helped me and hindered him.

He reversed the direction of his push with a suddenness that was quite literally preternatural. It was the kind of lightning-fast movement that no human could have possibly hoped to register let alone avoid, but I'd been expecting it.

The hybrid tried to flip both of us around, but I threw myself in the direction of his pull, and sent us through an extra half revolution. That put me on top instead of him.

I heard a soft gasp and smelled blood, but none of that registered. I was too caught up in the fight, too caught up in the fact that my right hand had come free. I killed the hybrid with a single slash to the neck and rolled to my feet looking for another foe.

A sudden pulse of light blinded me for a couple of seconds and I stumbled backwards in an attempt to avoid anyone who might not have been as affected by the flash.

"Enough!"

I didn't recognize the voice, but the fighting stopped with a suddenness that I wouldn't have believed possible.

"Shift back to your human forms now or I'll have you all killed where you stand."

I felt a rapid, many-pointed surge of power as half a dozen people shifted back to their primary form over the space of just a couple of seconds.

"Alec, it's my dad. We're safe now, go ahead and shift back."

My beast didn't want to obey, didn't view Shawn or Ulrich either one as being dominant to us, but I knew better. Ulrich wouldn't have left his compound without bringing at least a dozen hybrids with him, not if he knew he was coming to this kind of battle.

It didn't matter who was dominant to whom, the fact of the matter was that he could have all four of us killed without even raising a finger of his own. I'd come into his territory without asking permission, without honoring any of the normal forms, and my life was forfeit as a result if that was his desire.

I shifted back to human form. The change cleared my vision enough for me to take stock of my surroundings. My breath caught as I looked down and saw Brindi on the floor in a pool of blood.

She had been the one who'd come to help me when I'd been struggling with the Chicago hybrid. She'd helped me pull his hand away from my kidneys, but when he'd flipped us over his claws had gone through her stomach.

I dropped down next to her and pushed my hands against her stomach to keep her life from leaking out.

Chapter 12

Adriana Paige
Marauder's Gas Station
Central Wyoming

It turned out that having all of my energy drained away didn't kill me. At least not that time. Taggart was still alive two days after the fight that had nearly gotten both of us killed, which was good, but I still wasn't sure that he was going to make it.

I spent my days up in the store trying to keep anyone from realizing that the actual owners of the gas station had been killed in the supernatural equivalent to a Wild West shootout. I took frequent breaks to check on Taggart, but mostly he just slept. Occasionally he woke up enough for me to help him down a thousand calories and a pint of fluid, but other than that I was by myself.

AMBUSHED

There wasn't much in the way of traffic past the gas station, which made it harder and harder to justify spending my time up there, so after the first full day I put up a new sign saying we'd reduced our hours and started spending more time down in the bunker.

The last thing I'd wanted to do was clean up a bunch of dead bodies, but once they had started rotting I hadn't had much of a choice. I'd spent three hours during my second full night dragging them all into one of the bunk rooms and locking them in there. I left the exterior door up for an hour or so after that and it had gone a long ways towards making the air breathable again.

I'd had to get inventive when it came to moving the bodies, so I put that same inventiveness to work that same night moving Taggart. I got a second slick tarp, since the first one was now good for nothing but being incinerated, and used it to drag Taggart to Paulo's master suite, after which I'd been too exhausted to do anything more than shower, change the sheets on Paulo's bed and then crash for the night.

I tried to contact Alec again that night, and I'd even stocked up on extra calories during the day, but I didn't have any more luck than I had the first night. I once again made *some* kind of connection, but it never got to the point where I could use it to pull him to me or me to him. I tried to sever the filament sooner this time, but it was still too elastic.

I slept in for an extra two hours, almost missing my shortened hours up at the store, and still felt like I'd been run over by a freight train. I actually had two whole customers stop for gas and munchies that second day, but other than that I just spent a lot of time worrying about Taggart and stressing over the fact that I hadn't been able to make contact with Alec yet.

I spent another two hours that evening cleaning. I didn't try to address all of the blood and fire damage, but I did clean up the couple short corridors between the master suite and the tunnel to the store. I also grabbed some replacement batteries from the store and used the lantern to brave the semi-darkness in the kitchen.

I couldn't time Taggart's periods of wakefulness enough to make cooking for him worthwhile, but I at least was able to cook some rice and beans for myself. It wasn't anything fancy, but after the things I'd seen in the forty-eight hours prior to that I didn't feel like anything more adventurous.

I'd showered again before cooking, so once I finished up the food and checked on Taggart, who was still on the floor because I wasn't strong enough to pull him up into Paulo's bed, there wasn't anything left to do but sleep.

I wasn't up to trying to talk to Alec again, but luckily I'd had another idea during the long hours minding the store. I'd been wrong when I'd said that there was only one other supernatural being I knew besides Taggart. Alec and Taggart were the two I knew the most about, but there had been that girl at the away game who I'd saved from being beaten to death by the other team's cheerleaders.

She hadn't told me her name, but I didn't actually need a name to make contact with someone. It was risky, far riskier than reaching out to Alec, despite what Taggart might have said, but it also felt like the right answer, so after I fell asleep I sent myself back to the school where I'd saved her and closed my dream eyes so that I could concentrate.

Things went better this time. It didn't take the tendrils anywhere near as long to make contact with her, and I hardly felt like I'd expended any energy at all by the time I had a connection strong enough to use.

I took a deep breath, mentally grabbed the thick cable between the two of us, and pulled with all of my might. It was like trying to lift a house with a cable and a thousand-pulley block and tackle. I was pulling in the rope and knew that meant that I was moving her, but it was so hard and it felt like she was barely traveling any distance at all. That phase only lasted for a second or two though and then she was accelerating towards me at impossible speeds.

It would have been tempting to slack off, but I gritted my teeth and pulled harder. I knew what came next and I wanted to have all of the momentum I possibly could generate before she hit the wall I'd experienced with Taggart.

A second later, she hit the barrier. It was like trying to pull an elephant through a mailbox. She was moving so fast that it seemed impossible that anything could stop her, but I could feel reality flexing and shivering as it tried to keep from allowing her into my dream.

I pulled with everything I had left—even though I was pretty sure that nothing I could do this late in the game could possibly make any difference—and I felt myself start to lose my grip on my dream. That was terrifying. The last thing I wanted was to send myself into the gray plane of nonexistence that I could feel her traveling through, but I needed her here.

I gave one last desperate tug on the cable between us even as I clawed at my surroundings to keep from being pulled in after her. The universe tore and then suddenly she was standing before me, confused and wary.

"I'm sorry, I hope that wasn't an unpleasant experience for you."

She looked around at our surroundings, taking in the school behind me and the shop building we were standing next to.

"I've been here before."

"I know, I was there too. You were letting four girls beat you. I stopped them without realizing that you didn't need my help."

She nodded slowly. "And in return, I warned you that one of your companions was dangerous."

"You were right. Jackson was a vampire. That's why he was there with me. Before then he'd found me in the dream world, but at that point he hadn't figured out my real identity."

I hadn't changed my appearance, so I knew she recognized me, but she seemed to take a degree of comfort from the fact that we'd both described an event known only to a handful of people. I was realizing that there weren't any bulletproof guarantees when it came to the supernatural world, but this was as close as I could get to proving I was really who she thought I was.

"So you're a traveler then? I'd heard rumors of someone who could do this, but I didn't know that there was more than one of you."

"I call it dream walking instead of travelling, but you're right, there weren't two of us, at least not until a few months ago."

"Why have you brought me here?"

"I need your help again. I know I don't have a right to it, but I had to ask regardless. I've learned a lot since we last talked. I know you're a shape shifter, that's the only way that you could have known that Jackson was a vampire. You could smell him, but he and Tristan were standing so close together that you couldn't tell for sure which one was the vampire."

For a long time she didn't say anything. Her brown eyes seemed to be taking stock of me in ways that I didn't understand, that or she was just trying to see if I would crack under the pressure as the weight of the silence between us continued to grow.

"Let's say for now that you're right and I'm a shape shifter. What difference does it make?"

"I need to know about the Coun'hij. I need to know everything you can tell me about them."

"Why?" Her voice had changed. It wasn't that her beautiful accent had gone away, although for a second I thought that was the reason. It was because her voice had gone flat. It was like someone had stripped away all of the emotion and life from her.

For a moment I couldn't get any words to come out. I was skirting dangerous ground now. Everything I revealed could potentially make it back to the Coun'hij, could potentially be used against Taggart and me at a later date.

"You know the other one like me?"

"Dream Stealer?"

"Yeah, that's the one. Together we could be a much bigger threat to the Coun'hij than he's been so far. He's asking me to help him, to...kill the Coun'hij's agents, and I don't know if that's the right thing to be doing. I like Dream Stealer and I think I trust him, but it's hard to kill people based off of the word of just one man."

She sighed and then started walking toward the football field. "What's your name?"

"Adri."

"Very well, Adri. My name is Dominic. Let's go find somewhere to sit down, somewhere that will let us stay far enough away from each other that we're unlikely to attack each other, but close enough that we can talk comfortably. I've had a long day already."

I thought about creating a pair of benches out of thin air in front of us, but I didn't want to spook her. Besides, it was just as easy to let her lead me over to the bleachers. She waved me up onto the stands, then selected a bench several rows down from me and turned around so she was facing me.

"I've never heard anyone say that they liked the Dream Stealer. His methods are said to be brutal, but no more brutal than the Coun'hij. I'm not sure that you can fight a superior force without being at least as vicious as they are."

"So the Coun'hij is bad then, just like he said they were?"

"I'm not sure I'm the best one to answer that question, Adri. I come from somewhere much worse than here. I expected to live and die down there, probably at the hands of one of the self-styled rulers of my people. The Coun'hij is much less corrupt and murderous than my own father is."

"You're saying it's all relative?"

Dominic looked away from me for a couple of seconds before nodding. "I guess I am, at least partly. The Coun'hij is prosecuting a war against my people, a war that they had no real reason to fight. Hundreds have been killed already, many of them for nothing more nefarious than wanting to cross the border from Mexico so that they could lose themselves here in the United States where they might have a chance at a normal life."

I tried to remember everything that Taggart had let drop during the few short weeks that I'd known him.

"So you're a...jaguar then, not a wolf? Dream Stealer said that there was fighting going on between the wolves and the jaguars. I guess I didn't really give it a second thought. He's always seemed a lot more focused on the Coun'hij than anything else."

Dominic nodded. "Most people seem to find their own pet causes and ignore the rest of the bad going on in the world. It's like we can't simultaneously think about all of the terrible things out there so we just pick one and put everything else out of our mind."

I felt like I was in the middle of the ocean without a life preserver. I needed *something* to hold onto, something certain, something that could anchor me against all of the things that I didn't know.

"So what should I be doing then? Forget about the Coun'hij and try to stop the worst of the jaguars instead?"

"Are you really so eager to kill that you have to find a target?"

"No, I've killed before and I didn't like it, but I think that Dream Stealer is probably right. I'm a weapon. I didn't ask to become like this, but I have the ability to do things nobody else can do. If I don't chart my own course then sooner or later I'm going to end up manipulated into doing something I don't want to do. Besides, if I can make a difference and don't then in my own way I'm just as bad as the people who are making the world crap."

Dominic flinched a little at my last statement. I hadn't been trying to make her feel bad, but apparently that was a little too close to home for her.

"Very well, I'll tell you as plainly as I can, Adri. There are hundreds, maybe even thousands of wolves who live their life out in security, safe from any kind of harm other than what they deal with by being part of a pack. In almost every way the wolves live better lives than us cats, but you can't measure the Coun'hij by that one fact any more than you could say that they are good simply because they are doing their best to wipe out the vampires."

I opened my mouth, but she talked over me. "The truth is that the wolves are happiest when the Coun'hij doesn't notice them enough to interfere in their lives. Once you come to the attention of the Coun'hij things go badly. For them, might *is* right. There is nobody that the Coun'hij wouldn't murder if it was in their interest, no law they wouldn't break, no right that they wouldn't abridge if it suited their purpose. They surround themselves with murderers and thugs because, at its heart, the Coun'hij is the biggest collection of villains around."

"So you would agree with Dream Stealer then, anyone that works with the Coun'hij is someone who the world would be better off without."

"No, I think that is a step too far. I think people can end up working for the Coun'hij for a variety of reasons, fear being not the least of them. You can't blindly kill the Coun'hij's pawns without risking injustice, but you are more in the right to be fighting them than you would be if you were aiding them."

Chapter 13

Alec Graves
Club Pure Vertigo
Chicago, Illinois

The lights were back on, which meant that I could see the full destruction that had been wrought on the club. Ulrich had arrived with a force of more than forty shape shifters and he'd come prepared to contain the situation in more ways than one.

He'd had a group of hybrids march away the surviving Coun'hij loyalists who'd attacked Shawn and then turned his attention to keeping the humans out of the club until his people had cleaned up enough that nobody would know the damage had been done by six-and-a-half-foot-tall monsters.

Two hundred years was plenty of time to get really good at your chosen profession and Ulrich's medics had obviously been practicing their craft for a long time. One of them, a big male who communicated mostly in grunts with the occasional gesture thrown in for good measure, took over Brindi's care within seconds of Ulrich's arrival.

I'd been edged out of the way by another of the Chicago pack while the medic got to work running an IV drip and hanging a blood bag off of a metal rod similar to the one I'd used to impale the wolf that had been such a problem during my fight with the hybrid. My beast probably would have resented being managed like that, but I was too tired and shocky to protest right at that instant.

I stood with a vague plan of checking on James and the girls, but it took less than a second to locate them. They were all bruised and bleeding, but they each had a medic or two attending them and now that the bootlickers were all gone nobody seemed noticeably on edge.

Shawn got my attention and waved me over to where he was talking to his dad. I hid a grimace and nodded as I started picking my way over to them.

I could hear the white noise generators when I was still several feet away from the booth. There were several of them, which meant that Ulrich was serious about keeping our conversation a secret.

Ulrich and Shawn had already disappeared into the booth by the time I arrived, so I took a deep breath and followed them inside. Shawn was even bloodier than I was, but he seemed in good spirits, so there was a reasonable chance that most of it belonged to the other team.

I opened my mouth to apologize to Ulrich for having entered his territory unannounced, but he cut me off before I could even get started.

"Do you have any idea the kind of position you've put me in by coming here, Alec? By all rights, I should just kill you and your friends and save myself the headache."

Shawn winced, but I didn't wait for him to come to my defense. "You'd be well within your rights to try, but unless you're planning on executing the next Coun'hij enforcer who shows up on your doorstep unexpectedly, you'll be creating a dangerous precedent when it comes to your prized neutrality."

He didn't like that, but then again I hadn't expected him to. I was in as deep as I was going to get, and there wasn't anything to be gained by being timid.

"Don't push me, boy. I was here before your dad was born and I intend to be here long after you and he kill each other off, assuming that you're up to that kind of challenge."

We locked eyes, but I refused to back down. After a handful of seconds Ulrich finally smiled and leaned back in his chair.

"You've got guts, and not just because you were sneaking around in my backyard plotting with Shawn. I like that. Besides, I owe you for keeping Shawn alive."

Shawn looked like he was going to protest, but Ulrich stared him down.

"Despite what you might think, not even Vicki can pull you through against three-to-one odds, Shawn."

Satisfied that Shawn was suitably cowed, Ulrich turned back to me.

"You've earned yourself a bit of leniency this time around, but don't come back through here without permission again."

Ulrich worked his way around the table until he could stand and leave the booth. "I've got some things to check on. Finish up your conversation quickly, I can only hold off the police for so long."

I looked over at Shawn with a raised eyebrow. He ran his hands through his hair and sighed.

"Thanks for standing by me when we got jumped."

"I didn't really have much of a choice. Most packs will turn against the outsiders before they'll fight amongst themselves. Standing with you was my best chance of getting my people out in one piece."

"Was that really what you were thinking at the time?"

I hesitated for a second before shaking my head. "No, it didn't even cross my mind. You'd been good enough to talk to me without ratting us out. It just seemed right to fight with you guys instead of against you."

Sometimes not being able to lie was a real pain, but other times—like now—it was a lot easier. Shawn knew that I'd just told him the truth.

"That's what makes my job hard, Alec. Kaleb or Puppeteer would have turned on me the instant that they thought it might help them get ahead, but you're willing to stand by people even when it's likely to cost you."

Shawn tapped on the table for a second before looking up at me. "How's your sister? Did she make it out of Sanctuary with you okay?"

"Yeah. I'm surprised that you know about that."

"There isn't a lot that we don't find out about. Like I said earlier, we're the biggest unclaimed prize out there so I tend to hear from all kinds of people who are trying to convince me to stage a takeover of the pack. Somebody back in Sanctuary has been talking. Maybe it's your mom, but I can't be sure."

My throat tried to close up from emotion, but I forced myself to speak.

"I'm glad that everyone knows what Kaleb and Brandon tried to do; maybe it will help the cause if people know that Kaleb was willing to trade away his own daughter."

We sat there in silence until I realized that I hadn't answered Shawn's question. "Yeah, Rachel is okay. I'll tell her that Mom might be the source of the rumors; that will make her feel a little better."

"But not you?"

"I just don't know. I'm not sure you can come back from what my mother has done."

I could practically see the wheels turning inside of Shawn's head. He debated for nearly a minute before pulling out a business card that was blank other than a single phone number on it.

"This is my number, or it will be again in a day or two once I get a new phone."

Shawn pulled out a pen and scribbled another number on the other side of the card.

"This number is one that I think you should call. I can't guarantee anything for myself, let alone for this guy, but call him and tell him that I said the two of you should talk."

I accepted the card. It was more than I'd been afraid I might get, but it still wasn't what I was after.

"What is it going to take for you to roll the dice, Shawn? I know there's a risk, but you have to see that Kaleb and the rest are bad news. If nothing else, then what happened with Rachel should be plenty of proof."

Shawn clapped me on the shoulder as he stood to leave the booth. "Have you manifested a power yet, Alec? People have been talking about your potential ever since you were born, but the rumors have shifted into high gear since you cut ties with dear old Dad."

"If I told you it had, would that be enough to convince you to join me?"

"That would all depend on what form your ability takes, Alec. It's going to have to be something really game-changing if you want to have some kind of bloodless revolution."

Shawn walked away without looking back at me. I stuffed the card he'd given me into my pocket and tried to keep my beast from acting up. It always came down to the same question. Everybody out there was sitting on the sidelines waiting to see what kind of power I was going to manifest.

The Chicago pack was the big unclaimed marker, but in some ways they didn't matter as much as I did. I'd already picked a side. Now I just needed to manifest an ability the likes of which had never been seen before. Mallory had been convinced for years that it would eventually happen, but I wasn't so sure. If I was going to manifest something it should have happened by now.

James, Jess and Jasmin were all looking pretty beat up, but they were all mobile. They followed me over to Brindi, who looked like she was losing her fight with death.

The medic looked up as I approached and grunted at me. "She touched you before she was injured?"

"Yeah, a couple of times. She caught me by surprise and then there wasn't anything I could do to stop her during the middle of the fight."

The medic reached up and pulled me down to my knees so that he could move my hand over to Brindi's shoulder. The transformation was almost magical. Her color improved immediately and her breathing strengthened as soon as our skin touched.

Jess gasped, but I was too busy trying to wrap my mind around the ramifications to look back and reassure her. The medic packed up his gear with a couple of sure, quick motions and then stood to leave.

"You're going to need to keep in contact with her for a few days if you want her to survive. She's addicted."

The Ja'tell bond. After everything I'd seen Kaleb put my mother through, I'd sworn I would never addict anyone. In the end, it happened without me even realizing it.

Chapter 14

Adriana Paige
Marauder's Gas Station
Central Wyoming

Taggart's color had finally improved and one of his lucid moments had finally coincided with my break from the store.

"What's our situation, Adri?"

"Not really that different than when you lapsed into your healing coma. I've kept the store open during the daylight hours for the most part. I scouted the bunker from one end to the other and cleaned up some of the worst of the destruction and dead bodies. We're currently in the penthouse suite which has the benefit of working lights, running water and no corpses."

"Were you able to make contact with Alec Graves?"

"No, I tried a couple of times. You've been out for the better part of four days, but I didn't have any luck so I decided to try something else. When I was back in Minnesota I ran into a girl who tried to warn me away from Jackson. Looking back in hindsight, I was pretty sure she was a shape shifter so I decided to reach out to her and see if she could corroborate your stories about the Coun'hij."

"Did she?"

"Yeah, for the most part she did. She made it pretty clear that there were more shades of gray than I was going to like, but I guess I should have expected that."

"Does that mean you're fully onboard in the fight against Kaleb and the rest?"

I shrugged, but I knew I was going to have to give him a better answer than that.

"I guess I'm mostly onboard. I'm not willing to start assassinating random Coun'hij flunkies, but I'll do whatever I have to do in order to help you save Agony."

Taggart was obviously still in pain, but he managed a nod. "I'll do my best not to betray the trust that you're placing in me."

"So what do we do next? Are you even going to be able to move in time to help Agony?"

"I think so, but I won't know for sure until I've had a chance to check in with some of my contacts. It all depends on what the Coun'hij has planned for him, but I should only need another day or two of rest before we can at least resume travelling."

"Are you sure? No offense, but you're still looking pretty bad."

Taggart snorted. "At least you didn't tell me that I always look pretty bad. No, I'll be okay. I'm past the worst part of it. Once I doused Paulo in oil he didn't dare use an open flame against me, but he still cooked my insides a little bit. That all seems to be healed now, so I should bounce back from the rest of this pretty quickly."

I did a double-take. "How are you even alive? I never would have expected that a vampire could cook your insides without using fire on your outsides."

"Yeah, they are pretty nasty customers. There's a reason that we don't go after the really old ones unless we've got them outnumbered by a healthy margin, and even then we try to take them by surprise. As for how I'm alive, us shape shifters are a lot tougher than we look."

I shook my head in astonishment. "All right, so you'll be up and moving around in a day or two; what do we do then?"

"You're not going to like it, but I'm not sure that there is much else you can do right now. I'm going to be pretty busy trying to pull together the strike force we'll need to rescue Agony. Until that is all squared away, there isn't much I'm going to be able to do as far as training you. I need to pay a visit to Agony too and see what he can tell me about where he was captured and how he thinks they might be planning on transporting him."

"You're hurt. What if you run into that red hybrid again?"

"I'll be careful. I've got some contacts I trust a lot more than I trusted Eric."

"Even so, I'd like to come with you. I can stay invisible and then if things get bad I can surprise them just like I did with Eric."

Taggart gave me a long look, but I already knew what he was thinking. Taggart could afford to be nice to the girl he'd saved in Minnesota, but the Dream Stealer was another deal altogether. Part of Taggart's effectiveness came from the fact that he was feared. It was possible I was going to see him do something terrible to someone over the next few days as he tried to get the information he needed.

"Are you sure you're ready for that?"

I nodded. "We don't have much else in the way of choices right now, not if we're going to save your friend."

Chapter 15

Alec Graves
Roan Mountain State Park
Tennessee

The last few days had been difficult and terrifying on several levels. Brindi was still alive, which was a good thing, but that also brought with it a whole different bag of problems that I'd never expected to deal with.

Kaleb or Brandon would have let her die rather than be virtually chained to her for two days while she recovered enough to be able to sit up in bed and even walk around a little on her own, but that wasn't me. Especially not after she'd saved my life.

We picked Rachel up from the hotel where we'd left her in Montana, which took basically a full day of driving, and then I called the number that Shawn had left me and told the voice on the other end that I wanted to meet.

The person on the other end of the line gave me an address and a time two days later that I figured I could just make if we didn't waste any time on our drive. I almost made Rachel stay in Montana, but she begged me to let her come along and, in the end, I agreed to let her come as far as Nebraska.

We shape shifters don't do well in close quarters for an extended period of time, so I ended up renting another SUV so that we could split up. I spent the entire drive in the very back seat of one of the SUV's with one hand on Brindi at all times. Rachel spent most of the time when she wasn't driving looking back and forth between Brindi and me.

By the time we hit Nebraska, Brindi was doing well enough that she was awake for as much as a couple of hours at a time, which was astonishing all by itself. Addicting humans wasn't something that good little shape shifters were supposed to do. It happened, but it wasn't usually talked about in polite company, which meant that I didn't know whether Brindi's rapid recovery was normal for a human kept in constant contact with the source of her addiction.

We dropped Rachel off outside of Omaha and I left her enough cash to make sure that she would be fine even if something happened to the rest of us. At that point, all that was left to do was walk unarmed into a meeting with someone

I didn't know who might be planning on trapping me until the Coun'hij could come get me.

It wasn't the kind of thing designed to make me feel very safe, but I didn't have a lot of options. I needed help. Shawn might still come through for me and show up with a bunch of hybrids and wolves from the Chicago pack, but that was starting to look like a long shot.

The instructions for the meet had included orders not to bring anyone else, so I left James, Jasmin and Jess in a small town half an hour away from the meeting spot and drove the rest of the way there with just Brindi to keep me company. I would have left her behind as well, for her own safety if for no other reason, but she wasn't up to any kind of prolonged separation from me.

Even when I left for half an hour to shower she always got listless and her skin took on the pale white of someone who wasn't getting enough oxygen. Given that, there wasn't any option but to bring her along.

Our path took us up into the Appalachian Mountains and by the time we turned off into the overlook that was our final destination I was glad that I'd rented something with a decent amount of horsepower. I looked around the parking lot, taking in the other three cars present, and then got out of the SUV so that I could walk around and get Brindi's door.

I got a call a few seconds later.

"You were supposed to come alone."

"I did the best I could. She's injured and suffering from a skin addiction. I can't leave her for more than a few minutes without her vitals starting to drop off."

There was silence for a couple of seconds.

"You should have told me that when we first talked."

"I would have if you'd given me half a second to get a word in and if I'd had a chance to think through the fact that I wasn't going to be able to leave her alone. This is a rather recent development. You can call Shawn if you don't believe me, he saw it all happen."

"Fine, stay where you are."

The phone went silent before I could ask him how long he was going to be, but that wasn't exactly a surprise, not after the way he'd acted so far. I looked around and then pointed out a bench on the other side of the parking lot.

"Can you make it that far by yourself or do you need me to carry you?"

Brindi studied the bench for a second before nodding. "I think I can make it, it will probably do me some good to get a little bit of exercise in."

Now that she'd shed the club wear and heavy makeup, she looked a lot younger. I was betting that she was closer to my age than I'd originally thought. I should have asked already, but I'd been so busy trying to get the flow of money started out of the Caymans and into the U.S. that we hadn't actually talked much.

"I'm sorry we haven't had a chance to talk before this, Brindi. I've been neglecting you."

She didn't look up. Apparently just putting one foot in front of the other was more work than I'd realized, that or she wasn't ready to let me see how she felt.

"It's okay. I've been sleeping a lot, and you've been busy. I kind of feel like I should resent whatever you're working on, but I don't. It's a pretty odd feeling."

"Jasmin said you asked her about the skin addiction yesterday while I was in the shower?"

Brindi nodded. She was starting to breathe hard now, so I stopped and picked her up.

"Thanks, I guess I'm not up to moving and carrying on a conversation at the same time yet. Yeah, that was the first time that I realized your absence was the reason I felt so crappy."

"Do you have any questions for me?"

"So how exactly did this happen?"

That was the same question I'd been asking myself. I knew the answer, but I couldn't figure out where I could have legitimately taken a different action than I had.

"My friends and I aren't normal humans, we're shape shifters. I guess you figured that out the night that you were injured though. We give off a kind of constant low-level energy that is intensified when a human touches us.

"Usually it's not a big deal because for most people it takes quite a bit of exposure before they start craving that contact, but occasionally someone will be more susceptible or the sensation will be paired with some kind of traumatic experience, and addiction will happen much more quickly than normal."

We reached the bench and I gently set her down and then sat down next to her. She reached for my hand, apparently without any conscious decision on her part. I interlaced our fingers together and tried not to think about how odd it felt to be holding hands with someone I didn't know. I'd spent my entire life never being anything more than friends with anyone and now Brindi and I were essentially a couple.

"So when I got hurt I also got addicted to you."

"Yes, once again, I'm really sorry about that. I wouldn't have chosen to have that happen to you, but I appreciate your saving my life. How did you find me in the middle of all of that craziness, especially when it was so dark?"

Brindi started to shrug and then grimaced as the motion pulled on her stomach wounds. "It's kind of hard to explain. I could feel you out there fighting. Not at first, but once you changed to your hybrid form I could sense you. Everyone else was more...fuzzy...but I could feel them too. I was scared out of my mind, especially when that other guy crashed into the booth next to me, but then all of a sudden that didn't matter. All that mattered was that you were in danger. Is that normal for these kinds of things?"

I cleared my throat and then shrugged. "Honestly, I'm not sure. I've never had this kind of bond with anyone else before now and most shape shifters don't talk much about skin addiction. It usually puts a lot of strain on both sides of the bond."

"So now I'm your dirty little secret?"

The words should have been caustic, but there wasn't any heat behind them. Her tone had every indication of someone simply seeking clarification on their status.

"No, I'm not going to force you into that kind of an existence, but there are complications. I'm not a very safe person to be around right now. The best thing would be for us to get you healed back up and then help you break the addiction."

"What if I don't want to get clean?"

Once again her voice had the dead, emotionless quality of someone who didn't feel like they had any real input on the decision.

"Do you?"

"No, I don't."

"You don't sound very emphatic about that."

She looked up at me and for the first time I saw a hint of the fire that must have sustained her through everything else she'd gone through up until now.

"It's hard to get worked up about something I can't influence, but if you want me to display more emotion I can do that."

I resisted the impulse to rub my temples. Nobody had done anything overtly aggressive yet, but that didn't mean that we were really safe. I looked away from her, pretending to just be buying myself time to think, but in actuality using it as an excuse to try and unobtrusively scan our surroundings.

"I don't want you to feel a certain way just because it's what you think I want. Honestly, the thing that would make me the most happy would be if you could distance yourself enough from the addiction to make your own decision."

"You almost sound like you really mean that."

"I sound like I mean it because I do mean it. If I was the kind of person who wanted to have some kind of twisted subservient relationship I could have had it anytime in the last three or four years. If you remember, I did everything I could to stop you from touching me."

She gripped my hand even tighter, like she was worried that I was about to pull away, but there was a mixture of surprise and hope on her face.

"I've never met someone who wouldn't try to take advantage of an addiction. My suppliers, my competition, even me, we all did everything we could to get people hooked on our product so that we could suck them dry."

My free hand formed a fist, but I forced myself not to squeeze her hand. If I lost control even a little bit it would be almost impossible not to hurt her.

"That's not who I am. I've seen the effects of this kind of addiction firsthand. I don't *need* to take advantage of you."

"You don't like that I was a drug dealer, do you?"

"No, I honestly don't like it, but I was willing to pay to get you free of your suppliers before you became addicted to me. I'd like to see you get a fresh start; none of this changes that."

"How come?"

"Like I said, I've seen the effects of addiction firsthand. Maybe you getting clean and making something of yourself proves that it's possible and that gives me hope that someone else could make the same change."

Brindi stared off into space for a moment and I used her distraction to check another quadrant of our surroundings.

"I told myself that I didn't care that I was hurting people. Nobody had ever taken care of me or given me any kind of break in life, so I shouldn't have to worry about them any more than they'd worried about me."

"What do you think now?"

She took a deep breath. "I don't know. No, that's not right, I feel bad about what I did, but it's hard to separate my craving for you out from everything else. You despise the life I used to live and I'm terrified that you're about to leave me here all alone, so I *need* to be what you want me to be. I need to hate the things you hate and love the things you love because that's the best chance I have of continuing to touch you, of continuing to feel this way."

"I'm not leaving you here and I won't cut you off, at least not until after you've recovered enough to survive the withdrawal symptoms. Does that help?"

"Honestly?"

"Yes, always."

She shook her head. "It takes the tiniest bit of pressure off, but it's not much compared to the fear that you'll go away tomorrow or next week. I've been on a lot of different drugs and nothing felt like this. It's not just chemical, there's something else to it."

"Try to fight it, Brindi. I know it's hard, but it's important. You don't belong in my world. I can't protect you, I can barely even protect myself. The entire time we've been here I've been trying to keep an eye on our surroundings because this could all be one huge trap. I never would have brought you here if there'd been any way to leave you behind without killing you."

"Why are you here then if it's so dangerous?"

She didn't seem worried about the possibility of dying herself, if anything she was most concerned that something would happen to me.

"I'm here because there are things more important than whether I live or die. There are a lot of people relying on me to find the help this guy may be able to provide."

Brindi shivered, but she didn't smell cold. "Do you realize just how badly that rocks my worldview? If you're the real deal, if you really mean what you're saying, then I was terribly wrong to have done most of the things that I've done so far in my life. That's more frightening than anything else you've said so far. It's scary to contemplate having to worry whether people are trustworthy. It's a lot easier to just know that they aren't and go from there."

"How old are you, Brindi?"

"I turn eighteen next month. Why, how old are you?"

"I'm seventeen too."

She looked at me with astonishment stamped into her expression. "That's not very old to have the weight of the world on your shoulders."

"That's funny, I was just thinking the same thing about you."

Whatever response she might have had in mind was cut off by the sound of my phone ringing.

"Yeah?"

"I checked with Shawn. It sounds like you've had an eventful week."

"You could say that, but you might want to reserve judgment until you hear how my vacation went down."

That earned me a chuckle. The guy on the other end sounded like he was laughing in spite of himself, but he *was* laughing.

"There's a trail on the south end of the parking lot; follow it. You can bring the girl."

He hung up again before I could respond. I pocketed my phone and then stood.

"It sounds like we've got a hike ahead of us. It's probably best if I just carry you."

Brindi nodded. "I'm not going to complain about being in your arms, Alec, you know that."

I picked her up and headed to the other side of the parking lot. The trail wasn't immediately obvious, but once I'd gone a dozen yards or so in, it became more defined and easier to follow.

Brindi fell asleep within moments, which was good because it meant she was getting the rest she needed, but bad because I had to be even more careful. I couldn't afford to stumble and wake her up, or even worse fall and reopen her stomach wounds.

It had been ages since I'd gone on a hike in human form. I'd forgotten just how slow it was to navigate through any kind of wilderness on two legs. Normally when I needed to cover any kind of real distance I was either on four legs or in a car.

I hiked for more than an hour before I got to a spot where I could set Brindi down and stretch out the tired muscles in my back and neck. Brindi started to wake up, but I reached down and rested a hand on the side of her face, which made her smile and go back to sleep.

If we had to go much further food and water were going to become an issue. Not for me, I could probably get away with drinking the water from one of the streams in the area, but Brindi didn't have the advantages of a shape shifter constitution that could laugh off most of the parasites in a flowing body of water.

I pulled out my phone and debated calling my contact, but then just shrugged and put the phone back in my pocket. If he'd set this meet up with the idea that I'd be traveling on four feet then I could have hours of walking still ahead of me, but in the interest of keeping whatever goodwill I had garnered so far, I'd give it another hour before calling again.

I picked Brindi back up and started forward again. We were slowly climbing the mountain we were on. The path was mostly headed north with an imperceptible rise to it, but the air was getting colder as we ascended and I was grateful that we'd purchased Brindi the heavy down coat she was wearing.

The scenery was breathtaking and I realized that was what I would have missed if I'd been tearing along the trail on four feet. Everything was so incredibly green that it boggled my mind. There was a beauty to the desert around most of Sanctuary, but it was a more subtle beauty than what was before me now.

The sheer variety to the flora and fauna around me was amazing; I wasn't sure I'd ever seen so many different shades of green in one place before. I could have gladly continued walking for hours more despite the fact that Agony's—and therefore my—time was limited.

It seemed silly to say so, even inside the privacy of my own mind, but the cacophony of noise around me, the twittering of the birds I could see and the rustling of other animals that I couldn't, was actually peaceful. As I continued down the snowy path I felt reservoirs inside of me that I hadn't even realized were depleted start to refill.

No matter what else happened, regardless of whether Shawn's contact ended up helping me, the trip out here had been time well spent. I took another deep breath as the tension continued to melt out of my body and I couldn't help but smile.

Brindi was deeply enough asleep that her hands finally fell away from my neck despite the magnetic effect that the prospect of touching my skin seemed to have on her. She unconsciously started to thrash around as her body sought out the connection that it knew it needed even if her conscious mind hadn't noticed the lack yet. Rather than letting her wake, I simply adjusted my right hand, sliding it up underneath her coat enough that my palm was resting against the small of her back.

She was a complication and I knew we would both be better off if we could cure her addiction and send her far, far away from me, but Brindi was more than that. She wasn't the person I would have chosen to fill the hole in my life, but even so it still felt good for the gap I'd been feeling inside of me for so long to be at least partially covered over.

That was dangerous. I couldn't afford to keep her around just because she made me a little less lonely, but the urge to do so was something I was going to have to fight on a nearly constant basis.

We rounded a bend in the trail and were suddenly faced with the visual music of a waterfall trickling down from the cliffs above us. It wasn't a particularly tall waterfall and there wasn't all that much water coursing down the rock, but it was still perfect.

Maybe it was the sheath of ice that had formed on the rocks or maybe it was simpler than that, but the ribbon of water somehow turned the clearing into a winter paradise. It was so idyllic that for a second I didn't even seen the man waiting for us a dozen yards further into the clearing.

"My name is Carson. What do you have to say that's so important Shawn thought it worth introducing the two of us?"

Brindi moved a little in my arms but didn't wake up. I looked around for somewhere to sit, but it was really just an attempt to buy myself time to think.

"The Coun'hij has Agony. I went to Shawn hoping that he'd help me break Agony out. I can only assume that he sent me to you because he thinks you might be able to help."

Carson approached Brindi and me slowly so as not to be a threat, but he obviously wanted to be close enough that there wouldn't be any way for me to sneak a lie past him.

"Agony's death will be a profound blow for the resistance, but I fail to see what it has to do with me. He's fought a good fight, and lasted much longer than anyone expected him to, but his fate was sealed from the time that he broke away from the Coun'hij and started working against them."

"The Coun'hij isn't the kind of group to let anyone stand to one side. So far you seem to have managed to stay off of their radar, but eventually they'll find you and you'll either have to ally yourself with them or face the consequences of rebellion."

"Is that a threat?"

The words came out low and angry and his voice had changed pitches enough to warn me that he was only a heartbeat away from shifting forms. My beast surged forward in response, and although a part of me would have welcomed a straight-up fight rather than another round of verbal sparring with someone who probably wasn't going to help me, I stomped on my anger, forcing it down to where I controlled it rather than it controlling me.

It was harder than I expected it to be, and it wasn't just that my beast had gotten behind the emotion and started pushing. The tide of rage rising inside of me was deeper and stronger than anything I'd ever felt before and that was scary.

I'd felt something similar bubbling under the surface when Kaleb had told me that he was planning on giving Rachel to Vincent, but it hadn't been quite the same. Back then some kind of defensive mechanism had walled me away from my emotions, armoring me in stillness so that I could do what needed to be done. By the time my armor had fallen away, I'd already saved Rachel.

I reached for a similar measure of protection this time, but it wasn't anywhere to be found. I was furious and even worse, I *wanted* to be furious. The temptation to give into the rage was nearly more than I could withstand, but a tiny part of me knew that if I let myself be provoked that everything would be stacked against me.

I was on Carson's home turf and I had Brindi to worry about. I couldn't fight with her in my arms and even if I could, that went against everything that had brought me out here in the first place.

I started shaking from the effort of controlling my transformation, but unlike most of my kind I had another option besides shifting, an option that was still dangerous but less inflammatory than becoming a hybrid would have been.

I hugged Brindi tightly against me with my right hand and forced all of the anger and hate coursing through me into my left hand as it fell away from Brindi's body. My left hand exploded and then shrank back down leaving me with the hand and claws of a hybrid.

"It wasn't a threat. Kaleb and the rest won't learn about you from me, at least not without torturing me first. I was just speaking from personal experience. I thought I could stay in the middle and avoid choosing sides between Kaleb and Brandon, but I was wrong.

"People like them aren't wired to ever be satisfied. They always want a little more power, a little more influence, one last victory over an already battered enemy. It took almost seeing my sister sold into slavery for me to realize that I had to pick a side."

"Shawn said that you saved her, your sister Rachel, I mean."

"She's alive and I'll do whatever is needed to keep her safe, including letting you insult me, but don't mistake my willpower for submissiveness. If you were someone else, someone I didn't need, someone who knew me well enough to realize what I've done already to try and stop Kaleb and the rest, I might not have been able to avoid responding with the kind of escalation you would have gotten out of most other hybrids."

Carson nodded slightly, not necessarily in response to my words, but rather because of something else, some other question he'd been waiting to see the answer to. He gestured with his hand and suddenly my rage, which had been still on the edge of getting away from me, dissipated as though it had never existed.

"So you do have an ability."

Carson's smile was remarkably boyish and disarming. "Yes, and although it's not as overtly powerful as the kind of stuff the Coun'hij typically looks for, it's proven very useful over the years."

"Useful how?"

"Well, for one thing it allowed me to test your mettle in ways that otherwise would have taken months or even years' worth of time spent with you. I never would have guessed that you'd be possessed of such strength of will, not at such a young age."

I was suddenly tired and the only possible explanation was the emotional rollercoaster I'd just been put through. The emotions that Carson had pushed into me hadn't just been strong, they'd had a crushing weight to them that had taken everything I'd had to resist.

"So now that I've passed your test will you help me?"

Carson studied me for several seconds before nodding hesitantly. "I think I probably will at that, but it will take more than strength of will to buy my assistance."

He pointed at Brindi. "You saved her a few days ago."

He obviously already knew the answer from his conversation with Shawn, but I nodded anyway.

"Yes, but she saved me first. She stepped into the middle of a hybrid fight to help me kill one of the hybrids who attacked Shawn."

"And was injured as a result. What will you do with her once she's healed and doesn't need your touch to keep her from dying?"

"I'm not sure. We've only just begun discussing options."

"You and your friends?"

"No, her and I."

That earned me another odd look from Carson. "You love her then?"

There was an edge to his voice that should have awoken a surge of anger from my beast, but I felt none of that now.

"You're soothing my emotions right now, aren't you?"

"Indeed, I am. It's quicker this way because I can ask you questions without you getting up in arms at some perceived slight."

"And if I don't agree with you then you can just manipulate me into feeling like you're right?"

Carson frowned and shook his head. "That's not something I'd do. Right now there isn't anything for you to agree to. Whether we proceed as allies is entirely up to me and therefore I'm not manipulating you into *doing* anything. If we come to a point where you need to make a decision I'll release your emotions and let you get back to an equilibrium point before pressing you for a response."

"That's asking for a lot of trust for someone I met all of five minutes ago."

"Possibly, but I'd say that it's commensurate with the level of trust involved in agreeing to join a doomed rebellion against the Coun'hij."

"I guess you've got a point there. In answer to your question, I don't love her, but I don't have to love someone to realize that they have rights. I don't expect it to be easy, but we'll talk things through and try to figure out some kind of route forward that works for both of us."

"And if you can't find something that works for both of you?"

"I don't know. I guess if push comes to shove then I'll have to help her through withdrawal."

"Because that's the easiest option from your point of view?"

This time the rage bubbled up even past the calm he was projecting into my mind, but it was just the tiniest sliver of anger. I managed to respond to him without letting what I was feeling bleed through into my voice.

"No, because I have the right to my own body just like she has the right to hers. I'm not going to turn her into some kind of human chattel subservient to my every whim, but by the same measure I deserve not to be turned into a slave for her addiction."

I'd done my best to conceal the fact that I'd realized Carson had a limit to how much he could influence my emotions, but something must have slipped past because he held up a calming hand.

"That's fair. The best you can do in the really difficult situations is start from your rights as an individual and work from there. What's your plan?"

"I don't have one, not yet, not really. It's too soon. I don't know enough about where Agony is being held or how they are planning on moving him, and I'm still trying to gather enough fighters to have a chance at beating the Coun'hij's security detail. Even if they don't have someone like Brandon or Puppeteer down there we're still probably going to be up against a dozen or more hybrids."

"I guess it won't be the first time that I signed up for an impossible task because of an ideal. I won't betray you. How many people do you have so far?"

There it was. He'd just made an explicit statement, something that was firm enough that there couldn't be any gray area with regards to what he'd meant. I'd heard it and I'd been paying enough attention to detect any of the usual signs of a falsehood.

His pulse hadn't changed, his respiration hadn't wavered in the slightest, and his body temperature didn't seem to be moving around at all. Carson was either a masterful liar, the kind of psychopath who didn't actually feel things the way that the rest of us do, or he was telling the truth.

There wasn't any way to be positive which it was. I had to make a judgment call and if I was wrong then my friends, Rachel, Jack and every other person currently depending on me was probably going to die.

"So far I've got three hybrids and eight wolves in total. All of us have some fairly recent combat experience. We killed a group of five hybrids a little while ago and have mixed it up with vampires and werewolves as well not too long ago."

Carson frowned. "You're right, that's not enough, not nearly enough. Do you have any other prospects besides me?"

"I've got one other wolf that I expect to be joining me soon, but other than that it's just you and Shawn. I'll be reaching out to some of the independents who've been fighting on the border with Brandon, but I'm not very hopeful that any of them will rock the boat right now. They're all too worried that if they step wrong it will bring down reprisals against everyone else still down there, that or their families back in their home packs."

"That makes sense. You're not planning on getting much out of Jaclyn or the others because they are being watched?"

"Yeah. How many people do you think you can come up with?"

Carson was silent for a moment as he considered the question. I'd expected him to look off into space while he was thinking, but he didn't. Instead he looked at Brindi and his expression changed slightly. It was almost imperceptible, but his face softened a little.

"From the standpoint of raw numbers it's not going to be good. I think I have three or four hybrids that I can depend on, maybe a few more than that, but not many."

He held a hand up before I could despair. "I'm going to have to eat some crow, but I think I've got something better than a dozen hybrids though."

He didn't have to tell me what would be better than a dozen hybrids. The answer was obvious. He had access to a hybrid with some kind of extreme power. Someone like Brandon or Puppeteer, someone who could tip the balance of the fight all by himself.

"Do you think this…friend will agree to help?"

Carson was still looking at Brindi as he answered. It was almost like he knew her, that or maybe she reminded him of someone else, someone important to him.

"I think so, but there's no guarantee. The last time we saw each other…well, things were said. Even if he does agree to help he may not be able to make the difference. He's not always the most dependable in a fight."

"Then I guess I'd better keep trying to come up with more help. Saving Agony is too important to leave anything to chance."

Chapter 16

Alec Graves
Perfect Sleep Hotel
Omaha, Nebraska

I was disoriented and struggling to remember how I'd gotten here. I remembered talking to Carson, remembered walking back to our SUV with Brindi still in my arms, but I didn't remember coming back to Rio Rico.

Even odder, I couldn't think of any reason for Brindi to be here with me, but she was. Not only that, she wasn't injured anymore. It wasn't just the fact that she was moving around without wincing every time she breathed. Somehow she'd put back on the black club wear that she'd been wearing the first time I'd seen her in Chicago and her bare stomach was as unblemished and whole as it had been before she'd stumbled into my fight with the Chicago hybrid.

Except that was impossible. Her clothes had been little more than bloody ribbons when we'd left Chicago. She would have had to have purchased new clothes, but more club wear wasn't the kind of thing we should be wasting money on right now.

I tried to get Brindi's attention, but she ignored me, choosing instead to continue to rub her face against my arm like some kind of blonde housecat. That was when I finally realized I had to be dreaming.

I tried to make her disappear. We were never apart for more than a few minutes while I was awake. It seemed unfair that I couldn't at least have some privacy inside my own dreams, but apparently my subconscious was firmly of the opinion that she belonged here with me. Brindi flickered a little, growing slightly translucent before becoming solid again and returning to clinging to me.

I would have tried harder to remove her from my dream, but being here, aware I was dreaming, was awakening memories that were demanding my full attention. The last time I'd had a lucid dream there had been another girl, the one Brindi reminded me of...a girl named Adri.

It all came back to me in a rush. Her situation, our kiss, my fight against dream werewolves at the end. That was the kiss that I'd been on the point of remembering at the club before Brindi had distracted me.

AMBUSHED

The realization of what I'd forgotten rocked my world in completely unexpected ways. I staggered over to a bench that had appeared just a second before, apparently summoned by my need, and sat down. Dream-Brindi trailed along behind me, never losing contact with my skin, and sat down next to me. The bench hadn't been large enough to accommodate both of us when I'd sat down, but it stretched as Brindi lowered herself onto it, growing so that there was room for us.

I wanted to scream. There was no reason to believe that my dream had been anything more than just another dream, but I lived in a world that contained vampires and werewolves, a world where people could shift into terrible, fearsome beasts. Not only that, there was at least one instance of an individual who *could* travel to other people's dreams.

Besides, my dream with Adri had been too real, too detailed to be just another dream, which meant that she was really out there. She'd been in danger when I'd talked to her last, but I'd been so wrapped up in my worries about Rachel, Brandon and Kaleb that I had told her I couldn't help her.

That wasn't true anymore. I could help her now—I wanted to help her—but I didn't have any way of getting in contact with her. She was the girl I'd been dreaming about since even before I'd made my first transformation to a wolf, and I couldn't do a single damn thing to help her.

It was infuriating in the way that only complete powerlessness could be. I had resources now that I hadn't had before, but that still wasn't any kind of guarantee. I could find a sketch artist and pay millions plastering her face on every television in America, but that still might not be enough and it might even put her in more danger.

I started making plans, subtle plans to try and find her anyway. I'd hire private investigators. She'd had a hint of an accent, Minnesota or maybe Canadian. It was hard to tell for sure which it had been, but it was at least *something* to go on.

Even as my mind was picking and choosing amongst all of the different possibilities I knew it wasn't where I should be spending my time. I should be thinking about ways to find more hybrids and wolves rather than trying to find a girl who might not even exist, but I couldn't help myself.

My mind stopped thinking about her mid-thought and it took me nearly a full second to understand why. We weren't...I wasn't alone. Dream-Brindi vanished as I jumped to my feet and spun in a quick circle. Apparently my subconscious felt like she belonged with me even in the middle of my dreams but the urge to protect her, to get her out of danger was even stronger still.

I completed the scan of my surroundings, but there wasn't anyone out there...only there was.

Visually there wasn't anything out of the ordinary and I couldn't hear or smell anything, but I could feel someone nearby.

It was a little like the feeling you get when someone is staring at you, but magnified a thousand times. As I forced myself to control my breathing and clear my mind, the sensation grew until I could have closed my eyes and pointed at whomever it was.

They were moving, not quickly, but they were orbiting me. I could tell direction, but not distance, but the simple fact that I knew they were there had robbed them of their biggest weapon. Except that it had to be one of only two people. I couldn't believe that Adri would have come to me like this, not after our last encounter, which meant this had to be Dream Stealer.

I tracked him with my eyes for several seconds so that he would know I really did know where he was.

"I know you're there. Show yourself."

The air shimmered slightly and then he appeared in front of me, only he looked nothing at all like Adri had described him. He was huge, easily the most imposing man I'd ever seen, and he looked like he wasn't a day past thirty.

"How did you know I was present in your dream, Alec?"

"I don't know, Dream Stealer, I just did. Since when have you started spying on other members of the resistance?"

He shot me a look that awoke my beast with an accompanying surge of anger, but even here inside of my dream I ruled my beast, not the other way around.

"You're awfully quick to claim that title. Most spend years just trying to keep their head down. It's only once the Coun'hij has backed us into a corner that most of us choose to actively fight them."

"I don't believe in halfway measures. I spent the first two decades of my life trying to live in the gray and all it bought me was several brushes with death and nearly losing my sister. Once I decided to rescue her from Vincent I knew there wasn't any going back."

"The timing of that strikes me as being awfully suspicious."

My beast didn't like that, didn't appreciate being called a liar. This time I wasn't fully able to suppress the power that exploded out of me at the accusation.

"You can't honestly believe that I'm still working with Kaleb."

Dream Stealer responded to my burst of power with a stinging, lashing metaphysical wind of his own.

"By all accounts you'd finally started acting like a proper heir in the weeks leading up to your disappearance. You killed vampires in St. Louis and then flew down to the border and started volunteering for missions. You were even instrumental in killing an Ancient. I think that you found the power and acclaim addictive."

My lips pulled back from my teeth. It wasn't a smile, it was the human equivalent to showing my hackles.

"While I was down there, I rescued Jaclyn Annikov from a bunch of werewolves and told her that I wanted to know the truth about what was going on down there. She sent me to a small town called Naco where I saw Brandon's people slaughter nearly a hundred people and then stage the scene to make it look like it was the work of jaguars."

I needed Dream Stealer. We didn't have to like each other, but I needed him to trust me. I was still on the outside when it came to the real core of the resistance. If I could convince him to vouch for me it would help get me access to the people I needed for operations like the one to rescue Agony.

Dream Stealer shot me a sardonic smile as he continued to slowly orbit me.

"Ah yes, I've heard reports of your 'shocking' revelation, but it wasn't anything that most of us didn't already suspect. You breaking that particular story may have scared off a few independents who otherwise would have gone down to help fight the cats, but it's made no difference other than that. Brandon's little army hasn't shrunk appreciably and all of the sympathizer packs are still just as much in bed with Kaleb and the rest as they ever were."

"What are you saying? That Kaleb used me to intentionally break that story as a way of getting me enough street cred to set up the resistance for some kind of massive takedown?"

"You said it, not me."

I wanted to scream, but I knew that wouldn't accomplish anything. Dream Stealer seemed determined not to trust me.

"My friends and I nearly died getting my sister out of Sanctuary and we've nearly died several times since then. There was a hit squad of Coun'hij enforcers waiting for us the last time we got off of a plane."

"All that proves is that your friends are either in on it or spectacularly stupid. The kind of near defeats you're describing are less important than the fact that you've so far managed to come out on top. You can't honestly expect me to believe that you beat Brandon of all people."

Dream Stealer couldn't have done a better job hitting all of my hot-button issues if he'd had a script to read from.

"I stole Kaleb's sword before I left and I used it during the fight with Brandon, but even that almost wasn't enough. I dived to the side at the last moment during the end of our fight and he was swept off of the train by a metal girder."

"I stand by my original statement; that is highly unlikely."

His tone had gone from doubting to downright scathing and it was finally too much for me.

Maybe it was the fact that Carson had pushed me to the edge such a short time before, but I lost control of my beast.

My transformation exploded out from me with a blast of energy that knocked Dream Stealer back a full step and then he likewise shifted into his hybrid form with a roar of power that came very close to equaling what I'd just unleashed. For the briefest of seconds everything balanced on the edge of a knife and then I forced myself to take a step backwards.

"What is it going to take to convince you that we're on the same side?"

"Your death at the hands of Kaleb or Puppeteer seems like a good starting place."

I gritted my teeth and forced myself to take another step backwards instead of springing forward and trying to rip his throat out.

"I'm going to rescue Agony, but I could use your help."

That got his attention. "What do you know?"

"That he's been captured, but little else. My contacts are still trying to figure out where he's being kept."

Dream Stealer shook his head at me. "You don't know where he's currently located or when and how they are moving him?"

"No, do you?"

"If I did then I certainly wouldn't tell you. Kaleb must really think I'm an idiot."

My lips pulled back again, but this time they exposed hybrid fangs that were capable of snapping the neck of a rhinoceros.

"How many times do I have to tell you that I'm not working with him?"

"Fine, I'll bite. I think that Kaleb tracked Agony down months ago but decided to hold off going after him until he could set up the biggest trap imaginable. I think you were sent out to try and rally as much support as you can behind the cause of freeing Agony, but really you'll just be leading everyone who joins you into a massive ambush. With a single stroke Kaleb and the rest will gut the resistance and position themselves for another century or two of uncontested rule."

"Believe what you want, but I will save Agony even if it costs me my life."

"Brave words, but that's all they are, just words. Your actions tell another story."

He'd finally succeeded in confusing me, but the addition of another emotion into the mix didn't do anything to dilute the rage I was feeling towards him. My beast didn't like being outsmarted any more than it liked being made fun of.

"I shouldn't give you the satisfaction, but I'll go ahead and ask. How have any of my actions done anything but support the fact that I'm prepared to risk my life to better the situation of our race?"

"The girl you were dreaming about. I'm not an idiot, I can recognize the signs of a skin addiction as well as anyone else. No honorable shape shifter would choose to addict someone like that. That was the first sign that Kaleb wasn't what he seemed, the first sign that he was going to have to be stopped along with the rest of the murderers and thieves on the Coun'hij. It's one more indication that you're just like your father."

I wanted to argue with him, wanted to explain that it hadn't been my choice, that it had been a freak series of events, but I already knew he wouldn't believe me. I'd been convicted since the first moment that Dream Stealer had seen Dream-Brindi.

"I won't even dignify that with a response. Get out of my dream now and don't come back or we'll see just how deadly inside of the dream you actually are."

Chapter 17

Adriana Paige
Marauder's Gas Station
Central Wyoming

Sometime in the last day or two Taggart and I had gotten our schedules mixed up. I would have suspected him of doing it on purpose so that we'd be back to twenty-four-hour coverage up at the store, but that would have broken his primary rule.

In order to make dream contact with someone Taggart had to be asleep at the same time as they were, so moving his schedule forward would make it even harder to link up with anyone on the West Coast.

It was possible that he had some operatives on the East Coast, but even if that had been the case he wouldn't have needed to advance his schedule forward more than a couple of hours to sync up with them. The only other explanation was that he was trying to get ahold of someone on another continent, but given all of the time I was still spending up at the store, I hadn't had a good chance to ask him yet.

I came back down a few minutes after sunset as he was cooking up dinner. Taggart had been right about how quickly he'd bounce back from his wounds. He wasn't quite a hundred percent yet, his movements were still a little stiff, but he was up and moving around enough that he'd started repairing some of the damage to the bunker.

I arrived at a kitchen that had functional lighting for the first time since I'd come down into the bunker.

"Wow, how did you get the lights working again?"

Taggart shrugged. "I scavenged some of the wire from elsewhere in the bunker and ran new circuits."

"Where did you learn how to do that?"

"I worked as an electrician for a little while. You'd be surprised at how much you can pick up over the course of a couple hundred years, especially when you're around when something is invented."

His words were polite, but there was something about his tone that told me he wasn't a particularly happy camper.

"What's wrong?"

Taggart put a lid on the stew he'd been putting together and then looked up at me.

"I've spent most of the last day hitting up all of the contacts that I could safely go to while still not at full strength. I haven't managed to find a single person who's both able and willing to help break Agony out of wherever it is the Coun'hij has him locked up.

"Everything has become too static. That's part of how Agony and I have been able to stay out of sight for so long, but now it's working against us. All of the major players are too well known and the Coun'hij is keeping too close of an eye on them."

Once again I felt like I was swimming in waters that were too deep for my level of skill and understanding.

"I don't understand what you mean."

"I originally thought Kaleb was being stupid to wait this long to move Agony. If it had been me I would have moved him to one of the Coun'hij's secret bases immediately so that it would be that much harder for everyone to find him."

"Right, that makes sense to me."

"Yeah, it makes sense because you and I are both used to operating from a position of weakness. We have to move quickly and keep a low profile because if we don't we're unlikely to last for long. Kaleb doesn't have that problem and it was a stroke of brilliance to wait like he has. It means that he's got his people stationed at or near all of the big packs that would otherwise be willing to help me out.

"He's got wire taps up and running, he's monitoring their e-mails and texts, he's controlling the flow of information and he's basically got a knife to the throat of anyone who's ever even thought about resisting him."

I opened and closed my mouth a couple of times and still couldn't come up with anything truly helpful to say.

"There has to be some way to do this, something we haven't thought of yet."

Taggart shook his head, looking truly defeated for the first time since I'd met him. "I've gone over it inside of my head again and again and I can't come up with anything. I've thought about every single pack and come up dry, there's nothing any of them can do to help.

"The vampires can't be trusted even assuming I was willing to try and recruit them, which I'm not. The werewolves are barely even sentient and even if I had a way of getting them to the right spot and the right time there's no guarantee that Puppeteer wouldn't be there waiting to take control of them."

I interrupted him before he could say anything else. "What about the jaguars?"

"No, I thought of that too. The jaguars hate all wolves equally. They'd sooner sit back and watch us kill each other than lift a finger to help any of us."

"Sorry, Taggart, I said that wrong. What I should have said is what about *a* jaguar. The girl I told you about, the one from Minnesota, the one who tried to warn me away from Jackson. What if I asked her to help us?"

"It's better than nothing, but one shape shifter isn't going to make much difference either way."

"But what if she isn't by herself anymore?"

I had his attention now.

"Why, did she say something about having joined another group?"

"No, but she was really different this last time when I saw her. She looked healthier, like she'd been eating more regularly, and she seemed less scared—like maybe she's found somewhere safe."

Taggart started moving some of the dishes over to the sink, buying himself time to think.

"It's worth a try, but I don't think you should try to do a bunch of negotiating by yourself in the dream. There's too much you still don't know. We'd pretty much have to meet up in the real world with her and her friends."

"So that's a risk, right? But saving your friend would be worth taking that kind of risk, wouldn't it?"

Taggart's nod was reluctant, but we were back to having at least the beginnings of a plan.

"Yes, a real-life meeting is worth the risk, but try to arrange it so that it's just me who meets with them. There isn't any reason to risk both of us."

I looked at him doubtfully. "I don't think she'll go for that."

"I know, but at least try. It will help me sleep at night to know that we did everything we could to keep you out of the line of fire."

"Okay, I'll try and get her to meet with just you. It feels good to have a plan again."

"Yes, for however long it lasts."

I stepped closer and put my hand on his arm. "If this doesn't work then we'll find something else."

"I hope so. If we can't then I'll have no choice but to ally with Alec Graves and that will probably be the death of us all."

There was something about his voice. It told me more than he would have chosen to.

"You've talked to him, haven't you?"

"Yes, just a short time ago. I've had so much time asleep lately that I'd managed to talk to everyone I needed to so I went to him."

"How did you form a new connection so quickly? Usually it takes you a month of trying to find someone new."

"I'm sorry, Adri. I let you think that I didn't have a connection to him, but I sought him out years ago. I thought that it would be prudent to be able to spy on Kaleb's heir and when the necessity arose I might not have time to waste trying to establish a new connection."

I wanted to be mad, but at the same time I was almost giddy at the fact that I finally had some connection, indirect though it might be, to him.

"What did he say? Did he ask about me?"

"It wasn't exactly that kind of conversation."

My anger was starting to move to the forefront now. "What kind of conversation was it exactly?"

"A very strained one. We nearly came to blows on a couple of occasions. I'm sorry. I tried, I really did, but he just reminded me too much of his father. It wasn't just his face, it was the way he moved and his certainty that he was right. We struck sparks off of each other in ways that I hadn't anticipated."

"You didn't hurt each other then?"

"No, but there is something you should know."

I held a hand up to block his words, and talked fast in the hopes that he'd be too much the gentleman to interrupt me.

"I know you don't trust him, Taggart, but I do. I talked to him when he was at his lowest and I was nobody. There wasn't any reason for him to believe that he'd ever see me again or that I'd ever be any kind of player in his world. He doesn't trust his father."

Taggart sighed. "Nobody trusts his father. Even the rest of the Coun'hij doesn't trust Kaleb to do anything that isn't in Kaleb's best interest.

I'm sorry, Adri, but that really doesn't prove anything."

My bottom lip was quivering, but I wasn't going to cry. I hadn't been a child in almost a decade and I wasn't about to start crying just because Taggart didn't agree with me.

"I understand why you don't trust him. You have a lot of bad history with his dad and there's a lot at stake, but you're not going to stop me from believing in him. There's a bond between the two of us that I can't even begin to describe. It's like nothing else I've ever felt. All I can say is that I think we are somehow meant for each other."

Taggart closed his eyes as though gathering his strength. "That's what I've been trying to tell you. You haven't said so in so many words, but I could tell that your encounter with him was more than just a run-of-the-mill meeting. It's been obvious from the way your expression shifts whenever you talk about him that you feel strongly about him, but he doesn't feel the same way."

"You don't know that! There isn't any way you could possibly know how he feels."

I turned to go, but Taggart grabbed my arm. The grip was gentle despite the strength underlying his grip, but it was the first time I could ever remember Taggart physically forcing me to do anything.

"He's got another girl with him. She looks a little like you, but that's not the worst part. He's addicted her to his touch."

"I don't understand."

I was impressed with myself. The words came out almost normal despite the fact that it felt like I was dying inside.

"It's another side effect of being a shape shifter. We transmit a kind of low-level energy whenever we touch someone. With other shape shifters it's pleasant but hardly noticeable. For humans it's more than that. A human who has prolonged exposure to the touch of any one shape shifter almost always becomes addicted to the sensation. It's like they become heroin addicts, junkies who will do anything for another fix.

"He was dreaming of her when I first made contact with him. The signs were obvious. The way she was hanging off of him...it was shameful. No decent man, shape shifter or otherwise, would do something like that."

"I refuse to believe it is as bad as you're making it out to be. It was some kind of accident. They came together by mistake and now he's too good an individual to just send her away."

The compassion in Taggart's eyes was enough to finally push my tears over the edge and they started running down my face.

"He was ashamed of her, of what she represented. As soon as he realized he wasn't alone, he banished her in an attempt to try and hide what he'd done. That's better than if he was so far gone that he didn't care, but it's still not a good sign.

"I wanted to be wrong about him, wanted him to be a decent man, for your sake if for no other reason, but I'm afraid he deceived you just as he's trying to deceive everyone who is fighting against the Coun'hij. I think that's what pushed me over the edge with him right from the very start. I can understand trying to entrap the resistance, Kaleb has been trying to do much the same thing for decades now, but there was no need to shatter your heart along the way."

I turned and ran out of the kitchen without looking back. Taggart called after me, but I didn't stop running until I got to the small bedroom just outside of the master suite and locked the door.

Later I would go to sleep and do my best to contact Dominic. I'd hate myself for being able to function and do my duty when it felt like my insides were shattering into a million pieces, but I would do it. For now I was just going to cry.

Chapter 18

Alec Graves
Two blocks from the Rest Easy Hotel
Rio Rico, Arizona

Going from the cold of the Tennessee mountains to the dry heat of southern Arizona was a bigger shock than I'd expected it to be. For all practical intents and purposes it just meant that we made another quick shopping trip to make sure that Brindi had some clothes that would help her avoid heatstroke, but the heat seemed to drag at me with surprising strength.

I hadn't noticed the same kind of issue the last time I'd been in Rio Rico, which made me think that it was all in my head. Coming back, even after just a few weeks' absence, was harder than I'd expected it to be.

Part of that was the fact that we were walking back into the lion's den, but that wasn't the only reason. Purposefully putting myself within a mile of Brandon was a good reason to be jittery, but Rio Rico was more than just a place where I'd spent a week or two in between combat missions. Rio Rico was where everything had started to change for me.

I'd been here when I'd found out that my mother was lying to me and when I'd realized that Kaleb and Brandon were massacring people and then blaming the deaths on the jaguars. Even before that I'd told myself that Kaleb was a bad guy, someone who couldn't be trusted, someone who was capable of terrible things, but it was Rio Rico that had finally opened my eyes completely.

Rio Rico had even been where the seeds of Rachel's near-captivity to Vincent had been planted. Kaleb had been putting Brandon off until our pyrrhic victory at the end of my time down there had caused Brandon to start pushing Kaleb harder.

Everything had changed in Rio Rico and if I'd had my way I never would have come back, but I couldn't stay away and still pay off the debt I'd incurred while I'd been down here. I probably would have sat there lost in my thoughts, Brindi at my side, for hours if my phone hadn't started ringing. It was Jack.

"It's done, you're good to move forward with your side of things."

"Thank you, Jack. Your wolf got out okay then?"

There was a long pause as Jack tried to decide how much it was safe to tell me over an unsecured line.

"Yeah, so far. There have already been a couple of close calls, and none of us are in the clear yet, but the contingency plans we worked out should be enough to make sure that we get a clean getaway unless they chase us down in the next hour or so."

"Okay, best of luck to you all. I couldn't have done this without you guys."

"That's the understatement of the year, but it's worth it if only because it means Kaleb will get knocked down another peg or two. We need to talk as soon as you can meet up with us. There were some interesting developments up here."

Part of me was dying to know what he was talking about. He sounded a little rattled, which was unusual to say the least. Jack was usually a pretty cool customer; most older dominants tended to be that way. Jack was more than a hundred and fifty years old. He knew his capabilities and it took a lot to rattle him, but this was obviously something he felt needed to be shared in person.

"Understood, we'll see you all shortly."

I hung up and turned to James who was sitting in the driver's seat. "Any word from the girls?"

"Yeah, the target is following her usual route and she's right on schedule. You've got about sixty seconds before she'll be running right past us."

"Thanks, James. Tell Jasmin and Jess to get out of there, things could get awful hot in this town in the next few minutes."

I looked over at Brindi and sighed. She seemed to be mostly healed. It was hard to be sure without access to the advanced diagnostic equipment you'd find in a hospital, but she moved around without flinching now and she wasn't sleeping all of the time anymore. Unfortunately she still deteriorated quickly when she wasn't with me. She could make it an hour now before she started showing the outward signs of withdrawal, but that still wasn't much time to work with.

"I need to go outside for a few minutes and it's best if you stay here."

Brindi nodded. "Is what you're about to do dangerous?"

"Yes, but no more so than anything else we've done over the last few days."

I could see how badly she wanted to argue with me, to plead for me not to put myself in harm's way, but we'd already had that argument today. I owed Brindi a debt for saving my life, but I couldn't let my debt to her stop me from paying down the other people I owed.

Brindi nodded again and then I was opening the door of our SUV and stepping out into the harsh Arizona sun. James' estimate was spot on. Alison came jogging past the alley where we were parked right on schedule.

"Alison, we need to talk."

She turned towards me with the inhuman quickness and poise that we usually tried not to display in public.

"Alec? Are you insane? This is the last place you should be. We've got an op tonight. Brandon has pulled in everyone he can get his hands on for this one."

"I know, that's part of why we decided to come today. Brandon's going to be faced with choosing between going forward with the operation or trying to catch us."

She looked like she wanted to hit me, but that wasn't much of a change from how she'd acted when I'd been here the last time. She was skinnier now than she'd been when I'd last seen her and she hadn't much, if any, excess body fat on her then.

The red streak in her hair, a symbol of defiance that she'd sported for as long as she'd been down here, hadn't changed, but her black running shorts hung lower on her hips than I remembered from before and her white tank top revealed arms and shoulders that looked like they'd been carved out of rock. She was all hard planes and angles and looked like nothing more than willpower was keeping her from giving up. None of it pointed to anything good. Juan had been a great team leader, maybe the best, and in a lot of ways he'd been the glue holding Alison together.

He was dead now and that was one more reason for Alison to hate me. Juan had died protecting me from the Ancient that had been part of a trap designed to kill all of Brandon's people. Juan had died and then I'd been whisked away to Sanctuary to recover from my wounds in safety while Alison had been left here to be fed back into the blender.

"You just can't leave well enough alone, can you? You made it out, free and clear, but you have to come back here and drag me into some kind of asinine plan that is almost guaranteed to get me killed."

"It's not like that..."

She cut me off before I could get another word out. "I'm not going to help you, Alec. I'm done with all of that crap. It's past time for me to just keep my head down and try to last as long as I can. You may have inspired Juan, but that won't work on me."

"Your mom left Sanctuary a few minutes ago, Alison. Kaleb probably knows she's gone by now, but the people with her have been planning their escape route for the last week. They've got fallbacks for their fallbacks. It might take a day or two, but eventually she'll disappear and Kaleb will never find her. She's not important enough for him to dedicate the kind of time and effort that he spent looking for Agony."

"So that's your play? You came down here to tell me that you're going to use her to blackmail me? You really are just like your damn dad."

James turned on the SUV. It was a signal indicating that we didn't have much time.

"I'm here to give you a chance to get out. Some of my friends risked a lot to get your mom and Chloe's parents out of Sanctuary. There isn't anything holding you here now. Come get into the car with me. We'll leave and you don't ever have to come back. No tricks, no threats. I'd love to have you help me, I can always use another good fighter, but if you want to walk away I'll tell you where your mom is, give you a hundred thousand dollars and let you go to her."

She knew I was telling her the truth, but she was still having a hard time believing it. Alison was roughly my age, but she'd been down on the border fighting jaguars in one desperate battle after another for months. I'd always thought my life was pretty rough, but in some ways Alison had been through even more.

"You swear to me that it's not a trick?"

"I swear, Alison. I can't guarantee that we'll get away and every second we stand here talking reduces our odds, but we've got a plan. It may fall apart and we may all be caught and executed, but I'm going to do everything in my power to get us all out and then you can start making your own choices again."

She nodded jerkily and started towards me, but she only made it a couple of steps before her legs gave out. I caught her before she could hit the ground. She'd never been very heavy, but as

AMBUSHED

I picked her up and carried her to the SUV it felt like there wasn't anything left of her.

I was still hoping to get Agony out and eventually overthrow Kaleb, but I'd already accomplished more than I'd been worried I might. Saving Alison might have seemed like a small thing to some, but it had been important to me and it would make all the difference in the world to her, her mother, and the parents of her best friend, a girl who hadn't lasted for even two weeks in the hell that Alison had been facing for months.

Chapter 19

Adriana Paige
Downtown Parking Emporium
Houston, Texas

Things between Taggart and I were strained. It wasn't because I didn't believe him, and I didn't blame him for telling me about what he'd seen with Alec. He hadn't done anything wrong, but it was hard to know what to say or how to act around someone who had seen me humiliated so badly. I was pretty sure that most of the awkwardness would eventually disappear, but that wasn't particularly helpful right now.

I'd made contact with Dominic the night that Taggart had told me about Alec. Talking to Dominic had been odd on several levels. I kept wanting to like her but I knew that was dangerous in the world I lived in now. If we'd met back in Minnesota as two normal girls then things would have been different, but as they were now I couldn't afford to trust anyone.

If Alec had managed to pull the wool over my eyes this badly, then I wasn't a good enough judge of character to be selecting my own friends. Dominic seemed to be struggling with something as well, but I couldn't tell for sure what it was that was bothering her.

She was very coy when it came to providing details about where she was and who she was living with, but after I explained that I was trying to find people to help Dream Stealer and I free Agony, she finally agreed to take my plea to 'the rest of the group.' It wasn't a lot to go on, but it was better than nothing.

The next morning Taggart suggested that I spend some time inside the underground shooting range. I wouldn't have trusted me with a handgun if our positions had been reversed, but if he was worried he didn't show it.

He took me by the armory to grab some more ammunition and a selection of guns, and then once we arrived at the range he showed me how to load the gun, chamber a round, and get the bullets to hit roughly where I was aiming. All of that took a bit less than fifteen minutes including the mandatory gun safety talk, and then I was on my own.

I expected to hate it. The only exposure I'd ever had to firearms was when Benito and Pete had taken turns holding one up to my head. It was something designed for one purpose and one purpose only, and I still wasn't excited about killing someone in the dream world let alone in the real world.

All of that changed as I sent my first hundred shots down the range. There was something addictive about seeing my skill improve in real time, about blowing the center out of a target, but it was more than that.

I'd read somewhere in a history book that one of the early pistols had been called the great equalizer. That might have been true for fights between normal humans, but it wasn't true when the person with the gun was a human who was up against a hybrid. Even with a gun I'd still be out of my league when faced with a vampire or a shape shifter, but things would be a lot closer to even.

For the first time since my ability to dream walk had completely screwed up my life, I felt a degree of safety that didn't depend on Taggart, a degree of control over where I went and what happened to me. That was the most addictive thing of all.

I knew I wasn't going to turn myself into an expert over the course of one or two days, but I did the best I could. It took Dominic two more nights to get some of the others in her group to agree to a meeting. I spent a significant amount of time each day until then down in the range running exercises that I hoped would make me more competent and deadly with the pistol that I eventually settled on as my weapon of choice.

It helped that the range was built with tactical exercises in mind. It took some doing to figure out which buttons back by the shooting station did what, but once I got the hang of that I started running through shooting at moving targets that popped up seemingly at random. Things were so easy that I was worried at first that I was doing something wrong.

That only lasted until I remembered that I didn't function quite like a normal human anymore. Something about my fight with Pamela had souped up my time sense to the point where it was nearly the match of Taggart's. In an emergency I still couldn't move as fast as a shape shifter, but I thought as fast as one of them, which meant that I had all the time in the world to put rounds through each of the pop-up targets.

I was pretty sure that Dominic was going to tell me that she'd worked out some kind of meeting on that second night, so I knew that afternoon that I was going through my last round of practice. Once my slide had locked back and the last heavy steel plate had been knocked free on the last moving target, I set my now-familiar pistol down and walked downrange to collect all of the steel discs and remount them into their bases.

There wasn't any real need to clean up after myself, but I did anyway. Maybe someday this range would host another scared teenager who needed the empowerment provided by a gun, who needed a way to defend herself in a world that was infinitely more dangerous and deadly than she'd ever suspected. It wasn't likely, but if it did happen I didn't want to make her job any harder than it was already going to be.

I turned off the lights and then headed towards the tunnel up to the store so that Taggart could teach me how to clean my new gun.

That night I found out that Dominic had indeed come through for me. I had a location and a time, but just as I'd known she would, she told me that if I didn't come along with Taggart the meeting was off.

We piled some boxes in front of the secret door down to the bunker to help keep it hidden, locked up the gas station, and then started towards Texas the next morning. I brought my new gun, a backup weapon of the same size and caliber, and two hundred rounds of ammunition.

If Taggart thought that was overkill he didn't say anything and I didn't ask. I also didn't tell him that half of the ammunition was 'penetrator' rounds. I hadn't known what to expect when I'd tried out the first round of the color-coded ammunition back in the bunker, so it had taken me completely by surprise when I blew a hole through the metal plates that had so far laughed off everything else I'd shot at them.

I figured if we ran into trouble that the penetrators would be useful. Even a hybrid wouldn't easily laugh off a round designed to go through a metal plate.

I'd stocked up on guns and ammo because that was what I was most concerned about. Taggart had swiped all of the money from the cash register and three-quarters of the gold from Paulo's vault.

We'd made a single extended stop on our way out to Houston so that Taggart could stash the gold in a safe deposit box under both of our names. He kept a single bar, which he sold at a pawn shop in the same town. That one bar sold for more money than my dad made in several years. It felt almost obscene that something so small could be worth so much money, but Taggart didn't share my feeling.

"Money isn't obscene, Adri, it's just a tool. It's only obscene to those who give into their basest qualities once they have it."

It sounded eerily like something my dad might have said and I spent the next couple of hours pondering what I would do with millions of dollars. I finally fell asleep without having come to any kind of firm conclusion other than that I'd get some to my dad so that he could retire when the time came for him to stop working.

We arrived at the parking garage a little before noon, which meant that we had a little bit of time to kill. I'd adjusted one of the shoulder rigs in the armory down to the point where it mostly fit me, but I still had to fight the urge to fidget with it underneath my jacket. The last thing I needed was for a cop to realize I was illegally carrying a concealed weapon.

Taggart finally broke the silence five minutes before we were supposed to get out of the car and start walking.

"I'm sorry, Adri. I wish that things could have been different, I didn't want to have to tell you about Alec."

"I'm sorry too, but it's better to know than to go on blindly thinking he's interested in me."

I reached for the door, but Taggart stopped me with a gentle hand on my shoulder. "One of my contacts came through with a location and a route. We know enough to save Agony, assuming that Dominic and her friends are willing to help us."

"That's good news."

"I know, but it doesn't feel like it, does it?"

That stopped me more surely than if he'd chained me to my chair. "I guess you're right, it doesn't. Why is that?"

"Because it means we have a choice to make. We either rescue him or we leave him to his fate."

"Except we aren't going to choose to abandon him."

Taggart nodded solemnly. "Exactly. Having this information means that our options, the options we can live with, have narrowed down. Either Dominic and her friends will help us, or we'll go to Alec and take our risks with him."

"And either way everything is about to change. We'll either rescue your friend or die trying, but either way things will never be the same."

"Yes, exactly. The Coun'hij has looked for me for years, but it's always been a secondary concern. A jailbreak of this magnitude will cause them to shuffle around their priorities. Our lives will get very difficult even if we succeed."

"I guess I can understand why some people become paralyzed when faced with the tough decisions. If you don't make a decision then you can't be blamed when things go wrong. Only that's a lie too. Failing to make a decision is still making a decision; it's accepting whatever the universe throws at you because you failed to act."

Taggart opened his mouth to respond, but I tapped the clock in the dash. "We're going to be late. Come on, we don't want to make Dominic's friends any more jittery than they already are."

The parking garage they'd selected for the meet was absolutely huge. It was the kind of place that had seven or eight elevators, took up an entire city block and served four or five different stores. In short, if you were willing to black out a few security cameras, it was the perfect place for a clandestine meeting.

We'd both been wearing big glasses to disguise our faces from any security cameras that the Coun'hij might have access to. It was probably an unnecessary precaution while we were in the car and safely shielded by tinted windows, but it wasn't going to be enough outside of the car.

I flipped up the hood on my jacket, pulling it far enough forward that shadows would obscure most of my face, and then opened my door and slipped out of the car. Taggart had a neck warmer pulled up over the lower half of his face, which was ludicrous given how warm it was still in Texas, but it served to make him unrecognizable for any kind of facial recognition software.

It took us only a couple of minutes to find the appropriate section of the parking garage. It was a dead end that had been blocked off with cones and I was able to pick out several cameras on the way there that had been covered up, painted, or otherwise put out of commission. It was comforting to know that we weren't being tracked to the meeting place, at least not by any kind of automated surveillance system.

Someone did see us approach though because less than ten seconds after we arrived Dominic and the rest showed up behind us. They'd all taken similar precautions to make sure they weren't recognizable, but as they arrived they pulled off their glasses and discarded their wigs.

I pulled my hood back away from my face and moved my sunglasses up onto my hair as I looked for Dom. It shouldn't have taken me as long as it did to recognize her, but she seemed so different that I had a hard time believing she was the same person I'd saved from a beating back in Minnesota.

Her face was the same with lovely, dark skin and exotic brown eyes, but her bearing was night and day different. She no longer looked like she was expecting to be attacked at the drop of a hat, and she wasn't quite so gaunt. There'd been some hints as to the changes she'd undergone from our meetings in the dream world, but nothing like this. Apparently her subconscious image of herself was lagging behind the actual changes.

"Thank you, Dominic. I appreciate you arranging for this meeting."

A big guy to her left spoke up before she could respond. "It might be best to save the thanks until we all know whether or not you can be allowed to leave."

His tone wasn't overtly menacing, in fact the words were delivered with a calm certainty that almost hid the fact that he'd just told us that they'd kill us if they didn't like what they heard. I turned so I could get a better look at him.

He didn't look old enough to be the leader of such a large group. With him and Dominic included, there was a total of eight people standing in a half circle between us and the rest of the garage. Some of his people looked like they'd been through hell and back. I would have expected the leader of that kind of group to be some kind of heavily-tattooed biker complete with chains, piercings and a bewildering array of scars. Instead I was looking at someone who looked like they could have belonged to the ruling family of Saudi Arabia.

He had one of those thin beards that was little more than a series of lines that followed the bold planes of his face and the precise diction you only found in someone who had a passion for languages. I opened my mouth to introduce myself, but he didn't give me a chance.

"My name is Isaac. Dominic tells me that the two of you met in South Dakota and that you were wearing a band uniform."

I shook my head. "It was Minnesota and I was wearing my cheerleading uniform."

Everyone seemed to be waiting expectantly. It was Taggart who explained. "Ask Dominic something that only she should know."

"What did you tell me when I said I was in the middle of the field?"

"We were on the phone. I'd asked you how far away the nearest person was and you said nobody was closer than the bleachers to which I responded that would have to be far enough away."

I nodded to Taggart. "It's her."

Some of the tension seemed to leach out of everyone around me. "We're satisfied that you are who you say you are, but what about him?"

Taggart stepped forward half a step. "I'm the Dream Stealer. We've come to ask for your help."

Isaac shook his head. "If you want our help then you'll tell us your real name."

"The name I was born with is Taggart."

I could tell that Isaac was filing that piece of information away. It was one more sign of how desperate we were. Taggart had kept his real name a secret for decades. Giving it up now meant that he wanted their help badly enough to risk being found by the Coun'hij if Isaac or any of the others betrayed us.

"Very well, Adri, Taggart, Dominic says that you've come here to ask for our help in freeing Agony. Is that true?"

"Yes."

Taggart had answered, seemingly ready to take the lead in the negotiation, but Isaac held up a hand. "I'm sorry, but I'm going to have to request that Adri be the one to respond to my questions."

"Why?"

"Because as little as I trust her, I trust you even less. Adri is here because Dominic spoke eloquently on her behalf. You are here simply because Adri trusts you. If I'd had my way we would just be talking to Adri and you would have been left out of the conversation altogether."

"That's ridiculous. Adri knows next to nothing about what's at stake. She couldn't even begin to hope to coordinate an offensive of the size we'll need."

Isaac shook his head. "The first thing you need to understand is that you're not negotiating from a position of strength, *Taggart*. For us, character always trumps ability. Adri tried to save a stranger despite the fact that her actions put her in harm's way as well. Your history on the other hand, is filled with nothing but one bad decision after another. You're little more than a vicious bully who's used your gift to play politics without having to pay the kind of price anyone else would have had to pay."

I could see Taggart struggling to control his beast, struggling to contain the rage that I knew he would be feeling as the result of such a casual dismissal combined with a scathing judgment of his character. I jumped back into the conversation hoping that I could help distract him.

"I only know a little bit of Taggart's history myself, but you should know that it was he who saved me from the vampire Dominic tried to warn me about. He risked death to defeat not just one, but two vampires and in so doing saved me, my sister, and another friend of ours."

"Doubtlessly so that he could enlist your aid in his private war against the Coun'hij."

"No, he's let me pick my own way. He's asked for help, but he's respected my right to choose at every step along the way. That's why I sought out Dominic after so long. I wanted to know if the Coun'hij was really as bad as he had told me they were."

Dominic stepped up to Isaac's side. "She's telling the truth."

"I know, I can smell it on her as well as everyone else can, but just because she believes he's honorable doesn't mean that he's actually honorable."

For the briefest of moments Dominic seemed to be searching for the right words. "I can't dispute that, but given how well he's treated Adriana don't you think he deserves some respect in return?"

I wasn't an expert in shape shifter pack dynamics, but I knew enough about social dynamics between humans that I would have bet a sizable amount of money that Dominic wasn't dominant to Isaac. She treated him with a respect that bordered on reverence, and she was very careful around him as though worried about her actions being taken the wrong way.

Based on everything Taggart had told me about pack life, the normal response for a dominant being corrected by a submissive would have been anger and possibly even violence, but Isaac simply bowed his head.

"Dominic is right. You have my apology. Still, I would have Adri do the talking, at least for now. She's undoubtedly a less-practiced liar than someone your age. Once she's told us her view of things then you'll be given a chance to respond as well."

Taggart seemed to gather himself in with a titanic force of will, but when he nodded there were no longer any visible signs that he was struggling to control himself.

"Very well."

Isaac turned back to me. "Tell me why you're here, Adriana. Tell me why you think we should help you at great risk to ourselves, and tell me why exactly it is that you trust Taggart, the Dream Stealer."

I opened my mouth, unsure of what exactly I was going to say, and the words just poured out almost of their own accord.

I talked for nearly an hour. I kept expecting someone to show up to find out why the cameras weren't working, but nobody did. Maybe Isaac had bribed one of the guards to ignore the blank monitors for a few hours, or maybe he had someone acting as a lookout. It didn't really matter other than the fact that Isaac seemed to feel like we had all of the time in the world for him to get each of his questions answered.

By the time he'd finished teasing every event of the last few weeks out of me, I was in desperate need of a bathroom. Our last pit stop had been nearly six hours earlier, and it must have been pretty obvious that I was uncomfortable because Dominic volunteered to escort me up to one of the stores.

Taggart seemed for a moment like he was going to protest, but Dominic promised that she wouldn't let anything happen to me, which was enough of an assurance that Taggart apparently decided that it wasn't some kind of ruse designed to split us up.

I pulled my sunglasses back down onto my face and shifted my hood forward while Dominic put on a blond wig and glasses of her own and then we headed off as Isaac began interrogating Taggart.

We passed the trip up to the bathroom in silence, but by the time I finished up and we'd started back down to the parking garage, my curiosity had gotten the better of me.

"Thank you for arranging this meeting. It doesn't seem like you've been part of this group for very long so I suspect it was a little nerve-racking to have to push for something like this."

Dominic shrugged. She was a strange mixture of shy and confident now that we were away from the others.

"You're welcome. I appreciated what you tried to do for me back in Minnesota and I'm just sorry that I didn't figure out a way to confirm which of your friends was the vampire."

"No, you don't need to be sorry at all. Things ended up working out okay for the most part. I mean I nearly died and all of that, but all of the good guys survived and if Jackson and Pamela hadn't found me I might not have ever had the courage to pull Taggart into my dreams."

"Still, I wish I could have done more. The little bit of help I offered wasn't a very good repayment for your help."

I shot her a look of disbelief. "You could have easily wrapped all four of those girls into knots all by yourself. You didn't need my help."

Dominic's blond wig was positioned so that it obscured most of the right side of her face. She looked up at me from behind a curtain of hair as we stepped into an empty elevator and I pushed the button for our floor.

"You're right, physically they weren't a match for me, but I was at a real low point when you saw me. It wasn't that I *couldn't* defend myself, I didn't *want* to. I guess I'd lost hope. I came up here to your country thinking that I'd be entering some kind of paradise where law and order reigned supreme and the people were fundamentally different than everyone I'd known back home.

"Instead, I found out that people are the same everywhere you go. The ordinary people here confine their actions to something mostly within your laws, but most of them aren't any better or worse than anyone from my country."

Her smooth alto and beautiful accent didn't give any hint to what she'd gone through, but I'd seen some of the depths that people could descend to when they didn't think anyone was watching. My own sister had even tried to make my life miserable enough to quit the cheerleading team despite the fact that my joining had been her idea from the start.

"I'm so sorry. Things must have been really hard for you here. I can't imagine what it would be like not to have any support system, no family, no friends, nobody to make the bullies think that it might not be a good idea to pick on you."

"*Sí*, it was pretty bad. I was ready to give up, to crawl off somewhere and die, but you reminded me that there were other kinds of people out there, good, kind people. You gave me back my hope and convinced me that I just need to go back out there and find more people like you."

"I'm glad I was able to help, even if I didn't really do much of anything. It seems like you've found a good home with Isaac and the others."

Dominic's smile and nod were the most completely unreserved expressions I'd seen out of her yet. "Yes, they are like the family I wish I could have had growing up."

"I was surprised to see that Isaac was so young. He seems like he can't be much older than us. I thought pack alphas were usually older, more experienced but still in the prime of their lives."

"They usually are, but we aren't exactly a pack and Isaac isn't really our alpha."

Our elevator glided to a stop. I gave her a confused look as we stepped out onto the white concrete.

"I don't understand."

"It's hard to explain. I don't know that there's ever been anything quite like this before. Before Isaac was exiled there was no us. It was just a bunch of dispossessed who had all lived in the same area for long enough that they knew each other and had worked out a rough dominance hierarchy."

"Isaac changed all of that?"

"Yes. Some of the most dominant hybrids were as bad as any of the alpha jaguars back home. The only thing that kept them even slightly in check was the fear that if they pushed too far or didn't keep our existence a secret the Coun'hij would step in and kill them."

That was exactly what I would have expected out of a group of shape shifters without a central authority. It mirrored the things Taggart had described from his time as one of the dispossessed.

"Isaac wasn't like that. He doesn't have any kind of special ability like some of the hybrids have, but he was young and strong. The wolves in our territory expected him to come in and claim one of the better areas for himself. That would have forced whoever he pushed out to take another territory from one of the other wolves. Those kinds of fights, when a shape shifter has been robbed of their territory and have to fight for a new spot, are some of the most deadly. When we are away from home and operating without any kind of safety net we are the most vulnerable."

"So I take it that Isaac didn't do that?"

"No, he found one of the more submissive wolves and asked her if he could share her territory. She thought he was just going to edge her out over time rather than all at once, but he didn't and when one of the lesser hybrids came through and tried to steal from her, Isaac ran him off."

I could see where the story was going. Isaac already sounded like a standup guy. He was exactly the kind of guy I'd been thinking Alec was until Taggart had burst my bubble.

"So, I'm guessing that once Isaac beat that other hybrid everyone expected him to go in and evict the guy he'd beaten?"

"Yeah, pretty much, but instead Isaac paid him a visit and told him that he had nothing to fear as long as he stopped shaking down Isaac's friend."

"Only hybrid number two was shaking down more than just the one wolf..."

"Right, the other hybrid—Clarence is his name—kept robbing from the other wolves and in fact took more from them to make up for the fact that he couldn't steal from Isaac's friend, Zaire. Once word of what had happened got around to the other wolves, they went to Isaac and asked him to protect them from Clarence."

We were only a little ways away from the others, but I didn't want to go back just yet. I was pretty sure that once we were around everyone else Dominic would clam up and I would miss out on the rest of the story. I reached out and placed a hand on Dominic's arm. She stopped and looked at me.

"What happened next?"

"Isaac visited Clarence with half a dozen wolves at his back and told Clarence that his protection racket was done for."

"I'll bet Clarence didn't like that."

Dominic looked a little sad now. "He didn't, but not for the reason you think. He was shaking down the wolves because one of the other more dangerous hybrids kept coming around and shaking *him* down. He told Isaac what was going on and Isaac agreed to help him stand up to the hybrid who had been giving Clarence problems."

My mind was whirling in astonishment at what I'd just heard.

"Isaac just reestablished civilization among the dispossessed in your area."

Dominic nodded. "Exactly. It's nothing less than amazing. For so many years, back in my country, I thought that barbarity and lawlessness was unusual. I thought the natural order of the world was something like you all have here in the United States. I got here and found out I'd had it backwards the entire time."

"Right, the natural order of things is for the strong to prey on the weak."

"Even so. It takes a special set of circumstances and rare kind of person to bring civilization to something like what Isaac found when he first arrived in our territory. Most of it happened before I'd arrived, but even hearing about it secondhand was amazing."

I had so many questions that I almost didn't know where to start. "But you're not a pack and Isaac isn't your leader?"

"No, not in the traditional sense. Many of the dispossessed are dispossessed for good reason. Some of them don't play very well with others, so we haven't formed anything as rigid as a pack. Instead it's more like an...understanding. Isaac has a set of rules, simple things like no robbing from each other, no evicting someone from their territory."

"A basic legal code..."

"*Sí*, that's it exactly. The dispossessed are divided into two groups, those who have agreed to uphold Isaac's rules, and those who haven't. Isaac is the final arbitrator of any disagreements between two of us who have agreed to his law."

"What about conflicts between you guys and the ones outside of his law?"

"Isaac settles those according to the rules he's established. It almost always comes down to bloodshed, but no one hybrid can hope to stand against Isaac and the rest of us."

"And the Coun'hij doesn't know about any of this?"

Dominic shook her head. "We don't think so. They usually only monitor the most powerful dispossessed and we've tried very hard to keep a low profile. It helps that Isaac isn't the best fighter or most powerful hybrid in the area. Anyone looking in from the outside is unlikely to view him as being at the center of anything."

"Only he is."

"Exactly."

We started walking again. I still had questions, but we'd been away long enough that Taggart was probably starting to get worried. Besides, none of the rest of my questions really mattered, not compared to what I'd already learned.

We came around the corner just in time to hear Taggart finish responding to another of Isaac's questions.

"...so I've got the current location and the first leg of their route, but no idea what they'll do after that."

Isaac sighed. "Which means that you've got a very narrow window in which to strike; if you miss it you might lose him forever."

"I'm afraid so."

The tension between Isaac's people and Taggart had continued to ratchet down in my absence. Nobody was standing anymore; they'd all found cars to sit on. Some of the guys with Isaac even seemed to have relaxed enough that smiling at Dominic and me as we came back wasn't a capital offense.

Isaac stared off into space for several seconds before nodding. "All right, I'm in. You're either both telling the truth or you're the most accomplished liars I've ever encountered. Either way, you're right. If Agony disappears permanently things will get noticeably worse for all of the rest of us."

The last of the tension melted out of Taggart and, for the first time since he'd found out that Agony had been captured, he seemed to have a measure of hope.

"Great, how many people will you be bringing?"

"I'm sorry, but our group doesn't work that way. I don't just give orders and expect everyone to hop. Everyone with us here today now knows enough to make their own decision, and it will be *their* decision. As for the rest of the people who've chosen to live by our rules, it will take me a day or so to get the message out to them."

For a second I thought Taggart was going to say something he'd regret. What Isaac was describing went against everything Taggart had seen in nearly three hundred years of life and I could tell he was having a hard time believing it. I made a quick 'calm down' gesture and he fortunately chose not to take umbrage at what could have been considered an order.

"Another day when we don't have something more pressing going on, I'd be interested in learning more about your group."

Isaac's nod of agreement was accompanied by a smile that seemed to say that he knew just how much it had cost Taggart not to say something else, but it wasn't a mean smile by any stretch of the imagination. If anything I got the feeling that Isaac himself was surprised that he'd managed to accomplish so much with such a dangerous, disparate group.

"Still, I have two concerns that must be addressed if we're going to be able to work together."

Isaac waved for Taggart to go on.

"It is vitally important that news of this operation not leak out to the Coun'hij. If your group is as democratic as you say it is, then you're not going to be withholding any information from any of your people. Surely you can see my concerns from a security standpoint with that arrangement..."

"Of course, that is completely understandable. All I can say is that while there isn't any guarantee when it comes to these kinds of things, we've done everything we could to limit our exposure generally. Before we leave, each of my people will confirm to at least two other people that they won't share this information with anyone outside of our group, and that they will only do so in person after getting the same kind of promise from whomever they share the information with."

"That's not bad, but a ritual promise that bound their beast to enforcing the oath would be even better."

Isaac actually chuckled. "It would, but that isn't the kind of thing I can get away with asking. Most of the wolves and hybrids in our group have grown to love the freedom of not answering to a central authority. I'm afraid this is the best I can hope to get out of them. What was your second concern?"

Taggart didn't exactly look happy about Isaac's response, but apparently he decided it was satisfactory enough to move on to his second point.

"You must have at least *some* estimate of how much help your people might offer. If we're going to have any hope of pulling this off then I need—we need—to start planning today."

"Possibly as few as five or six, possibly as many as two or three dozen, but plan as though there will be twelve or thirteen of us. It's going to take much more than just a few years before most of the dispossessed will trust each other enough to fight for a cause."

Some of the air seemed to leak out of Taggart. "It's not enough. Even with fourteen hybrids we'd still be unlikely to win, not against the kinds of animals that the Coun'hij uses as enforcers. Even if they don't have someone really scary along like Puppeteer or Oblivion we still would be stupid to go in without more of a numerical advantage than that."

Isaac seemed to be debating his response, but before he could decide between whatever options he was considering one of the guys to his left stood and walked over to his side.

"It's okay, Isaac. You can tell him."

I felt Dominic go tense next to me, but I was too busy wondering why I hadn't noticed the guy next to Isaac before now. He didn't look like the others. They were hard men who looked like they were in their late thirties or early forties, which probably meant that they'd lived for more than a century already. He looked like he was all of fifteen.

"This is Heath and he's the real reason that our little group isn't constantly at each other's throats."

Isaac's words were obviously making Heath extremely uncomfortable. Heath looked like some painter's attempt at bringing an angel to life. He had straight blond hair that framed a face that didn't seem to have even the tiniest trace of guile, and his skin was as flawless as an alabaster doll.

He didn't have the massive shoulders of most of the rest of the guys, Isaac included. He didn't have any excess body fat on him, but he didn't look athletic. He looked like your best friend's kid brother, the one that you always had to protect from the neighborhood bullies.

"That's not true, Isaac. You're the one who makes all of this work. Everyone looks up to you or at least respects you."

The words had the feel of an argument that had been voiced frequently already, but there wasn't any heat to them.

Isaac smiled at Heath and then looked back at Taggart. "Even before I got exiled from Sanctuary I'd read enough books to realize that the biggest threat to any society, to any civilization, isn't the petty crooks or the second-tier criminals. The biggest threat is the human equivalent to an apex predator.

"The humans deal with that by making their own apex predators. They take normal men and women and put them in the military and teach them honor and duty before they unlock their ability to kill. Of course, that would never work for us. Our apex predators are born instead of being made."

"Heath is your apex predator." It was a statement rather than a question, and there was a kind of hushed reverence to Taggart's voice that I'd never heard out of him before.

"Indeed, he is. Heath is one of those rare hybrids with an ability. He can manipulate what people see. He's been standing there with the rest of the guys the whole time, but you didn't see him there because he didn't *let* you see him."

"You knew all along that the wolves would support you."

I was the last person who should be interjecting something into the conversation. I wasn't a hybrid, I couldn't even ante up for the game that Isaac and Taggart were playing, but I couldn't help myself.

Luckily Isaac just smiled at me. "Indeed, I did. The wolves had the most to gain from civilization. I figured I could get the second-tier hybrids to see the benefits as well. They were like me, predators but not apex predators. Whatever we were going to lose out on because we couldn't prey on the wolves would be more than made up for by the fact that we wouldn't have the first-tier hybrids preying on us.

"The first-tier hybrids were the problem just like in any other society. Nobody was preying on them. They had to worry about conflict with each other, but by and large they just stayed in their own territories. From a purely material perspective they wouldn't gain anything by following my rules."

Heath spoke up again. "Only I didn't want money or human women. I just wanted a home and someone I knew I could trust to watch my back. I've been on my own for years already and I spent a lot of time at the bottom of the food chain before I finally became a hybrid and manifested a power. I've had enough sleeping with one eye open to last me for a lifetime. I'm in."

Even I knew that meant we had a chance of pulling this off, and knots of tension that I hadn't even realized had been paining me unknotted in my neck and shoulders. The Coun'hij enforcers couldn't kill, couldn't even fight, people that they couldn't see.

AMBUSHED

Taggart nodded respectfully to Heath and I realized that for the first time I was seeing Taggart interact with an equal. He'd chosen to put himself in Isaac's power because it had been the only way to save his friend, but in his own way Taggart was just as deadly as Heath.

He couldn't blind someone, but he was capable of reaching people no matter how far or fast they ran. Heath could kill, but Taggart could make you *wish* you were dead.

They'd both chosen a path that put them at odds with the only people who could really threaten them. They were kindred spirits in a way that I could never be. I could kill in the dream, but I was never going to be Isaac's apex predator. I was just a girl, a human girl who wouldn't last one second by myself in the world that Isaac and the others dealt with on a daily basis.

Chapter 20

Alec Graves
Shelley High School
Shelley, Idaho

Seeing Alison and her mother reunite after so many months was worth all of the risks that we'd run getting the two of them out from under Kaleb's thumb. Their tears were understandable and nobody minded when the two of them disappeared into one of the white-walled classrooms to catch up.

My biggest concern on the drive up to Idaho had been that Kaleb would track us to the rendezvous point. My second biggest worry had been that something would happen to Rachel. I was incredibly relieved when she came running out of the theater where Jack and the others had set up and threw her arms around me.

"I was so worried about you, Alec!"

"I know, Rach. I'm sorry that you've had to spend so much time alone, there's just been a lot going on and none of it has been very safe."

Rachel wiped away a couple of small tears before they could make it all of the way down her face and then offered a shy smile to Brindi.

"I'm glad you made it back too."

"Thanks, Rachel. It will be nice to be out of the car long enough to stretch my legs for more than just a couple of minutes at a gas station."

It wasn't the first time that Rachel and Brindi had met, but I'd worried that things would still be strained between them. Brindi was fierce when it came to warding off anything that might take me away from her for even a few minutes, and Rachel had obviously not been sure what to make of the injured girl who'd attached herself to me out of the blue.

It was good that they were at least trying to get along.

Rachel took Brindi's hand and pulled her towards the theater. Given Brindi's viselike grip on my hand, that meant that Rachel pulled both of us into the theater after her. James, Jasmin and Jess followed the three of us in and a few seconds later we were all arrayed in a loose circle with Jack and the rest of his people.

I could tell that Jack was bursting to tell me whatever it was he'd learned while in Sanctuary, but I held a hand up, stopping him before he could get started. I looked around at everyone in the circle, both Jack's people and my friends, meeting each of their gazes for a second or two.

"I just wanted to say thank you to all of you. I know some of you are here more because of Jack than any other reason, but I still appreciate you going back to Sanctuary and risking what you risked to help reunite Alison and her mother. I pay my debts, and when you help me pay a debt like you just did then some of that debt transfers from the person you helped to you.

"If there comes a time when you need to cash in that debt all you have to do is tell me. Money is easy, but if it's something else you need I'll do my best to make it happen."

Jack let the silence hang in the air for a few moments before clearing his throat. "I have some news, Alec. While we were in Sanctuary I found out where they are holding Agony. Even better, I found out when they are going to move him and what route they are going to take. If Shawn or his contact comes through with a couple dozen hybrids then there is a good chance we can do this."

I didn't even realize I'd stood up until Brindi tugged on my arm. My shock was complete. I'd been trying to put together a jailbreak for Agony ever since we'd flown back to the mainland, but given the complete dearth of information, I'd stopped believing it was going to be possible to actually get him out.

"Show me."

AMBUSHED

With the biggest grin I'd ever seen on his face, Jack pulled out an old-fashioned, red three-ring binder and passed it over to me. He'd been busy, extremely busy.

There were topographic maps, weather data, satellite pictures of the enclosure where they were guarding him, and detailed information about each of the cities along the route from the Mexican border up into New Mexico. There were probably only a handful of people in the world who could have put together that much information by themselves along with three separate possible plans while on the run from Kaleb's people and all in the space of just two days.

I was extremely lucky to have recruited Jack to my side. We still lacked the numbers and the top-of-the-food-chain hybrid abilities that we would have needed to go head to head with a group of the Coun'hij's finest, but with Jack on our side we at least had a chance of structuring things so that we could achieve objectives without *having* to go head to head with someone like Brandon or Puppeteer.

Jack and the others waited while I looked through the binder. Once I was done and had handed it to James, Jack pulled out another map. This one was of a tiny stretch of road on the eastern edge of New Mexico.

"I've gone through the other two plans half a dozen times and if we had to we could give them a shot, but we'd need something like fifty people to have any chance of making them work."

I nodded. I couldn't have put options together like Jack had, at least not as quickly as he had, but I could understand what he was saying.

"How did Kaleb and the rest ever even find him down in Mexico?"

Jack shrugged. "Maybe the Brain Box found him. They've been working with Brandon for months now scouring every bit of intel they could get out of Mexico and parts south. Maybe Agony got sloppy, or maybe it was just sheer dumb luck. Honestly it wouldn't surprise me to find out that Agony has been spending a lot of time south of the border. It's the last place the Coun'hij would have been looking for him, so it makes a lot of sense that he would have gone down there whenever things started getting too hot here in the States."

"I agree with you, an open assault on the compound where they have him right now is too dangerous. Not only do we have to worry about any jaguars who might be in the area, I think the intelligence you've got is probably right that Puppeteer is down there."

"Yeah, it fits too well with everything else I've been hearing. Mexico's power grid isn't as redundant and robust as ours is, but there has been a definite uptick in blackouts down in that area and Puppeteer has been remarkably quiet for the last couple of weeks."

I shook my head in astonishment that anyone had managed to get Puppeteer to remain in one spot for that long. Kaleb relied on Brandon and the largest pack in North America to keep him secure. Puppeteer on the other hand relied on anonymity. He'd killed too many people over the years and his ability was too powerful. People from both sides were gunning for him. If his actual identity ever became common knowledge his life expectancy would drop precipitously.

"I should have seen it. Kaleb has managed to keep Puppeteer leashed pretty well for the last few years, but even for him it would have been an epic accomplishment to keep Puppeteer down there that long just to do a little jaguar hunting."

"Don't beat yourself up about it. Nobody else saw it either. In fairness, Kaleb was probably killing two birds with one stone. The pressure on Brandon and his people seems to be reaching critical levels. For every official op that they run there seems to be another one going on that nobody is talking about. All I can figure is that Kaleb is more concerned about looking like he has the situation there under control than he is about trumpeting his latest body count figure from the rooftops."

I'd known that Jack didn't like Kaleb, but there was something else there besides just the death of Jack's son. Now wasn't the time, but I needed to get him to open up. Jack has as much control as anyone else I'd ever met, but some pressures are too great to be contained indefinitely.

Jack moved his finger over to a small town on the map that was the most likely place for the convoy of vehicles to refuel.

"We could hit them here once they aren't moving, but then we'd have to worry about all of the humans around. I'm not just talking about the fact that we'd be on the six o'clock news either. Kaleb and the rest are going to know that this is their most vulnerable spot. If I was him I'd have at least another six or seven hybrids there at the gas station waiting for the convoy to roll in. If we get into some kind of knock-down drag-out fight with all of those humans around we're going to have some innocent people caught in the crossfire."

I wanted to argue with him. Fights involving wolves and hybrids didn't usually cause the kind of ancillary damage that you saw when you added modern weapons and explosives into the mix, but ultimately it didn't matter. He was right that the Coun'hij would have extra security waiting at the gas station.

All of which brought us to the final option. Jack flipped the map over and revealed another map and some satellite photos taped to the back of it.

"This section of the road climbs a six-and-a-half percent grade for a mile and a half, which means that the truck will be basically crawling by the time it hits the top of the hill. There's a stream that runs along from here to here which is important because it has fed some of the biggest trees I've ever seen all along this section of the road at the top of the hill.

"They don't provide any direct overhead concealment if you're standing on the road, but they will do a great job of giving us cover until the last possible second when we put tire shredders on the road."

"What if they've got run-flat tires on the truck? Brandon used a similar tactic against a convoy of jaguars while we were all down there. I'd be surprised if Kaleb hadn't learned from that little trick."

Jack smiled. "I almost hope they have, but it won't make any difference. By the time that truck hits the top of the hill it's going to be going slow enough that you, James or I could easily run it down in hybrid form and rip the door away from the cab. One way or another that truck will be stopping, and if it stops then the escort vehicles will have to stop too."

I nodded my agreement, and Jack continued. He had everything worked out, including an escape route, but there was one thing he hadn't dealt with. I debated raising the point with him, but ultimately decided against it.

Jack hadn't come up with a contingency for the one thing I was the most worried about because there wasn't a good way to deal with it.

Besides, I already had a plan for that particular issue if it arose. It wasn't Jack's problem to deal with, it was mine.

Everyone talked through the plan, asking questions and offering suggestions, and then just as things were winding down Alison and her mother entered the theater. They'd obviously been crying and Alison's mother had ahold of her arm as though trying to stop her from entering the room, but I'd known Alison for long enough to know that it would take more than tears to stop her.

Alison's eyes were red from all of the crying, but she looked better than she had in a long time. She was still too skinny and too tightly-wound, but there was an air of acceptance to her that hadn't been there before. I turned around in my seat so I could meet her eyes as she walked up to me.

"Whatever you've got planned, I want in."

"You don't have to do this, Alison. I meant what I said. If you want to go to ground with your mom you're welcome to do so. One person isn't going to make the difference in what we've got coming up. If I can't turn up another twelve or thirteen people all of this planning won't count for anything anyway."

"I know I don't *have* to help you out, but the fact that you're giving me the choice means that I don't really have any other option but to help. Guys like Kaleb and Brandon need to be stopped, but I'll settle for being there when Sam gets put in the ground. If a few of the pack back in Sanctuary had stood up to Kaleb then maybe Chloe would still be alive."

She took a deep breath and held it for a second. When she released it she seemed at peace for the first time I could remember.

"I'm not going to sit around and just let Kaleb continue to screw people over."

"Okay, welcome to the team."

I turned to the rest of the crew and gave them another nod of thanks.

"You should all take a long break and get some sleep once we get back to the hotel. I'll go see what I can do about rounding up some more help."

I tossed James and Jack each a stack of bills that I figured would be more than enough to get everyone settled for the night and then exited the auditorium as I pulled my phone out of my front pocket. It was pretty much a given that Brindi would follow me out of the theater, but I hadn't expected the stream of other people that were only a step behind her.

"We want to help too."

Chloe's dad had the look of someone who knew he was going to be refused, but who couldn't bear not to ask. The problem was I knew that I *should* turn him down. I needed all the help I could get, but I needed fighters and neither of Chloe's parents remotely fit that description.

They were both submissives who'd spent most of their adult lives avoiding confrontation by just giving into the demands of whichever dominants crossed their path.

Kaleb was a power-hungry monster whom you would have expected to turn everyone around him into living weapons, but no pack could function for long filled with nothing but battle-hardened dominants.

You needed submissives to serve as a pressure release valve, and the bigger the pack the more submissives you needed to offset the dominants. A pack the size of the Sanctuary pack, especially one that was as militant as Kaleb had made it, needed a huge supply of submissive wolves and they needed to be extra weak-willed to offset people like Brandon and Vincent.

In their own way, Chloe's parents were as much a product of their environment as Vincent was. In another pack Vincent would have still been bad, but faced with fewer hybrids gunning for the top spot he probably wouldn't have become the kind of heartless monster he currently was.

By the same measure, in a smaller pack Chloe's family would have still been submissive, but they would have been forced to become better fighters. A smaller pack couldn't afford to have as many non-combatants, not if it expected to survive in a world filled with vampires, werewolves and rival packs.

Chloe's parents were stronger and faster than any human could hope to be, but they would be barely more than cannon fodder in a fight against a group of vampires. Putting them up against other wolves, or even worse hybrids, would have been like signing their death warrants.

"Mr. Peterson, I appreciate the offer, but going up against a bunch of Coun'hij enforcers isn't going to bring Chloe back."

"Please, call me Dylan. You're the boss around here. Everyone is working together fairly well, but eventually you and James or you and Jack are going to have some kind of difference of opinion and you don't want to muddy the waters by showing a couple of submissives more respect than they deserve."

"It doesn't have to be like that...Dylan."

He looked at my hand, currently holding Brindi's hand, and shook his head. "I'm sorry to disagree with you, but it does. I've been alive for nearly two hundred years. I'm a submissive, but in some ways that just means that I understand dominance posturing better than most dominants.

"Eventually you're going to have to force obedience out of someone. You probably won't want to, it may even be for their own good, but it will eventually happen. You're not enough stronger than the other hybrids here to force the issue without a fight, not if you haven't played your cards just right."

His wife stepped forward and put her hand on her husband's arm. "Please. We know that we're no good in a fight, but we're willing to learn. Back in Sanctuary we would have been beaten down for trying. Even the other wolves would have resented us for trying to better our standing in the hierarchy, but that's not the case here. You need fighters. Let us help in whatever way we can while you turn us into fighters."

My beast had a very decided opinion as to what course of action I should take. She was right, I needed fighters, but if I said yes then their lives would never be the same. Even if they didn't die the first time I was forced to throw them into a fight, they would still be different people by the time I was done with them.

In a world where it was kill or be killed a pair of non-combatants were worse than useless, but I didn't want to drag them into my world. They'd had a taste already. Nobody could spend time around murderers like Brandon and Vincent without getting glimpses of the world that civilization was designed to protect us from. Not only that, they'd already lost their only daughter to Kaleb's pointless war with the jaguars.

They knew what they were getting into, but I still almost refused them. Chloe's mom loved her husband despite the fact that he wasn't the ultimate killing machine, despite the fact that he couldn't protect her from someone like Vincent. There was a chance when I was done with them that they wouldn't like each other, that they wouldn't even like themselves.

"Very well. Jack's plan was to pay humans to leave our vehicles at the bottom of the cliff, but it would be even better if some of our own people were to drive them there a few minutes behind the Coun'hij motorcade."

"Thank you very much!"

Dylan shook my free hand with such enthusiasm that it was almost painful to watch. Someone old enough to be my grandfather shouldn't be so overcome with excitement when I allowed him to do something he'd been wanting to do for years. It wasn't right for me to have this kind of power over other people and yet there wasn't any other way to keep my friends safe. Other than maybe Jack, I was the best killer we had.

I was the only one who could hope to keep a dozen strong-willed predators all moving the same direction, all working towards a common goal, but even that wasn't the scariest part. The scariest part was the question of what I'd become if or when my ability finally manifested.

Mallory hadn't ever been wrong before. Part of me was afraid that she was wrong now, that it had been too long and I wasn't ever going to manifest a power, but mostly I just hoped that I was going to manifest a spectacular, unbeatable power soon. That was the only way I was going to keep Kaleb and the rest of the Coun'hij from rolling over us sometime in the next few months.

"Go to Jasmin and tell her that I want her to begin training you. Given the lack of room and privacy it's probably going to be a while before she can do much with you, but she's the best we have and she might as well start thinking about what she wants to teach you."

"Thank you, Mr. Graves. Thank you."

The two of them backed away from me with smiles still plastered across their faces, and then they disappeared around a corner and it was just Brindi, Rachel and me.

"Alec, can we talk?"

I wanted nothing more than to call Carson, but I nodded. Rounding up the additional bodies we needed was more important than almost anything else right now, but a few minutes wasn't going to make any difference.

"Sure, Rach. What's up?"

"No, alone."

Rachel had the grace to look embarrassed. She reached out to take Brindi's hand and gave her an apologetic smile.

"I'm sorry, Brindi, but I really need to talk to Alec alone."

Brindi shook her head and latched onto my hand even tighter. "No, I'm not going anywhere."

Rachel shot me an imploring look, but that probably wouldn't have been enough to sway me if I hadn't spent far too much time lately worrying about Brindi's increasing attachment to me.

"Brindi, please go help James and the rest cross-load the supplies we bought into Jack's vehicles."

There was a flash of something in Brindi's eyes that disappeared so fast that I wasn't sure I'd correctly categorized it.

"They don't need my help. They're stronger and faster than me and I don't want to be there, I want to be here."

"Those are all true statements, but I want you to go help them regardless."

"I saved your life."

Her words came out in a low hiss, but that didn't surprise me. It was just the next step of the behavior I'd been noticing ever since I'd taken her with me to see Carson. I still meant everything I'd told him, but I hadn't counted on just how much her addiction would change her or how fast it would all happen.

"Let go of my hand, Brindi."

"Or else you'll hurt me?"

"Listen to yourself. You just tried to use the fact that you saved my life to compel me not to make you help James and the others. Did you even stop to think about the logic behind your argument? They have all saved my life dozens of times over the years."

It was like I'd hit her with a club. She was trying to come up with some rebuttal to what

I'd said but she couldn't seem to get any words out.

"Your having saved my life means that I owe you in at least some small way, but it doesn't make you more important to me than the friends and family who've been there for me again and again. I'm sorry if I've given you the wrong impression by keeping you so close since you were hurt in Chicago, but you're not the most important person in my life."

"So what, you're going to just toss me aside like so much trash now that it's not convenient for you to have me around? I would have done anything for you, I tried, but you told me not to."

I looked pointedly at her hands, both of which were now desperately wrapped around my bare arm.

"If you ever want to touch me again then you need to let go of me right now."

I could see the calculation going on behind her eyes. If she didn't believe I'd go through with it then now was the time to refuse, to play on my guilt for having addicted her and force me to back down. It was the surest route to some kind of twisted codependent relationship where she'd never have to go without a fix.

If, however, there was even the slightest chance that I was willing to cut her off completely, then she would be cutting her own throat by disobeying me. For the barest of seconds she refused to let go, and then she pried her fingers off of my arm with an almost tangible effort of will.

"Now what?"

She was refusing to look at me, so I reached out and gently pulled her chin around so she had to meet my gaze. It was risky, but I wanted to reward her for having forced herself to let go.

"Now you can go help James and the others, and when you are done moving everything I want you to stay out there and strike up a conversation with one of the others. If all else fails find the Petersons and talk to them, or listen to their conversation with Jasmin if they are having one. You can come find me once forty-five minutes have passed."

"You'll still be here?"

I could hear the impending tears. A part of her was convinced that I would leave and she'd never find me again. The fear was nearly all-consuming, but she was forcing herself to deal with it because she knew the alternative would be to defy me and watch as I walked out of her life.

"Yes, I promise. If I'm not in this exact spot ask one of the others to help you find me. I won't leave the school without you."

She nodded, a quick, choppy motion, and started for the door as if eager to start the countdown so she could return as soon as possible. I called out to her before she disappeared from view.

"I'm sorry, Brindi. I don't want to hurt you like this, but you've changed—even in just the last couple of days. I need you to be the strong young woman who saved me from death, not someone who will try to manipulate their way to an extended high. One of those people will be welcome in my life, the other won't be."

She nodded and strode quickly from view. I turned back to Rachel and found that she had wrapped her arms around herself as though trying to hold herself together. That or maybe force herself not to reach out and touch me.

"I'm sorry, Rachel. I didn't think about what it would be like for you to be all alone with only a bunch of shape shifters you can't ever touch for company."

She mustered a brave smile, but I could tell that my words had hit home. The revelation made a lot of other things suddenly make sense. She didn't approve of Brindi, but she'd still taken every possible opportunity to touch her.

Brindi was the only other human, the only other person Rachel didn't have to keep a careful distance from in order to avoid Brindi's fate. I'd taken Rachel away from our mother to save her from a terrible situation, but in a lot of ways her life had gotten even harder since leaving home.

"It's okay, Alec. I think a lot of it is just that seeing Brindi hang on you like that makes me think of Mom. I'm worried about her."

"Don't be, Mom will be fine, she always is."

"You're still mad that she didn't find a way to stop Dad from giving me to Vincent?"

My hand clenched into a fist and I suddenly had an overpowering urge to put it through a door. I took a deep breath and forced myself to relax.

"It's more than that, Rach. She didn't just fail to stop him, she wasn't going to tell you, wasn't going to even tell me. She didn't just fail, she never even tried."

"That's not fair, Alec. I understand why you're disappointed in her, but I also understand what it's like to be a human in a world filled with shape shifters. Mom's not perfect, but she's doing the best she can."

Rachel had moved towards me as though to wrap her arms around my middle in another hug, but I stepped back away from her.

"How can you even say that? I know she couldn't have fought off Vincent or Kaleb, but she could have at least told me what was going on."

"Why, so she could lose both of us? I'm glad you got me out of there, Alec, but even at the time I wasn't sure that I should be going along with your escape attempt. You and James both nearly died. If things had gone differently you *would* have died and I would have still ended up with Vincent."

My beast wanted to shout her down, but that wasn't fair. She'd turned away from me when I'd avoided contact with her so I reached forward and took her by the shoulders. She was trying to be brave, but I could feel her trembling underneath the thin material of her t-shirt.

"You can't live in might-have-beens, Rach. I could have died, or I could have been just a little faster and killed Brandon that night, thereby saving the world a lot of trouble. I did the best I could and this time things worked out. That's what Mom doesn't understand. I would have rather done my best and died than lived knowing that I didn't even try to save you."

Rachel reached up and brushed away the tears that were threatening to break free.

"I know, Alec, but she's all we have left and she's trying to do better. She's the one who got Jack the information about Agony. Not just that he'd been captured, but where they've been holding him and the route they are taking to move him back into the States. That had to have been dangerous for her, but she did it anyway because she knows that she's going to have to do better if you're ever going to forgive her."

I still wanted to be mad, but Rachel's revelation took the wind out of my sails. It was all still just straws in the wind, but they were all blowing the same direction.

I cleared my throat. "She's been telling everyone that you're the reason that I turned against Kaleb. I mean, there isn't any proof that it's her, but the evidence is all pointing that direction."

Rather than being happy, Rachel looked even more worried.

"That can't be safe, Alec. Kaleb will eventually find out that she's the one leaking all of this stuff and then he'll hurt her."

"Yeah, you're probably right, but there isn't anything we can do about it right now. Once we're through the next few days we'll see if we can find a way to warn her off. In the meantime, at least she's trying to do what she can to help."

Rachel studied my expression for several seconds before venturing to say anything else. "You haven't forgiven her yet, have you?"

"No, but I don't hate her quite as much as I did a few minutes ago and I can see a path to maybe eventually forgiving her."

"That will have to do for now."

I gave Rachel my best fake smile and then pulled out my phone. "I'm glad we had a chance to talk, Rach. We should spend some more time catching up once we get to the hotel, but if there isn't anything else urgent right now, I'd really like to make a couple of calls before Brindi comes back."

"Actually, there is one more thing. I want to come with you guys when you go to try and break Agony out."

"Absolutely not!"

"I'm not asking to be in the middle of the fighting, Alec, I just want to help. Let me babysit the cars with the Petersons. I'll be as safe there as nearly anywhere else."

"That's a lie and you know it. You'll be *safer*, but you won't be safe. Jack has contingency plans in case everything completely falls apart up above, but you'll still be at risk. You could be looking at a cross-country hell ride where you're trying to keep one step ahead of a bunch of Coun'hij enforcers who don't need to sleep as much as you and who have access to all of the NSA's satellite feeds."

"Which is no different at all from what the Petersons will be dealing with and a heck of a lot less risky than what the rest of you will be facing. I want to help, Alec. Please let me do this."

I could tell her no. She couldn't force me to let her into the operation and nobody was going to fault me for keeping her out of danger. A refusal was on the tip of my tongue, but I couldn't force it out.

Rachel had spent her entire life on the sidelines, wanting to help and having nothing to offer. If I told her no there was a chance that she would never offer again. Rachel put on a brave front, but she was more fragile than most of the rest realized.

"Okay, you can help with the cars."

"Thank you, Alec! Thank you so much."

That was the other reason it was so hard to deny Rachel anything. Her smile lit up the entire room.

"Just be careful, okay?"

A minute later it was just me alone in the classroom and there wasn't anything to stop me from making the calls I'd come here to make. I put a portable noise generator in front of the door and then dialed Shawn's number. He picked up on the second ring.

"Hey, this is Shawn."

"Hi, Shawn. It's been a little while. I'm hoping that you have some good news for me."

Shawn was silent for so long that I almost thought we'd lost our connection. "I've been waiting for you to call. The things you said have been on my mind a lot lately. This hasn't been an easy decision."

He wasn't using my name. That could just be because he was being extra security-conscious. If someone was listening in on our conversation they'd probably be running some kind of voice recognition software, but it never hurt to be careful.

Of course that might not be the case at all. Maybe he was trying to maintain some kind of deniability. As long as he didn't say my name he could always claim that he'd thought he was talking to someone else.

"I can't promise the kind of force you want, but I've decided that you're right. This is important, and if you tell me that you've got a good plan, one that will let us get in and out without leaving any witnesses behind, then I'll bring eight of my closest two-legged friends to your party."

That was code for hybrids. He was bringing a total force of nine hybrids down to the ambush. It was like a huge weight had come off of my chest. For the first time in days I felt like I could breathe. Shawn's people would make the difference for us. Even if Carson couldn't get his mystery hybrid with the game-changing power to join up we should still have enough people to make it all work.

"I'm not going to lie to you, Shawn. I think our plan is good. I fully expect for us to be in and out in minutes, and I'm not planning on leaving anyone alive to tell tales, but there's always a chance that we'll miss someone."

Shawn's voice was remarkably relaxed considering that I'd just told him there was a chance that his cover would be blown.

"That's what I like about you. You never pull any punches. If everything goes according to plan then I'll be back in Chicago two hours after we finish up and nobody but us will ever know that I even left."

"And if things don't go according to plan?"

"Then my friends and I will spend the next several decades on the run. It will suck, but like I said, this is just too important for me to just sit around and do nothing. Send me an address and a time—I'll be there."

"Thanks, Shawn. I appreciate this."

"No problem. Someday you can come bail me out of a bind and we'll call it even."

He hung up and I stared at my phone in amazement. If I hadn't been operating under a time limit I would have just sat there and basked in the sense of accomplishment. Shawn coming down with more than half a dozen hybrids wasn't an accomplishment on the same order of magnitude as bringing the entire Chicago pack out in open support of the rebellion, but it was much better than I'd actually expected to achieve.

I forced myself back to the present and dialed Carson's number. I almost thought his phone was going to go to voicemail by the time he picked up.

"It's me. Did you have any luck bringing on the star talent you told me about?"

"Yes, his name is Grayson and he's onboard along with six other hybrids and a pair of wolves. I must caution you once again not to depend too heavily on him. He's failed, quite dramatically, in the past and the consequences were...severe."

The force composition was odd to say the least. Shawn could bring all hybrids because he was cherry-picking the best talent from the Chicago pack. He was obviously concerned about keeping things on the down-low, so he'd brought the best fighters he could as a way of maximizing his group's lethality while still economizing on numbers.

Carson on the other hand didn't seem to represent any kind of big organization. I'd come away with the impression that he was drawing from a small group of close associates, probably dispossessed like him. Based on that, I'd expected a lot more wolves and fewer hybrids. It was one more oddity where Carson was concerned, but his worries about Grayson seemed the more pressing item to explore.

"What happened, Carson? Who is this guy and why are you even bringing him on the operation if he's so completely undependable?"

The silence on the other end of the line remained unbroken for nearly a full minute before Carson finally mustered a response.

"I'm sorry, there is simply too much there that I can't tell you. Suffice it to say that Grayson failed to protect people who were important to me. Among those people was someone who was important to more than just me. As to why I'm including him, that is a more complicated answer. I'm including him because we lose nothing by having him along, but it's more than that. He needs a chance to redeem himself just like I need a chance to forgive him."

His answer hung in the air for several seconds while I tried to decide best how to respond.

"I'm sorry to press, but the safety of everyone involved in this operation is my responsibility. Isn't there anything else you can tell me?"

"The king is dead, long live the king."

"I'm sorry, I don't understand."

"I know and I apologize, but I can't say any more than that. You'll have to accept my word that he's an acceptable security risk or we'll have to part ways."

I was tempted to tell him that what he was describing was a deal breaker for me. With the eight hybrids Shawn was bringing, the odds were good that I wouldn't need Carson or his people. Part of me didn't want to deal with the headache of dealing with someone Carson was so unsure of.

I resisted the temptation though. Even if I could get by without Carson and his people on this particular operation, I couldn't afford to offend potential allies that I might need at some point in the future.

"Very well, I accept your terms. Do you have an encrypted e-mail address that I can send a meeting time and place to?"

Carson's laugh was surprisingly boyish. "I'm afraid that using a cellphone is currently the extent of my technological prowess. If you'll give me a time and a place we can meet the day before the operation and I can review your plans then."

"Okay, that works for me. There's a city in New Mexico called Roswell. If you travel an hour and a half in the direction you had me travel from the car the last time we talked, you'll find me. I'll be in the hotel."

It wasn't bulletproof as far as making sure that nobody knew where we were going, but it was the best I could do.

I could hear Carson reaching for a pen and notepad and I waited while he wrote down my coded directions.

"Very good. Are you planning on bringing the item you stole from your father with you on this trip?"

It took me a minute to realize that he was talking about the massive two-handed sword that had been created back in the time of the monarchy.

"Yes, actually, it figures into my plans in a fairly central way."

"We'll need to talk about that. Such...items...aren't meant to be used under these kinds of circumstances, but bring it nonetheless. There are things I can teach you about its use."

Carson hung up before I could even begin to process the idea that he'd just told me that he knew how to use my sword, that he was familiar with a style of fighting that had disappeared centuries before either of us had been born.

Chapter 21

Alec Graves
Ambush site
Southern New Mexico

It defied belief that I'd been on such a dramatic high such a short time before. The rendezvous with Carson had gone just fine. He'd brought all of the people he'd promised to bring, but they were an odd bunch.

They were quiet, even more so than you would have expected from a group of shape shifters who were forced to associate with other moonborn they didn't fully trust. They were almost cliquish. It was the kind of thing that you expected out of a pack that had a long history together. It wasn't the right vibe to be getting from a bunch of dispossessed wolves and hybrids whose only common tie was Carson.

There was something there that I needed to figure out, preferably sooner rather than later, but the eve before a big fight wasn't the time to be picking at the threads currently holding our Frankenstein coalition together.

One of Jack's contacts, motivated by a hefty bribe, had come through for us in a big way. We currently had a live, scrambled, feed from one of the government surveillance satellites over the area, which meant that Rachel and the Petersons were watching—in real time—the progress of the motorcade carrying Agony.

We'd arrived at the scene of the ambush about an hour after sunrise. It was still cold enough that thermal tracking was a problem, but we'd spent the last hour and a half huddled under silver, reflective blankets which Jack said would break up our thermal picture if Kaleb currently had someone monitoring the area.

It was good that Jack's uplink was working because everything else felt like it was mere minutes from falling apart.

Shawn hadn't showed up. He was more than half an hour behind schedule and he hadn't answered the one call that I'd risked making on the satellite phone that I'd brought along. It was a bad sign, and Carson was smart enough to know exactly how much danger we were in.

"The other group you've been expecting isn't coming, is it?"

"It's not looking good. I can't say for sure that they aren't on their way still, but it's definitely not looking good."

AMBUSHED

I held up the small military-grade radio in my left hand. "Rachel has been watching the area for me and she says that there aren't many other vehicles on the road right now. If we were going to get any company, either expected or otherwise, they should be on the road right now, but Rachel said that there's only one or two vehicles on the road right now that could make it here before the convoy comes through."

"They could have split up their men to help disguise the fact that they are on the way."

I gave him a humorless smile. "We're not talking about the good guys anymore; you're worried that a bunch of enforcers are on their way here to spring a counter-ambush."

"I'd be lying if I said the thought hadn't crossed my mind."

I shrugged. "It's possible, but Rach said that the closest vehicles are subcompacts. Even if they had split up into three different cars they still couldn't move very many people in vehicles that small."

Carson pondered my answer for several seconds. You couldn't pack shape shifters, especially not the super-aggressive hybrids who usually ended up working for the Coun'hij, in tighter than maybe two per car when you were dealing with transport that tiny. It was persuasive evidence that our operation hadn't been blown despite the fact that Shawn hadn't shown up, but it wasn't a guarantee.

Unfortunately, we weren't in a business that provided those kinds of guarantees. The underlying math behind our situation hadn't changed. We had a large group of both hybrids and wolves and we had a secret weapon in the form of Grayson who apparently was capable of throwing large groups of hybrids into uncontrollable seizures.

If Grayson's ability worked as promised then we would be up against something like a dozen hybrids all of whom would be completely incapacitated for the period of time it would take us to close and deal with them. If it didn't work then we were going to have a pretty rough fight on our hands.

"All of the arrangements for our getaway are still looking good then?"

"Yeah, I had Rachel speed up a little so that she isn't as far behind Agony's moving prison, but I can't have her get much closer without potentially causing Agony's guards to get suspicious."

"Very well, I think we should proceed then."

I tried to maintain my composure; I mostly succeeded, but I couldn't completely suppress a sigh of relief at the news that I wasn't going to have to scrap the operation at the last minute. Carson didn't seem to notice though. He was eyeing the sword strapped to my back. He'd been doing much the same all morning, but so far he hadn't been ready to get whatever it was that was bothering him off of his chest.

I thought maybe he'd turn away again without saying anything, but he finally sighed and started unzipping the large, slender black bag that he'd been carrying around all morning. A few seconds' work revealed a sword that was eerily similar to mine.

His wasn't quite as ornate, not that mine was in any way ostentatious, but other than his lacking the complex royal sigil on the blade, the two weapons were nearly identical. They were both massive blades that no human, regardless of how strong, could have possibly wielded effectively.

My sword was the weapon of a king, and his had originally been commissioned for a lower-status hybrid, but they were both meant to be carried into battle by six-and-a-half foot tall hybrids. It was hard to think of many situations where a single hybrid wasn't deadly enough, but they existed and swords like this had been envisioned as a way of allowing my kind to meet nearly any opponent on equal terms.

"Where did you get that?"

The question burst out of me before I could second-guess the impulse.

"It was a gift from someone who meant the world to me. That same individual instructed me in its use."

"How is that possible?"

Carson gave me a sad smile. "There are many, many things you don't know, Alec Graves. You're heir to an incredible legacy but even you don't know everything that has transpired since your family fell from power. Suffice it to say that there are places still where knowledge that most of our kind believes to have been lost is still treasured and passed on."

"Do you know how to make more of them? The swords, I mean, do you know the secret to their manufacture?"

"Why? If I did know the lost art of making these weapons, what would you use it for? Swords like this were the basis for how the monarchy was originally established. Would you use them to return your family to a position of preeminence?"

"I...I guess I've never thought that far. I would use them to overthrow the Coun'hij. I'm not sure what would come after that."

Carson sighed. "Believe it or not, I understand your desires. When I was much younger than I am now I felt much the same way, but my instructor was adamant about one thing. He never wanted me to take up this weapon against others of my own kind."

"He thought they should only be used against the werewolves and jaguars?"

"Yes, vampires as well, but the key was that I not use the gift he had given me to slaughter other wolves and hybrids. I would ask a boon of you. Do not take your weapon into this fight, don't dishonor its legacy."

It meant a lot to Carson. I could tell as much, even if I didn't share his sentiment. The silence stretched out between us as I tried to come up with a response that honored his concerns without giving up the edge I needed.

"I'm sorry, Carson. I understand why you don't want to see me use this weapon against other hybrids and I think it's very admirable that you've honored the memory of your teacher, but I can't give up an edge that might make the difference between my friends dying or surviving what's about to come."

Carson looked away from me for a long moment and when he looked back his face was even more grave than it had been a second before.

"Very well, I see that I must offer something of value to you in exchange. I will not ask you to risk the lives of your friends. I would suggest a trade. If you will leave your sword next to that stream over there I will leave mine there as well."

I opened my mouth to refuse him, but he wasn't done.

"If the fight starts going against our people then the two of us can fall back to our weapons and I will help you save those you care about. In exchange for your doing this, once we complete this operation I will begin your instruction."

"You would teach me to use a sword knowing that I would use it against the Coun'hij?"

"I would agree to teach you now in order to avoid seeing your blade dishonored today and in the hopes that I'll be able to convince you later on to use it only for its intended purpose."

I looked out over the barren landscape to the west as I considered his words. Nothing seemed to be moving for miles. The closest thing to life that I could see was a plane that was high enough up that it didn't seem to be moving at all.

"I accept your proposal."

We walked over to the spot Carson had indicated a short distance from the stream that Jack had pointed out in his original briefing. As I gently set my sword down on the bag next to Carson's I notice that the stream was much louder than I'd expected, but it was the kind of inconsequential observation that couldn't hold my attention. I was too busy calculating distances and travel times to worry about how fast the stream was flowing.

It wasn't the perfect spot to leave the weapons, at least not for the purpose I thought we were most likely to need them for, but it was good enough and it would mean that I got to take over the most exciting part of the upcoming fight.

Carson and I walked back toward the road and everyone else. All three groups were starting to get antsy. It was nearly time for the motorcade to show up. As Jack shot me a questioning look, Rachel came on over the radio.

"We're in position and your target is inbound. You have about two minutes. The porcelain doll is struggling. Hurry every chance you get."

AMBUSHED

That last bit had been a reference to Brindi. She hadn't liked being forced to stay with Rachel and the others, but she had no place in the middle of what was about to happen. If anything went wrong there would be no way to get her out safely. By now she was deep in the throes of withdrawal, but I couldn't worry about that now.

I held up the radio so everyone could see it. It was an unnecessary gesture, we'd been close enough that everyone had already heard Rachel's message.

"We're a go. I'll take point on the semi. Jack, you're with James. Everyone get in position!"

Jack and James took off at a dead run towards the edge of the canyon while the rest of us moved further down the road. Carson gripped my arm—there was a reassuring solidness to the gesture—and then he turned to follow the main body of our group as I headed in the other direction at a jog.

I made it to James and Jack as they were dragging the first set of spike strips out on to the road. We'd run ropes to a nearby tree so it was just a matter of pulling on the free end until the slack on the rope was all used up. Once they hit the end of the rope, the collapsible, accordion-like construction of the spike strips expanded out and they dropped the strips into exactly the right place.

I crossed over to the other side of the road and crouched behind a rock as they ducked behind a tree and then there was nothing left to do but wait.

I knew we wouldn't have to wait long. Rachel's estimate had been right on; I could already hear the sound of engines laboring to pull the vehicles of Agony's moving prison up the steep grade.

A couple of seconds later the two lead cars, a pair of black SUV's, came up over the lip of the canyon and hit our spike strips. Neither vehicle went careening out of control, even though the spikes worked. They were equipped with run-flat tires just like I'd suspected they would be. That was okay though, we'd planned around that.

I felt Jack and James shift forms in twin surges of power and then joined them. My beast rose eagerly to the surface with a pulse of energy that forced me into my hybrid form with a flare of shadow pain that was gone almost before it even got started.

The semi-truck was almost even with me when I abandoned my cover and started sprinting towards the road. A hybrid was no match for a wolf, not across any kind of longer distance, but for short bursts it was hard to beat the sheer explosive power of a hybrid's muscles, especially when combined with the traction provided by the talons on our feet.

It took me only two steps to match speed with the huge truck, and then on the third I was overtaking it. The odds were that the driver was a shape shifter, but events were happening too fast even for one of our kind to process everything.

Carson and the rest had stepped out of concealment as soon as they felt the three of us shift forms. That combined with the panicked reports coming from the two lead vehicles had directed the truck driver's attention up ahead rather than right next to him where the danger actually was. Even if that hadn't been the case, it probably wouldn't have made any difference, the cab of the truck was too small to allow him to shift with any degree of safety.

I put my right fist into the back panel of the cab. There wasn't any way to know for sure what was underneath the shiny exterior, but it was a good bet that there was some kind of structural steel member in the corner.

My claws went through the thin metal like it was paper and then I closed my fist around something hard. I'd found the frame and I used it to give myself extra leverage as I pushed off the ground and spun clockwise so that my left fist went through the driver side window in a spray of glass shards.

The way his body moved as my claws hit his chest told me that he hadn't been wearing a seatbelt, so I pulled him out of the cab through the window that I'd just destroyed. I didn't look to see where he landed, he was already dead.

Hybrid claws hadn't exactly been designed with the idea of being capable of fine manipulation, but that didn't matter this time. I grabbed hold of the door and threw my weight against it. The back end of the door popped free with a squeal of overstressed metal, but the hinges on the front held just enough to save me from losing my hold on the big diesel entirely.

I rocked backwards and then threw myself into the cab as I shoved my beast down far enough to trigger another shift in forms. I hit the driver's seat in my human body and then made a grab for the wheel as I started to slide back out toward the road. A second later I had the brakes and the clutch depressed as far as they would go.

There was a sickening crunch and jolt from behind the truck as one of the tailing vehicles crashed into the back of the trailer, and then another black SUV pulled up next to me. Nothing about this operation would have worked in a world where my enemies used firearms, but luckily that wasn't the world I lived in.

I spared a thought to hope that James and Jack had been out of the way when that other car had crashed into the back of me, and then I threw the wheel hard to the left. Even moving as slowly as it was, my diesel slammed into the SUV with enough force to send it off of the road.

I hadn't put on my seatbelt either, and the force of the impact nearly sent me flying out of the cab. The metal of the steering wheel deformed slightly under the pressure of my grip and the stress of keeping me in my chair, and then the massive semi-truck finally ground to a halt.

I cut my arm on a shard of metal as I dropped down from the cab, but it didn't matter. I shifted to hybrid form before my feet even hit the ground and charged towards the closest SUV. Each of the black vehicles would have between three and five shape shifters inside which meant that we were facing somewhere between twelve and twenty of the Coun'hij's enforcers.

Depending on how many hybrids we were up against, it might still be a stiff fight if Grayson's ability didn't come through for us. Because of that it was vital that we kill as many of them as we could before they managed to get out of their cars and transform.

Hitting the SUV had slowed the big diesel faster than I'd originally planned. We wanted to get it to a stop as soon as possible so that James and Jack could get the trailer opened up and Agony out of there, so that was good except I was still a couple dozen yards away from Carson and the rest.

The driver of the SUV I'd hit was already stumbling out of his ride. He saw me coming and shifted forms, but I was already airborne. I cleared the twisted black collection of wreckage in a single bound and hit the driver like a ton of bricks.

He was a hybrid by the time I collided with him, but he didn't have any momentum on his side and I'd been moving at a full sprint. I led with my feet and my talons sank into his chest as my weight bore him to the ground. He got off a couple of weak slashes to my hip and side before hitting the ground hard enough to shake up even a hybrid.

I never gave him a chance to recover. As half a dozen wolves streaked past me, headed for the SUV that had crashed into the tractor-trailer from behind, I reached down and ended his life with a couple of well-placed slashes of my own.

I lunged back to my feet and threw myself at the SUV. The windows on this side hadn't been broken and the tinting on them was too dark to tell if anyone was still inside so I just put my right hand through the back window and my left hand through the middle window.

I'd been hoping to catch *someone* still inside the vehicle, even though that would tend to mean that there were more hybrids in each vehicle rather than fewer. The claws on my left hand came up empty, but my right hand tore through a frail human body. I closed my fist around the enforcer I'd just wounded and tried to pull him out towards me. The angle wasn't as good as it had been with the semi driver.

The crunch of broken bones and crumpled metal told me all I needed to know. I let go and spun around to block an attack as one of the other hybrids finally made it around the SUV and tried to engage me.

AMBUSHED

I could see another hybrid out of the corner of my eye. He was headed towards me from the other direction. I was about to be surrounded and outnumbered. I jumped up and backwards, landing on the top of the SUV as the first hybrid who'd engaged me sheared through the side of the vehicle with one swipe of his claws.

With the structural integrity of the SUV now having been compromised, the roof I was standing on started to give way. I threw myself off of it, but the roof wasn't sturdy enough anymore to give me a very stable launch platform.

I hit the ground, tucked my shoulder, and rolled. I came to my feet after the first full revolution, and spun around just in time to intercept another attack that would have probably severed my spine. I'd bought myself a second or two, but I couldn't turn and run again and two more hybrids were nearly within arm's reach of me.

I backpedaled furiously, trying to buy myself enough room to flee, and then suddenly Carson was at my side. He blocked another slash, but he didn't *just* block it, he blocked with enough force and the perfect angle to open up the entire left side of the other hybrid. Reflex took over for me and I stepped in and drove my claws into the enforcer's side.

It wasn't a clean blow. My claws penetrated, but they grated on ribs that were nearly as strong as steel and the angle wasn't quite right. I could feel his heart pulsing just out of reach, but he'd already recoiled from me. He reeled away, injured but not dead, and then it was Carson and I against two more of our kind.

At that moment I wished I'd argued with Carson and kept hold of my sword. There was a decent chance we could defeat two enforcers, but the third one would be back in just a couple of seconds. I hadn't killed him and that was going to cost us.

The enforcer on the right charged forward, juking at the last second to avoid my attack, and hit me with his shoulder at the better part of thirty miles per hour. It should have leveled me, but luckily I'd already been turning slightly to the left.

I felt muted stabs of pain as two of my ribs broke, and he sent me spinning away wildly out of control, but he hadn't managed his objective. I dropped down on all fours, claws and talons digging into the rocky ground in an effort to stop myself, and then it happened.

More than half of the enforcers suddenly seized up. I was positioned perfectly to see it. I'd been knocked over to one side of the battle and I'd come to a stop looking over at everyone else. We were outnumbered by a greater margin than I'd expected even in my worst-case scenarios.

They hadn't just packed five hybrids into every vehicle, they'd put another five hybrids in the trailer with Agony. We'd been up against twenty-five hybrids and they were some of the best the Coun'hij had access to. The wolves had made it to James and Jack in time to save them from being killed out of hand, but it had been a close thing. Even with the additional help, they'd been losing, but Grayson's gift leveled almost every hybrid from the battle that had been raging at the back of the convoy.

James and Jack each stumbled over to an enemy hybrid so that they could deliver a coup de grâce, but it was the wolves who really mopped up the enforcers back there. Carson's opponent hadn't been incapacitated, but both the hybrid opposite me and the one I'd nearly killed a second ago were down.

As I darted over to finish off one of the two downed hybrids I saw that our hybrids from the front of the caravan were dealing quite handily with the enforcers up there. Grayson's power hadn't knocked as many of them down, but Carson's people had been less heavily outnumbered to start with and the wolves he'd brought were gleefully pouncing on the incapacitated enforcers while the rest of our people held their own against the unaffected hybrids.

I ended the closest hybrid with a single clean blow to his neck, and then started towards the one I'd stabbed in the chest a few seconds previously. I wanted to go help Carson, but it would have been foolish to pass up the chance to kill two hybrids in exchange for entering what could still end up being an extended fight. I was just going to have to hope that Carson could hold out for long enough for me to make it over to him after the second hybrid was dead.

It turned out that I shouldn't have worried, about the larger battle or Carson either one. Something as massive as a hybrid takes several seconds to bleed out even from a lethal wound, but by now some of the enforcers who'd been injured first were dead, which apparently freed up some of Grayson's capacity.

As I killed the second hybrid, a scattering of additional hybrids at the front of the convoy were dropped to the ground by Grayson's ability. Carson had indicated that once Grayson's power was working that the biggest concern was that he'd lose his focus and the seizures would stop, but even if that happened right now the battle was ours. The Coun'hij forces had simply lost too many people to have any possible hope of winning.

I turned towards Carson and found that he'd wrapped his opponent up in some kind of complicated hold. I'd never seen anything like it, and apparently the enforcer hadn't either. It was like someone had modified human-style grappling and turned it into something that worked with a hybrid's unique joints and musculature. The enforcer was still struggling, but his efforts were more and more ineffectual with each passing second.

Before I could make it over to Carson he casually released his enemy and repositioned again. This time the hold left Carson's right hand free. Less than a second later Carson was rolling away from the other hybrid, but not before opening up several key arteries in the Coun'hij's enforcer. There wasn't any need to worry about that particular hybrid ever again. He might manage to struggle to his feet, but he'd be dead before he took two steps.

Carson took off towards the rest of his people, but there wasn't any need to hurry. As I watched, the last enforcer was dispatched and then it was only Grayson who was still thrashing about in the throes of the seizures that his power inflicted on him.

I hurried to the back of the trailer and as bad as things were back there I knew they could have been so much worse. James and Jack were both bleeding from dozens of wounds, some shallow, others not. Two of Jack's wolves had shifted back to human form and were doing their best to staunch the bleeding while their surviving fellows ran back into the trees to grab the first-aid kits that we'd left there.

Unfortunately two of Jack's wolves hadn't lasted long enough for first aid to be applied. Jess, Alison and Jasmin were all hurt too. They weren't bleeding as badly as Jack and James, but they'd all shifted back to human form already in an attempt to kick-start the healing process.

"Carson, we need some help back here if you've got anyone you can spare!"

I probably hadn't needed to yell, not considering how acute shape shifter hearing was, but it was gratifying to hear Carson instantly detach two of his people to come back and help with our wounded. Under other circumstances I would have simply stayed in hybrid form. I'd already shifted twice today, but I dropped down next to Jasmin, shifting back to human form so that I could help apply pressure to the nasty gash in her arm that was dripping an alarming amount of blood.

Jack's wolves made it back only a few seconds later and Carson's people weren't far behind them. A slender brunette whose name I couldn't remember shouldered me aside once she had a tourniquet on Jasmin's arm.

"It's only temporary until I can get her sewn up."

I stood, looking around to see where I was needed, but the medics seemed to have everything well in hand. One of Jack's people had grabbed the radio on their way back. I accepted it with a nod of thanks and then depressed the transmit button.

"The operation was a success, but we've got wounded, get up here as quickly as you can."

"We're on our way!"

I let the hand holding the radio drop to my side as I started towards the back of the trailer. I only made it two steps before Jack swore.

He was white as a sheet and it was obviously painful for him to raise his hand, but he was pointing off to the west. I turned to see what he was pointing at and my blood ran cold.

The plane that I'd noticed from before the attack had gotten closer, but that wasn't the worst part. The plane had loosed a thin trail of tiny black shapes, shapes that were descending with the blinding speed of an unchecked fall.

They were moving our direction as they fell and there were nearly thirty of them. It had to be the Coun'hij. Nobody else would have been sending in people this late into the fight. Shawn would have just stayed in the plane once it was clear that we'd carried the battle. It was ironic that they'd hit on the same delivery mechanism that Jack had been counting on using to get us out if things went bad. Ironic, but terribly inconvenient.

I did some quick calculations in my head. We were a hundred yards from the edge of the canyon and we had wounded. It was going to take time to get our people to the extraction point, but by the same measure, Rachel and the others were still a ways from the road. They had at least two or three minutes of driving cross-country across some nasty terrain before they'd even be able to start up the gigantic hill that separated us from them. We just didn't have very much time left.

I lifted the radio back up to where I could talk into it. "Belay that order. Go with the original plan, we've got company, we'll be coming to you."

Carson and his people must have overheard Jack's oath. They all arrived a couple of seconds later. Carson was supporting Grayson, who seemed uninjured but strangely disconnected from everything.

As Carson set Grayson down his people started picking up the wounded. I knelt down in front of Grayson. "Can you stop them, Grayson? We need your help or we're in trouble."

Carson shook his head at me. "Don't waste your time. Either he'll help or he won't. Either way our course is the same. We've got to get the wounded to the extraction point."

Our people were already moving. The uninjured wolves, who were all back in human shape by now, were lifting the worst of the injured up onto the shoulders of a few of the less injured hybrids. It was the quickest way to move everyone, but it was going to be close.

I looked over at the falling black-clothed figures and saw the first of the parachutes deploy. They'd waited until the last possible second in order to make sure that they would have the minimum flight time possible.

I threw myself into the back of the semi and sprinted towards the gigantic cage secured to the very front of the trailer by massive nylon straps. The tired-looking man who looked up at me had been beaten at least half a dozen times. The collection of mottled bruises across his arms had to all be fairly recent to not have already faded. Apparently the average Coun'hij enforcer was every bit as sadistic as Brandon or Vincent.

The cover that made it impossible for someone on the inside of the cage to open it up was incredibly complex, but the actual locking mechanism was dead simple. It took me all of two seconds to throw open the door to his cage and half support, half drag him out of it.

I could feel the clock ticking in the back of my head as we made our way to the back of the trailer. "Agony, I presume?"

"Yes, who are you?"

"Alec Graves. You may not have heard that I ran away from home a few weeks ago."

Agony stumbled and would have fallen down if I hadn't been supporting him. "When you say it like that you sound like a rebellious teenager."

By the time we reached the end of the trailer he was walking better and he actually just threw himself off the back, shifting to hybrid form a split second before he landed. I followed suit with an equivalent surge of power.

Carson was waiting for us just behind the trailer. All of our seriously wounded people were already back at the edge of the canyon and everyone else was spread out between us and the enforcers, most of whom had already landed.

I was just in time to see the last of the new arrivals undo their parachute from a height of about ten feet up. They too shifted shapes as they hit the ground, landing in a spray of dust and rock shards.

I turned on Carson to demand an explanation for the scattered formation, but he preempted my question.

"They needed to be close enough to quickly dispatch anyone Grayson manages to drop. I told them to keep enough distance that they can make it back to the extraction point ahead of the enforcers if it comes to that."

I opened my mouth to approve his decision and then it happened. Our people had done exactly as he'd ordered. They had plenty of separation between themselves and the Coun'hij's people. There was enough room that no normal hybrid could have hoped to run any of them down, except that they weren't up against a normal hybrid.

One of the figures in the front of the enforcer ranks suddenly exploded into motion so fast that even in my hybrid form I couldn't fully follow what had happened. One second our people were calmly falling back towards our wounded teammates and then in the next one of our hybrids had fallen, hamstrung by the one hybrid I'd been most worried about running into.

Brandon didn't even bother finishing off the hybrid he'd maimed. He left Carson's man lying in the dirt and sprang at another of Jack's wolves.

She was fast, but even her preternatural speed wasn't enough to save her. In two seconds Brandon had dispatched two of our people and everyone we had was in full flight back towards us.

"Jump!"

Both of the individuals Brandon had attacked had fallen without any sound louder than his claws rending their flesh. It was an eerie kind of near silence for such wanton slaughter. My voice shattered that silence, cutting through the air with all of the urgency I felt.

I didn't do any fancy estimates this time because I'd already done them. From the second I'd arrived at the ambush site I'd been worrying about what would happen if Brandon arrived. I'd already seen that the wounded hadn't started putting on their parachutes. They'd probably been worried about giving away the fact that we had an exit strategy in place.

Under other circumstances it wouldn't have been the wrong call. Brandon and his people would have moved towards us even more quickly if not for the fact that they thought they had the bulk of our forces trapped between them and a sheer drop of more than six hundred feet. That time had bought me the breathing room to get Agony out of his cage, but it was going to get a lot of people killed now.

Some of our people were hurt badly enough that they would need help putting on their parachutes and others were going to have to team-jump off because they wouldn't be able to jump far enough out to avoid the cliff on their way down. We needed time, time for people to get their parachutes on, time for the less injured to get back and help throw their fellows far enough out that they could clear the cliff face.

I was already in motion as I yelled the order for my people to get out in whatever way they could. The spot where Carson and I had left our swords was far enough away that there was a chance I could have made it there a second or two faster if I'd shifted to wolf form, but I couldn't risk it. I was already risking muscle cramps based on how many forms I'd worn in such a short time.

I couldn't court the risk of seizing up in the middle of what was headed my way, so instead I dug deep for every ounce of speed that my hybrid body was capable of mustering. I went from stationary to full speed within the first three steps and was still clawing for every bit of traction that I could muster.

Even for a hybrid, with our enhanced endurance, it still wasn't possible to sustain a full-out sprint for forever. By the time I'd covered half the distance towards the sword, my breath was already coming in big gulps. I wasn't out of gas yet, but my body was telling me that I couldn't keep up this ruinous pace for much longer.

The temptation to slow down, even just the little bit that would be required to make it so that I could keep the pace up for hours, was intense. It wasn't nearly as intense though as the desire to yell and tell Brandon who he was up against.

We hadn't spent much time around each other in hybrid form so there was a good chance that he hadn't recognized my single yell ordering everyone to flee. I heard him kill another one of my people in the time it took me to cross the halfway point. I'd expected the butcher's bill to be even higher than that, but apparently our wolves and hybrids were spread out enough now that it was taking him longer to run them down.

The sound of footsteps dogged me. I was almost certain that it was Carson, or maybe Agony behind me, but I didn't *know* that was the case. I'd whited out mentally from the exertion of getting so far so quickly. It was possible that the two of them had done the smart thing and headed for the wounded like I'd ordered. If it wasn't them I was probably okay, unless it was Brandon behind me. Nobody else should be able to run me down, not in the amount of time it would take me to reach the swords, but Brandon could.

I took another impossibly long step and decided the risk to my people was too great to wait any longer.

"Brandon, come fight someone who can give you a challenge. I beat you once, I can do it again."

Two more long seconds passed. I didn't hear anyone else die which meant that my ploy had worked. Brandon had stopped chasing my people and was after me instead.

I wasn't going to survive, but I'd known that going into this battle. I'd beaten Brandon because fighting on the roof of a moving train favored me in almost every respect. Even with those advantages I'd still almost died and it had been little more than sheer luck that had saved me.

Brandon would more than likely make quick work of me, but the simple fact that he'd detoured away to dispatch me would give my people the extra few seconds they would need to get away.

I started to lose my balance, but I used that to my advantage and converted my fall into a long roll that started almost directly above my sword. I came up winded but with a sword in my hand. I spun around to find that Carson had just finished grabbing his own weapon and Agony was only half a step behind him.

"Agony, run for the cliff! This was all to get you out of here."

"Sorry, Alec, but I'm staying. The way I see it the two of you probably have a decent chance of holding Brandon off. Even if we can't kill him, if I can get in a couple of good strikes I might manage to cripple him forever. Putting a monster like him out of the picture is more important to the resistance than I'll ever be."

I shot a frown at him, and then there wasn't time for any more talk. Brandon arrived,

AMBUSHED

blurring with speed, and his first attack nearly knocked the sword completely out of my hands.

Chapter 22

Adriana Paige
Ambush site
Southern New Mexico

Sitting motionless and quiet underneath the huge silver blanket for six hours was much harder than I'd expected it to be. Taggart and I had arrive at the ambush point in the company of Isaac, Heath, Dom and the others well before dawn and set up near the stream and then spent a mind-numbing amount of time waiting.

Our position was necessitated because while Heath could make us invisible and mask our scent he couldn't do anything about our heartbeats. He said that the stream would probably cover up any sound we might make, but he went even a step further.

When Heath had concealed himself from us in the parking garage there had been enough other heartbeats for his to get lost in the background noise. This time he'd brought half a dozen small electronic devices, all of which played recordings of running water.

It was eerie to lie on the ground and just trust that Heath would be able to edit the sensory feed of anyone else in the area. It got downright surreal when Alec and the rest showed up a couple of hours before we were expecting the caravan to come by.

I'd thought that my feelings for him had been strangled by the knowledge that he'd addicted some poor girl to his touch, but the reality was just the opposite. My feelings came back with a vengeance when I saw him.

The moment when he and the other guy walked over and set their swords down less than twenty feet away from me was the hardest. It took everything I had not to call out to him.

Taggart hadn't trusted Alec from day one. I was pretty sure that he thought Alec was there to ambush anyone who tried to free Agony, but I knew that wasn't the case.

Even before Alec and the others attacked the Coun'hij enforcers, I knew that Alec was there for the same reason we were. The fight between Alec and the rest was like a symphony of violence.

Before that moment I wouldn't have said that death and blood could be formed into a masterpiece. Even later on I was still sickened by just how many people had died in such a short period of time, but that didn't change the fact that there was an inherent *rightness* to seeing Alec and the others spring into action.

Hybrids were built for speed and strength and nothing tested the limits of their ability like combat against their own kind. From our vantage point I couldn't see Alec for most of the fight. Once he disappeared behind the truck I could only guess at what he did to stop the vehicle. I didn't stop worrying about him, but the fight between the two groups ahead and behind of the massive diesel captured my full attention.

For a second it looked like Alec's people were going to be overrun. I looked over at Taggart and Isaac, beseeching them to go help. I even went so far as to get onto my hands and knees to go help myself, but then one of Alec's people went into convulsions, which somehow sent most of their enemies into convulsions.

Isaac and Taggart waved me back down once it was clear that Alec's people were going to come out on top. It was obvious that neither of them wanted to come out in the open if they didn't have to. Taggart obviously didn't like the idea of Agony going off with Alec and the rest, but it was a safe bet that we were all on the same side which meant it would be much safer for all of us if we just stayed quiet until Alec's people had all left. What they didn't know couldn't be pulled out of them via torture or metaphysical means.

I thought my heart was going to stop when I saw the paratroopers. We were far enough away from everyone else that Taggart, Isaac and Heath risked a quick, whispered conference.

The key was obviously whether or not their guy who had sent everyone into convulsions could repeat his earlier feat, but by the time I realized that he was one of the ones that they'd dropped off with the rest of the injured, it was obvious that Alec's people were going to need a miracle.

Taggart motioned for me to hide behind a large tree and then he and the rest of the shape shifters started towards the group of injured people huddled up against the edge of the canyon.

I watched as they broke into a loose jog and then a few steps later they all disappeared as they moved far enough away from me that I was no longer inside of the area that Heath was shielding.

A few seconds later Alec and two more hybrids reached the swords they'd left behind such a short time before. Alec's hybrid was basically indistinguishable from any of the others to my merely human senses, but somehow I knew it was him as he stood a couple of dozen feet away from me, panting in an effort to fill his lungs with air.

He was magnificent, like some kind of pagan war god. Even his injuries, the long, bloody gashes that he'd collected while hidden by the massive bulk of the semi-truck, only emphasized the sheer strength and vitality flowing through him.

In the next instant one of the Coun'hij hybrids arrived and I saw something that dwarfed even Alec's strength and speed. Alec had yelled at someone named Brandon and I realized it must be Brandon that he and the others were fighting.

Brandon was death unleashed. My improved senses were capable of following a normal fight, even between two hybrids, but Brandon was simply faster than anyone else I'd ever seen. He attacked Alec with powerful, lightning-fast slashes that rocked Alec backwards and seemed to send a shiver of shock all the way up to Alec's shoulders.

Alec yelled for someone named Carson, but the other hybrid, the one with the sword, had already stepped forward, attacking Brandon with blindingly-fast slashes of his own. Meanwhile the third hybrid, who I was pretty sure was Agony since he was the one who had been locked up in the trailer, was circling around in an effort to get behind Brandon.

What followed was like nothing else I'd ever seen. It was like watching a trio of wolves try and bring down a grizzly bear. Alec and his friends surrounded Brandon and tried to lure him enough out of position to score a blow on him without giving him the opening he would need to kill one of them.

Alec was big, strong, and as fast as any hybrid I'd ever seen—other than Brandon—but it was obvious that he didn't know as much about using his sword as Carson did. Alec attacked with furious stabs and slashes that seemed always on the edge of committing him too much and thereby giving Brandon the opening he needed.

Carson on the other hand was all fluid grace. His blade was in constant motion. It was like a striking snake, licking out and back in before Brandon could respond to his attacks. Brandon was faster than Carson, but he was obviously having a hard time compensating for the greater reach Carson's massive sword provided him with.

It quickly became apparent that Agony was the one in the most danger. Unlike the other two he didn't have a sword to help offset Brandon's greater speed and strength. There were several times where only a quick attack or two from Alec or Carson kept Brandon from mowing Agony down, but Brandon seemed oddly reluctant to just bowl Agony over and take his lumps in the process of killing the smaller hybrid.

It took me nearly a minute to remember that Agony had the ability to permanently scar even another shape shifter. Brandon was obviously worried about being crippled.

It was a delicate balance. If Agony had been equipped with a sword then the three of them would have quickly killed Brandon. If Agony had been any other hybrid then Brandon would have overwhelmed him and then turned and killed Alec and Carson despite their weapons.

If Alec had been as experienced as Carson then they would have likewise been able to kill Brandon, but if Carson had been even just slightly slower or less skilled then Brandon would have overcome the trio facing him and gone on to kill the rest of Alec's people.

The four of them were moving so quickly that it felt like hours had passed, but when I risked a quick look away Brandon's people were still a few seconds away from the edge of the cliff. Alec's people were throwing themselves off of the edge in ones and twos. For an instant I thought they were committing suicide until I saw that they all had backpacks on and realized they had borrowed a page from the same playbook Brandon had used.

They were parachuting to safety, which was good for them, but it was obvious that they weren't all going to get away before Brandon's people arrived.

The clang of steel on claws brought me back around in time to see Alec reel back away from Brandon with blood dripping from his stomach. Brandon tried to follow up on his momentary advantage, but Carson stepped forward and his sword nearly took Brandon's head off.

Brandon changed directions instantly and threw himself towards Carson, trying to get inside the reach of Carson's blade, but then Agony was there and it was Brandon who was reeling away with a long set of gashes across his ribs.

Alec shook himself and sprang back into the fight without stopping to assess how badly he'd been hurt. Brandon knocked Alec's swing wide and then things were back to almost the same position they'd been a second ago. Brandon was in the middle of the three of them and they were shuffling around the perimeter trying to find an opening.

The only question now was whether the fight would end in the quick, lethal violence I'd seen so far today, or if it would turn into a prolonged battering match in which slow blood loss would eventually cause one of them to succumb to exhaustion and make a fatal mistake.

A flicker of motion off to my left caused me to risk another quick look over to the main battle. Isaac, Taggart and the rest materialized between one breath and the next and charged into the mass of Coun'hij hybrids before them with an abandon that should have gotten them all killed, but it didn't.

That was partially because Alec's people, those who hadn't thrown themselves off of the cliff already, realized what was going on and attacked from the other direction, but mostly it was because of Heath. Even from more than a hundred yards away I could see that Brandon's hybrids weren't reacting like they should have. They were stumbling into each other and they were slashing empty air in response to the faintest sound. In short, they were fighting blind.

It wasn't all of them—apparently there were limits to Heath's ability just like there had been limits to the number of people that Alec's guy had been able to throw into seizures at any one time—but it was enough to more than even the odds. I saw Isaac block a vicious but aimless attack from a big brown hybrid and then he stepped in and rammed his claws into the other hybrid's chest with enough force that he must have shattered the ribs between him and his opponent's heart. The other hybrid dropped bonelessly to the ground and then Isaac stepped forward to engage another enforcer.

Another hybrid, who I was pretty sure was Taggart, grabbed his opponent's wrist as the enforcer tried to slash him. A split second later Taggart was hanging from the enforcer's arm with the talons on both his feet embedded deep into the enforcer's chest.

The combination of pain and the weight of a full-grown hybrid, was too much. The enforcer collapsed to the ground as Taggart repositioned for a killing blow.

AMBUSHED

Dominic was the easiest person to spot in the entire melee. She was the only cat and she was bigger than most of the wolves. She waited until one of Alec's wolves started their attack and then she sprang at the same hybrid a split second later.

Her target heard the wolf coming and got his claws up to roughly the right area, but before he could firm up his grip on the poor wolf, Dominic hit him. She raked his back and shoulders with all four sets of claws as her powerful jaws clamped onto the back of his neck. It didn't look like it was a position from which she could execute a quick kill, but he couldn't get at her and he'd already dropped down onto all fours. Unless someone from his side intervened soon, he was as good as dead.

Our guys and girls were tearing through the Coun'hij enforcers like a chainsaw. Unless something catastrophic happened in the next minute or two, we were going to win at least that part of the battle, and once Brandon was outnumbered ten or fifteen to one, even he couldn't hope to win.

Only when I looked over at Alec and the rest it was obvious that their fight wouldn't last the minute and a half it would take for Taggart and the others to come help. Carson was bleeding now. His left arm looked like he'd had to use it to ward Brandon away and it had been terribly savaged as a result. It was dripping blood which

I was pretty sure would make it hard for him to continue to wield his sword, but he was losing even more blood from a long set of claw marks that had opened up from his left shoulder all the way down to his right hip.

Alec was in just as bad of shape. He'd taken a couple of nasty wounds to his legs and even I could tell that they were slowing him down. That was probably how he'd ended up with the new splotchy pattern of wounds dotting his upper chest.

Agony on the other hand seemed to have mostly stayed unmarked. He was still bleeding from a few places, but they weren't as deep as the wounds on Alec and Carson. Brandon still seemed reluctant to close with him enough to really hurt him.

It was obvious that Agony understood that more and more of the fight was falling to him. Even as I watched, he took the fight to Brandon, attempting to drive the bigger hybrid back into the reach of Carson's blade.

Brandon stepped to one side and sliced Agony's face open from just in front of his ear all of the way down to his chin. It was a vicious blow that came within millimeters of taking Agony's eye or opening up the carotid artery along his neck.

Brandon was bleeding from more than a dozen places and he seemed to be moving slower now too, but the blow he'd just landed on Agony was persuasive evidence of the fact that he was still incredibly dangerous. Once again, he'd been within inches of ending the fight with a single blow.

Agony backed up in an attempt to dodge Brandon's follow-up blow, but instead of pressing his advantage, Brandon turned and stepped into Alec. It was the kind of thing that Alec could have easily avoided just a minute or two previously, but he'd lost too much mobility and his sword was out of position.

Brandon's fist disappeared into Alec's chest and for a second I thought that he'd destroyed Alec's heart, but it was on the wrong side for that. Carson stepped forward, blade slicing towards Brandon's side aimed for approximately where the kidney would have been on a human, but Brandon intercepted the attack with his right hand as he let go of Alec and raked Carson's right arm from shoulder all the way down to his wrist.

Less than a second had passed and Agony threw himself forward in an attempt to save Alec and Carson. Even I could tell that Agony was going for the kill. Brandon's back was to him, which meant that all Agony had to do was latch on and then ride Brandon to the ground while Alec and Carson got out of the way. It was risky, especially against someone as fast as Brandon, but it was obvious that Agony couldn't hope to fight Brandon by himself.

For a second I thought Agony had done it. Brandon moved slightly, but not enough to deny Agony the shot at his back that the smaller hybrid was angling for. I expected Brandon to start thrashing about in an effort to try and buck Agony off of him, but instead the four of them stood frozen, motionless for nearly a full second before Agony dropped to the ground with Carson's sword through his chest.

Alec and the others were dead, they just didn't know it yet. Brandon had set up Agony perfectly by offering up the one target he'd known that no hybrid could pass up. It had been the perfect trap precisely because nobody, not even Brandon could have gotten out of the way in time, but it turned out that Brandon hadn't needed to.

Instead he'd just used his grip on Carson's right arm to angle Carson's blade up into Agony's heart.

As my mind registered what had just happened, I realized that I'd stepped around so that I was fully out from behind my tree.

It was a stupid thing to do, but that paled in significance compared to the fact that my gun was already out and rising up into the two-handed stance I'd spent so many hours practicing. I'd never even considered taking a shot at Brandon before this. The range wasn't too bad, especially against such a large target, but the four of them had been moving too quickly for me to guarantee that I wouldn't hit Alec or one of the others by mistake.

Only now that wasn't a consideration anymore. Agony was still between Brandon and I, but he was on his knees and falling. Alec was off to one side struggling to pull himself back up to his feet, and Carson's struggles to free himself from Brandon's cruel grip had moved him out of the line of fire as well.

My first shot took me by surprise. I'd acted out of reflex. I knew what my target was and my sights had finally lined up on it. I squeezed the trigger without even thinking about it and didn't even realize that I'd sent a round downrange until the gun bucked in my hand and I lost the sight picture I'd had on Brandon's chest.

Brandon was still insanely fast. He spun back around while I was still trying to bring my pistol back down so that I could get another shot lined up.

This time I overthought things. It was the first time that I'd intentionally fired in anger at a live target and I was scared that I wouldn't be able to get another center-of-mass shot before he started moving towards me.

Instead of waiting for my gun to finish coming back down so it was pointing at the center of his chest, I pulled the trigger again as soon as his head came into view over the barrel of my pistol. It would have been a perfect shot except for the fact that my hand tightened up slightly and pulled the barrel right at the last second. It was such a small movement that most people wouldn't have even realized what had happened, but it was enough that I missed him, creasing the side of his head rather than putting a round between his bestial eyes as I'd intended.

Brandon started towards me and his speed was mind-blowing. I couldn't have ever kept up with him except for the fact that he was still so far away. He needed to move his whole body more than two dozen feet. I only needed to move my hands fractions of an inch and with each step he took towards me he became a bigger target.

I pulled the trigger again and my nerves betrayed me a second time. The shot was low and right—it hit him, but it wasn't the killing shot that I'd hoped for.

I couldn't take a calming breath, there wasn't time for that, not when I was acting and thinking with the speed of a shape shifter, but I imagined myself taking in a slow, deep breath as I fought to bring the muzzle of my gun back down. It worked, I got another shot off and this one was only a quarter of an inch off where I thought his heart was positioned, but it wasn't enough. I was running out of time.

"Surround him! Don't let him escape!"

It was Alec yelling the words—I knew that—but they didn't mean anything to me until Brandon shifted forms and threw his slender wolf body to the side. I got one more shot off, one that went completely through his stomach and out the other side, and then he was lost among the rest of the trees.

The rest of our people were still a couple of seconds away, but Alec had bluffed Brandon into turning and running. By the time Brandon realized that he wasn't in as much danger as Alec had indicated, he must have decided that it wasn't worth the risk of circling back around to try and kill any of the rest of us. Even Brandon wasn't indestructible and he'd taken his share of damage over the last minute or two.

Chapter 23

Alec Graves
Ambush site
Southern New Mexico

I was trying to ease Agony's pain when everyone arrived. I turned to thank the new arrivals and was blindsided by a backfist that sent me sprawling.

"Stay away from him!"

As I came to my feet I realized that I still had my sword in my hand. I wasn't a match for what I'd been earlier, but by the same measure the big gray hybrid who had just hit me was no Brandon. If I hadn't already been in hybrid form my beast would have demanded that I shift. As it was, I sent out a pulse of power that exceeded anything else I'd ever displayed.

"Who the hell are you?"

"I'm Dream Stealer and you'd be wise to back down and do as I say."

My lips pulled back from my fangs.

"Please tell me that you're really stupid enough to threaten me in real life after all of the crap you pulled the last time you came at me in my dreams."

I stalked towards him on legs that weren't as steady as normal, but which I was confident would be more than up to the challenge of killing the infamous Dream Stealer if he didn't back down and show me the respect I deserved.

I was only a few feet away from striking range when the oddest surge of calm washed over me. The emotion was so strong that I almost accepted it, but my beast didn't like being manipulated. His emotions were simpler than mine and he knew now wasn't the time to relax and look weak.

"Carson, I thought you said you'd never use your gift to influence any of my decisions."

There was a moment of silence as Carson processed my words. Taggart was still trying to figure out what was going on, but then again he didn't know that Carson was more than capable of projecting any emotion he chose into those around him.

"You're correct, Alec. It's not right for me to manipulate you in that fashion, but I beg of you to reconsider what you're about to do. It not only dishonors your sword, it's incredibly rash. We've won today, but that doesn't mean that the Coun'hij is defeated. We can't afford to kill each other."

"Turn it off, Carson. No, don't just turn it off, put it back the way it was."

It was dangerous and not just because I was ordering around someone who was my superior when it came to weapons play and every other conceivable method of combat. Carson had come to me as an equal. He wasn't submissive to me, he was a partner, but by the same measure he'd been the one to escalate things.

I was either a dominant, a force unto myself, or I wasn't. Accepting his slights would just start me down a path that would result in me no longer controlling my destiny.

Another painfully long second passed and then my anger roared back. It was at least as strong as it had been before and possibly even stronger. It was a firestorm that demanded fuel. It wanted Dream Stealer as its first sacrifice, but that was actually the problem. The kind of rage I was feeling was never satisfied with one victim.

I would want another sacrifice and another after that. If I let it run unchecked, then sooner or later I'd find myself surrounded with nothing but devastation. I took a deep breath and then another. My beast reveled in the promise of glorious combat, but I forced my beast back down, bottled him up and crammed myself back into human form.

"Carson is right. I won't have the blood of potential allies on my hands."

Dream Stealer hadn't shifted and his anger was still burning so hot that he practically glowed even to my human vision.

"I'm not your ally, I'll never be that. Your incompetence has done nothing but get your own people killed. If you'd simply left things to us we would have easily dispatched everyone the Coun'hij sent to guard Agony."

A blond kid who didn't look old enough to shave yet stepped forward and cleared his throat. "That's not true. We couldn't have stood against Brandon like the three of them did. I tried to blind him like I did the rest of his men but I couldn't. It's something about his gift, it doesn't make him just physically stronger, it made him resistant to my ability as well."

Dream Stealer had practically spat his response at me, but if anything being contradicted by one of his own people fanned his anger even higher. He looked around as though expecting to marshal his troops, but he and Carson were the only two left in hybrid form. Everyone else had gradually shifted back as it became obvious that nobody other than Dream Stealer was interested in another fight.

A familiar figure stepped up to Dream Stealer's side. "Let it go. My people aren't going to fight Alec for you. He's done nothing wrong and risked a lot to accomplish the same end we came here for."

I did a double-take at the familiar face and the scent that up until now had been mixed in with everyone else's.

"Isaac? You're okay? I never in a million years expected to see you here leading a force like this."

Isaac gave me a tired smile. "I likewise never thought to be standing here opposite you. Your father was always harder on you than anyone else, but you were still his golden child. I never thought that anything could pry you away from his side."

His words were the gentlest recrimination possible, but they were still a recrimination. I'd stood by and let Kaleb exile Isaac for no real crime at all. Isaac had been creating a fourth power pole inside of the pack for no other reason than he'd been so much more controlled than most of the other hybrids.

Kaleb hadn't been willing to risk yet another faction inside of our pack and so he'd had one of the older hybrids challenge Isaac to a fight and then once Isaac had been beaten and humiliated, Kaleb had exiled him on pain of death.

There hadn't been anything I could have done to stop it all from happening, but by the same measure I hadn't even tried. I should have left then rather than waiting for two more years.

Carson looked at Dream Stealer with the kind of calm confidence that told everyone watching that he had no doubt as to his ability to defeat the other hybrid.

"I'm not going to let you hurt Alec."

Dream Stealer looked like he was going to throw himself at Isaac or possibly Carson, but he managed to restrain himself.

"Can't any of you see that he's not on our side? He lured you all here to make sure that you died. He's working for Kaleb; it's the only logical explanation for the trap that was waiting for us. He didn't set out to accomplish the same thing and the cost..."

Dream Stealer trailed off. It was like he was waking up from a terrible dream only the real nightmare was reality. He shifted forms and dropped down to his knees next to Agony.

I would have bet any amount of money that Dream Stealer would never show me, or anyone with me, his actual human form. Next to his name, it was the greatest secret he possessed, something he'd been guarding for more years than I'd been alive, but he seemed so overcome with grief that he'd forgotten all other concerns.

Dream Stealer was an old man. I'd expected that, but I'd never realized just how old he was. He took Agony's hands, hybrid claws and all, and tears started making their way down his face.

None of us needed a medic to tell us that Agony couldn't be saved. It was a miracle that he'd held on for as long as he had and it was a tragedy that Dream Stealer and I had let ourselves be drawn into that kind of dominance posturing while the man we'd both come here to rescue bled to death less than ten feet away from us.

Carson's sword, wielded by Brandon, had pierced Agony's heart. The smaller secondary organs scattered throughout his body had continued to constrict and relax, but they were primarily designed to help take over some of the ruinous load of keeping blood circulating through the system of a hybrid in the middle of extreme combat.

The sword in his chest was the only thing keeping Agony from bleeding out. If we removed it then he'd die in seconds, but if we didn't remove it he'd eventually bleed to death anyways.

"Someone get on the radio and get Rachel up here with the bagged blood we've got in the coolers."

I didn't realize that I'd dropped to my knees next to Agony until he reached up and gripped my arm. His claws could have easily ripped my arm off, but he was so careful that he didn't even draw blood.

"I appreciate the thought, but all you could do is prolong the inevitable. Even if you put blood into me the healing kick-start I'll get from shifting back to human form isn't going to be enough to repair my heart."

"You don't know that. Maybe it will be enough."

The words were torn from Dream Stealer, but Agony just gave him a weak smile. "We've had a much better run, you and I, than I ever expected."

Whatever Agony was going to say next was interrupted by a long series of weak coughs. He was bleeding more now. The movement of Carson's sword against his body as the coughs had torn through him had opened up the wound in his heart. His remaining time had just been cut in half. Maybe even worse.

"Send everyone else away. What I'm about to tell you is for you leaders."

I looked over and realized that Carson and Isaac had joined us at Agony's side. Even more astonishing, a slender blonde figure had taken a place next to Dream Stealer, next to Taggart with an ease that made it obvious that it was where she belonged.

My heart practically leaped out of my chest when I recognized Adri. I'd seen her shooting at Brandon, but somehow, in the heat of the moment, I hadn't realized that Adri was the shooter. Now that I recognized her, even the grimness of our circumstances almost wasn't enough to stop me from singing out in joy that we were finally a few paltry feet away from each other.

She made as if to stand and leave, but Agony shook his head.

"No, you should stay too, Adri. You're Taggart's heir. Alec, Carson, Isaac, Taggart, Adri.

You're the five who will be carrying on the fight once I'm gone."

Taggart looked like he was going to protest, but Agony silenced him with a look.

"Are they all gone, Taggart?"

"Yes, Cyrus. Everyone else is gone. They're out of earshot, it's just us."

Agony…Cyrus…nodded and then grimaced in pain. "I'm sorry, old friend. There is one secret I never told you. I would have, but I was always worried that they would find out and come after you. My silence was the only thing that kept you safe. As long as I didn't tell anyone about them, this could remain a purely shape shifter conflict."

"What do you mean, Cyrus? I don't understand."

There was an edge of hysteria to Taggart's question, but that was understandable. The things that Agony seemed to be implying were terrifying.

"There are layers inside of layers, Taggart. It goes back much longer than any of us initially realized, but by the time we understood what we'd gotten ourselves into it was too late to back out. You've all spent your entire lives thinking that the Coun'hij was the ultimate threat, but in many ways, they are just another pawn on the board."

Agony was visibly weakening with each passing second. He tried to get something else out, but another coughing fit came over him and when it was done his skin had gone an alarming blue-white.

We all watched, helpless, as Agony gasped for breath one last time and then died before our eyes.

Chapter 24

Adriana Paige
Ambush site
Southern New Mexico

Taggart's scream was a terrifying, heart-wrenching thing. I reached out to him, risking skin addiction by touching his bare arm, but he shrugged me off as he stood and pointed a finger at Alec.

"This is your fault. You caused this to happen. Either you're a traitor or someone on your side of the operation leaked your plans to Kaleb and the rest. Stay out of my sight. The next time I see you, I'll kill you with my own hands."

Taggart stalked off, heading towards the road and the battered Coun'hij SUV's that we'd always planned on using as our getaway vehicles. I stood to follow him, but Alec grabbed my arm, stopping me with a firm, but oddly gentle pressure.

"Wait, Adri. We need to talk, all of us really, but if Taggart won't talk to us then you need to be here to hear what Carson and I have to say."

My heart had started to soar when he'd said that we needed to talk, but as I realized what he actually meant my joy turned to something harder.

"Isn't one skin-addicted girl enough for you, Alec?"

He let go of me like I was burning him. His reaction was so abrupt that I almost fell over.

"How did you know that?"

I'd been cruel. I'd known that what I was saying wasn't fair even as the words came out of my mouth, but I couldn't take them back now. I'd defended Alec against Taggart, but now that I was here face to face with him I couldn't bring myself to give him the benefit of the doubt. It hurt too much to know that he'd bonded in that way to someone.

I'd thought that what we'd shared in the dream had been something special, some kind of one-in-a-billion kind of link, but the reality of things was that it had probably been nothing more than some kind of dream-land shadow skin addiction. Alec and I had never had any kind of chance of being together, not really, not as equals.

Alec shook his head. "Never mind. Taggart must have seen me dreaming about her and told you. It wasn't something I meant to have happen. I tried very hard to keep her from getting addicted to my touch but there were powers outside of my control working that night."

I shook my head. "I don't care about that. Say what you need to say. I need to go to Taggart. He's just lost his best friend, the only person he knew he could count on for the last however many decades, and he's scared of what comes next."

Alec ignored my request to focus on the business at hand, instead looking at me oddly. "Are you addicted to him?"

"No, I'm not addicted to him!"

"Maybe it's so subtle that you don't even realize it."

I stood back up and turned to go, but once again a hand on my arm stopped me. I turned to give Alec a piece of my mind, to lash out at him with all of the hurt I was feeling, but it wasn't Alec who had hold of me this time. It was Carson.

"Let her go!"

Alec's order came out in the kind of low growl that I'd learned meant his vocal cords had already started to lengthen. He was mere heartbeats away from a transformation.

Carson slowly released me as he made a calming gesture with his free hand.

"Please, both of you need to avoid doing anything hasty. Adri, Agony said that you are

Taggart's heir. Is this true? Are you able to enter people's dreams?"

"Yes. As of a couple of months ago, I'm a dream walker. It's not exactly how things work for him, but it's close enough."

Carson nodded thoughtfully. "Alec, you should know that while humans with powers are very rare, there have been incidents in our history where they came into frequent, extended contact with shape shifters. There haven't ever been any recorded instances of humans with these kinds of gifts forming a Ja'tell bond with one of the moonborn. Adri is acting out of concern for a friend, nothing more."

It should have clicked for me before then, but it took Carson's explanation to make me realize that Alec wasn't just acting like the arrogant alpha male that Taggart always described him as. He was acting *protective*. He hadn't been trying to control me, he'd been concerned about my welfare.

Carson didn't give me a chance to respond. "Adri, you should know that Alec was telling the truth just now. He didn't mean for Brindi to become addicted to him. More than just being able to sense the truth of Alec's words, I have it from another source who witnessed the events on the night when it happened. I've only known Alec for a handful of days, but I've never seen him treat her with anything less than complete respect."

I opened my mouth to tell him that he didn't need to lie for Alec, but that would have been the anger talking again. Luckily Isaac interrupted me before I could say yet another thing that I would have later regretted.

"They are telling the truth, Adri. It's not a hundred percent certain, but either they are both incredible liars or it all really went down like they are saying it did."

I shook my head. "I don't know how you all live like this. Always knowing when you're lying, always knowing what's going on inside of each other's heads."

Alec gave me a tentative smile. "It's hard, but not as bad as you might think. Mostly it just makes things easier unless someone decides that you're an expert liar. Then things get harder."

"I guess you know that I was lying a few seconds ago when I said I didn't care that you'd bonded to this Brindi chick."

"Yeah. I really am sorry, I never meant to hurt either of you."

Carson cleared his throat. "I'm sorry to interrupt, but maybe this is something that it would be best for Isaac and me not to be here for."

Alec shook his head. "No, you're right, but don't leave. We need to talk about Taggart's accusations. I haven't intentionally betrayed anyone, but he's got a point. Someone told the Coun'hij to expect an attack here."

Isaac looked doubtful. "But using a plane like Brandon just did is the perfect insertion method for countering an ambush anywhere along the route. It doesn't necessarily mean that we were betrayed."

We all sat in silence for a couple of seconds before Carson frowned. "No, I think that Alec is right. There were far too many hybrids with Brandon and there were more enforcers with the caravan than I would have expected. They came ready to fight a force several times as big as anything we should have been able to field."

"Exactly. They either knew about both our groups, or they knew about one of the groups and the fact that we had Grayson or Heath along to even out the odds."

Alec's words had obviously given Isaac something to think about. "It's possible it came from my side of things. I have a high degree of trust in my people, but all it would have taken is for someone to call the next point in the communication chain rather than meeting in person like they were supposed to. It's always much harder to tell if someone is lying over the phone."

The way that Alec closed his eyes made it seem as though for a second the weight of all of the responsibility had become too much for him. He looked like a man who wanted to drop his burden and walk away from everything. Hopeless fights to the death were something Alec could take in stride, but doubting friends and allies looked like it was a step too far for him.

It was only an instant. The three of us saw a rare moment of weakness and then it was gone. Alec opened his eyes and once again he was the strong rock that you could build something lasting on.

"Okay, please follow up as much as possible with your people. Do it yourself wherever possible or delegate to one or two very trusted individuals. We want to keep this as quiet as possible or we'll have people defecting back to the Coun'hij in droves."

Isaac nodded. "If it was one of my people I'll find out and they'll be punished."

"Thanks. I almost hope it is on your side, but I'm pretty sure it isn't. Shawn Bishop was supposed to show up with a bunch of help. Since he didn't, I can only assume that he got cold feet and decided he'd be better off running to the Coun'hij."

"That's terrible news on practically every level. If the Chicago pack has started to shift towards the Coun'hij, then there's nothing left to stop the Coun'hij from going after people like Jaclyn Annikov."

It was Isaac who had spoken again, but Carson seemed fully in agreement with Isaac's analysis of the situation. Alec gave him a chance to interject, but the older hybrid simply waved Alec on.

"Yeah, it means that the battle lines have finally been drawn. We might have a few weeks, maybe even a few months, but sooner or later the Coun'hij is going to try and purge all of the dissident elements. We need to come up with a plan before then that will let us get groups like Jaclyn and her people out alive wherever possible."

"And if it's not possible?"

Carson wasn't questioning Alec, he was just asking what we were all thinking.

"Then we have to make sure that the Coun'hij loses a lot more people than they kill. We're only going to get one chance at this. We need to ensure that the balance of power doesn't get any worse or none of us will live to see next year."

"We're going to have to come up with a counter for Brandon soon or nothing else we do is going to matter."

Carson stood and put a hand on his sword. "You're right, Isaac. I can train Alec in use of his weapon, but even that might not be enough. We'll either need another equalizer or we'll need the perfect set of circumstances. I will think on this."

As Carson gravely pulled his sword out from Agony's chest, Isaac also stood. The two of them picked up Agony's body and carried him in the direction that Taggart had gone. It was just Alec and I now and there weren't any listening ears close enough to overhear whatever we might choose to say.

"I really am sorry, Adri. That night we talked, when you came into my dream, it was the most amazing experience I've ever had."

"Then why didn't you come looking for me?"

"I didn't remember the dream until recently. It's the oddest thing, I've been having dreams about you for years, but they were just dreams. I remembered them, or at least remembered most of them when I woke up, but I didn't remember the one and only time that I actually met you."

I didn't know what to say to that. My emotions were such a tangled mess that it was going to take weeks to even begin to sort them out. I'd gone from loving Alec to hating him and back so many times over the last week and a half that I didn't even know which way was up anymore.

Alec seemed to be waiting for me to respond, but after nearly a full minute of silence, he took matters into his own hands.

"Come with me. I can't guarantee your safety, nobody can make a guarantee like that in the world we live in, but I want to get to know you. There's a hole inside of me. I don't notice it most of the time because I'm not some kind of broken shard of a person, but it's there. It's like a splinter that I can't help but worry at, only when you're around it's not a bad thing because the hole was perfectly designed for you. It's like we fit together, like we were meant for each other."

"So you just want me around to complete some kind of metaphysical ratchet set?"

"No, I want you around because of how I feel around you. You're good and brave. You risked your life to save Carson and me. You care about people and you try to do the right thing even when it costs you. I've spent less than an hour around you, but I can already see that. I want to get to know you better and yet I'm scared you'll send me away because how could perfection ever agree to spend time with me?"

Tears started to pool in the corners of my eyes. What he'd just said was incredible. Maybe it wouldn't have been right for another girl, but it was right for me. It was almost exactly how I felt about him.

That was why my emotions were such a mess. A part of me had never doubted him, had never believed he could be anything other than perfect, but another part—a very big, vocal part of me—had been convinced that someone like Alec could never want someone like me.

A pair of tears broke free and started their slow-motion race down my cheeks as I reached over and took hold of Alec's hand. I wasn't as confident as Carson was that I couldn't be addicted to a shape shifter's touch. Being dependent on anyone to that degree scared me to death, but somehow in that instant it didn't matter. I needed to touch him as much as he needed to touch me.

"I'd really like that, Alec. I can't think of anything that I want more than that right now, but Taggart needs me. He's all alone and he doesn't have as much self-control as you do. He's going to need someone to lean on and I'm the last person left that he trusts."

Alec closed his eyes as if to deny me the heartache lapping up from the depths of his being. It was still there, easily readable in the set of his mouth and the defeat in his posture, but somehow he was right. Seeing it in his eyes had been the worst part.

"You'll sacrifice your happiness, *our* happiness, for your friend?"

"Yes. He's not just any friend. He's saved my life twice already and he's never asked me for anything other than friendship, but even if that wasn't the case I'd still be going with him."

"I respect your decision; I just wish I could understand."

I reached up and guided Alec's face back towards me. He opened his eyes and I gave him a sad smile of my own.

"You already understand, you just don't realize it. What would you say if I asked you to come with Taggart and me?"

"I'd refuse. I have duties. To my sister, Rachel, to my friends and to everyone who wants to overthrow my father and the others like him."

The admission obviously cost him, but I already knew Alec well enough to know that he wasn't going to lie to me, not about something this important.

"See, you understand perfectly. It's no different for me. I doubted our fight for a while, but I'm every bit as committed to it as any of you are. The resistance needs Taggart and it needs me. The two of us will be infinitely more effective working together and by staying with him I can serve as a bridge between the two of you. He's going to need to learn to trust you if we're going to have any kind of chance of winning."

I raised the hand I'd been holding and turned it over. I looked at his hand, a hand that had killed today, a hand that had saved lives, and then I brought it up to cup my face. I kissed his palm and then I stood and walked away without looking back.

I almost expected him to stop me. Part of me wanted him to force me to stay, but deep down I knew he wouldn't. Alec couldn't do that and still be Alec.

Chapter 25

Samantha Graves
Graves Estate
Sanctuary, Utah

Samantha was sitting in her waiting room, enjoying the sunlight on the back of her neck while she played her piano, when it happened. Kaleb stormed into her suite without waiting to be announced, without observing any of the normal formalities that had come to dominate their relationship over the nearly two decades that they'd been married.

Kaleb picked up a potted rose, a miniaturized specimen that had been a gift from him in happier times, and threw it through the large window directly opposite the doorway from the main house. The pot was heavy enough that a human would have had to exert themselves to get it airborne.

There was a casualness to Kaleb's motion that was belied by the fact that the pot hit directly where four panes of glass met. The heavy earthenware container shattered upon impact but not before it destroyed the metal supporting all four panes of glass and caused a deadly rain of razor-edged fragments.

Anyone sitting underneath the glass would have been killed. The rose was sliced into dozens of pieces. It was a small thing against everything else that had just happened, but that miniature rose was one of only two that had survived so many years. Samantha had never possessed Kaleb's green thumb. Most of the roses he'd given her had long since died.

The nearest shard landed a mere four feet from where Samantha was sitting, but that wasn't the terrifying part of the experience. The really scary part was the fact that Kaleb seemed so controlled. He was always the most dangerous when he was riding his rage rather than letting it ride him.

"Agony's convoy was attacked an hour and a half ago. By Alec."

Samantha tried to keep her feelings off of her face, but it was so hard to play these kinds of games with someone with the native advantages that Kaleb enjoyed.

"You'll be happy to know that Alec's people wiped out my men quite handily. Their attack was well-executed and they seemed to have brought along someone with a rather unique ability."

"Maybe, or maybe Alec has finally manifested the power that you and Mallory have been anticipating for so long."

Kaleb's smile had a cruel edge to it. "I don't think so. If he had, he would have used it when Brandon dropped a secondary force in his lap and nearly killed him. I'm just sorry we didn't manage to get Oblivion down there too. He and Brandon would have made an unstoppable team."

Samantha couldn't help but gasp, but it was a small gasp and in its own way it served her purpose as well. It always paid off to make Kaleb think she was weaker than she actually was. It was one of the few advantages she had over him. He was conditioned to think of himself as superior in every way. It meant he underestimated her, not frequently, but often enough.

"It was a trap."

"Of course it was a trap. Do you really think I would have let you get access to that information by accident or out of incompetence? I worked very hard to make sure that you and Jack would think that the intelligence I'd passed you was clean. It was Jack, wasn't it?"

This time Samantha managed to keep her face even and her breathing unchanged, but that just made Kaleb smile.

"I had my suspicions when Alec was able to fight his way out of the welcoming committee that I'd arranged for him when he flew back from the Caymans. He couldn't have done that without help and he'd had very limited opportunities to make the kind of contacts he would have needed to pull off that kind of unexpected miracle. Brandon just confirmed my suspicions. He saw several of Jack's people before he was chased off. He didn't see Jack though. Pity, I'd hoped to kill my old friend myself."

Samantha waited. Kaleb invariably let more drop when she just let him talk than when she tried to get information out of him with leading questions.

"The most interesting thing out of all of this is that you knew it was a trap, but you didn't tell Jack or Alec that. I made every effort to convince you that you'd stumbled upon the kind of intelligence windfall that the resistance needed and yet you still knew what I was really planning and arranged to have a second group there to bail Alec out when Brandon tried to shut the jaws of the trap."

"Maybe I just wanted to protect Alec. Maybe I didn't know it was a trap but I couldn't help but make every arrangement I could in order to try and protect my only son."

Kaleb's laugh was a biting, caustic thing. "We've known each other for too long for those kinds of ploys to work on me, *dearest*. You're much too experienced a manipulator to let something like sentiment get in the way of your larger goals. You wanted to weaken me, both in real terms and with regards to my position on the Coun'hij.

"Just remember, I'm not the worst thing you need to fear. There are forces out there that are much less *understanding* than I am, but they aren't any more dangerous than me. Even when I lose, I still win. How likely is Dream Stealer to trust you next time you provide him with a tasty bit of information? For that matter, how much confidence are you going to have the next time you think you've ferreted out some piece that I don't want you to know about?

"All roads lead to me, Samantha. It's only a matter of time before you figure that out. It was obvious that Alec needed more motivation to manifest his power than I'd managed to provide him while he was part of my pack. I think that's all about to change though."

Kaleb turned and left without another word. Samantha rose and picked her way across the shards of glass. She managed to hold off the tremors until she got the door closed and made it into her bedroom. Once she was safe, she couldn't keep from shaking. The fit didn't stop for more than an hour.

Chapter 26

Shawn Bishop
The Bishop Compound
The Outskirts of Chicago, Illinois

Shawn and his dad were in his dad's office when the text arrived. Shawn looked at his phone and then slid it across his father's desk.

"Alec pulled it off. I don't have any idea how he managed it, but another group showed up and bailed him out at the last minute."

Ulrich read the text and set Shawn's phone down with the same impassive face that he usually displayed to the rest of the world. Shawn had heard whispers inside the pack to the effect that Ulrich only felt two emotions. Anger and a mildly-interested clinical detachment. Both emotions were potentially dangerous to those around him.

"You're angry."

"Yeah, but to be fair, I'm not really mad at you. This was as much my decision as it was yours, I'm just pissed off at the situation. If Vicki and I had gone down there like we'd originally planned we could have prevented some of the losses that Alec took and maybe we could have even killed Brandon."

Ulrich nodded. "I know. Believe it or not, I feel the same way. Alec Graves didn't save my life, but he saved yours, which counts for a lot with me. It was just too dangerous. Someone leaked Alec's plan to the Coun'hij, which meant that there wasn't going to be any hope of keeping your involvement a secret.

"If Kaleb and the others ever realize that we're actively working against them they'll risk everything in a bid to wipe out us and every other pack that's ever even looked at them sideways. Even repaying Alec Graves for your life isn't worth that."

Shawn dropped his head down so that his face was resting in his hands. "I know, I'm not trying to say that you don't appreciate what he did, it's...oh, I don't know. It's more than just his actions that made me want to trust him. He's the real deal, Dad.

"I think he's what Jaldul or Thanatas must have been like. I practically wanted to kneel down and swear fealty to him. I didn't of course, but the desire was there."

"He's not going to make it much longer, Shawn. You're right, his heart is in the right place, but he's in over his head, even more than he realizes he is. Kaleb and the others will eventually crush him, it's only a matter of time."

"Do you really think we can change things?"

Ulrich shrugged. "We're up against some of the best, Shawn. Kaleb has been manipulating people since before you were born and he graduated to the major leagues pretty early on. The fact that there are two of us gives us more options than I used to have, and the fact that our pack is so large gives us leverage, but when you get right down to it we're just treading water."

"I know. You explained the plan to me when I was twelve. I understand it and I agree with it, but that doesn't mean I have to like it."

Ulrich reached one massive arm across the desk and rested it on his son's shoulder. "It's going to happen eventually. No repressive government can stay strong indefinitely. Eventually they'll misstep or some young hybrid will manifest a game-changing ability. When that happens we'll be ready to throw our weight behind the resistance and make the overthrow much less bloody than it otherwise would have been."

"I sure hope so, but I worry every day that we're going to wait too long to act and find ourselves boxed into a corner we can't fight our way out of."

Acknowledgements

Being an author is one of the more solitary professions out there, but the process doesn't stop once the words are on the screen, and this book never would have seen the light of day without the help of numerous people.

My editors, RJ Locksley and Amy Jirsa-Smith did great work fixing my usual run of mixed metaphors and misplaced words. It took me a long time to find editors that I was completely happy with, and I'm glad they continue to work with me.

My advanced readers are a great bunch, many of whom do even more than simply reading my new releases looking for the spattering of errors I always end up introducing into the text while going through the editing process. I'd like to express a big thank you to my Mom & Dad, Mark, Shalese, Matthew, Mimi, Kim, Heather Tucker, Jenine Anderson and Janelle Gordinier.

As always, Katie has been incredibly supportive throughout this process. Not only has she continued to serve as my very first reader, she has recently gone back through nearly all of my covers and re-branded them in a herculean effort to help us achieve our dreams. Thank you, Katie.

About the Author

Dean Murray is a prolific author with dozens of novels across multiple pen names and more than half a million copies of his work currently in circulation.

Dean started reading seriously in the second grade due to a competition and has spent most of the subsequent three decades lost in other people's worlds.

Things worsened, or improved depending on your point of view, when he first started experimenting with writing while finishing up his accounting degree.

These days Dean has a wonderful wife and two lovely daughters to keep him rather more grounded, but the idea of bringing others along with him as he meets interesting new people in universes nobody else has ever seen tends to drag him back to his computer on a fairly regular basis.

Keep up to speed on Dean's latest projects at www.DeanWrites.com.

Broken

Adri Paige is too busy dealing with the emotional fallout from losing half of her family to deal with boys. At least she thought so until the two most intriguing guys in her new school take an interest in her.

Both boys are gorgeous and blessed with obscene amounts of money. They should have the emotional depth of note cards, but instead display undercurrents she doesn't fully understand. Rumors the pair destroys peoples' livelihoods seem ludicrous until she gets caught in the crossfire and her family almost loses their home. She's increasingly unsure either boy is really human, and their rivalry is rapidly turning deadly.

Torn

Shape shifter Alec Graves has spent nearly a decade trying to keep his family from being drawn into open warfare with a larger pack. The new girl at school shouldn't matter, but the more he gets to know her, the more mysterious she becomes. Worse, she seems to know things she shouldn't about his shadowy world.

Is she an unfortunate victim or bait designed to draw him into a fatal misstep? If she's a victim, then he's running out of time to save her. If she's bait, then his attraction to her will pull him into a fight that'll cost him everything.

CHET:
Whispers From The Past
By Larry Murray

30 years ago Charles Tucker lost everything that made life worth living. A brutal car accident killed his son. A short time later painful cancer took his wife.

The arrival of the Saunders family casts Charles' life into turmoil, tearing open unhealed wounds. Without his help the Saunders' financial troubles threaten to destroy them, but helping them risks destroying everything Charles spent a lifetime building.

Over all the turmoil looms Chet, the battered old '64 Chevy pickup that carried Charles' son to his death. For 29 years Charles blamed the old pickup for his devastating losses, locking Chet away in an old barn.

The most intriguing mysteries refuse to stay locked up. Solving this one promises an enchanting adventure for the whole family.

Frozen Prospects

The invitation to join the secretive Guadel should have been the fulfillment of dreams Va'del didn't even realize he had. When his sponsors are killed in an ambush a short time later, he instead finds his probationary status revoked, and becomes a pawn between various factions inside the Guadel ruling body.

Jain's never known any life but that of a Guadel in training. She'd thought herself reconciled to the idea of a loveless marriage for the good of her people, but meeting Va'del changes everything. Their growing attraction flies against hundreds of years of precedent, but as wide-spread attacks threaten their world, the Guadel have no choice but to use even Jain and Va'del in their fight for survival.

www.ingramcontent.com/pod-product-compliance
Lightning Source LLC
Chambersburg PA
CBHW031958060726
47497CB00015B/222